God's Last Giant

Rob Ghiringhelli

PUBLISHING, LLC

Rob Ghiringhelli

God's Last Giant
All Rights reserved
Copyright © 2019 Rob Ghiringhelli
All rights reserved
SDC Publishing, LLC All rights reserved.
ISBN: 9781072930921
Published and printed in the United States of America

DEDICATION

This book is dedicated to family and friends. Those here and now and those who have traveled on to where there is no here and now, only forever in the arms of the infinite. Their kindness, determination and courage, are the foundations for those you will find in this book.

God's Last Giant

ACKNOWLEDGMENTS

How do you acknowledge the essence of love and support? Either you have 5 pages of thank yuz... or you leave out those who might have been... with one word, or one action... a catalyst for change. So... I think I will be swift and simple in this recognition.

To my wife Lori – Thank you for your kindness and support in reading and correcting my work so many times that you really do not have to read it any more to make changes. Thank you for actually initiating contact with Suzanne, Randee and Allen and continuing to believe in this work's value.

To my sister Ellen – Thank you for hitting the nail on the head with the title. When you called it out... the angels sang.

To those who supported me in memory and spirit – Thanks for not giving up on me and after each time that I was too stubborn or clueless to listen, having the patience and sense of humor to give it another try. Hey ... At least Lori was listening?

To many others that thought the idea was worth the journey, I am very grateful for your support.

God's Last Giant

CHAPTER 1

Warm air as soft as satin, confirming the arrival of spring, glided over my skin as I walked along the shoreline of my favorite beach. Rays of sunlight danced across the waves, forging a sea of diamonds, which tumbled to the shore and were harvested by glistening sands. The rising tide worked furiously to hide any indications that I had passed that way, as if to protect its treasure from the children chasing shadows and seagulls off in the distance.

Up from the wash, where dry sand harbored withering seaweed, a man sat with his legs crossed, his back straight, his head folded in to the cleft of his chest. He sat eerily poised against the unceasing motion which surrounded him, as if in preparation for the overture of some grand concert. Seemingly, I was the final attendee to arrive, for as I approached, the man's left hand began to rise in a flowing gesture and gracefully rotated toward the sun, calling to order the assemblage of nature before him. At its apex his hand swung downward, turning in a cupping motion, passing just above the sand. Upon the upswing, a small vortex formed. Sand gradually scaled the swirling pipe, underneath a balanced and weightless palm. The vortex rose to eye level as it continued to spiral. I watched in amazement and wondered why this tempest chose obedience to its creator, rather than tearing off across the sand in wild fury.

The man's focus now elevated toward the sky, he repeated the action with his right hand and again a perfect funnel of sand, swirling ever so precisely rose to match the other.

A little girl who had been playing nearby, chased after her ball which uncannily drove against the gusts of wind to finally settle in a cavity in the sand just behind the cross-legged man. She slowed to a pace and then stopped a few feet away. She stood very still. Her eyes shifted uncomfortably from the swirling pipes of sand, to her ball which had begun to spin and roll around in the cavity, as if it was searching for a way to break free and pursue a new course. I choked back a nervous laugh as I focused on her expression. It was the same one I was wearing.

The man brought his hands together before his chest, interwove his fingers and allowed his head to fall forward at a gentle angle. It seemed like the surrounding light changed slightly, I remember in the back of my mind trying to figure out what the time was, while feeling like time had simply been turned off. The man raised his head and opened his arms as if casting something outwards. The sand began climbing again and at the top of the vortex, it was picked up by the wind and escorted away. The vortexes began to collapse, and the remaining sand was welcomed by a misty gust of wind.

Awoken from her stupor, the girl flinched as the man lifted the ball towards her. Although I could not see his face, I believed he smiled, because she smiled and accepted the ball. Freed from temporal bondage, she raced off towards the other children.

I became overwhelmed with a desire to sit down, entranced in this otherworldly moment. As I gave in to the desire and sank into the warm soft sand, the sun bowed to the horizon, retiring to the heavens, ending its vigil on the day.

As wispy clouds of fading peach, pink and purple, provided a backdrop, the man rose in a swift, uninterrupted movement and approached the sea. On bended knee, he placed his hands in the wet sand which was accepting its last bejeweled offering. He began chanting softly. His words were lifted by the waiting breeze, impatient to carry away the message entrusted to it. A subtle harmony, filled with soft tones and humming accompanied his chant. The vibration echoed faintly off the approaching waves and as they flooded on to the shore, they also flooded my awareness. I fathomed it to be a wondrous harmony, tying all things to the moment ... a melodious prayer. Somehow, I had risen to one knee with fingers extended into the sand. I realized that my body was cemented to the ground and my posture now matched the strangers. While my mind grew lighter and more buoyant, a solid, rigid quality engaged my body. I began to float on a current of vibration. I felt my form, but I was separate from it. I was aware of where I knelt, cemented in the sand, yet I felt free, endless. My awareness seemed to have no boundaries. Every sense was magnified, alive. The moisture in the air enveloped me in a light mist, causing the hair on my arms to stand straight up, electrified. Behind me, I sensed a seagull dropping to the sand to grasp a clam rolling in the foam at the head of the surf. Just off from the breakers, a school of whiting dodged in and out of the crashing surf. Underneath my outstretched fingers, I became aware of small sand crabs digging upward in the sand, drawn like moths to light. I could sense their attraction to the vibration, not just the strangers, or the reverberation in me, but the entire symphony. In all these impressions of nature surrounding me, I identified a purpose, a force or will that weave all things together.

This brought my attention back to the stranger. I could sense him, very distinctly now. Although his features were not clear, his vibration, his energy was. It was a beacon extending in all directions, far into a world I could not define, or explain in words. It was a world so crisp, so clear that colors seemed florescent. Vibration had dimension and purpose. It was so ... alive? The vibration generated sounds that rolled through me. The sounds were so garbled at first, I did not recognize them as words, but I knew they held meaning and a specific purpose. I could feel a part of myself comprehending, focusing on the surges, guided from some lost memory and in a flash of insight, I experienced clarity.

Michael... Michael... open your mind, just let go.

As if a magic command had been spoken, I stopped struggling to understand. I let go and let the energy carry me. Vibrations danced before my eyes like the afterglow of a sparkler, while excitement and uncertainty sought compromise in the hopes of achieving balance and flow.

Another clear statement flooded my awareness: "Awake my friend, your world is now greater in scope, than your mind could ever have imagined. From the sinew and bone that define your humanity, to the spark of the divine that defines your place in the universe, you will find there is... more!"

As if the words forming in my consciousness, were a returning tide carrying me out into a vast sea with no end, I watched as my wonder merged with the flow.

The communication continued: "Every day that we rise and venture out into the world, we take a leap of faith that we will return home to that which we are familiar. So, it will remain on this night, but as for where you may find yourself in your tomorrows, that is a choice you must soon make."

There was silence. I felt like I needed to respond, but I was not in control of my body and in irony, I somehow knew that a corporeal response would have been unworldly and far too inadequate in that moment.

The voice spoke again: "Perhaps we can journey together, exploring what truly lies beyond your humanity and help you to believe the unbelievable."

The vibration changed in some small way, became denser, more solemn.

"Michael... be warned, what is discovered, what becomes known, cannot be unknown. This journey will promote changes in you and your world that cannot be reversed. Once completely through the doorway, your world will forever be altered. The decision must be yours to make. I will wait for your answer. Simply wish to explore the many questions filling your mind at this meeting and we will write a new chapter, in a story that has no end." The last words were attenuated, then cut short with a loud snap that echoed in my mind.

The stranger had swung to full height and was vanishing into the mist. The mysterious song had ceased and nightfall was consuming the twilight.

****

As if woken straight from a dream, my body jolted. Specks of sand and ocean spray needled my face. I tried to look around quickly to see if others were captured in this surreal experience, but seeing only empty beach, I turned back towards the sea. The tide had made considerable advances and I hurried to pull myself together. The world suddenly seemed very small and the sound of the wind rushing past my ears was one dimensional. It was eerily quiet compared to a moment before, when a universe of vibration filled my awareness.

As if recovering from a trance, I rose and stumbled awkwardly forward, pulled by the void created from the departure of some unfamiliar universe. Moving as skillfully as a two-day drunk, I attempted to avoid the rush of foam and sea that enveloped my ankle. Uncoordinated, and more than slightly confused, I struggled back to my car. I was exhausted, yet for the first time in many years, I felt wonderfully complete.

CHAPTER 2

As I stumbled out of bed that next morning, I had no idea exactly when or even how, I got home. I did not remember driving, or walking through my door, or taking off my clothes, well some of them anyway. All I knew was that I woke up that next morning, rejuvenated and filled with a sense of well-being. For a child forged in a cynical world, that was unique all by itself.

The day before seemed more like a dream and without any tangible substantiation, my responsibilities and obligations overwhelmed the unique and separate nature of it. Still, the feeling that something life altering had occurred, dominated my inner dialogue. My thoughts kept returning to those short moments by the surf when some magical veil hiding the mysteries of life was drawn back. What had been exposed in that unveiling, was emblazoned and etched into my inner awareness.

Over that next week, I begrudgingly accepted the beach experience as more a flight of fancy that momentarily gained the upper hand in a world of stark realities. I remember thinking, if somewhere in the great beyond there existed angels, astral spectators rooting for moments of spiritual freedom for those bonded to the human condition, they were undoubtedly cheering as my analytical and cynical mind had surrendered to a… daydream? Merriment for those Godly guardians of hope and faith would be short lived though. Too many years applying prudent judgment as an adult, in order to avoid the mistakes and embarrassments of youth, had created strong patterns, rooted in tangible, physical senses. With that said though, a day did not pass where I longed to go back to the beach and relive the experience. A night did not pass that as I slipped beneath the veil of consciousness, a sparkle of magic from that day did not dance against the backdrop of my closed eyelids.

Inevitably, each passing day brought back the old familiar. While regimen began to suppress the creative, cynicism discredited hopeful possibilities. Rigid structures of feeling and thought replaced the newly germinated feelings of a life in harmonious order. I felt powerless to stop the re-absorption, almost apathetic, as a clandestine inner force skirmished to reclaim the old me. Yet on some inner level, I was petrified to let go of the experience and fall back to my old ways and expectations.

CHAPTER 3

Somewhere in my youth, during a psychology class probably, I must have tucked away information about dreams. In my filing cabinet of a mind, confirmation that dreams are the inner consciousness's conduit to communicate what the outer awareness has encountered and ignored, or just plain refused to accept. I understood that the inner psyche required expression, but since my dreams were commonly of a disturbing nature, I had always felt it much more advantageous to just leave them be, since thankfully most of them were lost upon awaking.

After the experience at the beach, my dreams had taken front stage and the disturbing nature of them remained lucid in my mind, well into the following day. Emotional and physical snippets caused bouts of Déjà vu, leaving small eddies of doubt over which memory was real and which was born from a dream. So, it was not totally unexpected as I drifted off to sleep one chilly, rainy night a few weeks past the beach experience that I found myself hovering in that twilight between both worlds.

I could hear the rain beating against my bedroom window and the skylight far above, but I could not move a single inch of my flesh. My mind flashed between realities, "Move pinky Move" and "Hey...am I floating?" Conscious control all but disappeared, as an inner world severed the tether securing my mind to the dimensions it was used to functioning in.

****

The day was hot. The dust from the dirt road the bus was traveling on billowed up obscuring the route we had traveled. A pothole jolted the bus and my head bounced off the window at my seat. As I rubbed the tender spot, I noticed a large structure ahead. It was not a welcoming sight, but it certainly seemed familiar. The bus approached the facility and pulled through a set of rather large gates, stopping in the courtyard within. As the bus came to a stop, a man in uniform leaped on to the doorway steps and scaled them with purpose. Like a marine drill sergeant, he boomed," Home all safe and sound, are we?" The words resonated in the dusty cabin. He stopped directly in front of me and looked down.

"Good try", he said with discomforting familiarity, then with huge volume… "Now get the …Hell…out!" As I stepped from the doorway of the bus, I saw three men standing in a line. I was directed to line up next to them. The first man I passed as I formed up, was noticeably agitated. Eyes buried deep in a scared face darted back and forth, body poised to defend an attack from any direction. The second man I passed, rolled his hands over and over as he stood in line. He talked to himself, repeating a list of things left undone. He was so consumed by his own thoughts that he had not lifted his head toward the uniformed man clearing his throat to gain attention. I took the first open position among the three, next to a man staring at me intently. His eyes completed the examination and then he just shook his head and focused on the heavy dust settling by his feet.

"Listen Up," the uniformed man shouted. "Pay attention and don't make me repeat myself!" The man seemed unduly pleased with himself, gloating, or self-righteous.

"Our playmate has returned. He, like all the rest of you rejects belong here, buuut… Some things need to be repeated for the slower learners." he aimed the words at me. The first man laughed like a hyena and stopped abruptly. The second man was buried in his own concerns. The third just smiled and shook his head again. Oddly, I noticed I was the only person that had departed the bus, which amplified a feeling of being a focal point.

"Escape is not an option," he growled, the badge on his shirt flashing in the afternoon sun. Just a dream you don't share… got it? The second man came to life with a jerk and began to recite a new list. The third man smirked as he nodded my way.

"Bullshit", he squeezed out of the side of his mouth.

I began to wonder about the possibility that I was actually in prison instead of my bed, since my mind held fast to the charade.

The guard's impatient attitude and grating tone shredded my

logical processing. "Let's move it you bone heads, your burning daylight here", he yelled and motioned the line to start moving toward the inner door of the prison. With each step, the environment became more familiar. To my astonishment, as each man passed through the doorway to the cell block, he vaporized into the same dust that followed the bus." Coooool," I said under my breath, just before I passed through the door. I felt a slight shudder and a chill ran down my spine as a clear view of the inside stuck me. The structure was massive. I had a clear vision of many of the rooms that lay within. Those beyond sight were not totally absent from my awareness. I could sense them. Each one held, or maybe stored, memories. They felt like rooms in a museum and seemed to be what was holding the structure together. At times, there was no clear separation between rooms, they seemed to merge with each other, allowing some of the contents in one area to combine with others. What was even stranger, was no matter whether the room was on the top, bottom, side or corner of another, each remained intact, yet blended. I continued to move deeper into the facility, as if on an escalator. The farther I moved into the structure, the more claustrophobic it felt. Breathing became more difficult, the dust was denser and more irritating, fog like. I could hear the other men entering their cells in the background and anxiety escalated with every movement. I reached out and grabbed bars that framed the doorway into a cell to compose myself. As I entered it, I was surprised to recognize it as being ... my cell. As I turned to face the entrance, a dense swirling cloud of dust floated outside the bars. It rolled and twisted like a vortex or tornado. The faces of the three men formed, dissolved and reformed in its turmoil. The forms spoke as they solidified.

"You... were gone way, too long," said one, eyes shifting side to side.

"Warden said you forgot who takes care of things around here," said the next face phasing in and out of solidity.

"No escape goes unpunished, you will see," said the third.

As if in defensive response to my rising apprehension, a humming similar to that night on the beach, drifted past me carrying the scent of the ocean and the salty taste of the sea. Relief flooded over me; I did not feel so alone. Anxiety and fear were swept away, like rain washes dust from the road. Tangible awareness reclaimed a portion of my mind, creating a strange duality. In the background I heard a loud laugh as the nightmare fought back, reclaiming some of its sovereignty. The vibration and humming grew a little stronger in response and the third man's face scattered into rolling sand and moist dust. I again reinforced in myself that this was just a dream, even though it felt so real. Thankfully, as long as the elusive humming resonated in the cell, the dust at the bars could not hold a shape. Another salty breeze caught the roiling dust and forced it down the hall and out of view. I opened my arms, tilted my head back, and let the humming surround me. The rhythm separated me farther from the dream's grasp. The air and my mind cleared, I began to intuit a deeper purpose to the experience.

If this was just a dream, then maybe it was trying to show me that I was trapped, not just in this dream, but in my life. The specters in the prison, were my own self-made limitations. Preservation and instinct had created barriers; safety and security had become prison. I had to be re-incarcerated, a repeat offender, a perpetrator of my own inner society's status quo. Accepting this self-created world, a construct with fear serving as the jailor and illusion as the warden, was critical. Access to the keys that could unlock perceptual and, therefore, true freedom was not allowed. Before me, were old prison mates, worry, fear and self-reproach. They were residents here. They occupied many cells, and at times they occupied them all. Their efforts were constant, their purpose clear. They were to occupy the room between my thoughts and feelings, so that the walls of the prison would not seem so confining, the prison so empty. They were to contaminate the room between fear and self-awareness, in order to corrupt motivation and secure an unchanging environment. Finally, they were to taint expectation and interest in "what might be", in order to subdue the potential for the future. Perceiving life through past experiences completed the cycle, leaving absolutely no room for new thought. Thought remained defined by memory. Perception remained conditioned by that which had already been. I existed in a locked loop, forever replaying the same themes.

I yelled out, "I am in charge. I control what goes on. I make the decisions that dictate my life and this … this is only a dream." There was no response. I was bound to a world of dreams, yet I was as awake as I could ever have been. I searched for a firm hold, on just one reality. A dream is supposed to remain real only as long as one is in that dream, not outside of it, awake. I let myself fall backwards onto a filthy and well-worn cot. A dust cloud exploded upwards as my weight hit the mattress, engulfing me, threatening to suffocate me. I closed my eyes and purposely reached out for the beach, the symphony, the smell of salt air. As the memory of that night at the beach took on depth and substance, the surrounding world dissolved. I heard the guard pass my cell, his night stick rattled across the bar. "You should have known better than try to escape, boyee," he said with disdain. "You've been here long enough to know the rules."

CHAPTER 4

I came out of bed so fast, the sheets that were tied in knots around my arms and legs, pulled the mattress half off the bed frame. I gasped for air and exhaled yelling, "What the Hell?"

I felt all of it, as real as any day in a life. A dream, without being aware that it is a dream, can be very real, but upon awaking you know it was a dream. This was not the case. I was still having a hard time differentiating what was real, from what was a dream. Both awareness's were tangible to my ordinary senses, both worlds definite, with depth and substance. My mind was frantically pumping the clutch and grinding gears, in an attempt to fully engage at least one solid reality. It raced to search for any past experiences that came even close to matching last night's adventure. The search came up empty. I was confident I had never had anything like this happen. One thing I knew for sure, the dream, the beach, the stranger... all were somehow responsible for whatever was happening to me. It was becoming clear that I had to find the person on the beach. Because of him, my world was changed, my perceptions altered and my expectations surrounding my future, ambiguous.

I spent much of that day trying to figure out how I was going to find this enigma of a man. I started by stereotyping him, hoping that would offer a few leads. What nationality did I think he was? Was he old, or young? Was he strong of body or frail? What exactly did his clothes look like... would that even help? As I called snippets from that day to mind, I began to remember bits and pieces which stood out. I remembered the world seemed small in contrast to him when he stood up. So... he was tall, large. Ok... that might rule out certain nationalities.

He almost levitated off the sand. He was fluid and nimble when he moved toward the water... so he had to be younger? His movements were so precise; possibly he was a dancer, or performer?

I began to become frustrated, how were these ambiguous aspects going to help me find this person?

Possibly, I thought, if I retraced my path that day, I might recall something that was eluding me. This all started at the beach, so that should be my first stop.

I loved the beach anyway and visited often all throughout the year. I was sure I had never seen the man there before, but finding him was crucial. So that afternoon I left work a little early, avoiding any competition with the light that remained in the day. If I found the man, there would be no vanishing into the darkness this time. As I approached the beach, my confidence peaked. I knew this was the right place to start.

The afternoon wind, was dancing with the grass on the bluffs beside the parking area, but the warmth of the sun kept the chill of the day at bay. Small clouds rushed to unite, gaining influence over the shoreline in preparation for a fateful journey that would lead them over mountain and field, finally to release themselves upon the land in realization of their purpose. I thought about the awkward analogy we shared at that moment and as I cleared the last remaining bluff, I was welcomed by the familiar tingling of the salt air on my face.

The beach looked empty today. It was a weekday and most people were off maintaining their schedules and following their routines. I was out on a beach looking for an answer to a questionable dream. I immediately felt embarrassed. I could feel the flush rising up my neck, as I examined my situation. Taking a deep breath, I scoured the beach, no one in sight... I could feel my confidence wavering. What was I really doing out here? As if in immediate answer to that question, a burst of wind and sand pelted my face. A clear vision came to mind of my dream. A sneering face rolled past my inner vision. No words were needed to express the ridicule embedded in that grin. A little out of terror and a little out of pride, I set out at a jog.

The tide was about midway between low and high, so I moved closer to the water to gain better footing on the more solid ground at the wash. I needed a firm feeling under foot, a solid foundation to thwart any reprisals from within. I walked a while with no one in sight and found myself lost in the turbulence of the ocean. Waves crashed in upon the beach, tearing at the shore. I knelt to touch the foam; it felt empty, without substance. It struck me that I, as all humanity, were exposed to the same form of attack from everyday life. Each day life pounds upon the solid structures we build and depend on. It smashes against us, forever testing our virtue, our resolve, our identity. Forever tearing away the weaker formations, ideas and constructs. Forever challenging our assembly. Oddly enough, we survive the demolition. We may change, we may look and feel different, but what remains is stronger in structure and better prepared for the next assault, the next wave of life.

A shadow passed over me catching my attention. I looked up. A perfectly formed squadron of Herons were side-slipping the wind, sailing along the edge of the water, their V form rank held effortlessly. Caught up in the symmetry, my eyes followed them as they sailed down the shore line. The flying V notched the horizon, like a godly arrow flying true to its target. At its pinnacle stood a vague shape too far away to recognize, but something in me... my hope,   my   expectation   ...   became   electric.

CHAPTER 5

An odd sense that this moment was preordained and paranormal rolled through my body and created shivers. Then as if on automatic pilot, my body started to jog toward the figure. I headed up from the wash and the sand grew softer under foot. It created an awkward sense of running in place. Each stride completed... with what felt like little, to no progress. My emotions hung by a thread that was steadily unraveling, along with my composure. I needed to grab that thread, take control of it before I came totally apart at the seams. I tucked my chin into my chest and pumped my arms to gain momentum. A duality played with my sensibilities. My body was on automatic, while my brain was precariously balanced between fear and excitement. A proverb I once read came to mind: "Fear arrives, not when one has the most to lose, but when one has the most to gain". Gauging by the anxiety that was rolling around in my belly, my subconscious must have had very high expectations over what lay before me.

With my focus so internally arranged, I lost track of where I was. A rat..tat..tat..tat..tat from the Jake brake of a tractor-trailer off in the distance, brought instant recall of the guard in my dream, rattling the bars of the cell. My legs and arms received an instant boost of adrenaline.

Arms driving forward, legs in full stride, head tucked in my chest for power, I began gaining ground on my objective. Feeling like I was finally getting somewhere, I looked up just in time to collide with a half empty trash receptacle tethered to a cement support. With the skill of a WWF titan, I wrestled the trash receptacle to the sand. The smell of stale beer and I think... a PBJ sandwich caught my immediate senses. I scrambled free from the twisted wreckage, flinging sand in all directions. Startled seagulls screamed and cackled appropriately at the spectacle, as I had gained access to the mother lode they had waited so patiently to raid. Recovering, I rubbed my thighs and walked in circles repeating, "ouchy ouch ouch", while I picked up items that had been ejected from the can. I was holding the wrapper that contained the remnants of the peanut butter sandwich, when an unexpected voice startled me. I turned on a dime, sandwich wrapper in hand, wielded like a sword against an unknown foe.

A deep voice said, "The way you dove into that trash, I am sure you must be famished. I would be delighted to buy you some food… prepared more recently… of course."

The sun was directly behind this person, so I could not make him out. I had to strain my neck upward to catch his face. Realizing how the collision must have looked from a distance, evoked an uncontrollable laugh. Wonderful, I said under my breath and I began to look around to see if anything else was out of order, clothes, trash… self-respect? In a flash, the reason for being there came flooding back. I again spun towards the man standing nearby. He had moved a little toward the water now and the sun was to his left, his back was to me. He reached down and picked something up from the sand. As he rose from his effort and moved toward me again, I could see him clearly. He was very tall. Actually, he was very tall and very big. Proportionately he was a little larger than say, well… anyone I have ever known! His hair was moderately long, but well kept, hanging in strands behind his head and mostly tucked under his collar. His skin was a few shades darker than mine, as if he might be Mediterranean. He brandished a huge grin as he moved toward me, which after my recent embarrassment, continued to make me feel a little smaller than life and much smaller than him. His face was soft though, with eyes that seemed to have seen a lot and lived even more. In his outstretched palm were my car keys, which had apparently traveled a distance away from the crash scene?

The closer to me he got, the larger he became. There was no sense of danger, a smile that broad, even possessing a slight smirk, could not hold danger.

"I believe these are yours", he said, as he handed me my keys and then held out his hand to shake mine. "My name, if I might introduce myself, he said… is Alton Gaynor."

Still a little in shock at all that was happening, I took his hand. He laughed as he shook mine, which seemed more like a child's hand, once in his grasp.

And you are Michael, he said. I froze knowing there was no way he was familiar with me. Unless… the beach experience had been all that it seemed? A chill raced up my spine, spun on itself and raced back down. I lost my breath for a moment and even contemplated running. Four of my strides would have been one of his. Not much chance of escape now, I laughed to myself as I released the impulse. As if in response to my feelings, he moved back a few steps and bowed slightly.

"I am sorry, that was rude," he said, "forgive me". He pondered a moment and then spoke." Everything seems a little crazy at this moment, I presume." He looked down at the remnants of the peanut butter sandwich I was nervously grasping and then the sand? He rubbed his forehead and laughed, hanging on for a response.

I still could not talk. I shook my head up and down in confirmation. Seemed crazy… I thought? For a realist like me… that was an understatement.

"Michael, I would like to assure you that I am a friend. I am also a friend in need. I need your help and for that to happen, I need your trust."

"I… uh… I …," was all I could say.

Alton focused intensely on me and continued. "Michael, most people go through their entire life searching for a reason that validates their existence. By the time they reach old age, they realize for the most part that the purpose of life was to live it. To learn it. To struggle against the unknown and in the end, hopefully, for better or worse, accept personal definition from living it. At some point… perhaps achieve enlightenment, awareness of the eternal. That in turn brings peace to the soul, happiness to the individual and renders a life complete."

"NO, no, no… that's too, too much. I am sorry again. Ahhh…," Alton groaned. "Michael, each and every life is precious and purposeful. Some lives have what would be considered, a more specific purpose, a time sensitive purpose. Their life affects many, like one of your society's great leaders. Regardless of the scope of purpose, every soul is gifted one. If you were to ask an elder about living life, they might say I wish I had known then, what I know now! I would truly live life. I might avoid some of the mistakes and enjoy the moments. Michael, life is an adventure and a gift. It is a mystery to be uncovered through the living of it. If we had all the answers, all the knowledge, if we comprehended who we really are on a universal level, there would be no mystery and very little learning in the experience. Oh my, I am rushing and making no sense," were his last words as he walked off a few paces running his fingers through his long hair.

He was obviously frustrated, but at this point I could not even contemplate a response. Was this man some kind of Shaman? My mind was crisp, sharp, aware and I had to make an attempt to say something, but all I could muster was, "What is? Uhmm… What is the purpose?"

Alton took a deep breath and then let out a booming laugh." Do you expect one of the most important questions surrounding your life, all life, to be answered out on a beach, by a complete stranger?"

Alton, bent back looked up at the sky and took a deep breath. "If I offered you the answer, would you believe me? How would you know I am right?"

"I… uh… I might… if it sounded right", I murmured, feeling incredibly ignorant. Then I began to notice it…my body was immobile; I could not even wiggle my toes.

"Michael, knowing truth when you hear it requires an open mind, one that has been opened through trust and faith. At this moment, you possess neither. Even if the truth of life were to be laid at your feet, you would question its validity."

Alton paced around me, then said, "I hope we will have the opportunity to discuss this further, but for now, the reason I started this conversation with you was to tell you that you indeed have a very special purpose, one that holds great import, for many, many lives."

I had lost my train of thought as I wondered why my body had become a statue, frozen in place. My mind struggled to move even the smallest of body parts from my shoulders down, with no luck. It was only when I realized Alton was silent that I shifted my focus back to him. He was staring off toward the sea, as if collecting his thoughts. Then he began to speak in a very serious manner.

"Will you give me the benefit of the doubt, just for a while at least? Listen to what I have to say and then I will give you a chance to walk away, free from any responsibility."

I could hear the sincerity in his voice. I could see how important this was to him and an inner force confirmed that it was important to me, as well. "OK, Ok," I said with gritted teeth. "If I do, will you help me, I am stuck, really stuck?"

A warm smile spread across his face, filled with compassion. It was also a smile of relief. My arms were the first to move, then my legs. I had not realized that while I was frozen in place, I had also been light as a feather. As function returned to my limbs, I fell to the sand under my own weight and collapsed on my butt.

Alton knelt before me and spoke again." You are not going to believe this at first anyway," he said, "so we might as well cover as much ground as possible while your mind is focused in this moment. My name, as I told you is Alton," he paused, "Alton Gaynor. I come from another place, another culture... another world."

My mind was up on plane now, like a speed boat across smooth water. It had reached an angle from which it could deftly maneuver. Mediterranean, smaller villages, less people, different culture, third world lifestyle and they had Shaman... right? Spiritual teachers were well respected in many parts of the world.

My sensibilities were converting his statement into understandable, safe parameters. Subliminally, I knew I was qualifying the unexplainable, but it was working. I was more at ease with the notion that the man before me was just that, simply a man. He was a very large man! From another country? With uhmmm... unnatural abilities? "Ohhh boy." This time I said it out loud while submitting to the possibilities before me. There was no way out of this.

Alton continued, "Did you wonder why you felt so compelled to visit the beach the other day?"

The question gripped me. I was drawn to the beach very strongly, especially over the past month. I just figured the colder weather and a bit of cabin fever, urged me to walk the shore and breathe the fresh air.

"You are quite stubborn," Alton laughed gently, shaking his finger at me. "Every effort I made to communicate with your subconscious was challenged by your constant inner dialogue. You had an answer to normalize every effort I made".

What was he trying to say, that he could control my mind? I was definitely not ready to accept that. My body maybe, but my mind, that was sacred and well protected ground. All of this... well it just seemed crazy. This was the 20th century. Magic and the supernatural were pretty much explained away by science. My inner dialog was interrupted by his next statement.

"I have been exposing you, to what your mind can not possibly interpret, cannot confidently write off, or explain away," Alton said. "Your logic, you see, is a double-edge sword. It may not accept what cannot be addressed by your scientific physical laws, but it also cannot ignore what it cannot explain. That is until it is logically resolved." Then he smiled with a wink. "Michael, all my efforts are directed at stimulating your awareness, not to control you, but to better communicate with you," with the totality of your consciousness.

The seagulls were calm now, as if they understood exactly what was going on. They shuffled a few feet in one direction, looked over as if to judge how far my sensibilities were nudged, then shuffled back the other way to gain a different perspective. It aggravated me somehow, like I was too stupid to get it. Pacing back and forth they would look at each other as if in silent communication, "wait for it... wait for it... he just might be coming around."

The giant of a man must have taken pity on me in a heap in the sand and burst out in laughter. The laughter scattered the seagulls, who screamed angrily as they realized their show was about to end.

"Let us go get something to eat," Alton said, helping me stand up. He brushed me off, then stooped down and looked me directly in the eye. "I am starving and you need something more substantial than a peanut butter and jelly sandwich." With that, he snapped the sticky wrapper out of my rigid grip, winked, turned and walked away.

CHAPTER 6

Within seconds, Alton was 15 feet from me and moving at a rate the softness of the sand would not let me keep pace with. My prior guess was right… it took about 4 steps to keep up with his one. He was talking, but I could not hear him, the sound of his voice was lost in the buffeting wind. I felt like a school boy running after a teacher. Embarrassed and frustrated I stopped walking, crossed my arms over my chest and waited for Alton to notice that I was not following. As if he were at least minimally aware of me, Alton stopped mid step and turned. I could see his mouth stop moving and the grin return. With a few strides he closed the distance.

My apology… so much depends upon so few and we have not as yet, found common ground. With that he turned to walk toward the bluffs and the parking lot hidden behind. He walked with an obvious effort not to outpace me. Every third step he would pause and look up at the sky, or breathe deeply, or move a shell in the sand with his foot, feigning interest. Each time as I caught up with him, he would smile again, look around and walk on. If he was at all aware of my frustrations, by the time we breached the bluffs and entered the parking lot, he was wise not to show it.

During the walk up from the beach, I promised myself I would act more like a thinking adult than a wide-eyed child at a circus. When we reached my car, the only one in the lot, I logically questioned how he got there. "Alton… did you drive here?"

He smiled and said, "No, I walk most places. Sometimes," he was upbeat as if finding a better way to answer, "I find available transportation" and he smiled very broadly again, this time conveying a secret or two. "When I need to contact someone, I just reach out to them." He blushed for a moment, as if he had said to much.

Not for nothing I thought to myself, it would be very unlikely that he could just hitch a ride. Number one... who would pick up a man this size, on the side of the road? He was a gentle giant to be sure, but a giant of a man, none the less. Second... he would be hard pressed to fit into a midsize car, less likely a smaller car and he would definitely not fit in a compact.

"When you reach out to someone, is that through the web? I said, still trying to build a sense of who he was. He looked at me with a slight tilt to his head. "I mean, do you talk to other people through e-mail... computers?" He looked perplexed. I felt stupid. Third world countries do not have easy access to technology. I changed the subject quickly.

"Would you like me to drop you off somewhere after we eat?" He looked up and off into the distance and shook his head no and smiled as if hearing a joke. He then walked around to the passenger side of the car assessing his chances at entry. I unlocked the car doors and moved stuff off the front seat. I slid it as far back as possible, giving it an extra push for additional space, just in case. Even then, I had my doubts that he could fit. I put the items from the front seat into the trunk and when I closed it, to my surprise, he slid into the seat with unexpected ease.

"Where would you like to go to eat?" I asked, while trying to figure out how he got in so quickly.

He looked at me and said, "Anything is good, I am starving".

"I have exactly the place," I said. "It is called the Sea Sheppard." Considering the circumstances, the irony in the name made me laugh. "They have hot soups and good sandwiches." I looked over at Alton, who was fidgeting with an air vent which was digging in to his knee. He shook his head up and down. It took about five minutes to get to the small diner just up from the beach. As we traveled, I realized how much more comfortable I had become with him in a short time. I also noticed how at peace Alton appeared to be. Happiness and tranquility just exuded from him. It was infectious.

CHAPTER 7

The diner was fairly empty and as we entered, a few people looked up from their food and conversation. Of course, it was Alton that drew their prolonged stares. He had to bow to get in the door, but once through, he deftly navigated the low hanging lighting. His body cast a significant shadow on the tables as he passed, which caused the waitresses in his way to scurry behind the dining bar as if they were dashing across a busy intersection. A few traded comments like, "I guess the mountain did come to Mohammad" and "Is the circus in town?" I took the second comment a little personally and shot the waitress a glance. She just chewed her gum a little more deliberately, while forcing her right hand down on her hip like a gunslinger saddling his pistol, smoke rising from the last shot. Once things calmed down, the wait staff got to it.

A timid young waitress brought our meals. She stared as she laid a plate down in front of Alton, as if mesmerized. She could not have been more than 18 and certainly not a world traveler. Alton looked over his food and then looked down into her eyes which were open as wide as the saucers she had just set down.

"I am grateful for your service," Alton said gently.

Trying with all her might not to run away from the table to a safe distance she squeaked out, "I asked the cook to double the serving because of your… I mean because you looked hungry". Alton's smile became broad and powerful. He took her hand which now trembling like a leaf in a fall breeze. He held it with three fingers, which pretty much covered everything from her wrist down.

"Your kindness and consideration humble me," he said. By the time he let her hand go, the young lady's face was lit up like a Christmas tree. She glowed from the blush red of her cheeks to the bright green makeup- laden eyes, to the pearl white earrings that swayed wildly in response to her trembling. As she walked away from the table her strides were stiff and uncertain but her smile remained a mirror of his.

The meal hit the spot. I had to admit I was more than a little concerned that like his "Big" strides, it would take 4 meals to satisfy a "Big" appetite. Luckily that was not the case.

As we sat across from each other allowing the meal to settle, I noticed him playing with the steam from a new cup of coffee just poured by the awestruck waitress. As it curled upwards, he stuck his finger in the mist and spun it. Instead of dispersing, the mist followed the pattern created by Alton's finger. As the pattern formed, it became denser and began to pick up speed. The speed elongated the pattern into a perfect cone while gravity drew it down to his empty plate. Once it had found its platform, it acted like a spinning top following the contour of the plate around and around. Alton rested his head on his hand in the most casual of ways and watched as the mini cyclone rolled over a seed on his plate, pulled it up, rolled it around its form and then popped it out the top. The seed fell back onto the plate and bounced to a stop. I stared like a dazed child watching a magic trick, while the fresh and therefore, hot coffee I had just gulped, lingered in my mouth. It was the temperature of the coffee that finally brought me back to my senses, my tonsils screaming for relief. I washed the hot fluid down with ice water and embarrassment.

"See," I said anxiously as I rolled the ice cubes around inside my scorched mouth. "That…," and I pointed my finger and leaned in toward Alton lowering my voice, "that is not normal… it is not. It… it is not possible… scientifically speaking". Then I sat back to force down another gulp of ice water. Uncomfortable with speaking my next statement from a distance, I again leaned forward looking awkwardly upward into Alton's face.

"I mean… come on… what is really going on here? I have been doubting myself, my convictions and even my sanity, since the other night at the beach. I have been having incredibly vivid dreams, or astral projections, or for all I know, psychotic episodes. I came to the beach today, pretty sure that all I really needed was a reason to schedule a good, long vacation. I was going to put this all to rest and start planning a getaway. A real getaway, one with a facility that instead of offering heavy, soft, white robes, offered heavy, strong, white strait jackets. But noooo, who is here, but... but... you." I sat back, crossed my arms, sighed and then put my head in my right hand. "This is not going to end well, is it?" Alton looked down at me and smiled a gentle, understanding smile.

"I thought you would never ask." He reached over and squeezed my hand in a supportive way, then shifted slightly to have direct eye contact and skirt the spinning steam racing around his plate. His eyes were big and bright, teeming with effervescence. I felt like I had just stepped into a spotlight.

"Michael, you are totally in control of where we go from here. I will respect your desire to drop your inquiry over what you have seen and let you walk out that door." Alton nodded toward the entrance behind him.

"No, no, you see that is not true", I said feverishly. "I am not free to leave! I am a scientist. How... I mean... how does any self-respecting scientist say, 'No... but thank you very much' to an offer to explore the unknown? ORRRR... No, I am very happy 'NOT' knowing things that could change the way we interact with the universe we dwell in. HA HA ... No, I am very content watching the unexplained unveiled before me and honestly, I care less for the reasons it is happening." I threw my hands up in the air and grunted. "You said you have been in my mind! You said you have been watching me, but for how long? I don't know. You say you have knowledge of my life's purpose, and therefore by design, you must have knowledge of my past and apparent future. AND... if that is true, I do not know whether to be scared or just plain embarrassed at what you know." I had to stop to take a deep breath to regain my momentum. All the time the vortex of steam continued to dance around the plate in front of me, taunting me. Once the burning in my mouth, which had spread to my depleted lungs subsided, I soothed it with a little more ice water, looked around the room to see that we were not generating any more attention than when we walked in, of course that meant making sure the rest of the circus had not joined us for dinner. "You are as big as a house, but you move like the wind. You seem to control forces mastered only by universal laws. 'BUT HEY', I have better things to do with my life than allow my most basic nature to get involved here. Thank you though and good night! Are you kidding me?

"This is a setup, right? I looked around inconspicuously and whispered, "Where did the guys at the Lab hide the cameras? Come on… let's turn this charade back on them and have some real fun." I focused back on Alton's face, on the intensity of his gaze and my mouth fell silent.

"Michael, our meeting, our fate, is far from a joke and the outcome of what we do, or do not do from here on out, will affect more than just your world."

"Ohhh come on," I yelled at whisper level, "The world? The world? I am nobody! I could not possibly impact the world in such a way, or on such a vast scale." I spoke half out of fear and half out of guilt, because of course, everyone wants to be important.

"Yet," I said with a laugh and more than a hint of irony, "Look at me! I still sit here hoping you can convince me otherwise". I threw up my hands. "God, I must have an ego bigger than I ever considered, or… or… I am so gullible and simple minded that I find this all plausible." Alton could not help but let out a chuckle, then spoke with gravity.

"Michael, I will say it again, this is no joke. Will it help if I offer irrefutable proof that I am worthy of your trust and friendship?"

"Have at it," I said. "It is the only way we are going to work our way back from the fantasy land we are parked on the outskirts of, now!"

"Ok," Alton said, as if he was asked to play a game of chance. "Let's start with something very familiar and work our way out from there. Uhmmm… how about let's talk about your grandfather?

Your grandfather's name was Hugo; he was an inventor, a scientist like yourself. Believe it or not, we were very close friends."

I was just feeling comfortable with drawing my cup of coffee to my lips again when Alton spoke his sentence. My grip faltered and coffee splattered on my napkin and the empty plate underneath. If I was a target, and the statement Alton had just made was an arrow… bulls' eye!

Demanding more out of myself than to be such an easy mark and prepared to make Alton work for a foothold on trust, I said, "Whoa… hold on there, big fella. My grandfather was a very important person in my life and I was with him until he left to investigate some new discovery. He was 78 and I was 22 years old when we found out he had passed. That was almost 10 years ago. You could not be that much older than me and I am 32 now, so the numbers are just not in your favor. I never saw you around. Believe me you would not have been easy to forget. So how could you have been his friend?"

"True," Alton responded, "You never did meet me, but I kept my eye on you and we will talk about my age at another time, but thank you for the compliment. Your Grandfather and I spoke about you all the time. He was quite impressed with your intelligence and your abilities of deduction. I was there when your father and grandfather were helping you work on your first car. I believe they called it a Camaro. Your grandfather was consistently amazed at how quickly you assessed situations and generated a plan to achieve what you wanted. Do you remember what he used to tell your father, when you did something impressive?"

"Yea," I said. "He used to say to my Dad, 'See I told you so, Robert. Talent definitely skips a generation'. For some odd reason they always found that funny."

Alton smiled and said, "Your grandfather, my friend, was a wonderful man with a generous sense of humor. What would you say was the most valuable gift your grandfather gave you, Michael?"
I hung my head, as soon as the memory formed. "It... it was ..." I could not finish the sentence.

"It was a very special stone, right?" Alton leaned a little more forward to confirm his accuracy. "That is right, isn't it?"

My head bolted erect, as I stared fiercely into Alton's eyes.

"How could you know that? The stone was a secret! No one knew about it, not even my Dad! My grandfather made me promise to never show or tell anyone about it. How could you know about it?"

"Because," said Alton, "I am the one that gave him that stone. I gave him that stone out of friendship and I gave it to him, to at some point, give to you. It was his idea from the moment he saw it in my village. He knew it would inspire you to become what you are now, a scientist and a discoverer."

"Ok, this is really getting weird," I said, concerned that insanity had taken root. "Describe it to me and tell me why I became obsessed with it", I demanded.

Alton, began to speak, almost before I finished my sentence. "The stone had a base of solid white quartz." As if describing directions to a secret gold mine, he moved even closer. "The quartz base was unique; because it was composed of small geometric crystals that have not been found to exist anywhere on your world."

"Go on," I said, looking at my coffee, to make sure it had not turned into a glass of Kool-Aid.

"A bed of bright sky-blue turquoise colored mineral, lay across the top portion of the rock. A thick seamless layer of clear quartz covered the surface of the turquoise, adding luster and a twinkling aspect to the whole stone, as if it were a deep pool of water. Exposed to any direct light, the turquoise and quartz shimmered, reflecting the light like miniature diamonds. On one corner of the rock lay a multilevel crest which looked like a waterfall. The quartz flowed flawlessly over it. The levels of the crest were formed from a multitude of miniature crystals which added a frothy look to the quartz above and along the fall. This gave the impression that the quartz was surging down onto the turquoise and then onward over the turquoise bed. On the opposite edge of the rock, the clear crystal quartz ran into a hollow in between two crossed gemstones matching the shape of the ones on the base, but much larger."

Completely bewildered, I demanded more out of the description. "You have described it perfectly," I said while clearing my throat, "but there is still something missing about your description."

"Yes," said Alton, "as you know, your Grandfather Hugo was intrigued by minerals and crystals, especially their potential for generating, enhancing and controlling energy."

"Yes," I said. "He believed that ancient civilizations had mastered the use of minerals, metals and gems, to harness and focus the ambient energy of our planet. He believed that at some point the world changed geographically and those changes somehow threw off a dynamic, diminishing the potential and performance of crystalline structures in our environment."

I looked down at the table, juggling emotions created by my grandfather's absence. I mumbled, "I loved him very much and it hurt him that I didn't give much credence to his ideas, until…"

"Until the secret within the stone was revealed," Alton said completing my sentence. He smiled, in satisfaction seeing that the fisherman had finally set the hook. He wasted no time as he began to reel me in. "Our people, called that stone 'Mira' which loosely translated means, 'Clarity or Truth'. We named it that because when it was held to the sun, the quartz seemed to move across the turquoise surface. It flowed like a river into the cavity between the crystals. It sparkled like diamonds and generated a small rainbow over the crossed crystals at the other end of the stone… like one might see during a rain storm, or in the mist at the bottom of some great cascade. It beautifully translated raw energy, into energy with pattern and function."

"Yes," I said amazed. "When I placed my hand on the quartz surface while the sun was on it, it was cold and I could feel the quartz flowing like cool water. It took me years to realize that the sensation I felt, was energy flowing across the stone. It transformed the sunlight into energy, like my grandfather had believed. In sunlight, it became an energy source, when not in the sunlight, it was a battery. It retained warmth when touched. If you began to contemplate over it, reach out with your mind to get a better sense of the stone, or the energy in it, it responded, embracing your thoughts, connecting to you. If I had only grasped the truth of it, before my grandfather was gone. He said it had been a gift from the truest of friends, but warned me that if the stone was ever discovered by the scientific world, it would create problems. He would never say why; he would just say 'observe it and learn from it, for it will offer a great treasure to one who can see it for what it truly is!' So, I kept it a secret. I handled it and observed it. I would watch it in the sunlight often. It relaxed me and excited me at the same time. The stone was a catalyst in promoting my studies into the use of crystals. First for controlling frequency in radios, then wave development and finally energy generation and management. We exist in a world held together by energy. If a person could only extract the potential of ambient energy, like the stone does and apply the knowledge, he could change the world. My grandfather was not so far off the mark, after all".

"Michael, your grandfather's theories were not only right, but those theories and that stone, hold secrets to the very patterns of the universe. If left to those with selfish intentions, the stone, what it is capable of and the knowledge that can be extrapolated from that potential, in the least, could upset the balance of power in your world. Your grandfather began to feel that he was being observed and was exposing those he loved to unknown dangers, so he left to go on a journey those many years ago and as you know, he never returned to his home and his body was never recovered."

I tensed up as Alton finished his last sentence and I struggled to answer him. No one could have stopped my grandfather once he was set on a path. I did not even try to stop him from leaving. I just thought it was one of his many journey's to far off places. Even more heart breaking was that he wanted me to go with him, but as we talked about it, he could see that I was engrossed in my studies at the university. I could tell that it saddened him that I could not go. He was worried those last few years. Consumed with dark thoughts, afraid of something beyond his scope. He would call me every other day and ask me if I had seen anyone that looked out of place or threatening. I would always tell him to stop worrying and that I loved him. At least I got a chance to say that to him. He tried to tell me before he left that he did not know when he would be back, if at all. I was too involved in my own life to really listen to him. The day he left, he cautioned me once again about the stone and told me to be very vigilant.

"As crazy as it sounds and seems, I bonded with it. I was in tune and in sync with it. At times, when I focused my thoughts on the stone, I could feel it responding, pulsing along with my heart beat. If I reached out for it consciously just before sleep, my dreams would take on very realistic and tangible qualities. I found myself uncomfortable away from it and yet uncomfortable with the responsibility of it. All of those feelings started to create incongruities with my work and friends, so I put the stone where I felt it would be untouchable, safe. I promised my grandfather I would protect it. In hiding it so completely, I felt I was fulfilling that promise and at the same time creating a little distance between it and me. I guess my hiding spot was so safe that it was even safe from me, because when I went back to get the stone, it was gone. I thought I had moved it and forgotten its hiding place, but that is not like me. Anyway, in the end I failed to protect the stone". I hung my head for a moment and then said, "I am still angry at myself about that. I am also afraid that someone may have found the stone and validated my grandfather's fears". I pounded my fist down on the table and growled, "I cannot figure out, how I could have lost it."

Alton's eyes conveyed compassion and a sense of understanding. Then his face formed into a gigantic smile, one that many years later I would translate into, "Hold on to your senses, your mind is about to be blown".

I stared at him, wondering why he would smile after I had told him the stone was lost. He turned and reached into the pocket of his long jacket. When he turned back toward me, he was holding the stone. He held it out to me and my heart leapt out of my chest. My breath was caught in between memory and reality. As if the stone were a long-lost companion eager to be reunited with me, it released short bursts of crackling light, which encircled my outstretched fingers. I could feel myself releasing trapped breaths in gasps of relief and happiness. Alton surrounded the stone with his large hands and I regained my composure. I immediately looked around at the other tables within view, but the restaurant had become very empty. As I reached out for the stone again, the familiar ambient light it produced created shadows in between the folds of my fingers. As I touched it, I felt the vibrations echo deep within my chest. I wrapped my hands around the stone to take possession of it and found the cyclone had changed its pattern, in an attempt to encompass the stone. As I took hold of the stone, the cyclone tugged against me, drawing energy out of the stone, prying my fingers from their purpose. Sparks of miniature lightning, imbued the cyclone and it became more dense, stronger, taller and magnetic. It was not until Alton took one of his hands and separated the cyclone from around my hands that it stood true again. It was much denser and more powerful, but for the moment content to follow its preordained path along the plate's edge. I pulled the stone the rest of the way to my chest, as tears washed the disbelief from my eyes.

"The stone is yours", Alton said as the transfer was complete. "It resonates with you now and for as long as you desire it to. It is more than a gift from your grandfather. It is a gift from me and my people as well. It is a gesture of friendship and trust that between us, begins anew today and will carry into the future for as long as our families inherit the gift of life. I wonder who it will go to next, he finished and winked."

"How... when... No," I stopped my mouth from moving. "I am not even going to ask how you have it".

Alton's face turned serious. "Your grandfather felt that a very dangerous, clandestine force had been working with some of his theories, uncovering their potential. If that were the case, they would know that there was a missing and critical component."

"The Stone," I said in disbelief?

"Not only the stone, but what the stone can do, what it is

composed of and how that composition influences the very substance of this universe. Your grandfather became immediately wary of your safety, but it was not until he was contacted repeatedly by other researchers that his convictions were confirmed. He feared you might be in danger.

"At first, they came to him as colleagues interested in discussing his theories and how he came upon them. You know your grandfather, always on guard, very rarely fooled, so when he sensed that there was something devious a foot, he clammed up. Then this group, sent enforcers to motivate him through fear and intimidation. They did small things at first: tampered with his laboratory, bank account, safety deposit boxes, all to let him know they could take stronger measures to procure what they wanted, at any time. When they began to threaten those he cared for, by sending pictures of your family at their home and you with friends at school, he knew he had to take drastic measures. He asked me to take the stone back to my village. Then he closed everything up, and left on his journey. I watched his house after his reported death and found it strange that his possessions were immediately confiscated by some undefined authority. I am sure they did not find what they were looking for, because you hold it in your hands. I am also sure your grandfather is still alive and well."

"Alton, I do believe my grandfather was your friend, but he left 10 years ago. If you ever watched him challenge the laws of nature during any of his experiments, you know it was only through the grace of God and a good deal of luck that he lived as long as he did. The odds are not in either of our favors that he is alive."

"One can only believe in the union we all share, Michael. For now, let us be joyful that the stone is back in your possession. It is a very important part of your future. So… do we have a basis for trust? Do we share common ground?"

"Yes," I said. "I am truly in your debt." I grabbed his huge hand and with a smirk added, "and you have sufficiently trapped me in this mystery."

Alton leaned back and took a deep breath. "I am very happy you have chosen to be a seeker of truth, like your grandfather. Hugo followed his inner will, his true calling and it transported him beyond what he could have fathomed. If you wish to follow in his footsteps and set your own in the sands of time, you must be prepared to walk a similar path, with the same conviction. This is not a decision to be made lightly. Once you open the door separating illusion from the light of truth, the world you live in will never be the same."

"So, there is no going back," I said recognizing the crossroads I had just arrived at.

"A fish that swims in a stream, but somehow finds its way to the ocean, will not be satisfied with the limits of the stream, ever again," Alton added.

The words he spoke reverberated in my head, I really did not have an answer for him, but my mouth opened and I said, "Yes, yes, I am committed."

Like a horse out of the starting gate, Alton spoke immediately and again, in a very serious tone. "For expediency sake then, I need you to unshackle your mind, lower your defenses and let go of logic and preconditioned thinking, so that I might open doorways into your perception. Doorways that at present, you do not yet know exist. It is a lot to ask but the universe moves at a preordained pace; we need to match it."

"The universe," I whined. "Can't we start on a slightly smaller scale, with simpler expectations?"

"I am afraid not," said Alton. "The path we follow is not without its challenges. The human condition, the human mind, can be very frail. We must make haste on the path to minimize undesired exposure."

I could feel opportunity knocking. If I declined Alton's offer, if I got up at that moment and walked through the diner door into the night, I knew I would truly walk into darkness on a multitude of levels.

"Ok...Ok...," I let my head fall to the table with a confirming thud. "Help me. I do not even know how to do the simple things you just ask me to do. How do I stop my mind from analyzing? How do I stop trying to make sense out of what I see? How do I relax my logical mind? Look at me... I am already lost, and we haven't even started."

Alton laughed and stretched in his seat, letting out a huge sigh. The cyclone on his plate expanded in response to the release of tension at our table. Taking advantage of the moment, it darted to freedom. It passed over a fork, which flipped into the air high enough to fall into the adjacent booth. It sent a napkin shooting upward, spun off the table, hit the floor and disappeared through a swinging kitchen door. Alton followed the miniature tempest's flight into the unknown and then watched as the napkin drifted like a parachute earthward in between us. He looked at me, we both laughed. He shrugged and continued.

"There is nothing immediate you must do, except remain open and pliable of mind and spirit."

"Is that the same thing as what you asked me to do before?"

"Yes," he said." I must disconnect a lifetime of conditioning which has blocked your potential. I must access your dreams and your daydreams. That is where true desire entertains fantasy, where your soul weaves ideas which drive your future."

He stopped talking and leaned back again. I must have looked dumbfounded at the rush of information, because he laughed so completely the bench shook. In response, dishes crashed at a table nearby. Our waitress shot nervous side glances at us, as she raced to clean up her mess.

I spun in my seat, as a frightened yell and curse erupted through the skewed swinging doors to the kitchen. I could see a dishwasher with a wet mop, haphazardly slapping at something which was moving around his feet on the kitchen floor.

I took a deep breath and looked down at the reflections shifting endlessly in my coffee. It mirrored my sense of reality, which was similarly skewed at this point.

Alton spoke again softly, "For you to overcome your conditioning, you will have to take ownership of a new and enhanced awareness. You must be confident, believe that it can free you and create a new way of looking at your world."

I could feel the stone, now hidden in my coat, pulsating as if in agreement to Alton's requests. Reunited with it I felt strangely empowered, strong. I finished his statement with, "and project a better future, right?"

"Truly," Alton said softly.

"So exactly", I said with a pinch of sarcasm, "what do I do next again?"

"From this point forward," Alton said, "Fight the urge to disbelieve, to pick things apart, or to fabricate explanations. Do not allow self-doubt. Do not interrogate yourself, or constantly question each and every action. In other words, do not own, the unknown. It is not your responsibility to define everything you experience, that is a mechanism of fear. Instead of digging into the annals of your past for direction, give each complexity time to filter clear. Before you sleep at night, prepare your mind for the same duality you have already experienced. Let it become natural, let your inner lens refocus and swing wide the door, to infinite possibility."

The last embers of my energy were dying out. I could have slept right there on the dinner table. "Whatever you say boss", I said and I yawned.

"I am sorry," said Alton," maybe it is time to retire for the evening."

"I hate to agree, but that sounds good to me", I said embarrassed at my yawn". Wait, I promised to take you home. Also, I do not have any way to contact you, once I drop you off."

"I will be in contact with you," said Alton confidently.

"What does that actually mean," I asked with a wry smile?

"It is a nice night for a walk on the beach", said Alton skirting the question.

The waitress happened to be standing right by the table and not by coincidence I thought. Throughout the meal she was noticeably self-conscious around Alton. Whether it was looking up at a man who was sitting down. Staring into eyes double the circumference of her own, or dropping a tray of dirty dishes, startled from the sonic boom of his laugh, she remained a trooper. I could see she was perplexed as to whom to hand the check to. Since I could relate to her unsettled nature and felt a little sorry for her, I whisked the bill out of her hand, paid it, dropped the tip and followed Alton out of the door, giggling a little each time he dodged a light hanging from the ceiling.

The night air was crisp, but comfortable. I was in no shape to join him on his walk though. We shook hands. It was then that I noticed Alton looking behind me, his eyes stretched wide. I turned to see what caught his attention. In the light of the open back door of the restaurant, I could see a man in white, feet outstretched in midair. It was the kitchen worker and he swung wildly from what looked like the handle of a gyrating mop. He yelled something that was lost in the distance between us, but his meaning was not. His grip slipped, he rotated one time in the air and landed in the gravel a few feet away from his dancing adversary. The mop's cloth fibers, which hung near the ground, floated in an upward motion twisting and turning as if to braid pony tails. Small flashes of miniature lightning crackled intermittently amongst the fibers, creating a surreal image for sure. Swinging in an unnatural rhythm, the mop continued to move silently off into the night to dissipate.

"Now that is something you do not see every day," I said with astonishment as I turned with a questioning eye, but Alton was nowhere to be found.

CHAPTER 8

S tanding outside the diner, as night closed in, I felt grateful to be alive. Spring still resonated in the air, crisp and fresh, robust. Even now, it carried with it smells of moist, rich earth and rebirth. The ocean not far away, added spice to the air and nature's potent recipe for new life. As my mind drew a solid connection between the new beginnings that spring demanded of many living things and the new beginnings that destiny now demanded of me, I found myself feeling a part of something much greater. I looked around. I was alone, but I did not feel that way. Instead, I was feeling renewed and invigorated. I carefully pulled out the Stone. I could feel the warmth that pulsed from it. I could feel the connection between it and the essence of life resonating from the earth beneath my feet. I closed my eyes, took a deep breath and allowed the rhythm to radiate into my body. Almost immediately an effervescence climbed beyond my hand, past my wrist and up my arm, along with warmth one might feel facing upwards soaking in the sun. The warmth infused into my bones and felt incredibly good. The blood coursing through my veins became palpable, as it drew the energy in like a dry sponge to water. I continued to let the energy flow into every part of me. Where fear resisted, vibrant warmth calmed and washed clean the trepidation.

My entire body was now in sync with the stone. No… I realized, not just with the stone, or the earth and air. The stone was resonating to some essential and crucial vibration that interlaced all things. Just like the bones of my body provided a frame for my flesh, the unifying principles of the stone provided a frame for the sinew and muscle of my awareness, my will. The stone beat like a heart common to all things, woven into a unified purpose, connected to all existence.

"Sir… Sir… are you all right?" said a small and concerned voice.

At first, I thought it was just another tone, mixed into a symphony that poured out from the energy coursing through my body and then the voice became clearer and more stressed.

I was standing upright, my head back. I realized my mouth had been wide open, because my jaw hurt and my mouth was as dry as a desert. The only words I could muster as I regained my composure was, "Yes, I am fine... uhm... thank you." Luckily, I had been holding the rock on the far side of my body, so I did not think she saw it. I placed it back in my pocket and turned to find our waitress from the diner, standing poised to run like hell, should I turn out to be 'out of my mind'.

I pointed up, awkwardly." I... uh... I thought... I saw a shooting star and was looking for others."

Ohhhkay," she said relaxing ever so slightly. "You had not moved for a while, so I just wanted to make sure you were all right. I heard you saying something... or maybe you were humming or groaning. I was worried you might be hurt or in pain. I am glad you are all right. Where is your friend, the big one? I ... I liked him; he was very kind."

"Oh, he had to leave... uhmm... suddenly," I answered quickly. Just then out of the corner of her vision, the waitress saw the kitchen worker stumbling around in circles at the back of the restaurant.

"I have to go," she said. "It looks like my friend has been drinking again."

"I ... I understand and thank you for your consideration." I sort of bowed a little I guess, because I was still embarrassed. I smiled and then turned toward my vehicle to skedaddle.

CHAPTER 9

As I climbed in my car, it was hard not to notice the front passenger seat. It was pushed as far back as it could possibly go and then some. The seat back was leaning toward the rear of the car, so that Alton would not have to double over to sit upright. I started laughing like a man who had just won the lottery. Was all this real? I reached in my pocket and felt the stone, it felt fuzzy with energy and my hand and arm tingled in response. Yes, it was real! Everything that was too fantastic to consider a few weeks ago, along with what had happened today and tonight, it was all real... or I was really insane. I felt normal though... well at least mentally. So how much farther did the real, reality stretch? What else existed right in front of me, that I was not aware of?

I was wide awake now. I was energized and awed by happenings I could not possibly have imagined. There was no way I was going home to sleep. So, I pulled out of the diner parking lot hoping for inspiration. I began to reminisce about my grandfather. He had been so important to me while I grew up. He was always searching for ways to spend time together and share experiences. How could I have let him go, in both flesh and memory? It was as if I had packed him away like memorabilia, in some cerebral storage box. Then stuffed that box in a rarely used closet in my mind. Considering how important he was to me, that just did not seem right.

An inspiration came quickly. I made a U-turn and headed toward his house. As I drove, I rolled the windows down to enjoy the rich spring air and let my mind drift back to memories long stored away. As I drove closer to my grandfather's home, my childhood conditioning retraced the short trip we took almost every day from my parent's house to my grandfather's. I remembered looking forward to seeing him, his smile, his sense of humor. He brought the child out in all of us. It was as if he held some magical secret. We all knew he had one, but we had no idea what the secret was. We were 'OK' with that though, because to me, my sisters and brothers and neighborhood friends, he was the magic. He could do things that to our adolescent minds, defied reality. We all believed he was the 'Keeper of the Secrets'. Anyway... who cared, he was our grandfather and when we were with him, we never felt alone. Maybe that was his true secret ability.

I rounded the corner at the end of the block and could see the side of my grandfather's garage. I parked the car underneath some trees far enough away from any house to arouse suspicion. Even in the dark, my grandfather's home was comforting and familiar.

My father had followed the instructions my Grandfather had left with his lawyer. The first lines read "If I should die and my body be claimed, please follow the directions in Part One of this document". If I should not make a timely return from a trip, or disappear without a trace, please follow the attached directions in Part 2". Since his remains were never recovered, the Part 2 directions were followed to the 'T' by my father.

Everything was to be maintained in the same condition it was before my grandfather left. He stated in his will that he planned on returning. He gave a date when the will should be considered a final document and the Part 1 directions carried out, but that was still 10 years off. I did not know what he had in mind, but my grandfather always had a purpose and a plan.

It was not until some obscure branch of the government closed off the property and blocked everyone, including my family, from gaining entrance to it that we sensed others were searching for a secret denied them.

My father went ballistic over the trespassing on his father's property and wishes. Then for some reason which he would never share, he went silent on the subject. When I asked who gave them the right to ransack Pap's stuff, my father simply quoted my grandfather by saying, "Men are never so blind, than when they believe they understand what they are not capable of understanding. They are driven by a focus which eclipses the most obvious."

"What are they looking for," I would ask?

"What they will never find, Mike," he said. "Even if they did, they wouldn't recognize it."

"What, Dad... what would they not recognize?"

"Why your Grandfather's secret, of course you dummy!" That would make us all laugh, and then the subject would change somehow, or someway.

I do not think my grandfather had expected the government to come in and confiscate all his belongings though. A detective had come to visit us around the same time and gone as far as to warn us not to return to the house for any reason. Then after 6 months or so, they removed the broad yellow "No Trespassing" tape, the wooden horses, the digging tools and whatever else they used to try to uncover what they were looking for and left. It took a few years for my father to get back much of the stuff removed, fix the yard, the interior, the basement floor and the destroyed patio, but my grandfather had left plenty of money so that his property could be preserved.

Everything seemed quiet now. The neighborhood had not changed that much in the years I had been absent and while sitting there, I became engrossed in more memories. I could feel the warmth of the stone and just touching it relaxed me. Leaning back in my seat, with my neck supported by a well-used Lab coat, I smiled as I watched favored memories, kind moments, difficult lessons and practical jokes that never lost their zing, march forward from the hidden recesses of my mind. They would then retreat from my inner vision to the secluded vaults, all minds store treasures in. Peace enfolded me and just before I fell into a deep sleep, I felt the stone I was holding gently surge with warmth and a brilliant flash of light.

CHAPTER 10

I was immersed in crystal clear water, a vast living mirror, reflecting the world above and around me. I looked down at my body to get a sense of where I was standing, but there was only water. I struggled to move and ripples splashed on to the rocks and shore. Spectacular vistas and majestic expressions of raw nature painted across the ripples contorted slightly. This had to be a dream I thought and I remembered Alton's words, his guidance. "Do not over think, do not try to define, allow the locks limiting your freedom, to be broken."

A waterfall creating an effervescence which filled the air above it with a multitude of rainbows and crystalline shimmering, drew my attention. Life flowed through me and everywhere about me.

Off in the distance against sparkling peaks, I could see a figure approaching. He passed under two massive crossed crystal spires and once by my shore, he kneeled and bent forward until his face was fully visible upon my surface. As I watched him, I could see that unlike all the other reflections, his reflection extended deeper than the surface. It projected into my depths. I was the turquoise blue sky, the lofty white clouds, the glistening summits, but now as this figure gazed into my waters, it was as if his gaze was reflected in my every drop. Each thought, each feeling this person had cast itself upon my surface and into my depths. He resonated like a pebble cast into and penetrating fluid stillness, asserting presence, petitioning established shores. He deepened his gaze, searching for something... illusive.

Although his nature was anything but clear, now that I was coupled to his nature, I saw him clearly. I saw his fear and I saw his darkness. I saw the gleaming jewel of his soul, as it struggled with the bonds and limitations of a physical world. I saw walls like that of a mighty fortress, formed from foundations rooted in bedrock to provide safety and refuge for all within. Yet these walls had been built beyond prudence and held out all that was different and new. The light within these walls was dim. It was difficult to see anything clearly. I could feel the yearning, the needs and cries, echoing off the walls, calling out for redemption and freedom.

His focus suddenly sharpened, as he fathomed his salvation amongst endless reflections. He witnessed that he was not alone in a universe as infinite as the one he existed in. He realized that by committing to his truest of natures, he would be free, cleansed.

As his perceptions gained form, darkness began to fall away. Sins were washed from the dark walls of his fortress so that they began to gleam. Washed clean, they were as they had always been, an anchor, securing his spirit to his physical form, the structure supporting his soul.

The simple sins of ignorant action and deed fell away first. The life-draining sins, the ones we perpetrate upon ourselves, the sins of self-hate, mistrust, self-abuse, pride and denial, clung to the mighty walls with a pleading nature. The figure grasped what was necessary. With glee and a gulp of air, he simply let go. He fell forward, arms spread like a bird taking flight, offering everything he was, up to everything that is. As his body became immersed in my waters, we became one. My infinite nature, my right of existence in a free-flowing universe, became his. My shores disappeared. My communal waters blended with the individuality of a single life. That life now paired in awareness, to a boundless soul. Now cleansed, he transcended his limitations and carried us both beyond the scope of mundane shores.

Emancipated, he stood upon a different landscape, a new reality. Our spirit, our being as it was meant to be, the same energy, the same life, just different reflections in a universe of existence.

CHAPTER 11

I sat up in the car in a start like I had overslept for work. Actually, a fairly common experience. I took a few deep breaths to connect my thoughts to my actions and then looked around. I drew a sigh of relief, confident that I was in the seat of my car and night time was solidly in possession of the world around me. The stone in my pocket clung effortlessly to my hand like a saltine cracker wrapper, after the contents had been removed. The last of some paranormal exchange, softly fading away.

I was good! Everything was OK. I was not late for work and I was secure, hidden by the depth of the night. The stone pulsed again, like a cell phone vibrating upon receiving a call. Tentacles of energy raced around my hand as it vibrated. Something was connecting with the stone, on some level, other than me. The energy that sparked the stone to life seemed to also spark a very clear memory, or vivid image. That image was of my grandfather digging in a tree across the road from his house. I watched as he showed me a small tin box that had once held my miniature race cars, but now held three odd keys. I listened to the echoes in my mind as he said, "Mike, three keys, for three locks. Let this stone show you where the keys belong and the keys will show you where the stone belongs. Once you have found where the stone belongs, I believe you might find where you belong. Hopefully you will find answers to some of your most pressing questions and I am sure," he smiled very brightly, "many more new ones." I watched as he slid the box inside a sap-encrusted cavity in the tree, then he covered it with a piece of soft rubber to keep the moisture out. He then added a covering of leaves and dirt. He took his favorite knife out of his pocket, bent low and began scratching at the tree. A squirrel high up on a limb was upset that we were encroaching on his territory. He barked and chattered running up and down a branch, chastising us. My grandfather stood back up with his 'I have a secret' grin on his face. He put his arm under my arm and said, "The future is not always unknown."

Strange, I thought. I had not recalled that memory until now.

I could see the tree from where I was parked in my car. As I pondered on the remembrance of the strange looking keys, the stone seemed to magnetize more firmly to my hand as if giving direction, 'yes, find the keys."

I looked around; all was quiet. I got out of my car and wandered aimlessly down the street, trying to look inconspicuous. Late at night? In a residential neighborhood? Right… definitely more like creepy! When I reached the tree, I took another look around and slid behind a bush that lay between the road and the tree trunk. I used the face of my cell phone to illuminate a small area, as I circled the tree looking for evidence of where the cavity might be. I sunk to my knees and dug around the base, but there was no cavity. I stood up, rubbed my hands on my pants and scratched my head to get a little brain power into the effort. The rich smell of moist soil filled my senses while gritty dirt that was jammed under my fingernails, fell into one eye.

I shook my head and ruffled my hair looking up to let it fall away, then it hit me. I was a young man and hiding the box took place maybe 12 years ago? The tree had certainly grown, since then! I started walking around the trunk looking about shoulder height, guessing that would be 12 years of growth? Still, there was no sign of the cavity. Again, I stepped back and scratched my head, assessing the potential for growth to the tree. As I looked up, I saw a split in the tree, about 5 feet above me. Just to the left and below the split, my initials… 'MG' had been carved at a right angle to the cavity, so I would see it from the ground looking up. So that was what my grandfather was doing with his knife. How could he possibly know I would come looking for the tin in the future, or even remember it?

The cavity was just outside my reach. I needed a lift. I looked around and saw a pile of cut up wood, a recent road crew had left while clearing debris from the power lines along the road. Two large round pieces would serve as a fitting stool! I placed the first one solidly on flat ground, no need to prove my ability to join the circus here, I laughed to myself. I mounted the second piece upon the first and started to test my weight upon it. The stone seemed to sing with vibration as I climbed up on the support. It was too dark to see what the inside of the cavity held, but I had gone this far, so I started cautiously feeling around the edges of the opening and then slipped my hand further inside. An odd feeling of soft fur and warmth met my exploring fingers, just about the same time that I realized I was an intruder in someone's home. Between the racket caused by a startled animal and my fear of being bit, I lost my balance and was on my back before the home owner could make it fully out his door. After inspecting my body for damage, I looked up to see a fluffy tail darting in every direction. It belonged to a rather angry squirrel, mad at my lack of consideration and timing. I climbed to my feet and the squirrel darted for a higher platform to throw its intense condemnations. OK… I thought, I might as well get the job done. I jumped back up on the supports and dug into the hole, still concerned about what else might be in there. To my surprise, the box was wedged right behind the furled knot opening that made the mouth of the cavity. I grasped it, jumped to the ground, waved to the squirrel and hurried back to my car.

Just before I opened the door to my car, I looked around again. Besides the constant thrumming of the stone in my pocket, all was quiet. I climbed in my seat and rolled up the windows. I giggled to myself, a little giddy from all that happened up to this point and now to be reconnected with my grandfather in some kinetic way, was simply amazing. I took a moment and just stared at the box while rolling it over and over in my hands. It was just as I remembered it. Stored in the tree trunk, it was no worse for wear. The front of the box, held a little rotating clasp that secured the top to the bottom. I moved it with my finger and it slid easily off the lip. Rolling my eyes and taking a deep breath, I lifted the top all the way open, surprised at what I saw. Glistening in the minimal light, were three hexagonal crystals. Each crystal was the size of a pencil you would use to fill out a lottery ticket. Each one was fused to a round flat head-stock, like any other key might be. The crystals were grayish, and were fibrous in structure, as if made from a combination of crystal and metal strands. As the light from the stone pulsated, each key responded in a different way, with a slightly different color. It was unmistakable, a dull rainbow-colored luster flowed across the keys and disappeared, animating the keys and sending shivers up my spine. These were no ordinary keys. So, it followed, they were sure to unlock something extraordinary. As I moved the keys toward my left to get another perspective, I looked down. The stone in my pocket was now emitting a more intense glow, as if synchronizing with the keys was enhancing its intrinsic power. They were somehow communicating. I remembered what my grandfather had said, "Let the keys show you where the stone belongs". Then a thought came to me.

What if the people who were looking for 'whatever' did not find it because they did not have the keys? I knew my grandfather well. A wilier man as he... never existed. So, was it possible he left more than the house behind? Maybe he left the answers he promised, maybe a legacy?

I looked at the key ring that was hanging in the ignition. On it was a key to my grandfather's house. It was the one my father gave me to check on things when he could not get there.

Using that key, I spent many hours in my grandfather study. Pap's mind maze we used to call it. Oddly, it seemed to enhance my ability to think and concentrate while doing my homework. It was also not uncommon to have to fight my brothers, or sisters who showed up searching for privacy and desk space, having realized the same benefits. Hoping maybe for some of Pap's family secret recipe hot chocolate. We never found anything unusual in that room, but believe me... it was not for lack of searching.

A dull sheen surged across the keys again, keeping cadence with the stone. The energy continued into my mind, igniting the enthusiasm of a gold miner on a sure trail to discovery. It took everything in me, not to leap out of the car and dash to my grandfather's house.

CHAPTER 12

I took deep breathes to control my excitement. Once in my right mind, I began to check off what I needed to be conscious of before I took a next step. I remembered clearly what my father had said, as he bit back anger, years after the seizure of my grandfather's home. "This world has many predators, do not allow yourself to be easy prey. Be vigilant when you are at Pap's, they are always watching." This told me my father knew something more about my grandfather's secrets than he admitted, but he held his secrets like Fort Knox and would say no more. From that point on, I watched everything that was happening when I visited my grandfather's home. One day, I noticed one of the lawn sprinkler heads was stuck up above the ground. I thought that was odd, because it was fall. The water that supplied them had been shut off for the winter, so the head could not have been pressured above the soil. As I walked up to it to investigate, the head let out odd squeaks and squeals, like a fax machine. I thought to myself, sprinkler heads do not have complex electronics in them, so I bent down to get a better look. Just at that moment, a service van came to screeching halt in front of the house and two men leapt out of the van and moved quickly to the sprinkler head wedging themselves between myself and the device.

We have this son, said one man as the other grabbed my jacket and pulled me back away from the protruding head. As I fell off balance, I saw a red power light flashing on the sprinkler head. The first technician grabbed me before I fell flat on my back, he seemed very powerful for a sprinkler service guy. The second technician blocked my view.

"Nothing here boy, go on with what you had to do and we will take care of this."

I blurted out, "hey... what the heck... and then, what is that light and how can the sprinkler head be up, if the water is off?" The technician kneeling by the head turned and gave me a stern look, one that told me to "SHUT UP". I could only guess at what was going on that day, but I understood what my father was warning me of.

That was then, this now, I said to myself and I am no boy. As night moved silently on toward dawn, I slipped out of the passenger side of my car, locked it and began to follow a path through the woods we used when we were kids playing 'Capture the Flag'. The path had been well worn into the brush and grass years ago, no such luck now. It took me more than just a few minutes to work my way around to the rear of the house. Considering the new foliage on the pricker bushes, I was none to stealthy either. Next to the garage was a basement entrance covered by old metal storm doors. As a kid in the middle of a life and death struggle to capture the opponent's flag, it was crucial to know how to access that hiding place by opening the doors so they did not squeak. A talent only myself and a select few possessed. Staying to the shadows, I crept up close to the doors. I swung around to the front of them and working with the skill of a safe cracker, gaining access without any noise. Not as slim as I was as a child. I had to open the door wide to slip in, but I made it. The smell of mildew and spider webs filled my senses. Ahh... just like I remembered it. I was brought up in this house. I was familiar with all the nooks and crannies, the hiding places and the 'off limits' places. My Paps might be able to hide stuff from those who were unwelcome, but from me, 'No Way'.

I reached for the key to the basement door that hung on my car key ring. As I extended my hands to unlock the door, I noticed I had much more light to work with than I should have. I looked down at my side; the stone was glowing, but it only emitted a small amount of light. I looked at the wooden box holding the three keys. There was only ambient light sneaking through the lid. Perplexed, I sat on the steps and closed my eyes. I took a deep, patient breath. As I looked at the back of my eyelids, I allowed the myriad of geometric shapes to flash, rotate and then dissipate. I rubbed my eyes allowing the remaining shapes and light to fade. Soon, all I saw was black. I opened my eyes slowly, hoping to control their sensitivity. I sat still on the steps and looked down. To my amazement, the whole wall shimmered with a flowing sheen just like the keys in the box. I quickly opened the box and found that the luster from the keys was synchronized with the wall and the stone. I held the keys closer to the wall. It glowed brighter as particles matching those in the keys resonated in luminosity. I burst out laughing. A homing beacon! Again, my Paps words rung true. "Let the keys show you." I laughed out loud again, then covered my mouth giddy with possibility. How many times had I sat upon these stairs, lying in wait for an opportune time to jump out and scare my brothers and sisters, or Paps? I never would have imagined!

Ever the inventor, I was confident my Grandfather had to have designed a way to allow simple access to his secret places, while providing the ultimate in safety and security. Now… what could that design have been? I looked up at the doors above me, then pulled the stone out of my pocket and held it close to edges of the metal monoliths. It seemed to me that Paps would not want anyone opening the door, while he was accessing whatever was here, so maybe…? There in the corner by the original latch was a locking slide. In the dim light, I realized it was as large as the door was long. Boy, I guess he really didn't want anyone barging in. I turned around on the steps and pulled the latch handle out toward me to move the mechanism both forward, toward the entry and backward, toward the foundation, just like a submarine hatch, I thought. Once the lever had been moved in the opposing position, it snapped into place. I heard a thunk from somewhere underneath me. Excited, I backed down the steps and waited for whatever was to come next, but nothing happened. I jumped up and down on the steps, thinking they were stuck from the long years of disuse and needed a little persuasion, no luck. Discouraged I turned and sat back down on the third step. Ok… lets go back to what I knew of Paps again. If I could find that latch, he knew someone else might also find it. So, there might be a combination of actions needed, maybe three, to match the keys. So, combo one… is one and done. Combo two… I said to myself, hmmm, let's see… two entrance points, two ways for an intrusion, sooooo… I went down to the basement door. I worked my way from the top of the door to the bottom, left to right with the stone, looking for any reaction. As the stone passed the door knob there were two key holes, where there had always been just one. One key hole was on the knob itself, but the other, unfamiliar to me, was on the brass plate that held the entire knob assembly. It was an old style key hole, like from the twenties, round with a slot at its base. As I passed the stone over the key hole, a faint glow highlighted the edges of the hole and slot. I pulled the stone away; the keyhole went dark. Aha… this must be key one. I took out the keys and flipped one of them into position, but as I pushed it into the lock, the glow dimmed. I pulled it out and held it to the lock, it also was dim. I repeated the process with the second key on the ring and the same thing happened. I placed the third key next to the brass plated key hole and the pulsating light became a solid light. I ran it smoothly into the lock and held my breath as I turned it. It spun 180 degrees and stopped. An additional thunk sounded, just below my feet, as if large gears had unlatched. Combo two I said, like a safe cracker on a roll.

Again, I waited for something more to happen… yet nothing did. "Ok… Paps, what's next?" I said out loud rubbing my hands together and blowing on the fingers of my right hand for luck. I allowed my grandfather's nature to guide me. All entries secure, hmmm now … he probably would create some way to confirm that the person seeking entry was not just clever, but truly qualified to enter. What would they need to validate themselves? As I sat on the steps with only the luster of the stone, the keys and the walls to stave off complete darkness, I saw the outline of small hands in the concrete of the entry way. I remembered when we made those impressions, all five of us. There were David's imprints, he was the youngest. His prints were smeared a bit, as we had to hold him tight while he was kicking and screaming to get the imprint. He can't stand the feel of cement on his hands to this day.

Next to his prints were Ellen's, along with one and half foot prints, she was all about it. She had to put her toes in too and then she came back with her crayons to color in nails on her cement toes. Hugh's were the next, no fear there. His prints were deep and firm, along with the outline of a large cricket he had caught, now captured in cement for posterity.

Mine were… hey … where were my prints? There were Gina's. Ten inches from where Hugh's were. She was the oldest, her prints were the biggest and matching her personality, they had to be juuuuust right. She had earned the nickname 'G FORCE TWEEKER' because she loved to personalize everything, but mine… mine were gone. "That is not right," I said out loud. When the investigators left the hatch open during a hurricane, I helped my dad clean up the water and muck that plugged up the drain and sullied the hand prints. The drain in the bottom was really plugged up, so we had to... hey, the drain was plugged up? Maybe... I put my hand down flat in between my brother and sister's print. The floor began to glow and I pulled my hand away. In the center of the drain where the screw to hold it down would have been, there was a distinct glow. I reached for the matching glowing key, plugged it in and the floor vibrated ending in another thunk. The steps shook a little and I grabbed hold, just in case the whole floor fell apart. From under the basement door jam, the cement started to drop down. It continued to drop, until the floor matched the slope of the steps I was on. I could not see below, or how to climb down, but I knew there was a way. Light from the walls spread to down below, like halogen bulbs warming up in a large stadium, dull at first, becoming brighter as they charged. Soon the entire stair area was visible. As I waited, I thought how clever the clues were in guiding me on a path intended for me. It had to be for me, who else had imprinted the cement there, but me. Just below where the floor had been, there were handles on each side. I reached out grabbed one and pulled. Like a fire escape ladder, steps pulled up and latched into the ones I sat upon. Even though there was not a lot of room, there was enough to walk almost upright down the next flight of stairs. The steps went down for about another 12 feet and stopped upon a landing made of a clear crystal stone. It looked like cracked glass, or maybe polished granite, but it was made with the same metal/crystal composition as the keys. Each fracture in the floor began glowing in sync with the stone I held. It was clear they supplied a path for energy not just light. It looked like a network, or nervous system. As I stepped on to the floor, I felt a vibration very deep below me, as if a massive engine were running underground somewhere close. I bent my knees and reached down to feel the floor with my hand. Power vibrated right up through me and my hair crackled. When I looked up from the floor, I was staring into a wall of fractured light. The walls to either side, along with the floor and ceiling, were sending veins of light and energy through to a point in the middle of that wall. I stood up slowly and reached out to touch the wall of energy. My hand began to tingle and ripple with static energy, as my fingers touched the convergence. Where I touched it, my hand actually passed through the wall and the sensation was that of passing through silk or tepid bubbling water. With one hand holding the keys and the other ... somewhere else, I could feel a surge in the last key in my hand. It was pulsing brightly and vibrating with the same intensity as the floor, the walls and the convergence. I pulled my hand back, switched the key to my right hand and pointed the crystal key at the center of the convergence. Before I could make another move, the key was sucked from my hand by magnetic force and disappeared into the convergence. There was a surge of light which moved out in all directions from the center and the wall began to spin, like the cyclone or vortex Alton had created. It started from the point where the key entered and expanded outward quickly. It took on depth and the center warped away until there was no end in sight.

Even though the vortex seemed so violent inside, all was calm where I stood. I leaned forward, dumbfounded by the sight, sound and feel of what was occurring. I wanted to get a sense of what the vortex felt like. So, I leaned in a little and my face began to tingle. A little uncertain, I tried to lean back away. My face seemed to be caught in the energy swirling before me. I realized that as the vortex had expanded outward, it had also expanded forward and I was now in the event horizon of the vortex. I began to struggle to separate myself from what was unraveling and I became dizzy. I reached up to feel my face and saw my hand and parts of my face begin to fragment. From that point forward, there was no struggle, no balancing act, teetering on the edge of one reality while assessing the nature of another. I moved quickly along an intangible corridor. I could feel its size and dimension. I could feel massive power both magnetic and gravitational, but there was nothing solid in its construction, or in mine for that matter.

Within a few seconds, I was outside my normal world and looking at a landscape I was not familiar with. I felt a little out of sorts, but unless I had lost my ever luvin mind, I was in touch with every tangible, physical property available to my senses. My surroundings were blisteringly clear, as if what I saw held far too much information and definition for my brain to process. It almost hurt to look at it.

The smell of fields in blossom was carried by a breeze, dancing past my senses. Rolling plains filled my vision. As I absorbed the landscape before me, I was awed by its beauty. The plains resembled an ocean. Gusts of wind flowed like waves across its surface, cresting over small hills and disappearing just as the next wave carried forward through gold and crimson shafts of waist high grass. As the grass moved, it took on different shades, exposing patches of brightly colored flowers and bushes. Iridescent blues, reds, yellows and colors no physical description could do justice to, flashed like sparkles, reflected off a sea of gold. The grass which looked very much like wheat, was very pleasing to the eye. Off in the distance were vague structures. Set against hills and a lake, as if part of a painting. The whole vista was hypnotic.

At first, and as my conditioning dictated, I tried to define my location and surroundings in terms that made earthly sense. I knew I was just bargaining with my psyche for time to deal with what I had just come through. I might be… hummm… on the outskirts of a Plains Indian village, I said to myself. A better look at structures off in the distance, proved this thought wrong. The buildings I could see, were different in structure, solid with sharp angles. Off to my left, I heard distant voices obscured by gusts of wind, that rolled through the waist high grass, generating a hum, or rattle.

As I finished taking in my surroundings, my mind shifted back to me and I realized, compared to the cooler breeze blowing onto my face, the wind blowing against the back of my neck was far warmer and very moist. A warm ooze began to slide uncomfortably down my neck and beneath my collar. Before clear thinking could intercept fear, I had turned my whole torso, arms raised to defend myself.

Pink, wet and wide, a rather large tongue retracted past impressive pearl white fangs, flinging drool across my face. Before me stood a humongous wolf. Rich, thick, brown fur stood on alert up his spine and at his shoulders. Sharp, clear gold eyes stared directly into mine, searching for submission, but hoping for challenge. I was fixed in place. I could no more have turned my gaze from his in that moment than return to my world, where ever that was?

As I slowly moved back from the immediate threat, my foot slid backwards. I caught my balance and looked behind me. I was on a large mound. I was also about to step backwards off of it. My observer on the other hand, was standing on level ground and had to bow his head to focus on me. This animal was huge!

I had no idea what to do. If I was going to run for it, I would have to jump off the mound. Which of course, the wolf could just walk around... what next, I said basically giving up. The animal shifted his weight. That signaled more of a 'let me get comfortable while this strange thing figures out his next move', than 'Dinner... Yipeee'. As I stood there trying not to look desperate, the wolf turned to his left and smelled the air. Not exactly a move a predator would engage in unless he was really confident, I thought. He returned his gaze to me, then turned completely away from me and sat for a moment. At first, I did not know whether to be insulted by his actions. I mean, was I too small to eat? Then it struck me. I sensed no true threat from him; it was my own fear that inspired impressions of a few spare bones of mine dangling from a nearby tree. I only sensed diligent interest. He was cautious, yet bold. He was not aggressive, nor was he threatened by me in any way. Suddenly, an exhilaration, or excitement erupted from deep within my chest. Call it relief at not being eaten alive, or happiness that I met a friend, not a foe. Maybe he was overgrown, just like Alton. Maybe this was where Alton was from? I do not know. I laughed with the spontaneity of a child being tickled and I had absolutely no control over it. He turned and rotated his head slightly at an angle, as if he was thinking... 'Oh boy... this one is crazy'. That made me laugh even harder. It was also, just about the time when I am sure he began to wonder whether he should be the one afraid.

Without any warning, the grass in front of us burst apart. Two young wolves came crashing through. The younger of the two was being chased and in his haste to get away from his pursuer, tripped on the mound I was sitting on, knocking me to the ground. His head landed solidly in my lap. He continued his struggle against the larger one's pursuit, his back slowly rising up my chest, his head finally resting against my neck and shoulder. As the young wolf pushed his attacker away with his front paws, his head fell toward me, tongue hanging to the side in exhaustion. Our eyes met; you could see the world freeze in his. They were the spitting image of his fathers. Unfortunately, so was the drool which coated my shirt, neck and cheek. You could see his young mind grasping his position and then the place he lay. He let out a yelp which startled his sister, who was plunging her razor-sharp teeth into his defending paws. In less than a second, he had spun, gained his legs and vaulted away from me, landing with a thud, squarely on his father's back. Instead of running, the female in front of me backed up a few steps, lowered her head and with flattened ears, began to circle me and growl. She was smaller than her father. Yet the intensity and power in her low rolling growl, vibrated throughout my chest and head, bringing the reality of nature in the raw to my awareness and sparking true fear. She shifted her gaze to include her father. I could feel no movement from him, which brought some relief. With an apparent return gaze from him, she split off and circled around behind. Now that the children were involved, I was unsure what would happen between us. To my surprise, when I looked toward the adult to gauge my plight, he was gone. Then, so were the young ones. I spent a few minutes arranging my thoughts, assessing my surroundings and checking my underwear, before standing up. My canine hosts were not entirely comfortable with my suspicious arrival. I am sure they took the breach in their perimeter, personally. So, in order to avoid any more drastic responses, I rose slowly from my semi-hidden position.

Every facet of my awareness felt heightened, hard wired. The air was electric, the breeze was filled with rich smells and velvety smooth, as it dried the sweat from my skin. The sights and colors, were so vibrant, so... alive. Ten cups of coffee could not generate this level of intensity. I felt itchy, anxious. I needed to move around. I went to wipe my forehead and found that drool had worked its way down my arm and now after wiping my forehead, it oozed into one eye. I quickly pulled my shirt up to wipe it off, while growling at myself.

The air next to me changed temperature and I again felt that moist warmness, just to my right and shoulder high. All I could think of was, how does he do that so silently? As intense as all my senses were at that moment, I should have been aware of him. Good thing I am not a turkey.

The wolf turned to face a path in the grass. He then took a sitting position by my leg. Even seated he was massive and dwarfed me. He was waiting on something, but his stealthy nature hid all indications of what, or whom it might be. Dropping my arm and adjusting my shirt, not wanting to raise any concern with my actions, I faced the same direction. Almost immediately, a person came into view. With hands outstretched, palms forward, finger tips stroking the grass, a flowing figure approached. It became obvious as the person drew nearer that she was a female. Once directly in front of me, I was impressed by her height. She was approximately 9 to 10 feet tall, lean of structure and undoubtedly fit. She was dressed in ornate weaves and beads. Gold and silver jewelry of stunning artistry, bound her clothes. With a massive wolf standing next to me and this towering person standing before me, I felt miniature. Her face was calm and beautiful. She was similar in color to Alton, not light, not dark, but a shade of tan that deepened her beauty and brought out the hazel in her eyes. She stood motionless as if waiting for me to initiate a conversation. She looked down at the wolf, who had obviously notified her of my arrival. He looked at her and then to me, then back to her for direction.

I could imagine him saying... "See, I told you... and be careful, because he is crazy." It was then that I noticed something unusual. There seemed to be a silent, but discernible form of communication between them. Even more unusual, was that to some extent I had felt it earlier. Exhilaration again erupted in me and I did my best to choke it back. There was a joy, an excitement when the wolf's eyes connected with mine. I just had been too scared to recognize it. His thoughts, or at the least his intentions, were clear to me and he expected them to be. Giggles bubbled up in my throat and out of the side of my mouth. His head shot back towards mine, eyes connecting. He knew I finally got it. He had the advantage though. He could connect with me instantly, while I flopped around in my own mind like a fish out of water. His attention shifted to my leg; ears peaked. He leaned down swiftly and bit into a large bug that had crawled on my pant leg. He licked it off and looked at me as if to say, "They bite". The young wolves came rolling around the tall hosts legs and barreled into their father, who looked up to me again, this time his thought was something parental, like ... "kids", with a mental sigh added. It was then that my silent host, who I am sure, had been taking this all in, made a small movement. The wolf spun in response. She looked at the wolf calmly. I could feel the interaction between them, but understood nothing. She then waved the wolf off on a task that I could not grasp. As her arms came back to her waist, the colorful cloth on her staff floated to rest. I presumed these were identifying patterns, like Scottish weaves. She stepped forward, bent down and looked me very directly in the eye. She spoke no words, but I could sense her nature and her purpose, there was no threat. This time instead of exhilaration in eye contact, there was a sense of peace. A welcoming feeling rose from within my chest and spine and wound its way to my brain, where instruction to relax spread throughout my consciousness. Confident I was not threatened, she reached out and placed a gigantic hand, thumb down on my forehead. Her hand enveloped my head and part of my neck. She ran her thumb across the middle of my forehead and between my eyes very slowly in a circular motion, as her fingers cupped my neck for support. Peace flowed through me, from my head to my feet. I could only explain it as a homecoming, a blending, or reconnecting to what might have been essential universal energy. Tears welled up in my eyes. The feeling was so profound, that my body shivered as if it was throwing off dank armor, allowing fresh air to rush across stifled flesh. She took her hand back and I began to fall to my knees. She raised my chin with one long, supple finger and looked deeply into my eyes again. She shared something native about herself and in return accepted some subliminal aspect of myself. I knew immediately we had common ground for understanding. Through her eyes, an entire universe had opened up in my mind. In this universe, thoughts were words and feelings were the spices that flavored each thought. Communication was almost effortless. In an instant she had supplied me with the structure necessary to understand and communicate on a new level. I felt like a computer and she the programmer that had just downloaded newer software. My mind was suddenly a better instrument. I did not have the coordination, or physical ability to control the new upgrades, but I understood how.

Then, being the paranoid participant in life that I am, I thought… what if this advanced person should see something in my thoughts that was … not good? How would I protect myself from this exposure and more importantly, how would I keep her from incorrectly perceiving me? My mind retracted and the shared world all but snapped shut. The abrupt change created a shuddering in my mind.

It dawned on me in that moment how things must have ended in the Garden of Eden. One moment, complete harmony with all existence, never alone, never separate, a part of everything. The next moment, alone, hiding and separated by fear, mistrust and embarrassment.

A soft whisper, melodious and song like, swept gently into my thoughts and brought my attention back to the woman before me.

The communication was in ideas, rather than words.

You are not your thoughts, she projected. It is natural to have a thought follow a feeling like fear, they are spontaneous. It is action based upon a negative thought, which is unfortunate.

A weight lifted from me. I felt relieved, understood from a level deeper than my flaws. A thousand questions flooded my mind. I looked up to ask her the first of many, only to see that her back was turned and she was moving at an unhurried pace the way she had come.

The afternoon on the beach struggling after Alton, hampered by sand and wind, hit my mind with stunning clarity. Ohhh... NO.... not again. Now I was in waist deep grass and forced to struggle to keep pace.

This is getting ridiculous, I thought, as I started after her and climbed a rise that allowed only the top of her head to be visible as she moved down the next slope. I knew I could move no faster and that frustrated me, because I could feel her making an effort to move slowly like she did for others.

Others? where did that come from, I thought and ... what others? Just as I was about to call out, my four-legged overseer poked his head through the grass. His look was patient and proud. He was a majestic creature, fur flowing in unison with the grass. I wish I had a camera I thought, as the feeling of being abandoned began to dissipate. In truth, I felt like a lost pup and would have run to him without hesitation. That is, if my manliness had not weighed in. "Haven't we embarrassed ourselves enough for one day" ... I could hear my prideful nature chastise?

The young male ran up from behind. Nudging me with his head while on the move, knocking me off my feet. He stood over me for a second and looked about. Then he raced a few feet ahead, turned and crouched close to the ground. He looked at me, as if to say watch this, then a rustle in the nearby brush confirmed his target and in one leap he disappeared. I could not gauge his age, he was obviously still a juvenile, fit and very fast. His height was naturally deceiving because of the way he moved and the spring in his step, but he was almost as tall as a pony at this point in his growth. If he was going to end up the size of his father, no body, even his sister was going to dictate to him.

The young female slipped in and out of the grass to my side, casting a wary glance at me each time she surfaced. It was obvious she just barely tolerated me and she wanted me to know who was in charge. Her father's eyes gleamed at her prowess as he slipped away from sight, recognizing I was in good hands. Although intimidating, the young female was beyond gorgeous. She was all things beautiful in nature, including a glow that seemed to radiate out from within her. In that moment it took all I had not to run to her and wrap my arms around her.

"OK" … I chastised myself "that is twice. Get a hold of yourself big guy". I said it under my breath, but her intensity suddenly disappeared. Like a rise in temperature, I could feel her nature change. She looked at me, head tilted to one side. She relaxed her posture and loped closer to me, taking a stance of protector, rather than guard. I felt acceptance from her and I almost reached out to pet her… almost. As we came to the next rise, her brother made sure to knock her down a notch or two. Charging from the brush, he took her down at her front legs and in a tangle, they rolled down the rise we had just ascended.

CHAPTER 13

It was not too long before we were all heading down the path in an orderly fashion. As we walked, the path began to widen and become a road. A hopeful sign that we were heading toward civilization and the structures I viewed from a long distance away. I felt somewhat relieved because my lungs had begun to burn and with each breath I took, it got progressively worse. I guessed it was from the exertion, but the air seemed so... rich and unsuitably dense. It was clear that the environment was beginning to affect me in ways I was not familiar with. My head was starting to spin and I felt dizzy. A buzzing, both in noise and vibration permeated my body and the volume was increasing. The sun's rays assaulted my skin, generating heat down to my bones. I felt paper thin, with my skeleton bare for all to see. Instinctively, I knew that if I remained exposed to the elements in this environment too long, there would be more serious repercussions.

The young male loped along in front of me. Responding intuitively to my unease, he looked back at me on an increased basis. After a few minutes, he slowed until he was walking beside me. He looked down at my face and then ahead down the gradually expanding trail. I could sense his growing concern, as he shifted his attention continually from ahead of us, back to me. After a short while, he spent most of his time focused just on me. There was strength in him that flowed to me every time he focused on me. His gaze felt more like the beam from a light house in the darkness. Each time I was losing balance or control, the light of his evaluating gaze revolved around to shatter the darkness and cut through the twilight I was falling into. I felt a part of me reaching out and drawing upon him for support. After a few more minutes, my young guide swung directly in front of me, just in time to watch me collapse in a heap on the trail. I tried to stand back up, but I had lost coordination and started floating in and out of consciousness. The buzzing was unbearable and had begun to sound like static from a radio. Even so, I could hear his thoughts as if they were my own. He was trying to tell me to stop struggling... stay down!

"No problem," I tried to verbalize, as I fell again and felt my chin bounce off my knee. I was numb, but that shot I knew was going to leave a mark. To my frustration, I could not tell what position on the ground I was in. Odd thing, when all else was spinning, tingling, buzzing and shifting from light to dark, the one constant was the young male's thoughts. They remained clear in my mind. I could feel his desire to cover me, to draw and balance. He came up next to me and sat. He then laid down stretching out across me. Again, I got the impression of cover, draw and balance. My physical body was a buzzing mass, but I could feel his strength, merging with my crumpled form. As if a huge sponge had been laid in a puddle of water, I felt his body absorbing whatever it was that had set mine on fire.

I was like a baby wrapped in a fur blanket. My body relaxed and I began to feel a little better, a little more aware. He gave a low rough howl towards the trail ahead and his sister came immediately into view. She took one look at me and instantly went into action. Like a nurse focused on triage, she came directly up to me, face to face, nose to nose, oh no... tongue to nose. With a wide sweeping motion of her tongue, she coated my nostrils and the left side of my face.
A taste test... really? Oh well... I was too woozy to stop her. How appropriate that feeling should start to return just in time to embrace that experience, I thought. She continued to smell me and nudge my face. Then she began maneuvering me into a sitting position. Once that was done, she walked around behind me and sat, pressing the back of her body against my back. I felt a pull, or tug, almost magnetic and I let my body fall back on her for support. My very small spine, pressed up against the solid muscle and fiber surrounding her spine. She sat motionless against me. I could feel the dizziness lessen. It was as if we blended, or possibly became one energy. I experienced a flowing from locations in my spine. They felt like centers, or collectors that were overcharged and about to explode. An image of water being drained out of a reservoir before the dam could

break, resonated in my mind's eye. As the minutes passed, the flow between myself and both of my caretakers, became natural. I could feel the energy being pulled from me, similar to the static charge one felt when pulling clothing apart fresh from the laundry. I slowly regained feeling and balance. I was wonderfully cocooned in threads of life, woven by brother and sister. They were helping my physical body adjust to their very alive and dynamic environment. My human structure was apparently too fragile for this world, a world powerful enough, to sustain giants.

With the male stationed on my legs, his presence generating pure comfort and his sister's soft, thick, furry, back cushioned against mine for support, I could have just let go and gone to sleep. I was captivated by the unity of our three lives. It was an incredible sensation. I honestly did not want to let go.

As I relaxed, words repeated in my head, "My physical body… my physical body… my physic…". What about those words bothered me so much? "Come on… let us be somewhat logical" … a part of my brain pleaded. How could my physical body be here…? When I was at my grandfather's home…? The dried drool on my collar scraped my chin as I tried moving my limbs, it sure felt … physical. "This makes no sense. I have got to get a grip… on all of this." I forced my back straight.

Vigilant to the core and realizing I was feeling better, my young nurse stood up. Stretching effortlessly, she smelled my neck and licked my head. I guess I passed the taste test because she walked in front of me and looked me straight in the eyes. Finding the doorways to my soul open with the lights still on, she rolled her head and gently brushed the side of her face against the side of mine. The whiskers tickled at first, but as she rubbed in a circular motion, I could feel the concern a mother might have for an over stressed pup. A long sigh slipped from within me… well, maybe I could relax just a little longer.

After a moment, I could feel the pack leader begin to reemerge in my caregiver. Her pupils contracted and she swung her head around, ears peaked to listen at some distant sound. With a few sniffs and a nudge under my shoulder, the female got me up and back to the business at hand, which I was pretty sure was to get me to the village. Once on my feet, I waved my escorts on. There was no need to make a physical gesture, but in this world of intangibles, it felt good to keep things real. As we started forward, I reminded myself to investigate further the curiosities of this experience. What had they both done to me? How did they draw upon my energy and basically balance what felt like my life's force? As I asked that question in my mind, I could still feel at least five densely rotating areas running up my spine pulsating from the exchange. They were generating, or refining energy ... life itself maybe? Yes... I would have to find out about these centers of power, as well.

CHAPTER 14

In a short while we arrived at the village. The first buildings seemed formed out of stucco or something like it. Upon closer examination though, they proved extremely intricate in their composition. As I walked past them, I could sense a flow of energy that complemented or enhanced the elements. Maybe as Orientals would say, "Chi".

My initial impression of the village, was that it was an excellent example of a society that organized its existence around the nature of things. It just seemed easy to progress toward our goal, where ever that was. We were still alone in our trek and except for the unwanted growls of my stomach, which challenged in volume those generated by my friends, all seamed eerily quiet.

As we came over a small hill, I could see a park or city center nestled between shimmering channels of the lake I had observed upon my arrival. Drawing closer, I could see a larger building next to the lake, with bridges and walkways that traversed the two slender peninsulas. Standing before a building with a high spire that looked more like a work of art than a shelter, was a number of people, maybe 100 or more. They were quiet, almost reverent as we approached.

The young male wolf and his dominant sister had fallen back to walk beside me. I could tell from the male it was a gesture of unity, brotherhood, trust. From the female... well now it seemed I was something akin to a baby brother. We began to pass groups of people standing in family units. The eerie thing was the children that looked between 8 and 10 years old were my height. The adults, by my best guess, were about 10 feet tall. The men were dressed plainly. They looked serious and I could sense concern, or uncertainty from them. I was an outsider... duh... was my return thought. Then I remembered, thought was as tangible as words here.

My alter ego kicked in. "Hey, they are the pros at this. What about what they are thinking?" The young male wolf looked up with a … you are spoiling our entrance look and I brought my thoughts back into control. "No Inner dialog…? No… Inner dialog…". I repeated it a few more times to organize my inner thoughts and impressions.

Amongst mind readers, I had no idea what was good or bad etiquette. "Oh well, too late now, another query to ponder once I return home." Then it dawned on me, how am I going to achieve that? Was this a one-way trip?

We came to a halt abruptly. The woman I had shared consciousness with, stepped from the terrace of the building where she stood slightly elevated above the rest of the community. She gave a gentle nod that asked me to turn to face the crowd. The young wolves turned on queue with me and then sat down by my feet. Feeling a little uncomfortable with the attention and so as not to fidget, I let my hands down to my side, where they rested in the thick fur of my trail mates. The contact brought immediate comfort. I could tell both of them felt happy. Like it or not, I was one of the family and regardless of my age, I was not the supreme commander here. The young female looked up at me with a passive glance, but I got the drift, "You are mine, so behave."

A saying from a cartoon I watched as a kid, "Deputy Dog", blasted up from the buried chambers of my youth… "A dunnnnn you fergit it!" With that thought escaping my failing control, I swear I could see her smile.

In a song like voice the woman began to speak. "We are honored to be visited by a friend of Alton's. We have been asked to welcome this human into our community. In doing so, it is our fondest hope that we may offer guidance, enlightenment and understanding."

I turned to look at her. She was speaking out loud. She saw the confusion on my face and smiled. It was a beautiful smile. I remember seeing that smile on my mother's face as a child, when she had a surprise for me, but told me I had to wait. I loved the smile, because it was full of humor, excitement and sharing. More impressions ingrained in my memory were surfacing, but the woman aimed her intent to burst my reminiscing like a balloon.

"Of course, we must keep vigilant as to how best to guide him, offer insight and support his ability to learn."

She faced me again and said, "Michael, I am Kayla. I am the leader... no," she turned her head a little sideways looking off in the distance. I could tell she did not like her choice of words. "I am the counselor of our village. Alton spoke with me before your arrival and asked if we could work as a group to help you gain familiarity with our and ... other worlds."

There was a hesitation in her statement. It held a cautious quality, something inevitable. I knew instinctively she did not wish for me to perceive dishonesty; it would open the door to mistrust and I could feel that trust in this environment was a foundation for interaction. Yet, she moved on quickly as if to avoid something that did not fit in the moment.

Her voice was melodic and unexpectedly hypnotic. As she spoke, I could feel parts of my mind folding back like petals on a rose. I tried to pay attention to her, but it was like trying to pay attention to a lecturer, while a circus was going on in the same room. My mind or subconscious took control and individual thoughts linked together arm in arm, like a game of barrel full of monkeys. They just kept streaming out of my brain.

The stream of my thoughts started with recognition of the nuances of the telepathy we were all sharing. How it traveled on so many different levels at the same time. Talk about multitasking! I was beginning to zero in on several different levels of communication though. Sort of like gears to shift in a car.

1st gear was everyday thought. If you were a mind reader, you could see that coming a mile away, because it was built from emotion, sensing and feeling. The process took a second or so to transmit to the brain, be assimilated and then a response formed out of it.

2nd gear was inner dialog, chain thought, or conversation within oneself. That was harder to see in another because it entailed many thoughts and feelings, all continually wrapping around each other until a solid principal popped out the other side. If you had a hold on the stimulus, you could somewhat follow the train of thought.

3rd gear was when the brain and emotions were following patterned or conditioned thought. Things moved down the road at a faster pace here. The only way I could figure a person could assimilate a pattern of thought, was if he was familiar with the other person and kind of knew what to expect. Sort of like friends or partners that could complete another person's sentence. Logical trains of thought sometimes skipped stations. Those thought destinations had already been programmed from the person's past, via personality and conditioning. So... the train skipped the track at places where programming took over and then rejoined at other places.

Communication between my new canine brother and sister were examples of familiarity and response. For some reason, it was much easier with them. I think because I saw myself as more intelligent than them and therefore, more confident. Although I know the female would have found that concept ridiculous and possibly insulting.

4th gear and the farthest I had been able to gain insight into through Alton and now here in the village, was where a mind was immersed in islands of thoughts. The mind could be working out a problem, or a new experience on a deeply internal or subconscious level. That level of thought was a mystery. The best way I could define it was... as every person knows there is a point in reading a book where you just disappear. It is not until you pop back into awareness that you say to yourself, where was I? What was I thinking? I remember pieces... but... and where was I in the book? What page... where did I lose focus? You then have to go looking for the place you disappeared from. All one can do is go back to the place left off. Unfortunately, once the door is open, it usually begins to happen more frequently. Some people put down the book here, because the subconscious recognizes a hole in the fabric of thought and continues to probe for release. Leveraging the book as the vehicle to subdue conscious thought, the subconscious can claim rights to the mind and its potential. Probably a good time to roll over and go to sleep for some, but for others it is frustrating. Then there is me, I just want to scream at my mind's lack of discipline. A key here, is that as the conscious mind relaxes its hold on the present. Our inner co-pilot takes over and the subconscious rises to the occasion. Once the trail of subconscious matter is spent, the conscious mind kicks back in and takes over, a lot like the goal of transcendental meditation, or REM sleep and dreaming. So, If you can skip rocks across water, you can retain your conscious momentum by skipping thoughts across your subconscious. It works, believe it.

I was engrossed in this AHHAAA... moment when the young

female nudged my hand. She moved closer and leaned on me, but only a little. That brought me back to the present.

The tall counselor, Kayla, as she introduced herself, had been addressing the crowd when she turned to me and said, "You will be interacting with some of these worlds on a very personal level, Michael." Her last sentence carried definite undertones and it was again clear she was communicating with me and only me with certain comments.

Out of the corner of my eye, I saw the large male wolf approach and sit by Kayla's side. He looked at his children and felt pride. An equally large female approached and sat beside him; she was a magnificent animal as well. She radiated prowess, intelligence and acute awareness, but most inspiring was the quality of motherly love. As she rubbed shoulders with her mate, she raised her head in a regal gesture, acknowledgment of all present. There was no doubt she was revered, she was royalty. Her eyes penetrated me and her influence flooded my mind, spreading out in refracted patterns, light hitting a prism. I was immediately an open book. A simple creature exposed and vulnerable. From that moment on, it was hard to find anything particularly special about myself.

I heard her thoughts, like Kayla's. Thank you for honoring my children. We welcome you. We are here to serve. The impressions her thoughts left resonated like mental message, completely enchanting me.

Once as a child, I had watched a presiding President of the United States walk past me in an airport. He was surrounded by Secret Service. As he approached, he looked down at me, smiled and ruffled my hair. I could sense his power and magnetism, his authority. It felt as if he could stop the world from rotating if he wished. So, it was with this female, the mother of my new companions, who had accepted me as their own.

Not many people know that females are the leaders of the pack. They take on this mantle naturally and when they are in charge, they are more than a leader. They are the heart and soul of the pack. They are the glue that binds them and the spirit that drives them. They are the great mother and they are absolutely devoted. Without question, this female was the leader of her pack, but she was also more. She was a leader to these people, like Kayla. I noticed her glance toward her daughter, that same prowess was reflected back at her. "The apple does not fall far from the tree," I said in my mind as I observed them both.

Oddly, I was the one that was proud. I was proud to be cared about by such creatures. I was grateful to be accepted by them and amazed that I was of importance to them at all. My ego chimed in... "Ohhh brother... this is one messed up... dream."

I jumped to curtail the thought before it was complete. If I had a bag, I would have stuffed my ego into it and ask the young female to bury it somewhere far, far away. I hoped I blocked it in time. I cringed inside. It was then that I noticed how quiet it was.

Everyone was staring at me. I looked at the young male whose head was tilted up and slightly to the side. "I have gone off the reservation again, haven't I?" His blank gaze said it all. "You got nuthin... do ya brotha," I said, "Well... I am on my own on this one."

I could feel everyone's eyes on me. Where was Alton when you needed big help? I was already so red with embarrassment that I am sure I could have been seen from orbit. A giggle was the first noise I heard. It sounded so loud in all the silence that I immediately looked toward it while thinking, how am I ever going to get used to a world where one's thoughts are out on the table for everyone to rummage through? In my case, like a favored junk drawer. I wonder in a society of mind readers, if inner dialog was like a teenager carrying a boom box down the street, the volume turned up to... BIG!

I heard the giggle again; it was a girl. She was smiling at me and wobbling in small circles. I had to do something, or else I was going to melt in place. I stepped over to her. When I say girl, I do not mean little, for she was already taller than me and glowed with inner beauty and innocence. She continued to smile and I knelt down in front of her. I do not know why I did that, because now I was looking up very uncomfortably. I took her hand and said, "Hello, my name is Michael. What is your name? "My male companion passed to my right and brushed his head and shoulders against the girl's arm and body. He licked my face and then leaned up against her. She staggered a little to the side, off balance and giggled again, calling the young male by name.

"Luka," she said with feigned anger. I could feel the influence of an impending thought in response to my question. Instead she slowly enunciated, "My name is Lauren. I have seen you before, but you do not remember me."

I was confused, there is no way I could have missed a girl this tall, in my world.

"Do you remember my ball," she asked, pulling a colorful ball out from behind her body and placing it in between us.

I leaned back and the memory flooded through my mind. Wait... It was not my memory; it was her thought forming the picture in my mind. I could actually feel it being built, complete with sand, sun, spray and ... Alton? "You were the girl with the ball on the beach.... no... that girl was much smaller."

I felt Kayla's mind chime in. You saw her up against Alton, who is as you might say in your civilization, her uncle.

"Yes," the girl said with unbridled enthusiasm. "First time to the beach in a long time. Uncle promised we could all play in the sand." The memory of a little girl's awe and gracious smile, when receiving the ball back from Alton, penetrated my confusion.

No wonder she seemed relatively unaffected by what she saw. Grasping for balance, I asked in a patronizing manner, "Lauren... how did you get to the beach with Alton?"

"Well, the same way you got here," and she giggled. This time the giggle said, "You silly person."   I looked up at Kayla, her ear to ear smile let on that I was soooo... totally out of my league here. Oh my, I thought, trying to gain knowledge from a child and being out matched. Ahhh... Who needs an ego anyway?

Hoping for something solid to hold on to, since this world kept casting me out like a bug on the end of a fly fisherman's line, I continued.

"You travel through the spinning tunnel, too? I mean when you travel away from here?"

"Well I do not travel alone," Lauren said. "I usually go on trips with one of the travelers, like my uncle or Kayla, or Stella," and she pointed to the adult female wolf.

Somehow a wolf with exceptional abilities, mastering a dimensional portal, made more sense than some of the other stuff I had encountered.

"Can you... they... anyone travel ... whenever?" On this question she looked at Kayla and then at Stella, who was moving to stand beside the girl and opposite her offspring. Stella sat passively and looked over at Kayla, then she rubbed her face against Lauren's and spoke directly to me through thought.

"Lauren may be able to answer your questions, but her answers may not be complete. They may create a false image for you, since you are still assimilating so much."

The clarity and directness of meaning were exhilarating. Not to mention, I was talking to a wolf of prehistoric proportion... conversationally... and I... felt stupid? I answered back immediately. "You are right, I am dealing with a lot at present and at this point, I probably could not understand a simple nursery rhyme. Hummm... maybe she is just the person I need to talk to". Kayla smiled, understanding my jest.

"Thank you Lauren for introducing yourself," I said as I stood up and shook the hands of her parents standing behind her. It took two of my hands to move one of theirs, in a shaking motion. I could tell they were unfamiliar with the gesture. They did however see the meaning in my mind. They looked at each other, smiled and exaggerated the movement in return. I was not ready for jumping jacks, but I did what I could to make it work.

The large male wolf drifted gently up to my side, passed by and turned to look back at me. It was clear he desired for me to follow, but I sensed hidden intentions. For a second mistrust rose in me, then I felt a hand take hold of mine. It was Lauren. She spoke out loud to the male wolf.

"Let me take him, please?" The male wolf dropped his head slightly in a respectful gesture and stepped back. Lauren started pulling me immediately toward a group of four structures, one very large. Her strength took me by surprise.

"Where are we going?" I asked.

"I love surprises," she said "They make me so happy."

"Ok," I said back to her." I love surprises too, are we going to one?" She just looked into my eyes, giggled with a child's innocence and dragged me forward.

CHAPTER 15

Speaking as a normal male, there is something disconcerting, almost unnatural, when a girl can over power, out think and... well basically, control you. It is not that you are outmatched so much, as it is that you were no match to begin with.

Two females had taken control of my independence this day, each in her own way, and I was no closer to becoming comfortable with the situation than when I first arrived.

"Ohhh... stop being silly., I can hear you, you know," said Lauren.

"I know you can," I said, "but I can't help it."

"You will learn, Michael," Lauren said. "I will teach you and so will Stella and Kayla and ..." just at that moment a wet nose found its way across the back of my arm, creating a static discharge. Already a little out of sorts with the thought of added mothering, I was not prepared for Luka. He was excited, so much so that he began bouncing on his front legs as he walked along beside us.

We wove through two, or three sections of structures before we reached a shelter set off from the rest. It was not totally segregated, yet it was obvious this structure was the beginning of a different section of the community.

The entire community seemed to have been built to enhance natural order and unity, but the structure before us was less artistic than the rest, with thick walls and covered entries. It seemed more a shelter from the elements, than one that flowed with them.

The day had taken its toll. I was pretty worn out by the time we rounded the structure, following a path to the doorway. The burning in my lungs and the buzzing in my head was just starting to return. I contemplated the telepathic and physical nature of this new world. How all of it put together, seemingly overwhelmed my native resources. Not wanting to collapse again, I resolved to monitor my condition.

My male companion was still bouncing on his front legs like a ball, when I noticed it was not Lauren and I that he was so animated about, it was whatever or whoever was inside the structure. Lauren also seemed giddy with expectation and her head bounced in unison with Luka, as she completed her last few steps. I could feel a strangely familiar energy inside the structure, but I just could not place it.

I felt dizzy and out of sorts. I was looking for a place to sit down, when the door of the building suddenly swung open. Luka could not hold his exuberance any longer. He barreled inside. I could hear a voice inside laughing and items being knocked to the ground. Then Luka dashed out of the door, made a wide circle at full speed and headed back toward the entrance. Before he could get to the door, Alton strode out.

"Ahhh," I said. "Now I know why he is so excited." Alton walked to me offering a warming smile and a large hug, while Luka's never-ending enthusiasm was visible through his continued bouncing.

"Well, I am glad to see you followed the breadcrumbs laid out for you."

I backed away and said, "It was not that hard, especially with a little help from the stone. It called up memories and let me know whether I was hot or cold. On the trail, or off." Then I grabbed Alton's arm.

"Alton, I think you were right. My grandfather may still be alive. If the technology I found at his home is real and this is not all just some crazy dream, then he would have found a way to use it to protect and provide for himself."

"I have done more than that my boy. I have found the keys to the kingdom. The doors they open, will shake the foundations of present-day humankind."

Walking out of the doorway, ambled my Grandfather. His smile warm and familiar, brought incredible joy to me and I ran like a child to him and hugged him. I did not want to let him go. Then the reality of everything unbelievable in that day came crashing down. The strength in my legs drained into the ground. The air seemed way too thick and electric to breath. I was overcome with vertigo and fell to my knees. The world took on a spin worthy of a youthful all-nighter and Lauren's face slipped in and out of focus above me. I could feel her pick me up as if I was a scarecrow made of straw. Then Alton's face passed before my eyes and began to distort like a fun house mirror.... I blacked out.

CHAPTER 16

Muffled voices drew my conscious mind out of the darkness it had vanished into, while waves of tingling effervescence flowed from my chest outward, stimulating the tips of my fingers and toes. Rushes of air filled my ears and moisture coated one side of my head. As the rest of my senses came into balance, I realized the sound of air flushing in and out of my head, was Luka's massive nostrils stuffed against my ear, wet and gooey.

"No… no wet willies," I tried to speak but my vocal cords felt coarse and stiff. I struggled to control my arm and push him away, but his head was so weighty that I didn't achieve much. Luka's tongue dropped out of his mouth and like a wet mop, slapped across the side of my head.

"Okay," I croaked, "that is enough." I struggled to my elbows and looked around. Lauren was leaning up against Alton, who was facing my grandfather. Lea stood vigil next to them, her stare creating a sense of guilt in me I could not validate. I turned to refocus on Luka and said, "Why are women soooo good at that?" He looked at his sister, swallowed and looked up at the ceiling. I guessed that was his answer.

Alton and my grandfather were immersed in a serious conversation. Lauren heard me chastise Luka and studied me with the same intensity as Lea. Both wore a frown of concern.

"He is awake," Lauren said to them both.

"What happened, did I pass out?" I asked as I looked down and saw the stone centered on my chest. It glowed brilliantly. Intense flashes lashed out at the shadows in the room from the apex of the arch above the pool of crystal. I could feel the stone shifting my body's life force around in waves. It had pulled me back to consciousness and seemed to continue to heal me.

"Yes, you did. Just too much happening at once," said Alton with a parental smile.

"No... No, I said, it is not just that. I seem to be incompatible with this world. It feels like it is somehow, too potent. The air seems super charged. The colors are so incredible, it almost hurts to look at them. Everything here is very intense, powerful". I wanted to say so much more, but I left it at powerful, as I collapsed back on the bed. I immediately looked to my side knowing that Luka was likely coming back to stand guard over my ear, tongue poised and ready.

"No," I said. "Put that thing away," and I placed my hand up between us as a barrier. I heard a slight groan but he acquiesced and I laid my head back on the pillow.

My grandfather came over, pulled up a stool and looking over his glasses, started an examination. He shifted the stone on my chest, tuning it like the knob of a radio. I could feel the energy I had become familiar with warp to the left and then to the right, or in and then out, or both at the same time. Anyway, in response to his adjustments, intense tingle followed.

"Ok, Paps, that is beginning to bother me in ways I can't begin to describe!" Without acknowledging my discomfort, he began to speak with necessity, as if he was late for a meeting and had to get going.

"This world, Michael, is like our world was during the age of the dinosaurs. The air is super saturated with oxygen, which given time can strip the enamel off your teeth. Magnetic energy flows through everything, leaving unexpected static charges, which if you are not careful can taze you when you touch conductive objects... like hummm... a bed post while pulling your shirt off." My grandfather grunted under his breath as if reliving a bad experience. Recognizing a smirk carving out the corner of my cheek he added, "I have the scars to prove it! Gravity here is of course stronger, drawing further upon needed bodily resources. Everything on this world, like on our prehistoric earth, is more potent. An environment like the one on this world, is dangerous to you and me. Our present-day world, unlike this one, aged differently. Bombarded by a young sun, the magnetic fields surrounding our earth have been tempered. Massive movement in tectonic plates buried crystalline structures that were created as the planet itself formed. Those structures, similar to the stone on your chest, acted like tuning forks for the universe's energy, or as Alton's people refer to it, 'Gods voice'."

My grandfather had always been an incredibly spiritual man, but he had an aversion to religious dogma, so he must have known what my reaction to that statement was going to be. He stopped examining me, looked over the rim of his glasses and answered my question before I could ask it. "Alton's race has been around a millennium before us. They know far more about the universe than we do... so... yes... I am good with that." The humor in his response made me smile as he continued.

The assimilation of universal energy slowed on our world. Dynamic forces became less imposing and far less potent.

The vibration flowing to and from the stone kept generating waves of both calming energy and sustaining energy. My body seemed to absorb it like a sponge, but my mind still struggled to focus.

"OK... Ok Paps. I am sure there is a far more compelling reason for telling me this now than at a time I might better grasp it, but ...."

"I am telling you this, my son, because your body is under a form of attack on this world. It is a world that supports a far stronger race, with much greater physical capacity. The environment has driven their genes to perform and evolve to what you see." He pointed to Alton, then to Lauren. Lauren in kind, stood up and curtsied in a complete circle laughing all the way. Luka who had finally calmed down a little under the watchful eye of his sister stood up, but met the stern look in her eyes and with the same groan as before, lay down.

"Your body, your system, is immersed in an environment here, it will struggle to adjust to and certainly not in one visit. Lea acted as a buffer for you earlier, but the effects of this world are cumulative. Each cell that is created while you are exposed to this environment is supercharged by this environment. Each cell that dies, is a lost buffer to what your entire being is familiar with. You will need to return home soon, very soon, because even the stone cannot reverse the massive damage done through prolonged exposure to the elements here.

"Here...," I said. "Paps, where exactly... are we?"

"Where indeed? That question invokes profound consideration, which cannot be limited by earthly definitions. So, I do not think that is a good question for the moment. Maybe when you have recovered fully, we can engage Alton with that one. Until then, let me set the foundation for it. This world, the system it is a prime member of and the Galaxy it flows within, like trillions of others, are all essential elements in a structured cosmos."

"Are you saying cosmos instead of universe because it is somehow different than ...?"

"Yes, my boy, that is it. As usual, you are right on it! Suns, pulsars, countless worlds and the more than occasional black hole, are more than just rock and collected gases haphazardly strewn around in an uninspired universe. Each celestial body plays some important role in regulating, communicating, or generating a cosmic plan, a unified purpose, a universe, that is itself, consciousness. Imagine a massive universal circuit board, not just 3D, but multi, intra and inter dimensionally capable. Everything is timed to perfection. A pulsar acts as a power center, casting energy outward on a magnitude inconceivable by our understanding of energy. A black hole stands as a gate keeper reaching across dimensional rifts, folding time and space so elements can be transferred to different dimensional platforms. Vital universal life blood, shifted from where it is in abundance to where it is needed most. A sun might be recognized as a transformer, turning raw energy into light, heat and power. A planet acts as a resistor gathering energy and slowing it down as it moves through denser substances. An entire galaxy driven by dynamics we cannot begin to understand, becomes a functional platform for a universe on the move. That living consciousness suffers no dimensional limitations. The most important aspect in all of this though, is that there is an ultimate design and purpose to it all. I have seen the soul of it through inspired glimpses. Guided by Alton and those here, I have only begun to realize the magnitude of my ignorance and that achievement in itself, is something to brag about!"

"The God Aspect... can you describe it or tell me something about it?" I said.

My grandfather looked at Alton, who after the briefest of seconds nodded.

"There is matter and there is ... the opposite. There is consciousness and then there is nothing."

"What do you mean? I said. "Are you talking about dark matter, anti-matter?"

My grandfather nodded and then turned his head a little to the side, as if what I had said was close, but not exactly right. "The cosmos is aware. It occupies both time and space. It also occupies time in space, where we exist. Yet, the cosmos is not the entire universe. Where the cosmos is not, is where the universes still is. The universe is not limited to time in space. The cosmos can be, just as matter is. Dark matter on the other hand, is and is not definable as one or the other. It exists in everything and it is mutable. It is the Ying, to the Yang. It is the anode to the cathode. It is the negative or common potential, to all that is positive or charged. Electricity would not flow through a switch or a light bulb, unless the energy had a place to return to, which in all cases is back to the original and overall source. It is where all energy once used returns, a universal storehouse of potential. You might say it is essence, stored outside of time, in space, sort of like a zipped file for compacted energy, ready to take on any form as required by...."

"God?" I asked.

"Well... yes. The intelligence of the universe, the magic that awakens the seed, thus the mighty oak doth grow". My grandfather looked down at me from some distant place his thoughts had carried him away to. Then said, "What brings light to darkness, structure to chaos? Why? Purpose, awareness of what a seed might become?"

My grandfather reached over and placed his hand on my wrist to emphasis a point. "Michael, life is everywhere, existence in more forms than you, or I could ever imagine. It is in forms like us, Alton and Lauren, or Luka, or plant life, or beings of unimaginable variations. We live in a microcosm, within a macrocosm, connected in every possible way to a cosmos that is alive with potential."

My grandfather shook my arm with excitement. "I have wanted to talk to you about this for so long, but I was afraid it would interfere with your life. You would have thought me crazy as a loon, showing up out of nowhere, starting in on metaphysical concepts. I was sure of that and if I had provided proof, it would have altered you permanently. I had no right to expose you in such a way. You needed a teacher, one that understood on an objective level, when and where you should best be enlightened."

"You mean Alton," I said as I shifted my weight from one elbow to the other feeling like a bug under a microscope, as Lauren and Lea monitored my every move.

My grandfather reached over and gently removed the stone from my chest. As it was lifted upward, I could feel a web like structure stretch outward from my body. "This stone is an excellent example of universal connectivity and transformation. It is a stone, a crystal. Yet, it not only accepts the latent energy of the universe around it, but it transforms that energy. It recognizes patterns that indicate a structure that is in balance, or one that suffers from imbalance, illness or in your case, over exposure. If the structure is not too badly damaged, it can bring it into balance and repair it. It is more than just a semiconductor, like earth crystals that are used to tune radios. The stone is a vibrational sequencer, a universal communication center that can interact with other life forms."

"But, Paps, it is a stone, a crystal, not a life form. It may perform a more complex function than an ordinary crystal, but how can it be a life form?"

"Can you say that with absolute certainty?" my grandfather responded. "It acts and reacts with autonomy, with awareness. It can enhance your focus. Turn a thought into a physical form. For example, if you were depleted, it could pull latent energy from around it, transform that energy into a form your body can use and deliver it to an area with the same vibration and frequency. Who are we to say what constitutes life, when we do not even recognize the possibility of life outside our own world?"

"I am not sure, Paps, I guess the scientist in me must have enough evidence to outweigh other conclusions. Evidence like what I felt Lea do before. She balanced out my energy through wells or centers within me. I could feel her sense my situation, then react to move energy. It was amazing and it also bonded us on a deeper level."

"You have a bond with her now, because she chose to share her life force with yours, like a transfusion to help you to adapt and endure," my grandfather answered. "Beings on this world have a slightly different genetic structure than we do. Their DNA has crystalline compounds superimposed and bonded to the carbon that is the basis for their life form and ours. They actually are in some ways, the energy itself. Alton will undoubtedly explain more about this, but they can transform, control and regulate latent universal energy. Just like a prism can precisely refract light, or a singer can hone his voice to create a perfectly tuned note. Lea knew which of your nerve plexuses or energy centers were overloaded and failing. She then used her abilities to bring them back into balance. Those centers are also referred to as chakras, on earth. They are responsible for transforming the energy all around us, into energy the body, mind and soul can use. The metaphysics behind the chakra is the simplest form of demand and supply, but on a level we as human beings have lost touch with."

"Are you implying, that we are like them?" I said. "We are not crystalline in structure."

"Not like they are, but our bodies assimilate, digest and create crystals as part of its function. Look how quickly Kayla was able to modify and tune your metaphysical system to communicate more efficiently. That could not have been done, unless your structure was compatible with hers."

"Paps, are you trying to guide me to a conclusion? Are we related to these people?"

"Well, in fact, they are our predecessors, but that is far beyond our focus today."

I looked at Alton, who just smiled and winked. "As if told something truly out of this world," I said with a growling laugh. "Come on!"

Alton nodded to my grandfather and said, "As we discussed briefly before Michael, humans are one of the more complex life forms in the universe. They are more versatile and more independent from their progenitors than any other race to date. In other words, humanity has stepped outside of the parameters their forefathers existed within."

"Okay, but what exactly does that mean, Alton?"

"To make it easier, I will say it like this... Imagine the universe was woven together by say... music. A song of sorts and no matter where you stood within it, you could hear the music flow. You could touch anything and feel the musical vibration. You could sing to it, hum to it, sway to it, or dance to it. At night, it could soothe like a lullaby, creating a sense of belonging and security, shepherding you off to peaceful sleep. In the morning when you woke, it would be there anchoring your nature, connecting you to everything else. You would never feel alone, searching for..."

"God?" I asked.

"Yes, but not as you are meaning it. The "One" ... simply put,

"IS". Without the "One" there is no being. He is the music and the music defines the flow of existence. It confirms that we are an integral aspect that adds to the melody, the eminence. We are part of the orchestra, creating, divining,
perpetuating."

Although Alton's words were soothing, the scientist in me bulldozed ahead.

"Alton, that sounds so completing... but are we talking about a universal intelligence... God?"

"We believe, yes," said Alton. "To our benefit, our race is connected and sustained by that intelligence. We have free will and a free spirit, but we are an instrument of its intention."

"I am sorry, Alton. I have lived in the scientific world for far too many years. How can you be free, yet dependent at your core, on another? I mean... please do not get me wrong, mankind has always searched for the essence or true nature of the cosmos. I... I am on another world with other races and I have the audacity to say I am not sure I believe, but..."

"It is ok, Michael. That is why your race is so special. The universe has cut the umbilical cord. You live outside the music. You learn to hear it over lifetimes of experience. You were gifted something special, a capacity for independence, growth and faith. You have limited years of physical life to hone that faith and to make the universe your own. It takes physical death to release the soul, clear away the shroud of your physical existence and reunite your consciousness, to the 'One'. In those short years of life as a human, you have the potential to live like gods."

"Could we really be that different?" I asked.

"Yes and No," said Alton. "Most life forms are biased by evolutionary demands specific to their environment and therefore they are limited in how they can evolve. Life forms can expand their potential through connectivity or grouping, but not necessarily on an individual basis. The human form on the other hand, is basically unlimited in potential as an individual life form. Each individual is a spark of the divine, a newly created star with the capacity to become anything. Imagine a billion of those sparks of creation uniting for a greater purpose. The last time that happened, this cosmos was created. You, Michael, along with millions of other human beings, happen to have a strong genetic memory. Kayla, with a little help from me, has awoken in you that potential. The door to understanding that potential stands before you, but it is up to you to walk through that door and accept what waits beyond."

I just lay there with my mouth open, while my mind spun completely out of control.

My grandfather giggled at the dumbfounded look on my face and said, "Let's stick to rudimentary concepts, shall we?" He slapped me on my shoulder and laughed out loud. "Since the sleeper has awoken, in more ways than one, it is time to get you home."

"No way, Paps. Not now, I lost you once... not doing that again!"

My Grandfather smiled a satisfied, grateful smile. "I never lost you, boy and you never lost me. I knew where you were and how you were doing. I even had some fun with those ridiculous secret service scientists in the process. They continued to search for a key. A key that would open a door to power that they planned to solely control. They had no idea what that key looked like. They had no idea where the door was. Most importantly, they had no idea what truly lay beyond that door."

"Well... Until..." Alton added with a frown and looked down, "someone, or something offered an infinitesimal piece of knowledge about the nature and power of the universe."

"Yes, Michael," said grandfather. "That is what we have been discussing. That leaked knowledge has inspired covert organizations on earth, to exercise their arrogance and greed. The same greed that has destroyed many a civilization."

"And race", added Alton." Humanity... your world... functioning just outside the continuum of consciousness, can effect change for every world within it. So, whether by coincidence or by grand design, your world seems to have become a pivotal component in a universe we all share."

"Wait, that does not make sense to me," I said. "If you are in communication with the big guy and the flow of the universe, why can't you or some other race with the right connections, just stop the presses and put the genie back in the bottle?"
"We do not control or direct the 'One'. It is the ultimate definition of free will. If this situation exists, it is for some purpose we cannot envision. We are bound to protect and serve. So, we must make an effort to fix what seems broken, in hope that it was our destiny to do

so. Remember what your grandfather taught you years ago. All matter and structure, have purpose. If that structure, or the matter it is built from is changed, everything associated with it will be affected."

"Or," my grandfather added, "destroyed. Our world could be the catalyst to a potential universal Armageddon!"

I was numb. Our conversation had gone from the difficult to believe, to "Holy Shit". I felt like I had been sucked into quicksand and was already over my head. "Ok... I get the need for caution, but it seems like you both are working on a level much greater than I should be a part of. I have no experience with any of this. I mean why am I here? Why was I shown what is behind the proverbial universal curtain?"

"Like it or not, Michael," Alton said. "You play an important part in all of this. We are still uncertain about what is happening. We want... no... we need to figure this out. We want to keep your family and your world safe, along with millions of other worlds. As far as why you, why now? We do not know. Your Grandfather and I have always felt you had a special purpose; we did not realize you would be called upon in this manner, but here you are.

My grandfather added, "And I will not let you roam far from me again." He smiled that 'All Knowing, I am the keeper of the secret'" smile, which had won him so many debates between us.
I fell back on the cot, in just the right position to lock into Lea's determined gaze. Her eyes, half open/half closed, gleamed like the razor-sharp mind that filled them with light. Luka let out a small whine as if to say, "Tag... your it!"

There was a moment of uneasy silence that followed. Odd, it was not just a silence between people, but it was a silence of the mind as well. It was a silence that magnifies where something should exist, but does not. That silence reminded me again that my thoughts were part of the complexity of this new world and now my abilities had been reconfigured to be part of it as well.

Lea re-positioned herself; then sat absolutely erect resuming her vigilant pose.

Feeling a little embarrassed at my ineptitude I grunted at Lea, "Why are you so mad at me? I didn't do anything wrong. It was not my fault that I messed up... I mean this world messed up your handiwork, right?" I received a reply via thought. It was simply... "Child."

"Well," my grandfather said, with a sigh and a slap of his legs while standing to his feet." It is probably best that we send you back home right away. This building was built to defray a majority of the natural energy flowing along the meridians of this plane. But, even I after acclimating need to be watchful of over-exposure."

With that, Lauren reached over, grabbed my wrists and began to lift me off the bed. Lea turned her head to the side and cast a glance at Luka who was starting to bounce again slightly on his front legs as if expecting everybody to get up and go play.

Lea looked back at me and added to her thought, "Need I say more?" Alton boomed with laughter, Lauren flopped on to the edge of my bed, Luka just looked confused.

I rubbed his head and said, "Looks like we have to stick close together here, buddy." Luka laid down and put his head on his front paws. I began to laugh just as hard as everyone else.

CHAPTER 17

Pastel colors, reflected off the aqua blue surface of the lake, in the center of the village and made every building near us shimmer with life. Standing in the doorway of my grandfather's home away from home, I closed my eyes and enjoyed a moment of steadiness, something that only a few hours ago was as foreign to me as the world I stood upon. To complement that sense of equilibrium, a feeling of being intimately connected to everything around me, fostered welcome sanctuary. In those moments, I understood Alton's analogy of the music, the common thread in all things and how fulfilling it was to be a part of it.

Alton and my grandfather had been in intense conversation for about half an hour, shooting sidelong glances in my direction. Something about my pending departure left them uneasy. As expected, Lea was not far off. She still seemed peeved at me, but I was not about to be bothered by her attitude. I had so many questions and needed more defined answers than I had received. So, I walked over and interrupted my grandfather. I put my hands on his shoulders and directed him to sit at his work bench. I nodded at the stool next to him for Alton to sit down. I went to put my arm around Lauren's shoulders, sort of for moral support, but I had to settle for her waist, her size was so deceptive.

"Ok, I do not know how I am supposed to get home, or what is supposed to happen when I get there. But, before I go, I need a little more information. I need to ask a few questions that will help me to understand where I stand in all of this."

Alton smiled and leaned back against the bench. My grandfather laughed and looked at Alton while saying, "Shoot."

"Ok... I am wondering how much of this I am involved in

because I am closely connected to you, Paps. Your work is obviously real and has significance that humanity will come to a screeching halt over. Is it possible that I am only a right time, right place participant in all of this because of you?"

"No, my grandfather said. "That is wrong. Alton, would you care to answer this and keep in mind, he must leave within the hour."

"Yes, Hugo," Alton shifted his attention to me. "Michael, as I told you before, I am different from a human, but our race has been involved in human evolution since man was first conceived. I have had the pleasure of guiding many on earth down through history. We are usually aware when a pivotal soul is incarnating and sometimes, we seek to support his purpose. When you arrived, we observed your development. As we have told you, it became evident that there were other forces at work, destructive in nature and intent. If by being involved in your growth and development to help prepare you for some focused destiny, we brought attention to you, we might have made matters worse. I looked for a way to be present, but not draw attention, so I made contact with Hugo, your grandfather. He was as stubborn as you". Alton smiled at my grandfather who proudly nodded and winked. "As expected, he required irrefutable evidence, proving that I was not a mutant in mind and body. Over time, we reached common ground. As the years passed, we noticed subtle changes in you. Changes in how you learned and applied what you learned. Your aptitude with metaphysical mechanics and vibration technologies are just a few. As you matured and our conviction over your talents were validated, so were our concerns over interference in earth's destiny. Technological leaps became commonplace and largely without the ground work supporting those discoveries. Advances began to create a potential for chaos and destruction, while at the same time fostering avarice and greed. Since your grandfather's friendship had brought me much pleasure over the years and his council much support, we agreed to intensify our focus as a team in the hopes of exposing a culprit. There was a point when we felt that whatever intelligence was actively interfering with human evolution had also caught wind of a paradigm, an anomaly in humanity's evolution which would signal change on an unprecedented level. We believed that anomaly would be human. We believed that anomaly was you."

"What?" I said.

"The 'KEY', Michael, we are not sure, but we think that you might be a key, a catalyst for significant change. The earth has had many. Some that are well known and remembered in your history and some long forgotten. Not every person that is a key or catalyst for change, yields a positive cycle. Hitler, Nero, Alexander, they were all notable men in earth's history, but their lives created havoc and catastrophic change. Jesus, Gandhi, Mohammad, Buddha, were also notable for their contributions, especially for shepherding enlightenment. Negative change brings the most growth, because it forces the human spirit to fight against what is considered unacceptable and corrupt. Positive change usually follows periods of time when humanity has amended the corruption and has the need to reconnect to that which might be considered godly, or in balance. Although, we believe you are one of those 'Key' individuals and a critical component for change, the timing is wrong compared to earth's patterns. Either you are here to address some imbalance or inequity, or we have misjudged your significance concerning events to come."

"Can I ask how you know, what you know, I interrupted?"

Alton lowered his head as if gauging what to share and what not to, then he continued. "Every race seeks to identify itself against an ever-expanding cosmos and will eventually unite with other races. Races in their own dimension and in the countless other dimensions which add form, depth and substance to our universe. We all came from the same seed and one day we will all be consciously united by the energy that endowed that seed. Until then, we follow those who have come before us. Those who guide us into the light. Beings who are more closely connected to the source, to the 'One'."

"Now that last statement you are going to have to explain in detail, but let's stay on my involvement specifically for the moment. Let's say, I am this catalyst. What can I do about it?" I asked.

"We are not sure how you will evolve to complete your destiny," said my grandfather. "There are challenges ahead which will better define what you can ultimately achieve."

"We are here to guide you as best as we can," added Alton. "I have been a guide to many of your race, as I have said. Others of my race have served as well. Your grandfather and I will confront future challenges and experiences with you where possible, but some exploration will be self-defining, dangerous and will involve only you.

I am hopeful we can help you find your true universal voice and rise to meet your destiny."

"I find it hard to believe that I am somehow important in all of this, but as I said before, I am on a different world with a different race of people, sentient wolves? What is there not to agree with? I am with you. So, what is next?"

"We will begin to explore what your evolution, genetics and potential purpose have in store", said Alton. "You made the portal you came here with. The stone just amplified and balanced your energy. They were a mechanism for you, until you learn to do it yourself."

"Wait... you mean you think I made the portal to get here?"

"Yes, Michael, you did," answered Alton. "In time you will come to accept a new view of life and where you stand within it. We must be vigilant, as we believe another effort is being made to destroy a plan, millennium in the making."

"Evolutionary genetics? Along with words like, millennium in the making? That sounds like manipulation and well, I don't mean to be cynical, but it sounds like a plot in a bad science fiction novel.'

"You know the old saying," my grandfather snickered... 'Could not have imagined it, even in a book'?"

A soft, but firm growl rose from Lea, as she stood up and looked at my Grandfather with intensity. Before I could connect to her thoughts, my Grandfather spoke up.

"It is time, Michael. You must go home."

I rose in response, feeling sad over the thought of leaving. The intensity of that feeling hit me like a sledgehammer. Here were people, beings I was intimately connected to and the thought of leaving them tore at my very core. As if in response to my sadness, Luka forced his face in just over my shoulder, I could feel he shared my sense of loss. Still, he nudged me toward the door.

"How am I going to get back? I have to leave the stone here for safe keeping and I am a little short on the know how... to get home."

I stepped toward the doorway and noticed Lea was looking at me intensely, even more so than when we were out on the trail. I would not have thought that possible. The world around me suddenly seemed to buckle and warp, like a reflection off a thin piece of tin. The folding of the fabric of space caused me to feel queasy and I wobbled backwards. As I did, I noticed that the light around me seemed to darken. A shadow was emanating from behind me. It moved over and around me, where the shadow cast, the world was not. I turned to look back over my shoulder, just as the force of the portal grabbed my torso and off I went. No time for goodbyes. The world dissipated in swirling confusion, with a final view of my young female governess, the hair on her spine standing erect, a sense of sadness emanating from her eyes. For a split second, I hoped she would dive in after me, save me, but I realized I was not in danger. I was going home and she could not interfere with that. I could still feel Luka's fur on my cheek. The weight of his head on my shoulder, but he was not there either. It was just some sort of sensory reflection. I felt faint as the process accelerated and as I was drawn fully into the forces at work, I lost consciousness.

CHAPTER 18

Alton stood just outside of the boundaries of the portal that carried Michael back to his home. He felt the same sense of emptiness, but he had more serious concerns to deal with.

Turning to Paps, Alton said, "Well my old friend, it seems your grandson is every bit you and a little more for good luck."

Paps smiled, but his smile turned to a frown as he sat back at his work bench. "I am very happy to have him back in my life, but I wish I were sure he was safe. I think we both can see the progressions evolving. Soon, he will have to accept his purpose and therefore, his path. I do not know if he will survive it. Hell... knowing what I know now, I do not know anyone that can survive it."

"Maybe that is why your grandson is so very special, Hugo, and as far as we know, there is no other that is gifted like him."

"Gifted," said Paps, "I would think it more a curse, no matter who, or what the being.

"Yes, but I think the stubbornness he inherited from you will carry him through", Alton added, trying to help lighten the moment.

"Alton, Did you see how the stone responded when Michael was unconscious and put in balance? At one point there was another signature, almost an echo of another person exploring the energy transfer."

"Yes, I did my old friend. I have always been afraid that once Michael left his home and arrived in our denser dimensional matrix that others might sense his uniqueness. Although, I do not believe there is anything that can be done about it. He is not what he will become yet, and once he has made the transfer, there is not much they or anyone can do."

"Yes," said Hugo cautiously, "but the fact that another

consciousness was aware of an anomaly like him, tells me we are not alone in our pursuit of the truth."

"Possibly," said Alton. "Either that, or there is another who's need might require Michael's ability. It was clear by the reaction of the stone when it rejected the probing, that the energy searching was not in harmony with us, or Michael."

"I am afraid for him, Alton. He has not yet made the journey into a darkness none of us are familiar with, but he has already drawn attention from something that lurks in a darkness... we are familiar with!"

"Faith is our redemption, my friend, and patience will be our guide," said Alton. "But just in case, this is the perfect time to ask Stella, Thor and Kayla to go off world and follow up on any trails that have that curious energy left in them."

"That would make me feel a lot better," said Paps. "I will take the stone to them, so they will have a vibrational footprint to track."

CHAPTER 19

The buzzing that sawed at my semi-conscious brain as I stirred, was to say the least, annoying. Gradually, I realized I was in my own bed, in my own apartment and the buzzing was in fact, outside my own head. So, it had to be… yep… my alarm. I did not like that sound. No wonder the buzzing that rattled inside my head in the 'Other World', was equally annoying. As memory slowly coordinated with my immediate thoughts, I remembered my car was near my grandfather's house, or did I drive it home somehow without recalling? Feeling mentally sluggish frustrated me. Then, I had to laugh. Let's give ourselves a little credit here. We have been on quite an adventure; a little jet lag should be expected. "Jet lag… ha"! I laughed again as I pulled an arm out from underneath my pillow and stretched. Worm hole lag… is more like it, now that is what I call crossing time zones!

I heard a sudden low growling, could it be possible, could Lea be here? She was the last vision I had as I left Alton's world. Could she have leapt through the portal at the last minute? A mental reflection of her remained clear at hand, I sat up quickly. I looked around the apartment; I was alone. The collar on my shirt rubbed my cheek and I realized, no starch on earth could match the gooey cohesiveness of the wolf's drool. If I needed solid proof that I had ventured to a real, material, world and was not crazy, here it was. I laughed out loud in a response to my thoughts. Again, I heard the low growl and this time I felt it. It came from my stomach. Wow… I must really be hungry. I nodded my head in an autonomic response. I needed food and I needed it now! I was out of bed and dressed in no time at all.

The world I experienced was real. The environment had

certainly drained my vital energy and my body wanted it back. I went out the door so fast I did not take a coat to defend against the cold morning air. I leapt down the stairs, two at a time and flew out the door. I turned to my left, visualizing eggs, bacon, pancakes, toast... Alton? In front of me, blocking my path and a large amount of the bright and warming daylight, was Alton. Before I could compose myself, I threw my arms around... OK... well... I threw my arms up... there was no around on this man. I grabbed his clothes, squeezing hard.

I know... again, not very manly, but I was truly happy to see him. I could feel joy and relief from him as well. He was happy and he laughed. I stood back looking up. Instead of asking him how he was, I immediately started offering my thoughts on the journey and when I took a breath, Alton said, "Wait, wait... where are you going? If I know you, it is to eat. It looks like I am going to have to make sure you get fed again." He smiled as he shook his head.

"OK let's go," I said. "You are right... I am famished. I think it has to do with the environment in...". I had no idea what to call where I had been. Then Alton's comment about making sure I was fed rang home.
"Hey, I bought you the food last time, remember?"

Alton chuckled, "Yes, I do. I was hoping you didn't." He started to turn in the direction I was heading when we collided.

"Alton," I said, dodging a suit on a cell phone. "I have so many questions. Some that may be easy to answer and ones well, I do not know if I can ask in words." He smiled again broadly.

"I know, Michael, we will talk before you return to our four-legged friends," he said with a wink.

"You are right," I said, as a vision of the female supporting me back to back on the path to the village blazed in my mind. "They are my friends," confirming his words and meaning." It is as if a piece of each of them is inside me and right now those pieces are, very distant."

Rising from my thoughts, I said, "Her name should be, Bossy, though... you know, she is really bossy." I looked up at him for confirmation.

He just smiled again and raising his hands in a posture of surrender. "Well, as is the mother... so is the daughter."

I shook my head up and down as Alton was doing, saying, "I can believe that!"

I turned and walking fast, headed in the direction of my original intent. Alton was having a tough time trying to keep up, as he wove in between the human traffic that flowed against him. Every once in a while, a person caught up in cell phone conversation, or walking on auto pilot, would confront Alton as he tried to side slip around them. Their heads would rise, then rise some more. Once they realized that there was no head at an acceptable level to focus on, they would strain ungracefully upward. All of this would happen within a second, or two. Realizing the scope of the person in front of them many just melted down. Some screamed, a few dropped their coffee, or jumped to the side as if avoiding an imminent threat. I felt a little ashamed watching these people being shocked out of their mundane thoughts, but boy... was it funny. Even funnier, was Alton's efforts to apologize to each person as he attempted to help pick up something dropped here, righting a hat there. It was so comical I could not stop looking over my shoulder at his plight. From that moment on, the day was slated for remembrance.

I liked this advantage I had on Alton. Just for fun, I stopped, looked down at a chip in the sidewalk and scraped it with my shoe. I walked a few paces and looked up at the sun as if contemplating something important. When Alton caught up, which was only a split second later, it was just in time to catch my intention. He burst out laughing.

CHAPTER 20

My favorite diner was about 7 blocks away. The streets around it were jammed with every type of person imaginable. People from all walks of life counted on that diner to be the place to find food, friends and good times. Artists exercised their talents nearby, some painting, some eating, all of them talking and laughing. Musicians crowded the corner and the outside tables, some singing, some dancing, others playing instruments. A few vendors peddled their wares as the crowd moved back and forth past them, like fish in a school. An old friend, who turned me on to the diner, lived on the third floor of the corner building. From there, we would spend hours sitting on the window sill far above it all, pondering the world and watching the ebb and flow of people, cars and everything else on those vibrant streets. At times, the sounds would synchronize into a strangely hypnotic melody, resonating across buildings and buses, people and voices. It was also a place where I can remember never, ever feeling alone.

My friends name was JD. He was also a physicist, musician and writer. When I asked him how he found such an incredible place, he smiled and said it was partially due to quantum mechanics, but mainly like all good discoveries, blind, dumb, luck. He said he rented the apartment rather than buy a house because it was a nexus, a physical convergence of all the energies of the city. This way, he said, he was never far away from the action. He swore he was going to be on the first expedition to Mars... that way he could get first hand from an outside perspective, what the universe was really all about. JD was just good, that explains him in total, down to the bone.

The crowd in the diner was as eclectic as JD. Sitting next to a group of throw backs from the 60's, would be a group of Hells Angels, or a carpenter heading to or from work. The local vicar might be trolling for new recruits, while a few well-known actors would be discussing ridiculous... or not... tabloid articles about their lives. Everyone was welcome, down to a couple of street kids who would not be refused space to belly up to the bar, to claim one of the diner's special shakes. The food in the diner was very simply, just down home, feel good fixins. The bacon was crisp, the eggs perfect, the toast hot and the pancakes were so fluffy, that a scoop of melting butter and a coating of maple syrup was the only thing that could hold them down to the plate. The coffee... well ... I could swear it was made using some exotic ingredient. You could drink cup upon cup, without becoming the toast, they served. The aroma of it was so thick that it blended with everything you ate, defining the diner's ambiance.

I watched as Alton took the scene in. His eyes went wide, his stomach grumbled and the ground shook. A few people turned around to look, while laughter spread out across the diner.

"I can see we are going to need to contain that before someone gets hurt," the waitress said. We all called her D, short for Dancer. She got her nickname because of the way she could move among the crowd with full trays of food, or at night... with beer. Nobody knew her real name. We just copied what Mel yelled out. He would growl, "D, get a move on... 2 specials for number 4... I am sure they want their food... hot... right?" She would just laugh, and say something insulting back, like "Shhhh... they fell asleep waiting for you to cook it?" Dinner and a show, was the local joke about the place.

"Another rumble like that and we're likely to lose the neighborhood," D said as she swung the tray with her notepad around her hip and over the head of those sitting at the next table. She turned her attention to a passing patron, a construction worker heading past her out of the diner with coffee for his coworkers. She hip checked him as he passed and yelled, "Don't forget to settle up with Mel and before the week is out", she added with emphasis. "You know how crabby he gets when you guys hold out. He's making your lunch tomorrow, so don't piss him off". The man dodged the hip check with poise and a smile, then moved around another table.

"See what you teach me D." My wife thinks I am having an affair, cuze I can move sooo smooth". He smiled broadly as the nearby tables joined in with laughter. D smiled... and as quick as a snake added, "Tell your wife she has less than nothing to worry about, unless you don't pay Mel, then she might be very unhappy with what he makes next week's soup out of". The crowd groaned; Alton sat very still. It was obvious the entire environment was overwhelming to him. I laughed so hard out loud that a baby, startled from his stupor in a high chair nearby, flung a gooey spoon all the way to the bar. Alton looked at me like I was crazy. I could not stop laughing at him and the tears began rolling down my cheeks.

"What... what is so funny?" he asked.

In between the laughter I choked out," I just spent... I do not know how long with that same sense of confusion and wonder on my face. It is just too funny to watch you in the same spot". As the tears began to subside, I could see just enough to capture Alton smiling.

"Ha... Touché,' he said as his chest began bouncing with laughter. It was not until I saw Alton look down, as if he were a scolded child that I noticed D was standing there looking at us like we were both crazy. That broke it. I fell over on my side in the booth we had climbed into, with another bout of uncontrolled laughter. I could not see Alton's face from there, but from underneath the table his legs were bouncing just like his chest was. I would have expected to hear booming laughter, but somehow, he was holding it together. Thank goodness for that, the baby would really have been a mess!

I could sense D was getting impatient, as I used the last of my strength to gain composure and pull myself back upright. She turned away for a moment and as she turned back, I could see she had done that to hide her own smile and protect her reputation. It was no secret that even the roughest of patrons, bowed to her authority.

She bit her lip and said, "Come on, boys, I do not have all day and by the size of this one," she pointed the tray at Alton," it will take us all day just to cook his meal, or meals?" I had not realized the tables to our right and behind us had been caught in the infectious laughter and things were unraveling fast. D caught the sense of it. After years of carrying drunks and herding troublemakers out of the door, she had a keen eye for the progression of things.

"Ok... OK ... let's get this moving. What do ya want, Mike? I know you want coffee to start. How about you, sir", she said to Alton with a mischievous smile. "If you would like, I can bring your coffee in a bowl." The table to our right lost it again.

"Yes, to both," I said feeling the hunger bite, "but just bring two cups, leave a full pot though...uhmm maybe two? To make this a little faster D... we will both have the special."

"What else is new," she said as she moved off.

"Make sure the cakes are hot," I yelled after her. She looked back with a note of disdain, then smiled and swished her rear-end.

Conversation was not even a consideration as we devoured our food. It was interesting to watch Alton eat. He had good manners, dined slowly and you could tell he savored every bite. He actually ate very little for a man his size. When we received our third refill on the pot of coffee, we began to speak to each other, beyond the sporadic, hey...could you pass...? Hey... anymore of...? The neat thing about it all, if someone from a distance watched us eat, we would probably have resembled a tag team of wrestlers, attacking our food and devouring it in unison. It was a true example of efficient man-cave eating. After all was said and done, there was little left of the food but stains on the plates. As my thoughts oriented to a more civilized exchange, a nearby chair scraped the floor with a low growl. My mind drifted back to the wolves and the less than timid female.

"Alton, can you tell me about the wolves? Let's start with Lea". He choked a little on his coffee, as if interrupted by something unexpected. Since a cup of coffee for him was a few sips, maybe two, he was constantly refilling his cup. I caught him draining the last in his cup, neck extended and hatch open with the question.

After clearing his throat Alton said, "They are highly intelligent, as sentient as any life form I have ever met. The females are dominant, but I am sure you recognized that," he added with a sly smile. He leaned forward as if sharing a secret, he did not want anyone else to hear. "Make no mistake about it he said in a warning tone, Lea is just like her mother, Stella." I recognized a hint of both fear and adoration as he mentioned "Stella's" name.

"I sipped my coffee and said the name means Star in Latin, right? How did she get a Latin name?"

Alton looked at me, then put down his cup and adopted a lecturing tone. "Mike, our cultures are intertwined. As I have said previously, we have been here on your Earth since the beginning of mankind. We were ... Uhmm... positioned to bring mankind forward in evolution. Our history is yours to some extent. We are in your Bible. We are in the logs of Captains who sailed the vast seas of your world. We can be found in your museums."

"Wait a minute, Wait … a… minute," I said as I set my cup down ready for a little reasoning. "What museums? If that were so, I think I would have known about it, I am well read. I have not heard of any… 9 or 10-foot human… I mean 'Like', human like," I repeated still trying to make my meaning clear, "remains in existence."

Alton sat more erect challenged to prove his statement true. "The museum in the capitol of Peru has remains of not one, but two, of our revered and well know leaders. They left our world to dedicate their lives to the spiritual direction of yours."

"No way," I said.

"Yes," he said with defiant confusion. "Way!"

As he emptied the coffee urn into his cup, I pulled out my cell phone and looked up "Giants in Peru". Within seconds, articles came up showing sarcophagus over 9+ feet in height, dressed in robes with jewelry and metals. I shook my head in disbelief. Now… not only was I a stranger in a new world, I apparently was also a stranger to my own. "Unbelievable," I said.

"Way," Alton said in absolute seriousness. I laughed and shook my head.

"I need to walk… all of this is making me feel light headed, but first I will be right back. I ran to the rest room in preparation for our departure, all that coffee consumed having laid waste to my bladder. Upon return, I found "D" in conversation with Alton. On her tray was our bill, with money laid on top.

"You scooted out of this one, Mike," she said. "Good thing you have this skyscraper to cover your ticket. Mel is not in a forgiving mood today." I looked over at the barrel shaped owner, leaning forward across the bar with a not so happy look on his face. He shot me a glance of… "Look what I gotta deal with" then turned back to a customer in the hairs of his sights, digging desperately for salvation, in his pockets.

"Well at least you are always in a good mood, D," I added patronizingly.

"I am the smart one… remember?" she said with a wink and a tap of her pen on her temple. "You men are all alike. I can see ya comin around the corner before you have even thought about what your gunna order. Except you, Mike, I do not have to see you coming. I know what your order is. It is the same thing every time."

"What can I say, D," I jibed, "when ya find a good thing, you gotta stick with it".

"Funny," she said looking straight at Alton. "None of my old boyfriends saw things that way. I guess I am lucky there."

We all laughed. "Come on, D," I said. "What would Mel do if you went soft on some guy and left this place to have a hoard of your own? You know we are all your children. Well, you feed us like it anyway." I laughed nodding with a little embarrassment at the mess on our table. "Who would control the crowd?" I added quickly.

"Well, I am thinkin…uhm… this guy," and she pointed the tray again at Alton. "Not too many that would stand toe to toe with him. What do ya say, Big Boy… need a job? It comes with perks," she said with a smile and an ever so subtle swivel of her hips.

"No concern for hiding your intentions there, D," I giggled.

"Just takin' your advice, Mike. I can recognize a good thing, too," she said with an even more pronounced swivel in Alton's direction.

Alton was speechless. He had been watching the banter but had no intentions of saying anything. Now that a question had been posed to him… he was stone. D and I both laughed in unison. Alton smiled, while turning brighter red than humanly possible. He tipped his head in a quick bow and walked out into the sun and down the street.

D and I laughed out loud again, along with the nearby table taking interest in the towering figure that had been looming above them.

"I had better get going. He is a hard man to catch once he has a lead."

D jiggled a little and responded, "If you need some help just whistle. I have chased enough men out of here and down that street, so that people know just to step aside. The table next to us chimed in with yells of… "She ain't caught me yet, not me," while maintaining a chain of laughter.

D shot a side glance over at them and the table went silent.

CHAPTER 21

A lready in motion, I flung a wave over my head and hit full stride. I ran two blocks before I caught up with Alton. He was waiting on a corner for traffic to pass before he moved on.

"Hold up there, freight train", I gasped, out of breath from running two blocks, while dragging a pot of coffee, eggs, bacon… well you get the picture. I bent over, hand on knees to catch my breath. "Where are we going?" I asked. Alton took a few deep breaths in through his nose and out through his mouth like he was preparing for a race.

"We are going to let the universe guide us, Michael." He tilted his head a little to the side, like he was listening to something far away. I stood up straight while taking another deep breath of my own, then turned to face him just as he turned to look me directly in the eye. For a split second, I felt oddly out of sync with the rest of the world. Then Alton said, "Once you get comfortable with all the new places you can go, Michael, you will begin to see where you want to go." Those words seemed dangerously open-ended and vibrated in my head. Pressure pushed out on my temples, as I was absorbed by Alton's stare.

As if from an old movie I had once seen on the cure for malaria, where upon surveying the dark, dank, suffocating ward the patients suffered in, a doctor passionately began ripping curtains off the windows and throwing them open to let light and fresh air in. So in comparison, I could feel Alton shredding unforeseen barriers. Opening up not just cerebral territory, but a vastness that brought a climax of intense sensations and frightening exposure? Inner space was expanding like a bubble, my skull pounded, warning of an impending explosion. Alton was looking right through me and it seemed like he was focused on something deep inside me. Just out of the corner of my sight, barely visible, I could see a light, or a lustrous pearl, growing far faster than I could judge. My natural inclination was to try to get a better look, but even though the light originated from somewhere else, it was growing within me. As I contemplated exactly where the glow was coming from, I was seized by fear. An inner voice repeated… "Do not look… do not look at the light!" Too late it seemed. The inclination became a desire, the desire became a need and then an overpowering attraction which drove that need beyond my conscious control. I closed my bulging eyes, squeezing hard, trying to place the opalescent light in one realm, or the other. Inner sight brought the glow into better focus, but it was never quite in full view and the glow continued to overpower my senses. My eyes began to respond to the ever-increasing vision before me and started to rotate 180 degrees in an effort to look towards the back of my brain. I could not stop the physical turning sensation. My eyeballs felt like they would pop out of their sockets, or be ripped from my head. All the time, the glow was incredibly attractive, irresistible.

Familiarity fought the unknown, for footholds on a mindscape that was being reconstructed before my own eyes. Since I could not fathom what exactly was happening and I was obviously losing ground in a virtual tug of war, I attempted to find a path through it. I reached out for the light, swimming madly in my mind, as a person caught in a flood might seek something, anything to grasp for survival. My wish was instantly fulfilled. I floated into alignment with one of a multitude of silken paths that resembled 'Angel's Ladders' in the sky on a cloudy day. I felt the light and energy pass through me, but I was disappointed that simply contacting the light did not unify me with it or its' source, as I had hoped. I was bathed in the light, but not part of it. I could intuitively tell that I was not in harmony, or resonating with whatever energy had originated it. Like a tracker, finding footsteps or disturbed undergrowth in a familiar forest, I had memory of my mind's landscape to sustain me, but that forest was quickly being ravaged by an expanded world. As I passed into another tunnel or beam, I could tell it was newer, more recent than others.

A picture of jet engine exhaust trails crystallized in a magnificent blue sky, slipped into my radically altered mind. Right behind the jet, the trail of exhaust was always tightly formed and finite, but as time passed the trail would begin to become misshapen and dissipate. The same principle was evident here. Whatever formed the paths of light was gone and the energy that formed it was gone as well;" there was nothing left to hold the path and its dimensions in place. The more I focused on the beams, the more of them I could see. Some were almost undetectable, used, or spent. While some remained cohesive, held together by energy not yet dissipated. The visible or active tunnels took on depth and contrast, resembling passageways. Certain ones were spinning peacefully and in a controlled manner. Others were spinning wildly, as if struggling to contain tremendous power forced, or pulled down it. They traveled in all directions and at all angles.

"Oww," I said, reeling a bit as I gained a small amount of temporary balance and stability. I had been drawn in fast and deep, into whatever world this was. It was so engaging that it had almost blotted out the entire tangible world. Like a movie theater, lights out and screen alive. I reached outward intuitively to Alton for support.

"What did you do?" I moaned.

I knew before I spoke he could not explain it to me, but I needed to hear his voice as an anchor to the physical world. There was no response.

I spoke again, "Timing… timing … is important with that… whatever… you did," I stuttered to Alton while repeatedly opening my eyes widely and then shutting them. "I am glad I am not behind the wheel of my car." I shoved the heal of my hand into my eye sockets, in hopes that physical pain would pull me to the surface and away from inner pain. Alton did not respond, but I could feel him standing beside me, his hand resting gently on my upper back. I could also sense that he felt bad for me. Like a coach would feel bad as he popped a dislocated joint back into place for his athlete. Painful, but necessary. Alton also knew, I was back peddling from the process he initiated. He was not about to let that happen. I could perceive him struggling to keep me pointed in the right direction, inward. I could sense how he had utilized a moment when my mental guard was down. Chosen a precise second to slip beneath my conscious mind and open something… doorways? How my mind responded from swinging those doors wide was a whole other story. I felt like I had lived in a home with false walls and one day, someone kicked a few down. My mind and awareness went from an 1800 sq. ft fixer upper, to a country mansion with way too much space to explore in a lifetime.

"Ohh," I groaned out loud again. "Alton, what just happened?" I wanted to look him straight in the eyes but a duality confused my attempt. He was in this experience with me. Not his body, but he was there in mind, my inner world. I must have started to collapse out on the street, because I could feel Alton taking hold of my shoulders, his huge hands held me up as I began to sway. I could hear his voice as if it were in a huge auditorium.

"I am sorry, my friend, changing the way a person has learned to see the world and his own potential in it, is always a little challenging. There is no easy way to dislodge a lifetime of conditioning, except by pulling out its foundation and letting the whole structure crumble. Soo... I have opened things up a bit and let some fresh air in. You were given an excellent brain, with incredible power and well... you just do not know when you may need all of it."

I clearly sensed that he was biding time with that comment. I presumed he was doing so in order to allow me to recover from the initial shock to my psyche. There was an air of extreme caution in him, as if that very same fragile human psyche could crumble, crash and burn. Collapsing into realms not even he could salvage it from. I was beginning to see him physically again, but I was also standing in the middle of nowhere, no ... make that everywhere!

"What... fresh air... extra room?" I asked. My voice echoed inside my head. In truth, I was scared. Coordination with the spatial distortion began to bring relief. Vertigo began to subside and anger took its place. "Did you have to expand... do whatever, while my belly was about to burst?" I sputtered. "I think... I think I am going to puke."

Of course, I felt like a huge baby and was immediately embarrassed. Alton got the memo though; he saw I was shaky and struggling to stay composed. I was seeing a little better and watched Alton surveying the horizon while rubbing his belly.

"Well, now that you're more composed," he looked at me sheepishly, "we will just need to walk that food off."

Obviously, that was not the answer I was looking for. I still struggled with functioning in a duality. One reality was corporeal. That one, I was skilled and proficient in, familiar. The other reality provided no form, no familiarity and absolutely no defined physicality.

"Whaaaa," I said, "I am not even sure I can walk in a straight line. Ohhh… I really do not want to throw up out on the sidewalk."

Alton laughed while setting his direction, then headed off.

I groaned and somewhat blindly followed him off the curb.

CHAPTER 22

In general, our brain runs on automatic. We do not sense it like other members of our body that we tangibly interact with, say... a hand, or a foot. Only a headache, fatigue, or brain freeze from a frosty... stuff like that, reminds us it is a tangible organ. So, it was, that my brain and the conscious mind that I was pretty sure filled it up, or at least... had filled it up before, was putting me on notice... not nice!

Head in hand, I followed behind Alton for a block negotiating around people and structures, while watching my own internal version of "Extreme Makeover" in progress. It was apparent that Alton had tampered with familiar cognitive boundaries that define the breadth and depth of my conscious self. Now everything was out of relativity. Coming to terms with how integral my brain was in every single function it reasoned over, was truly an insight.

Imagine expecting to sit in a chair that is behind you. Unfortunately, the chair does not happen to be in a familiar place. It is only as you are falling backward, nowhere near the support you are familiar with, that you get a sense of everything being out of relation to what you believed it to be. That is, of course, until your rear-end inevitably and painfully crashes onto the floor.

Where once my thoughts followed familiar well-worn paths, they now floated untethered, groping for that chair, that solid structure, which could stay the pain of an unexpected fall. I began to feel increasingly anxious and panicked. As we reached the next street, Alton must have seen how unstable I was and moved behind me. This time he guided me over to a bench at the entrance to a neighborhood park. Once we reached the bench, he sat me down and again looked into my eyes. I wanted to reach out to him with mine, but I was not all there and what was there, was confused and embarrassed. Passing people, children's laughter, the not so distant traffic, all seemed to be taunting me, defining a world no longer my own. Inside my newly evolving world, I stared down into an abyss. There was no end. As a matter of fact, the nature of this abyss was nothingness, emptiness, a void. I groped for Alton who was now sitting next to me and the only other element that existed in both worlds. His presence, for the moment sustained me above that vast, empty space. Alton's voice reverberated in the crushing inner silence.

"Michael, it is time. You will have to let go now. You will have to let go of the many things that limit you. I know they serve as your shield in times of fear, but they are limitations none the less. They are physical and perceptual, emotional and psychological. They give the world of illusion form. The memories of who you are as an original being, as a dynamic of the universe, need to be restored. This evolution is premature and will be dangerous as... what you depend on your world to be, what has supported you in this life, will be forever changed. Your mind, your psyche, will be pushed beyond what your existing senses support. What is most difficult and for which I am sorry, is that I cannot help you here. Only you can navigate through and then dismantle the barriers placed on your awareness. They were placed there when you chose to live this physical existence. I believe in you and your ability to make this journey. Allow your sense of self, your will of spirit, to guide you, to navigate for you. Michael," Alton's voice dropped in tone. "The universe is forever, the distances between that which we know and that which we do not know, are very large."

I could feel Alton moving farther away from me as he spoke. Struggling to keep from falling beyond a point of no return into the void below, prompted me to cry out "No shit ... help me," but Alton continued.

"Trust yourself, accept what is born out of that which will be broken." His voice ended suddenly, but it ended with a hint of "sink or swim". Then it was as if Alton just let go. The last strand of the world I knew slipped from my grasp, into the embrace of all that was not. I began to tumble, or free fall in the expanding abyss. Orientation was a luxury of the outside world. Curled in a fetal position, I was a child conceived fully aware and driven from a peaceful coexistence with life, down a dark path of no return. Could a babe being born into the physical world, forced from all it had known as it developed and grew, feel any different than I? Could its fragile psyche, comprehend the incredible pressures of the birth canal and the icy cold burn that replaced its perfectly warm, static and unchanging world? Purged, was the steady beat, the melodious and methodical rhythm that reassured it of other life nearby.

There was no turning away, no running from the transition, no protection from this assault on my psyche and the approaching unknown world. Adrift and abandoned, I was awash in heartache. I refused to unfold and look out upon my surroundings as isolation crept into my mind, cold as ice. I was not being held up by my feet, or slapped on my bare ass, but this was a birth, or maybe… a rebirth. I had survived being born, yet I remained undelivered.

With fear as my companion, time passed and the impression that I was imprisoned in nothingness, confined in my own universal amniotic fluid, dissipated. I finally unclenched my mind… nothing happened? Nothing was happening? A unique thought came to mind. While existing in nothing… maybe nothing was going to happen. I laughed at the thought. It was an insane laugh, a feeble sign of defiance, but it felt good. Then the concept of "me" hit … me. I was still there. "I" was still aware. "I" was certainly not… nothing. "I" was… something. I was thinking, assessing, I existed. Nothing… to it! Again, I felt lighter from a spark of laughter. If I was life, a small piece of God, a small seed of His consciousness, should I not be the center of all that is, in a universe of all that is not? I mean… what else is out there, but me? I did not die. The light of my soul did not… blink out. The purpose of my being, whatever that was, did not stop… being. Maybe… the space between what we know and what we do not know, the space between understanding and emptiness is us? We are there… the essence of a seed yet to be sprouted, of a force of life yet to be realized. So, if we embrace our existence, if we engage the inspiration for the life that originated in the heavens above. If we strive upward like that seedling searching for sunlight, then as we grow, the unknown is just the soil in our garden. Could "GOD" have felt this way, as he created our universe? Could I … be that seedling expanding into all that is not, changing it into, all that can be?

My past programming revolted… you are not God! You are not

the hope and the light, you idiot, you ass, you... are... not... GOD. The intensity of this response by some part of my consciousness, my inner voice shocked me. There was no mistaking it though... in all that was not, at that moment... "I was". My response was swift and out loud. I am not God, but I am his love, I am his creation, I am his spark, his child, I am life never-ending. Especially right now, where there apparently is none, you simple minded bigot!

I probably was not going to get anywhere insulting the only person I had to talk to at the moment, but the added disdain was a welcome release. Not to mention that facing a universe of nothing, I certainly had nothing to lose. Still no response, only a silence as loud as any noise I had ever imagined. Fear and negativity had no foothold here, in a world without form. There were no excuses to hide behind. I could remain a tumbling blob of consciousness, or... I could take possession of that which I was, make my mark! I don't know... rebuild my own world?

My inner voice fought back again. You are not God... you do not own, you rent. I laughed, this time out loud and with a lighter heart, for I had zeroed in on the location of my inner heckler and he reeked... of fear. He could no longer hide from the unknown, as it was all that surrounded him.

"I see you now," I uttered in a growling whisper. "You can run, but where would you possibly hide?" Again silence. I spoke, whether it was mental or actual spoken words, I could not tell, it all was the same.

"What do you say?" The silence, coupled with the truth of the statement brought the emptiness of the void a little closer. "When faced with nothing, isn't doing something... anything better?" I screamed. This time, I had focused on the words and projecting a voice. Still only silence. Frustrated with nothing, I fully unfolded from my fetal position and began assessing.

"Bold move," my inner voice finally... anteed in, even though it was only a whisper.

I laughed and answered, "Bold how? This is... nothing," and I waved my hands outward to emphasize my point. "It is however, time you pitched in," I admonished. "I know now why I am here." Confident now in my voice, I spoke out loud, though the words trailed off with far less audacity than I had envisioned. I made another attempt at establishing my will upon the unformed space where I floated like a cloud.

"I am a point, a place in time and space where the essence of life exists. I exist, not nothingness... me. I exist and the void, well... it is exactly that! I have been focusing on what is not, instead of focusing on what is... life, me."

As I gazed out into the infinite blackness, I could not shake the feeling that I was missing something obvious. The weight of the blackness, the substance of the void was tangible. If nothingness was nothingness, then what was I feeling from it, when I should be feeling nothing? A childhood memory, incredibly real, beyond a holograph, but not corporeal, became visible against the depth of the backdrop.

The memory took flight and my mind sharpened. I remembered learning that the color black was not void of all color. Instead, the primary colors of the spectrum brought together, created the color "black". The color white was also a combination of colors, but it was a combination of all colors. I learned about colors from a teacher named, Mr. Baker. I had been in detention with my friend, Levi, for throwing paper airplanes out of a third story maintenance closet. Levi had built an awesome paper airplane that sailed far out into the parking lot. The wind had carried it far beyond our imagination and as it sailed through the air it turned sideways to us, gliding gracefully above parked cars. We watched in awe, eyes wide and jaws stretched to maximum. The flight was captivating and beautiful, up until the tip of Levi's aircraft buried itself firmly in our school principal's beehive hairdo. Caught up in the beauty of the flight and the unbelievable landing, we remained hypnotized as the perpetually composed Mrs. Finch, began a battle royal with an unknown assailant. Armed with only an umbrella and an unopened box of Twinkies, she spun, dove and swung, defending herself with impressive ninja-like moves. The Twinkies, once freed from the confines of the cardboard box, also took flight, landing unfortunately, in varying degrees of ruin on the pavement. Spellbound by the incredible battle scene, our outpost lay vulnerable. It was not until Ms. Finch concluded her final dynamic defensive posture and came to rest in a crouched stance, umbrella angled to defray the next attack, body tightly wound, hair bun flopped across her forehead, that the paper plane slipped from its docking station and glided effortlessly to the ground in front of her. Since this was not the first time Levi and I had challenged the Wright brothers' initiative and from that very same closet, the principle knew exactly where to look. There we were, frozen in simple childhood awe. During our ensuing detention, Mr. Baker, the only teacher who truly appreciated what Levi and I had achieved that day, asked us to recreate the scene in crayon.

He said, "Guys, in order to remember what you are being punished for and at the same time appreciate the magnitude of your achievements, I want you to draw in vivid color, together… since you were in this together, what happened as you saw it". Over that week, I had never had more fun in detention with anyone, than with Levi and Mr. Baker. We laughed and drew and laughed some more, describing over and over the snake like moves performed by Mrs. Finch. Mr. Baker was obviously concerned about authenticity in our efforts, as he asked us to repeat many times what had transpired. Each time our story grew a little and each time Mr. Baker had to blow his nose and wipe tears from his eyes, before he could stand up from the table that supported his doubled over frame. Every afternoon as we walked home, Levi and I passed the remnants of the failed flight of Twinkies, now crushed to the pavement by passing cars. Levi's mom had replaced the box and Mrs. Finch parked around the back of the building from then on.

As we drew and redrew the infamous events, Mr. Baker would explain how important it was to remember things that impacted our life. "Make them VIVID," he would say, spreading his arms and raising his voice. "It builds the mind and strengthens concepts". I really did not understand then, but later on in my life if I ever had trouble understanding a concept, or process, I laid it out in vivid texture in my mind and my abilities were transformed.

In our drawings, Levi and I drew black around Mrs. Finch's head. Mr. Baker said, "Good job, boys, but why is there black around Mrs. Finch's head." We said, "Because she was sooooo mad. It was like there was a dark storm around her." After Mr. Baker stopped laughing and shaking his head, he asked about other parts of our artistic rendition. He would suggest colors and add a few here or there for himself, but he liked the black the best. He would talk about the colors and how they had a language of their own; how they conveyed feeling and meaning. He then told us a story. He called it the story of "The One Tree".

He started, "In the center of all things, there exists a tree. It is the tree of life. The roots of the tree are what hold the universe together. The trunk of the tree carries life from the roots and supports the limbs and branches, which hold the fruit of the tree. The fruit of the tree of life are the planets, suns, stars and galaxies. All is held solidly in place, so they do not spin off and hit each other. The tree protects and fosters all life. One day, as the earth was born out of one of the flowers of the tree of life, the tree noticed how blue the sky around it was. The tree noticed the oceans and the green grass and it was in awe of how vibrant all the colors were. So, it decided to give the inhabitants of this new world, as much color as the world itself. Since the color black was all the primary colors combined, it created a being dark in color, to exemplify how vast the tree was and how precious each color was to the whole, for if just one color was missing the whole world would be diminished. He created yellow beings to represent light, the glow of all the worlds that warmed the tree. Without that combined light, life would exist in darkness, alone and vulnerable. The tree created brown beings to represent physical matter, a joining of energy in a focused purpose. The host of life the tree gave to all. The tree then created red beings to exemplify the essence of that light, as it wove its way through the tree. Glowing embers, the burning desire of life eternal. Finally, the tree created beings very light of color. This color, although pale in comparison to the other colors, was to represent the interdependency of life, as it took all colors to create and maintain the lighter color. The tree could not live without its' roots, the branches could not grow without the trunk and the fruit could not flourish without the limbs to bring forth new life. So, the light color beings could not live without all the other colors unified in their creation.

Once the tree was done creating the earth and its inhabitants, it allowed it to be the only planet in its sun's system that supported this type of life. The earth stood as an example of how interdependent, unique and precious, life can be. All the existing worlds on the tree began to receive sustenance from their new sibling, for the light from this world carried the essence and meaning of what all existence was designed for. Life, focused through purpose, toward an ever-refining organism of growth and awareness."

It was a great story. I never forgot it, or the value of expression through color. On our last day, Levi and I were sitting on the school's front steps before heading home. Our detention, our prison, our fantasy island had become the best part of school. We just sat there and commiserated. We did not say much, just kind of huddled close to each other, afraid of losing our union.

I broke the silence first. I said, "School is never going to be the same."

Levi said, "We could get in more trouble. No… no… my sister would only have more to tease me about."

I responded, "Yea… and Mrs. Finch will kill us, if my parents don't beat her to it." Huddled next to Levi for strength, I felt the sting of imminent separation, along with the emptiness that a changing reality created.

That barrenness swept profoundly over me now and I struggled to find a connection to what surrounded me here in this seemingly disconnected world, this black void. According to the story of the one tree, all of the building blocks of the universe were here. They were waiting for the painter, the builder, the creator, the spark of life, a consciousness to bind and structure it all, to "Make it vivid".

I began to rally. How does one go about building and coloring a new world, a new universe, a new awareness out of this nothingness? What would be the most valuable, the most enduring building block that I could start to color this world with? What generates substance and makes life worthy of being? My mind responded on cue: love, happiness, faith, values, the embodiment of all of those. I considered a concept fostered by a priest I once knew.

He said, "God is life. Hell… is life without God. Hell is life without purpose, without the glue that connects us to each other and to everything else, a void. Our spirits are eternal and so is our struggle for enlightenment. Yet, this struggle is no simple labor, unless it becomes a labor of love, then it becomes effortless."

If God's effort were structured from love, then any act of love I generated, would put me in harmony with the flow, the mechanics of life itself. A voice from within added, self- love and self-respect must be first on your list. "Proper foundations create enduring structures."

"Chalk one up for the logical mind," I shouted as an infectious enthusiasm took hold. My thoughts gained substance and linked together. It was as if the power fueling the cascade into the abyss lost momentum. I could hear Mr. Baker's voice call out from the past, "Make It vivid." "Make it mean… something."

CHAPTER 23

The void still encompassed me, but it seemed more like a fertile field for dreams now. "Lead, follow, or get out of the way," my grandfather used to tell us when we were avoiding doing our chores as kids. It was time for me to take the lead, accept the possibilities and apply them in a way that made a difference.

"Why be a victim, when you can be a victor?" Another of my grandfather's sayings reached out from the past to reinforce going on the offensive and overcoming uncertainty through applied expectation.

A child's scream from the nearby playground resounded in the vast space around me, reminding me there was a duality to this experience, a home to return to, if I could. As I listened to the echo, I was overwhelmed with a feeling of empowerment. Minus a few scruples and a sense of location, I was still a solid form, a man, a human being, part of a physical, tangible world. I began to hear Alton's voice as he conversed with someone close by.

"Yes, Officer, my friend is fine. We had a big meal and he feels sick. As soon as he is well enough, I will walk with him back to his apartment. No… no, I am sure he will be OK… he just fell asleep. No need for an ambulance."

By the tone of his voice, I could tell Alton was uncomfortable. I heard footsteps move off and I could feel Alton's body relax. Demanding a stronger connection with both worlds, I reached out with my thoughts.

"They should have arrested you for what you did to me," I poked in his direction.

I felt an immediate sense of relief from Alton as he said," I would not like jail, the benches are far too small and the cells smell very bad."

His honest response to my dig took me by surprise. "You mean you have been in jail before?" Trying to visualize how Alton might have become incarcerated and the sight of him scrunched up on a bench in a cell, seemed as surreal as what I had just gone through. "I cannot imagine what you could have done to be put in jail, Alton."

His response was simply, "It is a terrible thing to be misunderstood." A mixture of innocence and honesty generated a warming laugh, which swung open the door to daylight. For the moment, my inner voyage was ending. Baggage in hand, it was time to disembark. The fresh air, the trees, the world at large, was beginning to materialize.

"I have had other wards in my days," Alton said with a sigh. "The climate for tolerance for someone as different as myself, is far greater now, than a century ago, or... longer."

Feeling was slowly reaching my fingers and toes. My mind still buzzed with the noises that surrounded me, so I tried to sit erect. I understood that Alton was creating a diversion, to ease my journey back into the physical world, from a consciousness altering experience and I was eager to participate.

"Is that what I am to you, Alton, a ward?" I said as I felt my muscles begin to respond.

"In a way, yes, Michael, but you are far more to me than that. Before we talk about our relationship, and before your logical mind begins to rationalize your experience, let's talk about what has changed for you." I needed time to recover, so I relaxed a little and just listened.

Alton sighed as if relieved as well, then he said, "Some of the normal barriers and boundaries that are put in place when a consciousness transitions into flesh, have now been removed from yours. These barriers normally vanish upon death, or possibly while transcending through what you might call karma, life's lessons. It is dangerous for a person living a physical existence, to know his true spirit and to unravel the nature of the universe. The more enlightened, the greater the difficulty remaining within physical laws and boundaries."

"In other words, who would want to struggle in an earthly existence, when they can be free to explore an unlimited universe?" I responded.

"Freedom for some… insanity for others," said Alton and he moved uncomfortably, as if recalling a personal experience. "I have seen many a tortured soul whose eternal awareness, eclipses their earthly one. How does an infinite being, fit willingly into a finite space?"

"Claustrophobia?" I said with a mental shudder.

Alton cleared his throat as if in unspoken agreement. "Michael, what you become in this world, in your tomorrows, is pivotal for others who remain on their paths, fulfilling their own destinies."

Did he finally begin to explain what this was all about, I thought? I began to sit fully up and steady my body but, I had to keep shaking my head to clear the cob webs. It was obvious I was not ready for that much movement and I began to black out. My mouth was not coordinating with my mind and I mumbled to Alton, "Why does my mind feel so slow, so dense?"

Alton leaned over and put his right hand on my forehead and his left on the back of my neck. Almost immediately warmth, like the sun coming out from behind clouds, flowed over my mind and then to my body. It felt good. I laid my head back and as the warmth spread, I could feel multiple levels of awareness vibrating back and forth in an effort to mesh into harmony. The denseness in my mind slowly disappeared, while aspects of the inner world remained recognizable and separate.

"It will take time but once your new awareness is unified and assimilated, you will learn to use it like any other part of you," Alton said. He shifted his fingers up to the base of my skull. The warmth flowed anew and my head tingled in response to his touch.

"I think I would have a better handle on all of this if you could explain what you did to me. What… exactly happened? I asked. Alton sighed and removed his hands from my head and neck as if he had completed what he needed to. The tingling in my legs and back became feeling, which in turn became pain, noticed most prominently in my rear end.

"OUCH…. I have been on this bone breaker for way too long. Let's get up and walk." I started to stand and as I did, the world spun radically.

Alton, grabbed my arm and asked, "Are you sure you won't fall?"

I laughed and said, "Weebbles wobble, but they don't fall

down." I did not look up to confirm Alton's confusion, I could feel it anyway and it made me smile.

"Never mind," I said, "I will be fine. Just don't let me make too big a fool out of myself. I may know some of these people." I started taking stiff and unbalanced baby steps. Alton placed each of his huge hands on my shoulders, I picked up a little speed and we were off. He moved his hands down to my arms, to keep me from sliding sideways, which I did less frequently once we acquired momentum. I knew by Alton's less than silent giggles that I must have looked like a total fool, or maybe just a recovering drunk. I could also tell he was having a little trouble avoiding stepping on my heals and he would mumble something low every time he did. I laughed and he knew what I was laughing about, he smiled broadly.

"One of us always has to slow down for the other," I chuckled.

A little girl said out loud to her mother, "Look, Mommy, the big man is playing puppet with the small man." With Alton's large hands grasping both my arms, I could only imagine how it must have looked. Alton and I both started laughing uncontrollably.

CHAPTER 24

The sun was gloriously warm and well into the midday sky by the time I returned to my normal self. The breeze was gentle, the sky blue, by all accounts, a perfect day. The park we were walking through was huge. It took up about 20 blocks square. There was a lake in the middle, with many rock outcroppings for people to sit on and children to conquer. The trees were majestic, reaching heights that had inspired many an artist. Well-worn cobblestone paths where moss challenged the stones for rights to the soil they both were bound too, wove in and out of the ancient sentinels, promising adventure as they trailed off.

Alton and I stuck to the smooth main paths at first, allowing equilibrium to return to my body in earnest, but my mind was not as cooperative. Although I was no longer grasping wildly for structure in it, a feeling of walking along the edge of a cliff with a drop into wide open space, still plagued my awareness. Anxiety drove my sight inward to avoid a fall and instead messed with my depth perception, leaving me with vertigo.

I was uncomfortable with the expanded aspects of my consciousness. It was as if the buffers and filters that protect a mind and its psyche, from the million fragments of stimuli that assail it every second, of every day, were removed. If a voice echoed in the background, a part of me was immediately connected. It was almost automatic to explore the energy, then the personality and condition of the person owning the voice.

A young couple sharing the richness of new love, walked slowly toward nowhere in particular. A grandmother chased her grandchildren around interconnecting paths, while her daughter had gone to work. So many people, so many lives and all of them were interacting as seamlessly as the cobblestone paths, with the ancient elms and oaks.

We ventured onto one of the well-traveled cobblestone paths and I caught a glimpse of a man squatting against a tree, just at the edge of sight. I recognized immediately the disarray in his mind, it resembled what my mind had just gone through. I could feel his sorrow, his sense of isolation. He was homeless and living in a world between memories and nightmares. He had lost all that was valuable to him due to alcoholism, but like all stories, his was not that simple.

His alcoholism developed due to the loss of a child and the subsequent crumbling of his marriage. He had detached from the world. As he lost his will to fight, to survive; his ability to focus on anything in particular, had disappeared. Yet, deep below the surface, beyond the influences of his daily world, I could see his inner person, his soul. He was a kind man and in his early days he realized he had a talent for art, but no way to apply it. He had searched, but found no other worthwhile purpose for his life beyond his desire to draw, or paint. So, he just walked along with life and what it brought to him. In time he found a soul mate, a caring partner that he fell in love with. She provided reason and purpose for his life. She created a world with him, where he found personal comfort and companionship. In time, they gave birth to two children and their lives were full. He worked hard to provide for his family, while his wife stayed home to take care of the kids. The economy battered them, but they had remained a happy and purposeful team, partners and a family strong. Then the unbelievable happened. Their son, drugs, the wrong place, at the wrong time and their world was torn from its foundations. His wife began to drink heavily. As he watched her shrink away from the world, he was left alone to battle for them both. The world tore at him, like the surf tears at the sand on the beach. During a particularly savage and stormy time, the shores of his life eroded from the constant battering and were carried away. With his foundations fragmented, his own demons caught him off guard and he sought refuge in the same bottle that his wife did. The second child lost her way, watching the structure of her family decay. She moved out at an early age and cut off all communication.

His wife, having lost both children and being adrift in her life, searched for a place to hide from her hurt. She found another who fought with her to understand and overcome her challenges. Ending her marriage, she moved on.

After he lost his partner, he lost his job, mostly due to his addiction. His daughter would not allow him back into her life and he was left truly alone. Faced with inconceivable odds, he just gave up and drifted into a fog of indifference.

Two joggers, focused intensely on the path they were traversing, bumped past me as I stood in the middle of it all, totally consumed by the history that was unfolding before my eyes. Alton brushed up against me to offer room for the joggers. I realized he was there with me in the moment, in the unfolding pages of the book of this man's life. We looked at each other. I saw tears rolling down Alton's face. I could feel the same on my own.

At that moment, I felt three things very intensely. The first was anguish over how a person could fall so far and lives go to such waste, without intervention from some greater power. The second was how the hopes and dreams of a person could become so shattered and the effect upon others be so substantial, yet it all pass in silence. Where were his friends and family? The third was wonderment. I was able to share in this man's world, yet I felt shame at the same time, shame for being so small that I was not able to help a person afflicted by such despair. What of the abilities that were becoming part of my life? What do I do to employ them here? For Christ's sake, I didn't even know what they were, much less how to use them. I was consumed with these thoughts, when I heard Alton's mind speak to mine, the connection was clear and precise.

"Do not take responsibility for the lives of others," he said. I froze. I was shocked at the stark coldness of his statement. How could he say such a thing? A being as kind and passionate as Alton? It just made no sense.

Alton saw my reaction, waited a few seconds and said, "Remember that we are all on our own journey. If we interfere in someone's pain, we may remove a motivation that drives critical change. Wanting to eliminate the world's ills is noble, but unrealistic. For this world is the proving ground for the soul, the school for the spirit. Each soul has lessons to learn in support of becoming a greater presence in an expanding universe. The ability you now experience is not to be used out of guilt, or ego. If this man were to stand up one day, overcome his past and create a new world, one that brings him pride, happiness and purpose. How significant would your crime be to have stolen that opportunity, that experience, those lessons from him? The path this man... his consciousness, is on is his own. We would be wrong to interfere."

"But... but ... you helped me?' I said with confusion, "Look at how my life has been altered."

Alton continued as if I had not uttered a word. "Look more deeply. Follow what we both hope will happen for this man. How will his destiny be altered? Where does that vision lead, if you provide an easier path?" Alton looked up into the trees and whispered, "We are what we are and what we were meant to be. What we do with it, is what makes us... who we will be." He watched gusts of wind cascade through the tree tops, swaying one tree after another. The unified motion brought a sense peace to the moment.

"Lessons are gifts," he said. "Learning to embrace your lessons in life, is the equivalent of overcoming them. With faith and patience, we can transcend the limits imposed upon us. Destiny is designed to guide us to triumph. Each lesson learned, is a small step toward the greatest step in each individual's physical existence, which is to transcend physical bonds and limitations in exchange for a much greater and rewarding existence." He looked down at me with a gaze that bound me completely.

"So it is with death," he said, "the release of a consciousness from the limits of this life, reborn, awoken, into that which is eternal and beyond description." Alton took a deep and intentional breath and then said, "Michael, like I told you when you began your inner awakening, once you know where you can go, you will then know where you want to go. We all have personal designs. When you are in harmony with yours, then you are in harmony with the universe and the road will unfold before you. Simply take steps down the path," he finished and looked back over at the man whose head was now forced tightly against the bark of the tree. His hands reached around his body, as if he just received a chill.

"I understand what you are saying, Alton, but my path would have been to help this person somehow, to open his mind like you did mine. Then he could remember his family, his value. Now you tell me that is all wrong. How... in the name of everything holy, will I know what is right and what is wrong?"

"I cannot tell you that, Michael," Alton said with a slight grimace. "I can only tell you how to recognize an opportunity to help."

"OK," I said with frustration, "that would certainly be a good place to start. Otherwise, I am as good as a loaded gun in the hands of a child. Which… if you haven't noticed is not that far away from the truth of it, right now."

Alton smiled gently and continued to stare at the man. "It takes practice and experience to see clearly to the end of changes you initiate and to know when it is in the hands of greater powers. Look at the man. Look into his soul. Why did he choose this life? What are his lessons? Look with the vision you have awoken. What do you see?"

I followed his direction and I let my sight move inward. Where there was a void before, there was now a tapestry of multiple visions giving account of this man's life. As I stood there, I hoped for positive change for this man and one of the tapestries came more clearly into focus as if a lens had been tuned.

As the tapestry unfolded, I saw a sister find him. She had actually never stopped looking. They had been close their whole lives until his wife had left, that is when he fell off the map. There was another woman with her, it was his daughter. They found him in winter two years ahead, in a homeless shelter on the south side of town. When he saw them, he thought he was hallucinating and feebly turned to leave, so he would not have to face a familiar delusion, one that had battered his psyche untold times over the years. It was not until he felt his daughter's hands on his shoulders and heard her voice that he fell to his knees in tears and shame.

It had been a year or so, since he had stopped living his life in a bottle, but not out of discipline, or self-respect. He simply had lost the energy to drown himself in his misery. He became apathetic and could not muster the desire to punish himself further. Without any additional self-destruction to show for his sincere efforts, and with the extra time on his hands, he began visiting area shelters, surrounding himself with other troubled souls living outside societies norms. There, he did not feel so alone.

At one shelter, he observed a young teen lost in a world of sorrow. His heart ached for her and the pain he knew his own daughter was overcome by. As he watched her, he became aware of the others who flowed in and out of that shelter. He related to their suffering. He realized they were souls trapped far beyond his own torment, lost without a way to share that suffering. He wanted and needed a way to show those afflicted that they were not alone. He wanted to somehow lift the isolation, the barrier that imprisoned some and cast others adrift in a sea of heartache. Then one day while he was drawing with a piece of discarded charcoal, he received inspiration. He could draw pictures which exposed suffering and it would be visible to all who had become invisible to themselves, their loved ones and society. His self-reproach, was replaced by a clear passion.

At some point, a very astute and caring community activist noticed his renderings on the walls of the shelter, cast from pieces of spent coal he had gathered from a nearby glass factory. His murals were captivating and at the same time, haunting. The activist connected with property owners in the neighborhood, who were eager to revitalize the community. They pooled resources and purchased paint and other supplies. With his vision supported by others, the man began painting at a desperate pace. The murals drew immediate attention. People stopped to look and drawn to introspection, identified their own pain, or the pain of ones they loved, embodied by the mural's themes and intense illustrations. Knowing their pain was laid bare, shared with any who could relate in some small way, set them free for the moment from sole ownership of their burdens and brought them a sense of relief.

He worked feverishly from one building to the next. People soon began to call the area, "The Walk of Souls". Many tried to compliment him, but he refused to be approached based on his work. His art was life. His life and the lives of others. Their failures, losses and suffering, cast across the buildings-scapes for all to see. His desire to share in the only way he could, was not a cry for personal recognition. It was his way of apologizing to the world, to those he loved and to whatever greater being he had failed in his attempt to live his life well. It was his way of calling all those who suffer in isolation to a refuge, where life's darker nature is exposed and neutralized, no longer powerful hidden in shadow, shame, or fear. He often would respond to well-wishers, "Fear and suffering can only survive, where it can hide from the light of each new day." So, he approached each one of his new days with a warrior's passion. Here was his sanctuary, his daily prayer, his soul's expression fulfilled.

His work brought pride to a beleaguered community, as people from all walks of life came to experience the art and recognized it as a place of value. It inspired other artists, who began sharing in his work, each aspiring artist adding a small scene, a note, or a poem, their gift, to his gift. The collaboration endowed the art with the magic of hope and affinity, making the murals an evolution from darkness to light and priceless.

By fate, his sister had seen the images on the web, had watched the story on the news. Something about the artist's style captured her attention and plagued her inner thoughts. It was not until she visited the "walk" that she saw herself in one of the murals. There as a child, she and her brother were trying to reach an apple hanging just beyond their grasp, from a tree in their yard. She, kneeling on the ground, arms desperately trying to keep two old wood boxes which lifted her brother to within inches of the apple, from bursting apart and dropping her brother to the ground empty-handed. She instinctively knew the artist was her brother and for the first time defined her despair, for she had failed to prevent him from falling in his adult life. She contacted her niece; the man's daughter and their years of searching were rewarded.

As his daughter stared into tortured eyes, she watched as her tears fell to his cheeks. His eyes were crystal, through which she felt she could see down to his soul. As a child, she remembered how she would tell her father that he could never hide anything from her because his eyes were so clear, she could see all the way through him. Now, she could see all the way through him into his hurt, his desperation and finally to the frail strand of hope for salvation that bound his spirit to his flesh. She could hear the repeated prayer just under his breath, "Please be real, please forgive me, please …?"

Kneeling now before his daughter, the man battled within himself, hope claiming ground that doubt and fear tenaciously refused to relinquish. After years of wandering in a barren and scorched world, the tears were manna from heaven. As he buried his face in hands bound in worn dirty gloves which exposed fingers that were cracked and red from exposure to the cold, the daughter fell to her knees and embraced her father. The man's sister already there, face in hands reciting the same words.

The tapestry moved out of focus and another came into clear view. It showed him at his daughter's house smiling and playing with his grandchildren. An enclosed back porch overlooked a beautiful garden, which he had planted. On the porch were a multitude of paintings, many of his daughter and her husband, the grandchildren, his sister and some of his wife, who had since passed on. Other of his paintings though, were intense collages that conveyed life and its complexities. He had achieved fame for these paintings, for he was able to weave the essence of a soul's struggle into them. He created magic through color and canvas, as he chronicled life's struggles for hope, faith and purpose. His creations brought relativity and understanding to human suffering.

One painting, depicted a beleaguered, undefined figure, standing before a mirror outside a store window. Surrounding the main mirror were many smaller mirrors, price tags barely visible. Each mirror, caught the reflection of light from the main mirror and a portion of the figure. Each reflection bore a price tag and each manifestation was slightly different, capturing time and the cost of choices in endless reflections of existence. At the bottom of the painting was a title. It simply said, "Profit & Loss".

The tapestries changed again, the last one I viewed, was of his granddaughter in her first exhibit, both art and sculpture. In each creation, a hint of her teacher survived.

I did not look any further. I stood nakedly corrected. My face was wet and I felt cleansed somehow. I looked down at Alton, as he was squatting on the path next to me moving the moss around like puzzle pieces that still had not found their home. When he looked up, his large and peaceful eyes were reflecting the sky, deep pools of blue, the banks of which were red and swollen.

CHAPTER 25

Sparkles of light in the distance resembling polished gems, glinted off the lake at the center of the park. The sun and the water seemed so refreshing and inviting that I stepped off the cobble stone path which wound indirectly toward it and started down a well-worn grassy path that ran more directly. The trail spread out into a large field, which was free of the towering oaks and elms that had covered the cobblestone paths. I could feel Alton stand up and follow. In two steps, he was next to me. There were other people on the path walking toward us, but we both required a little privacy after our encounter and we moved farther afield, wandering in a casual manner toward the lake.

Feeling as if I had just walked out of a movie theater at midday, my mind adjusting to the bright sun, the crisp air and life outside of some dramatic story, I spread my arms and yelled, "Wow... this is some day!" I could hear Alton laugh, as he as well, was letting the heartache pass.

I sensed that Alton was still vigilant, but he was also confident that I was past any unexpected reactions to the morning's adventures. I was very glad he was aware and confident of my sanity, because I was not so sure. I turned to him and spoke with the intentions of relieving his fears.

"I feel good, ok? So... you know... stop worrying."

Alton rocked his head in acknowledgment. "For someone as stubborn as you, Michael, he said with some feigned contempt, "I am afraid I will never stop worrying."

As we reached the lake, the smell of the water coupled with the warmth of the sun, compelled me to sit on a nearby bench and take time to absorb it all. Alton stood behind the bench and watched a group of young people lay out a blanket on the grass.

"Alton," I said, adding a questioning aspect to my voice. "I do not understand why you have chosen to awaken me. Is that even the right terminology? I am not a brilliant person. I am not a spiritual person per say, either. I have never been a believer in the supernatural. As a matter of fact, my line of work has been to find fact and science to explain the unexplainable. I have no confidence that I can make right decisions empowered with the knowledge and understanding I have been exposed to. What if I end up misusing what I have learned and create ... bad things?"

Alton walked around the bench and sat down. For a moment, we simply watched a family feeding geese not too far away.

Then Alton said, "Michael I did not choose you. I was guided to you, to watch over you. Like I mentioned earlier, by knowing where I can go, I knew where I wanted to go. I watched over you for a period of years, as your destiny progressed. I was hopeful our lives would coincide in such a way that I might become your guide. I was excited when I knew they would. I was sure you could make the transitions necessary to accept your future."

"Can you define what you mean by transitions?" I asked. "I want to make sure I understand."

Alton weighed his response and said, "Let's talk instead about the nature of your existence, as opposed to mine. That will give you some insight."

"OK," I said, wondering why I was still following crumbs in a forest of understanding.

Alton moved some soil at his feet around in a circle and asked, "If you had all the worlds riches at your feet, if you knew how to never, ever be alone or afraid, or experience pain, would you let experiences that created them happen?"

"No," I said, "of course not. They are not good experiences and if I had the where-with-all to avoid them, I would. I obviously am not happy with fear," I smirked. "I surely can do without pain. Thank you very much. I kind of like being alone. People confuse me and are usually the catalyst for the unexpected. So, I would probably at some point in my life become more of a hermit, like gramps, to avoid the inevitable. Work on the mysteries of the universe... maybe?"

"What about loved ones," Alton asked, "or even for a passerby like the man earlier today?"

"No, of course not. I do not think I could let bad things happen to anyone... if I could stop them."

"Exactly," said Alton, "but you learned today how your good intentions, could have interrupted and negatively impacted the man in the park. Sooo," Alton looked down at me to cement his point, "it would be futile to take on physical form and attempt to live with the realities of this world, if you knew you could just step out of the experience when it became too challenging."

"Or," I said in a drawn-out manner, "if instead I could step in and change my or another person's destiny?"

"Yes," Alton said, "and if you had absolute certainty of a greater universal consciousness, where all things are in balance. Where there is no pain, no fear and you are surrounded by love and belonging. How eager would you be to abandon that difficult physical existence and simply go home? No one would judge you the lesser. Your spiritual life is yours, God given as it were. There is no judgment, because there is no time frame, or scale for it. Only experiences and lessons that increase your awareness of the greater universe.

"You mean..." I began to ask?

"Exactly." Alton answered immediately. "Once you know where you can go..." I finished the statement, "I can go, where I want to go."

"Yup," he completed the thought.

"OK, I might be getting a little tired of that statement, but Wow... I do believe you have a valid point. Why sweat it out, when you can hang out at the beach all day?" I laughed as Alton smiled.

"My friend," Alton said very directly, "every spirit that takes on human physical form, must accept a barrier in between his true spiritual self and his incarnated self. Call it imposed amnesia, a blocking of universal knowledge and awareness."

"Every time? I asked.

"Yes," Alton answered, "whenever the spirit takes on form and becomes a soul." I looked at him questioningly when he mentioned the soul. He finished his sentence saying, "The soul being the spirit woven into a physical form."

"Wait... hold up... how does the universe brainwash a being of his creator, if every fiber of his being is made up of that creator?

Shouldn't we be able beat that?"

"Yes, and some do and others find a temporary form of universal unity and love through physical relationships. In fact, many physical relationships hold a great volume of that universal essence. The earthly form of universal love requires faith, hope and forgiveness, qualities in short supply at times. Anyway, it is hard to recreate perfection." Alton raised his eyebrows and winked.

"Well," I said, "there are many here who do not feel that subliminal universal need for a spiritual home and do not recognize an essential drive to seek out a greater intelligence, spiritual or otherwise. They seem hell bent on the take, rather than the give."

"True," Alton said, "but that is taking a snapshot of that person in time. During an incarnation and over years in a life, there are none whom do not begin to yearn for God, or hope for enlightenment. All beings come back to the source in whatever time they were meant to. They may have a different mindset before transformation, but once the veil is removed and understanding is complete, they are awake and glad to be so."

"Quite a shock for some of them I will bet," I joked. "Wake up, bud, smell the coffee. By the way, look at the crap you did while you were on walkabout." I laughed to myself as I imagined what I would have to review when I woke up from my visit to human existence. "Is that why they say you see your life pass in front of your eyes when you die? Is it because you are remembering what it is like to be universal and the nearest part of remembering, is the trip you were just on?"

Alton let out a huge laugh that scared the daylights out of two small dogs playing with a stick nearby. They ran over each other to get under the nearest bush.

"I had not looked at it that way." Alton leaned forward to breathe back in. "It makes perfect sense."

"Ok," I continued. "You keep talking about humanity... humanity... like we are different than you. Besides being a much larger version of us, I think you are not that different".

Alton responded. "In form, Michael, maybe, but in other ways we are as different as one species is to the next. As I stated before, we are not built to live a life as independently as mankind, but each of us in their own way, is an extension of universal will.

"Our race existed before mankind, when the universe was

younger, so we were created differently. As the universe expands, each new race is different from the next in some way. Yet, there are commonalities within expansion periods. Our race is from a prior period or epoch and we retain an intimate connection with the universe. We are gifted with certain abilities that transcend physical form. We have been called angels by some races, but we are not. That race existed well before us in an earlier epoch. In all races, even the earlier ones, there have been those that have rebelled and sought to control, dominate, destroy, rather than build. Even the race you call angels, went through their rebellious period and battled for dominance over younger races. They were driven by common principles evident here on your world. Our race went through very dark times. It was mainly due to separation and isolation on worlds not interwoven with the same universal thread needed to keep us balanced and healthy. Like a wilting flower, diseases of the mind and soul affected our race. Jealousy, possession, incompatible reproduction and dominance, inspired destructive endeavors.

"Giants were supposed to help refine humanity and lead them to enlightenment, which we have done over ages on earth. We were learning to be good stewards and some learning curves, are much steeper than others. For a time, we failed horribly, but that was before the cleansing."

"Cleansing, what was the cleansing?"

"In universal terms, it was too late to fix what had gone wrong. There was unthinkable behavior, perpetrated by anomalies generated from corrupt breeding. Foul and depraved actions and intent. Sickness of body, mind and spirit plagued mankind. So, a power greater than ours, cleansed the earth for a new start. It removed us as a dominant species from this planet. You know it from your biblical history as the great flood. Since that time, although giants still survived here, our race was no longer dominant and we, nor any other of the races, were allowed to directly interfere in your world, accept when extreme measures are required."

"Holy cow, so are there any of those races still here, on earth?"

"That is a disturbing possibility," Alton said moving on swiftly. "Genetic makeup can coalesce in such a way as generations evolve, as to accentuate or magnify uncommon talents and abilities. In many instances, people endowed as such, are special and can create positive change. In other situations, the potential is misused or abused and humanity or any race, can experience... unfortunate consequences."

A gust of wind, fresh and cool after passing over the surface of the lake, woke us both out of our inner contemplation.

Alton's next words held a warning. "Those that are different, special, exist on other worlds as well as this and some are driven by very dangerous needs! We will need to discuss this at length, but later. For now let us enjoy the remainder of the day."

"Wait, you said something earlier that I wanted to ask about, you said involvement by higher powers happened when there was a need for 'Extreme Measures'. What does that exactly mean? That sounds thoroughly ominous. What constitutes the need for 'Extreme Measures'?"

"Not now, Michael, let's talk a little more about how closely we are connected. We are the building blocks of your race. The entire universe is structured by building upon what already exists, using it as a platform for that which is to come. We are a creation that is closer to the beginning of all things. Part of our genetics and our destiny is the beginning of yours. Therefore, we are builders and designers, to some extent, of your world. As a builder, we know the foundation, the structure, the bones of your world. If you know how something works... he started..."

"You can always fix it," I finished.

"True, but no longer. Remember, we are not allowed to interfere. I mention this, because your nature, Michael, is as a designer, a builder, you have a God given talent for the building blocks of things and how to use them."

"Well," I interjected, "maybe I did before you renovated my psyche, but I have no idea what I am capable of now. Everything has changed."

Alton laughed and said, "The more things change, the more they stay the same. The universe is not overly complex. It is governed by the same laws that rule here, just on a much larger scale. It is magnificently intricate, but simple in its process."

At this point, I felt like I was drowning in concepts. The more I struggled to pay attention, the deeper I sank. I was awash in questions and they kept popping up like a game of "whack a mole". I was suddenly very tired.

"Whew," I said as I leaned forward and ran my fingers through my hair. When I looked up, I could see by the curve of Alton's brow that he was aware I was flailing in the deep side of the pool and without swimmies to keep me afloat. I could also tell he wanted to finish his thoughts, so I sat back on the bench.

Alton took a long look at me, then said, "How about let's work our way back to your apartment."

"I agree," I said without delay. "I feel overwhelmed." I stood up and thought about being alone back at my apartment and shared my thought.

"I am kind of anxious to be back at my place, alone. I am not confident living with an expanded consciousness. I couldn't create something … I don't know… maybe otherworldly... right? I mean what else could happen? What if one of those vortexes happen and my apartment and the block I live on, end up materializing next to your village? Boy would that be a surprise!" Even though it was meant to be a joke, my concern was sincere.

"You will be fine", Alton said. "You are just at the beginning of your journey. There is much to be done before you have the potential to do yourself or others harm. Anyway, I think you will be sleeping soundly tonight."

"If I start walking first you will never catch up," Alton said with a smile and a wink, then he ushered the way with a sweep of his arm. We walked in silence for a short while. As we passed a grouping of park benches that were arranged around a convergence of paths, we encountered an older couple sitting near a tall slender oak. They sat peacefully, hands placed one over the other, arms entwined. They seemed to be enjoying all that surrounded them. The woman stared up at the clouds with a wistful expression that flowed across a content face. Just as those clouds she stared at, flowed across a perfect blue sky. The man was watching his partner with a sense of wonder, his eyes open to absorb the total of their moments together. As I watched them, I felt Alton's mind touch mine, his words were soft. "Look closely at the man. Tell me what is different, between him and the woman."

It was then that I noticed the strain in the man's eyes, as if he were trying to capture the last rays of sunlight by staring directly into them. Even though the intense gaze hurt, it was worth the pain to catch the last light of something so valuable to him. Rather than enjoying the moment as she was, he was desperate to not lose a second with her. His forehead was strained, as if to keep thoughts from flowing out of control. He was sad and struggling to hide the emotion from his partner. I felt agreement from Alton and at the same time, I felt him move away from my side. My focus shifted from my inner thoughts and vision, to the outer world. Alton had moved toward the couple. In two steps, he was standing directly in front of them. His frame dwarfed the bench and the two sitting upon it. At first, I was afraid for the couple, thinking that Alton would scare the daylights out of them. Then, I felt worried for Alton, that his feelings might be hurt by the couple's gut reaction to him. A feeling of peace came over me as I remembered who he was. I was reminded by her response, how infectious his smile was, how caring those gigantic orbs were and most of all, how tranquility radiated from him. He knelt by the woman and joined her gaze. No words were spoken. She simply looked back at him as if she was staring into the eyes of a child. I could tell when his consciousness harmonized with hers, because there was a glow, a light that sprung from her eyes and merged into Alton's gaze. She leaned attentively forward, but remained relaxed, as if to welcome an old friend. My attention switched to her partner. He looked at Alton, as a child would become engrossed in a puppet show, his mouth began to fall open, his jaw relaxed, as if mesmerized. Alton reached out and wrapped his huge hand around the frail, tiny, hand of the woman. I could feel the woman begin to understand what he was doing, as they paired for a dance of soulful expression. A gentle, clear flow of energy continued to develop between them. It did not originate from Alton, but he was the… outlet, so to speak. I heard Alton's voice in my mind again, all but a whisper… "Life is filled with moments that belong with each other, pieces of a puzzle that complete a picture." I began to see the woman's concerns and sense that something unexplainable was wrong in her. I was coupled with Alton's psyche and therefore to some extent, I could perceive their interaction. The stream between them was tangible now and growing into a river, similar to my first moment with Alton on the beach, yet uniquely different at the same time. The current was stronger, strong enough to carry the woman's consciousness along its path. The river of consciousness rushed faster and faster, picking up speed and volume. She was not afraid, she was ecstatic, thrilled as her spirit added life to the flow and rode with it like a roller coaster around bends at break neck speeds. Climbing to a point of perfect balance, boundaries fell away and she knew instinctively to just let go. I felt her giggle in delight, as she was carried by a cascade of life which flowed into a universal sea... a sea of understanding, harmony and enlightenment. A euphoric smile formed on her face and her head drifted slightly back. The feelings emanating from her were peace, comfort, joy and a release from pain. Barriers of perception were peeling back. Her being, as it grew in understanding, was growing ever brighter. She was letting go of physical world perceptions and seeing as a part of something much greater. I could also feel her letting go of the fear of being alone... lost. It was clear she worried greatly for her husband. He suffered from an overwhelming sense of loss, a dam holding back emotion, far beyond bursting.

She welcomed the limitless consciousness, infinite ocean of life, the universal family that embraced her now. As a drop of water returns to the sea, she had returned to her origin. Her chest heaved in a wonder filled sob. Tears of joy and awe flowed down her soft cheek, to pool in the creases of her husband's hand. In a way, his unconditional love for her resembled that very same vast, never-ending ocean that cradled her now. In some unexplainable way, I knew she had been set free. Her head rose. Her eyes were so bright that the blue in them, was almost lost in the light of her spirit. A portion of the wrongness was also now diminished, not exactly physically, but everything about her glistened. Alton lifted his bowed head and I watched the woman convey the remaining fear over her husband. In response, Alton reached out with his hand to touch the hand of the man, as it rested on his wife's shoulder, trembling. As Alton's fingers wound around the man's hand, I heard him take a deep breath, a sudden inhalation. I stretched my awareness to touch his. I could see that Alton had joined the couple in the experience. He had opened a doorway and enabled the man's soul to join his wife's and... flow, play or dance, it was hard to define. The man now fathomed what his wife was experiencing. He had joined his partner in this liberation, sharing and so much more. In that moment of mutual understanding, he could see her soul was beyond harm, her spirit was connected to the unlimited, never alone, never separate. He could see their love as a tangible force that bonded them, not only in this life, but in all life. His expression was magnificent. It was happiness and excitement, relief and joy, hope and fulfillment. A renewed strength radiated out from him, for what better place for his beloved to be, but cradled in the hands of love itself. Alton pulled both sets of their hands together in one bundle and let go, for both the husband and his wife were joined, free from fear by the knowledge of what lay ahead for them. The husband looked at his wife and leaned his head forward to touch her cheek. It then slid down into the nape of her neck. He was sobbing gently, but not out of sadness, although it was part of his feelings. Mostly he was crying, as a father might cry for a child who had been lost in an accident, only to find the child alive and well in the wreckage. The burden of loss removed. "Wreckage that life brings into every existence, I thought", remembering earlier in the day.

As Alton began to rise, he responded to my thought… "and only answered by faith, my friend."

The woman reached out for his hand and with a look that could fill volumes if put into words, squeezed. She then let go of Alton's hand to caress her husband's head, stroking lightly his hair and kissing his forehead. As she moved her body a little more closely to his, her hair caught on the park bench and slipped ever so silently off a perfectly smooth, bald head.

CHAPTER 26

Alton and I followed the paths and sidewalks back towards my apartment. It wasn't until I recognized where the sun was in relation to the buildings I was familiar with that I realized it was late afternoon. We had walked for what seemed a relatively short time, but it had been hours. So much had transpired since the morning and the walk back was cathartic for us both. We had not shared words since we left the couple on the bench. Although I had not seen all that had happened between Alton and the older couple, I comprehended much. The reconnection of the woman with what I could only presume was the universal oneness, heaven. Sharing in her husband's joy, where he found that his most precious possession was going to be loved and protected in a way that told him his prayers had been answered. To be gifted with an experience which allowed me to view universal consciousness, love and to share emotionally and be intimately connected? After that, I just did not have the energy necessary to push words past my lips. As we turned the corner onto a block in my neighborhood, I heard Alton speak through our minds.

"You had a very full day, Michael."

Even through our mental telepathy, I could only say, "Yeah..." with an accompanying cerebral sigh. When finally I could generate words from my thoughts, I did not. I wanted to savor the parts of the day that deserved to remain memorable, not limited by explanations, descriptions or words. I had not assimilated any lessons or the implications of what I had experienced; I did not know if I ever would. I knew, however, that initiating conversation at that point would somehow return us from the magic of much deeper reflection, to the mundane. Part of me intensely wanted to ask Alton, why he chose to involve himself with the older couple, but I knew if I asked, it would mean that I failed to see the reason, the greater purpose. Which in fact, I do not think I could have possibly grasped.

I could tell as seasoned as Alton was, he had been deeply impacted by what had transpired. Alton looked down at me, and then back at the fairly empty streets nearing my apartment. I still was not used to the open lanes of communication and the immediate contact shared through our psyches.

As if perceiving that frailty, Alton, spoke out loud. "Thank you."

"Your welcome," I said, "but thank you for what?"

"Thank you for allowing me to linger in those moments," he said.

"Yes…Yes… I understand," I responded. I felt the same way. I did not want our experience to end. I did not want the connection to end.

Alton spoke slowly as he looked off in the distance. "You do not realize how independent humanity is, Michael. You… your people, remain so apart, so disconnected from the source of all things. It frightens me to think of being that separate. Our species and others before us, could not survive that way. We would perish without our constant bond with the universal consciousness. To share in the joy of a homecoming, as with the couple back there. To participate with another soul, as affirmation of a union with all things and a belonging to a consciousness of unlimited love, is realized … it is … well, an affirmation for me as well.

"Remember when I drew the analogy about being in concert with the flow of the 'One'?" Alton asked. "You, mankind, hear that music. You cannot see the musicians, or the instruments, but the music plays. We giants, as we have been called, are part of the music, the notes. We are an extension of the music. We participate in the melody, we flow with the rhythm, but we can never step outside the music and experience it like you. We can never play the instrument, because we are the instrument. Do you understand? The basic fact is that mankind is a new breed, separate, and therefore, uniquely strong for it. Humanity can and will experience the universe in ways beings like ourselves cannot. If the music were to cease to flow, we would cease to exist. God, the universe is to us, like the air you breathe, is to you. Without air you would suffocate and then die."

I wanted very badly to participate with Alton in this conversation, but I could not, I could only listen.

"The angels I spoke of before, were created much earlier in the evolution of the universe than us. They are even more closely connected to the 'One' God than us. They also would perish without the rhythm, the universal pulse, energizing and sustaining their life. They are like embryos in the womb. They are connected so intimately to the heart beat of the universe, that they are almost one with it."

His last comment sparked a response in me. "So, angels exist here and now, as real beings?"

"Yes, they are messengers of change and purpose, universal directors," Alton said. "They can only be away from their natural environment on a temporary basis."

"If there are angels, are there demons?" I asked.

"Not so much as you understand or define that type of being."

I looked at him like he had not given me the whole truth.

He looked back at me and said, "This is a very complex conversation that could take many hours to discuss correctly, so let's just say that the universe is a balance of positive and negative energy. There are powers that work to build and powers that work to destroy, Powers that preserve and powers that demolish. One cannot exist without the other. The universe cannot exist without balance. Examples are everywhere. The pattern is the same, no matter where you are.

"There is no focused universal effort to create alone and none to destroy alone. There is effort to destroy what has existed beyond its purpose, so that something new can be built in its place, from its ashes. For those who have built meaning and purpose around such a structure, the destruction of it would be catastrophic... right? Sometimes labeling good and evil can be as simple as a matter of perspective."

"I get that," I said, "but there is evil. In people, purpose and in action, I have seen it!"

"True," said Alton, "but what is born out of an evil act, is not necessarily evil. If viewed against the backdrop of a single life, or a multitude of lives, or lifetimes, the act can have a positive purpose and effect."

I let out a cynical grunt. "A viewpoint like that would take a lot of work. I, unfortunately, am an eye for an eye guy."

"When you have the right perspective, the work is not in the point of view, it is in how best to mold what is created by evil, into something of greatest value."

"Okay... so... angels.... does that mean no demons, or really bad JUJU?" I questioned again with a little disbelief.

"No," Alton answered firmly. "It just means from the right perspective, there is no concerted effort to destroy solely for destruction sake. No agenda against any world, race or species, only variations that exist in a universe in transition. Where you are when change happens, defines how you experience it."

"What you say makes sense, but as I said before, in this world, what I have experienced proves otherwise."

"Exactly," Alton said. "It is your perception, from your place of experience, in your time and space."

"Wow... I have to think about that one," I said as we came to a familiar cross street. We turned the corner of the block my apartment was on, just as the sun turned the corner on the day and angled down the avenue in search of tomorrow. I was relieved to be home, yet sad that such a significant day was coming to a close. I looked at Alton, a being that must have lived an untold number of these types of days. In his return gaze, I found comfort and brotherhood.

"What next?" I said with a false sense of... I can handle anything ... now.

Alton let out a sigh as he looked up into the darkening sky. "I think a little sleep, maybeee... another one of those fantastic breakfasts," he said with a wink and shrugged, "who knows." He then smiled that wondrous smile of his, which sparked intrigue and nurtured curiosity.

"Oh brother," I said, with feigned unease. "I can't wait to see what comes next."

Alton smiled again, put his arms around me and gave me a huge hug. "Whatever it is, we will meet it together." He slapped his hand down on my shoulder as he turned to leave. For a second, anxiety over being alone with what I had learned, surged through my bones. I began to reach out to stop Alton from departing. He was already looking back with that incorrigible smile. A little embarrassed, I looked down at the steps to my apartment, turned and began my ascent.

CHAPTER 27

Alton walked directly to the corner and headed down the next street. His strides were solid, purposeful. Once around the bend in the block, he moved quickly into an alcove. There he stood absolutely still, his head slightly raised, his eyes closed and his senses roaming, like one of the wolves upon his home world. Alton searched for anything that might expose, even in some slight way, the threat he intuited.

He remembered the way the stone had responded when Michael was on his world. He remembered the quality of it, the strength of the footprint left, when he handed it over to Kayla, Stella and Thor. It was the same one that he sensed now. Near, very near, but any being with nefarious intentions from another world would have been savvy enough to cloak their presence. A hint of an ambush accompanied another impression, but the ambush was not for now, it was a plan for future action. The energy disappeared, as Alton had pushed the search to hard exposing himself, but not before he gleaned that the agent of dark deeds, was determined not to be compromised.

With the scent of his prey no longer traceable, Alton turned and moved quickly down a small set of steps. Descending from the alcove into a vacant basement storefront, he also vanished in a whirl of dust and long discarded papers.

CHAPTER 28

Paps sat on the landing outside his building, a sense of anxiety rising in him. He dug his hand deep into the fur along Lucas's flank and shook it, then patted the muscular thigh. Luka, laying with head slightly lowered nuzzled Pap's hand, then went back to his patient vigil. Paps knew that Lea and Luka were anxious since Kayla, Stella and Thor had left the village. On top of that, he could tell that the normal level of telepathic communication they shared, was interrupted or impeded. That was something to be concerned about. Paps picked up the stone and began to ponder the strange and unexpected changes in its frequencies since Michael had left.

He noticed the stone begin to resonate, just as Luka shifted from his position. He stood up and watched Alton approach.

"He was there, Hugo," said Alton as he rubbed the top of Lukas's head. "I could tell he was very near, still just watching for now. He was not alone. He was cloaked, or surrounded by a human form, but it was no one I could identify. If I am not mistaken, I got the impression of the place where Michael works. I cannot be sure. Whoever this being is, he is very powerful and skilled at using the power he commands."

"What of the power that he does not control," asked Paps, "like the stone? What does he know of that?"

"Again, I cannot be sure, Hugo, but I am sure there is a valid threat here."

Paps held out the stone. "I have been watching it. It indicates Michael has made contact with the dark matter side. Did he come back changed?"

"I know your true question, Hugo. The answer is yes; you would have been very proud of him. He was strong even when he was lost.

He shut down for a time and his consciousness began to disperse, but the stubborn streak you endowed in him, pulled him through."

Lea had followed Alton and stood in front of Paps now. Paps sighed in relief, grabbed Lea and hugged her. As proud and dominant as she was, she melted in Paps arms.

"There was something else, Hugo," Alton said with a serious tone." Michael was not alone in the void. It was not the person that we have been concerned over either, they would not be able to enter or remain there. I could not identify the presence I felt there either, it was barely familiar and my memory of the being is very foggy, which meant I was not supposed to share knowledge with it. I can tell you, it was the presence of a being of old."

"Of old...?"

"Yes, an original. Nothing else could live in that dimension. Only builders, or ...?"

"Or ... what, Alton?"

"I have only met them a few times in my life., maybe a Seraphim... maybe?"

"A Sera... of what, life... death?" Paps grabbed Alton's wrist.

"It was not my journey and I was not allowed the essence of it, but I felt better that the being was there, observing. It would not be there if it were not intended by the 'One'."

"Did the being contact Michael?"

"No, there was no contact and Michael had no clue that he was not alone. Through him, I was able to watch much of his awakening in the void. It was his sense of humor, logic and resilience that carried the day."

"So, does this mean he has transitioned completely?" asked Paps.

"No Hugo, he has not. I am new at guiding one who can go where I cannot. I am unable to truly provide for him, but I am doing my best."

"He came out, he survived the change, why is the transition not complete?" asked Paps.

"I do not know that either, Hugo. He seemed to be in a battle with himself. He did not have faith that what he was experiencing was real. Can you expect less out of him, having you as his mentor? He is a scientist through and through."

"I understand that," said Paps with a smirk.

Alton sighed deeply and placed his hand on Paps shoulder. "In the long run, he will realize his talents. That may require a battle for his own survival, one that will be fought beyond the trenches of his mind and even beyond the limits of his soul. Until such time, he is vulnerable. It is clear now though, that he is destined to be a creationist, a builder, which means he is a child of the Void, the dark matter side. Yet, he is a human, which means he is a discoverer, explorer and founded in the material substance of our cosmos. This is a very incompatible mixture."

"That is true," said Paps, "and right now he has dominion over neither."

"And that makes him a danger to himself and others," finished Alton. There was silence for a moment then Alton changed the subject.

"Lea is very worried over Kayla, Stella and Thor. We must find out why they have not returned, nor been heard from since they left. This is very odd. I have never known this to happen."

"The stone," Paps said. "Look at the stone. See, it is not vibrating as it normally does. I put it on the resonator this morning; it is as if it is being diminished or shut down bit by bit. This new resonator I built, is far more refined than the one those pin heads stole from me on earth. It can isolate signals, classify and separate individual qualities and locate points of return. I began to study the anomalies we observed when Michael was present. There was a definite intrusion or probing that looped through the stone to enhance information sent out there." Paps pointed to the heavens, "At some point, the intruder knew we became aware of him and terminated the connection. I am not sure, but it is possible that whoever was on the receiving side of the information is cutting off communications, one frequency at a time. Who could do that, Alton? What could do that?"

"There are many beings that possess power beyond what we may control, but they are far older races, with even stronger connections to the 'One'. They would have no interest in the stone. If there were a negative or destructive force at play, originating from an older being or being of higher vibration, then I am not aware of it."

"What should we do? How should we respond?" asked Paps as he walked inside to his bench and lay the stone down.

Just then Lea leapt up and took a few steps towards a building called the sanctuary. Luka assumed a defensive posture, to cover her flank. Lea whined, growled, then lowered herself to the ground and turned her head to the side. She looked at Luka and he came and stood beside her. Together they leaned forward and lowered their heads, making their spines rigid. They aimed the crown of their heads in the direction of the sanctuary and a portal began to form. The formation fluctuated and then began to dissipate. Luka leaned more forward to match Lea and the portal reformed. Like whirling sand in a desert, it continued to fluctuate and move uncontrollably. For a split second, Alton could feel Kayla and the wolves within the portal, they seemed physically OK, but were distressed. There was urgency and danger, then the portal collapsed as if it had been slammed shut.

Lea howled, while Luka ran around smelling the ground growling.

Alton walked over to Lea, bent over slightly and stared into her eyes. He stood up straight and rigid for a second then turned to Paps.

"Get your things, Hugo. We will be leaving as soon as you are ready." Lea came and stood by Alton's side; Luka remained prepared for whatever was to come next.

"You and Luka must stay here, Lea. Paps and I have a trip to take and we need to make sure the village is guarded. Especially Lauren, you know she is going to be upset, when she gets wind of what just happened."

Lea looked surprised and took a few steps back.

"Yes, I know that paths are being destroyed," Alton responded to her questioning gaze. Lea turned her head to the side.

"Yes, I know that the village and the planet could be cut off and I know that Kayla sent warning of more danger to come," Alton said. "I am sure I can get to them and together we can get to the bottom of this, but we cannot afford to leave the village without your and Luka's help here. The villagers can normally protect themselves, but what we have seen here today tells us that things are not normal. They may need help that you and Luka can provide."

Lea took a few more steps back and then sat down. Luka came up and rubbed his head under her neck. Then he walked under Alton's hand and rubbed up against his leg.

"Thank you, my sentinel," Alton said to Luka. "If something unfortunate should befall the village, take Lauren into the sanctuary, along with any other young people that might be in danger."

Lea whimpered. Alton smiled and said, "Luka, you know your sister when she is mad. If a stranger does present himself, someone has to protect him from her wrath." Lea looked at Alton and twisted her head to the side, then snorted as if sneezing out something irritating.

CHAPTER 29

Once in my apartment, I tried to relax and let the experiences of the past weeks settle into place, but there was something at the base of it all that bothered me. I grabbed a cold beer and sat in one of my favorite spots. As I sat there by the window, watching the world slow down from the day, I realized what was bothering me. Our world is as we see it. There are so many other parts of it that we cannot assimilate. Those other parts are either things we have no interest in and therefore, do not pay attention to, or they are vague and hard to relate to. Anyway, why if the Giants had been part of our history and actually been instrumental in the development of many cultures, had I or others not heard more about them? Why were they not a common theme in our schooling and education? Why were they a secret? We are all familiar with David and Goliath. We are all intrigued by the 8-foot teenager from China that has being studied for some rare genetics that causes massive growth at early ages, but what about the history of a different species? Where they came from? Where they lived on our world?

So, I grabbed my laptop and started to look for information that documented and illustrated proof of a race of Giants on earth. The computer screen filled rapidly with information. Some was scientifically verified and authenticated from institutions like the Smithsonian, whose scientists and investigators brought back both physical and historical proof of their existence. There were stories relayed by local Indian tribes and other cultures around the world, confirming the presence of cities and societies of giants. Those tribes knew where to find remains and examples. I was amazed, the

Smithsonian? How could so much information be ignored? I guess maybe because we do not find Giants in numbers anywhere in the world at present, the fact they no longer existed, turned them more into mythology. Maybe it was like many dinosaur species that did not hold the significance of Tyrannosaurus Rex and therefore, the average person is not aware they even existed. Still, the scientific community should have been all over this. The specimens recovered dated back from Neolithic man, to the Bible, to the South and North American Indian tribes that traded and lived near Giants, all the way up to about 1000 B.C. Scientific review of skeletal remains confirmed that the Giant race was not of human origin, possessing an extra skull plate. Giants were obviously another race, not human and therefore possibly not from earth at all.

The information was incredibly compelling, whether substantiated or theoretical. Many cultures on earth had an accounting of the race of giants. Some of them described abilities that mankind did not possess. Further research turned up eyewitness accounts from many of the most respected early explorers, including those coming to the New World: Magellan, Vespucci, Coronado, De Soto, and Sir Francis Drake to name a few. The 12th Annual Report from the Bureau of Ethnology to the Secretary of the Smithsonian published in 1894 and written by Powell and Thomas, who were agents for that bureau, contains several verifiable accounts of large, 7-9 feet tall humanistic skeletal remains found in the US. How were these facts withheld from history books?

Driven by the feeling of being intentionally deceived by those responsible for correctly chronicling history, I became angry. I pushed the computer away. "This is going to be counterproductive," I said out loud. My anger being stoked as if hot coals, by energy I imagined seeped in from the void. It is human nature to look right past a paradox as though it never existed, but to purposely remove proof of a paradox for some ulterior motive, smacked of deceit. My hand felt hot all of the sudden and I noticed that I was holding the now empty beer bottle in my right hand with a rigid grip. Steam was billowing out of the mouth of the bottle and the neck where I was holding it, was elongated and stretched as if it had become taffy long enough for gravity to distort it. I threw the bottle in the trash like it was about to bite me.

"That's it," I said. "Bed time for Bonzo," as I walked into my bedroom. I collapsed on my bed like a pillar of stone. I do not remember falling asleep, but I do remember worrying a little over being utterly crazy.

CHAPTER 30

From deep within a very restful sleep, the sound of a phone ringing badgered me awake. As my conscious mind began to pour into my physical body like cold molasses, rather than fresh steaming hot coffee, I caught the sound of a familiar voice leaving a message.

"Mike... Mike... you there? Mike ... this is Bill. This is Bill your boss...? Remember, your boss... where you work, or at least... used to?" There was a pause, then in keeping with Bill's natural default to humor, "Mike, help me out here. If you're dead, make the phone click twice before the fires of hell start to blister your ass. If you're not dead, you better be on your way into work, cause... if you're not on your way, your gunna wish you were dead when you finally get here." The phone hung up with noted impact. I began to move slowly, stretching a little here and a lot there, although the effort did not last long. I was drifting back into wondrous comfort when ringing interrupted my free fall. Again, the answering machine picked up. "Mike... Mike... geez!" Hearing Bill's frustration, I reached out to pick up the receiver. Dropping it twice while trying to maneuver an unresponsive body, I finally perched the phone between my shoulder and the pillow my face was buried in.

"Yeah... uh...uh," I grunted, clearing my throat. "Yeah, I am here."

"Mike, what is going on... and where the hell... is here?" Bill blurted out.

My mouth, not yet coordinated with my mind, I offered the best response I could. "Sleepy... but no uppy... no uppy."

"What...what the hell is... no ... uppy?" Bill probed incredulously. "Where the hell are you and whatever you have been drinking, bring it to work for the next Christmas party."

"Uhmm… bed…. Yea… I am in my bed," I said, my awareness warming up. I instinctively knew I had said the wrong thing and the bed was the wrong place to be, but it was too late to retract it now.

"What are you doing in bed? That is obviously not your job, I can guarantee that! Are ya coming back to work? Do you know that you have used up every free day you have?" Dead silence accompanied the low humming coming from the phone lines. For some uncanny reason, it sounded so… peaceful.

As a boss, Bill knew he had spent way to long coaxing me out of bed and into work. As a friend, I could hear on the other end of the line, that he was worried.

"All right … look … there are a bunch of people here that are wondering when you are coming back, because they need your help. Conversely, there are an equal number of people here, who are wondering how long their good fortune will last and how long you are going to stay away, so they can actually finish their work? Me… I am siding with the latter … so would you mind telling me … when you are coming in to take care of your responsibilities?"

"Uhmm." I struggled to think more quickly and respond with some acceptable answer.

"Mike," Bill said, void of patience. "Get up… and get… in …to… work!"

"Ok, boss," I said, getting the message clearly. "Uhmm, by the way… what day is it?" I asked. Appreciating way too late the idiocy of that request, I cringed in preparation for Bill's response.

With a gasp of total frustration Bill answered. "What day? What … daaayy? It is ass whoopin day if you do not get your butt in here … pronto… Rip… Van… Winkle!" Those were the last words I heard as the receiver resounded from a sharp and definite thud.

CHAPTER 31

Bill and I had been close friends and co-workers for many years. I first met him at a symposium on the composition of simple matter and the relation it played in regulating form and function. As fate would have it, we were assigned the same chair, at the same table. Bill's first comment to me as we both reached for the chair was, "Hey ... Mike... right... your Mike from the Daystar institute?"

I said, "Uhmm... yes." Not familiar with Bill yet and wondering what I had screwed up bad enough, that someone I didn't know at all, would know me. I repeated, 'Yes," in a guarded manner. Scientific types tend to be more introverted, spending most of their time exploring their own minds and the thoughts and inspirations that originate from them. Bill conversely, was gregarious and outgoing. He was a real live wire, possessing bold mannerisms and at that moment he wore a huge 'cat ate the mouse' smile, which made me nervous.

Aware of my cautious responses, he shook my hand and said, "This is... hum... the seminar on simple matter... right?"

I just shook my head up and down.

"Well, then by all means, this chair has to be yours."

His jibe caught me so of guard, I burst out in laughter. I was so loud the whole room stopped to look. We crumbled into adjacent chairs. Thankfully, there was plenty of room, as this seminar's concepts were considered outside the mainstream of accepted science and well-known scientific types might have been embarrassed to be seen in attendance. Anyway, I remember being amazed at how Bill assimilated the concepts and possibilities conveyed. He was very intelligent and had a vast, clean thinking open mind. We sat together, pondered, argued and combed through many, many concepts the rest of that day and the next. As we became more familiar, I came to sincerely appreciate his passion for life, his competitive spirit and his endless sense of humor. Open moments, where we could slide in a jibe, or crack the other up, made even the dullest lectures a blast. By the end of the symposium, I am sure we were the most unwelcome attendees present.

Bill became a true friend. His trust was very important to me and as the years moved on, we became as close as brothers. We worked loosely on several evolving technologies and made every attempt to include each other in personal projects. Then one day, Bill called me. He told me he was heading up a group studying the building and testing of thermal imaging equipment, to be used by NASA. Bill's group was going to be the nucleus for a cluster of well-known universities and private enterprises around the world, funded for similar purposes. The project was set up in pods, each to their own specialty. Their main research encompassed tracking, capturing and documenting changes on specific metals, caused by combustion, or excesive compression in alternative atmospheres. Some of the research was geared toward studying the effect of fast-moving particles, impacting a structure that was also moving many miles per second. My first thought was of a vehicle of some sort, exposed to space debris. So, I jumped at the opportunity, as it also offered a chance to learn more about emerging energy and propulsion technology. Both Bill and I soon recognized the highly segmented and separate nature of the research. Someone… did not want any of the parts, to be aware of the whole.

As I walked down the unnervingly long halls at the research center, I felt like I had been gone for years. To confirm my feelings, some of my coworkers gaped wide-mouthed as I passed. Some shrunk away slightly as I passed them, like they were watching a dinosaur that had risen from some discarded petri dish, in a dark forgotten lab in the bowels of the facility. My smiles and open gestures did nothing, to resolve their unease. Others came by and offered high 5's, as if I had overcome some devastating personal challenge. Maybe an experience great office gossip is birthed from? Turning down the hall to the wing I worked in, I could hear Bill's voice resonating off the walls.

As I slid my security card past the reader and entered our section, I could hear Bill's voice again, echo from the second office ahead.

"Alex, where are the results from the testing we completed Thursday?" I could not hear her response clearly, but I could tell by the sound of Bill's voice he did not like the answer. "Come on... tell those guys down in ops to wake up and smell the coffee. We all work together here. He sounded fairly bearish this morning. Did I mention Bill ran his facilities like a drill sergeant? Well, pretty close anyway. As I passed Alex's office, I saw her at her computer.

Alex had been introduced to Bill years earlier as a security specialist, first class. She managed a technology contingent overseeing a collaboration of military and civilian contractors. In actuality, Alex was part of a Special Forces initiative out of Langley, protecting evolving technology and preventing sensitive information from reaching undesirable hands. She was much more than she seemed at first glance. Bill, being no mental midget, recognized from the get go that there was much more to Alex and to her agenda. Always thinking in chess moves, he decided to leave the pretext alone, knowing he might be able to use it to his advantage in the future. He did however, recognize how quick, perceptive, trustworthy and loyal, Alex was. She was a doer, a provider and just about a half step ahead of almost everyone else. Everyone else that is, except for him.

Bill, being no slouch in the sharp category, knew he needed an insider on the military side and they needed one on the civilian side. Their work was incredibly productive and after time passed, Bill asked those he was connected with, to place Alex on assignment with him permanently. So, Alex became a permanent fixture on Bill's team. Everyone got what they wanted. Confidence on both sides grew quickly and production continued at unparalleled levels. Almost all of Bill's projects were, 'Connected'. Funding came from many sources and often I would see memos marked with scribble, noting, DOD, INR and NSA. Over the long haul, Alex became indispensable and an essential part of every achievement. Beyond that, she was our mother hen and we all adopted her as our own. Like all families with very strong personalities, there was argumentation and struggles for autonomy, ours was absolutely no different.

Noting the tone of Bill's voice, and deducing the probable mood that would put Alex in, I decided to move quickly past her door while she was occupied.

Mid-step past her door, I heard her comment, "You are welcome to borrow my body armor if you want. I just had it cleaned. It might be a little small on you, but if you don't show him your full profile and," she hesitated, "if you're lucky, he might not hit any vitals." There was dead silence, as I placed my suspended foot down on the floor.

"Nawww ... forget it," she said, with a slight sigh. "You are dead man walking... regardless."

"Shit," is all I could squeak out. As I continued on to Bill's office I could hear her giggling.

Approaching Bill's door, the hall way was eerily silent. I peeked inside his office.

"Ohhh... sleeping beauty has finally graced us with his royal presence," were the first words out of his mouth. Muffled laughter came from behind the door. "You did not really have to come in to work you know, even though it is so thoughtful of you!" A sarcastic tone emphasized his intent, as he leaned back in his chair folding his hands across his chest. "We all just needed to know," he feigned a deep sigh, rocked forward in his chair and slammed his hand down on a pile of papers stacked haphazardly, "If it was OK to go on breathing while you were not among us!"

The first sign something was really up was Bill's desk. It was always as orderly as his mind. The mess before him meant change was imminent. The laughter escalated in the back side of his office and I could not help but crack a smile myself.

"Ok...Ok, I am here," I said, committing to step through the doorway keeping Alex's comments in the back of my mind. "What is so important, what is wrong?"

"Why nothing... now that you are here, everything is just perfect," Bill said." I am beginning to feel better already. How about you, Jim?" I followed his gaze to the corner of the room by the bookshelf. Jim smiled, then the smile turned to laughter.

Pushing a button on the phone, Bill yelled to Alex. "Alex, bring the packages that arrived this morning in and then hold all calls while I am in conference."

"Yes, Bill," Alex replied tersely, adding "and no more espresso in the morning for you." Bill smirked and another muffled laugh drifted from behind me.

I turned to look at James again, as he fumbled with the books in the bookcase. He looked sideways at me and then nodded toward

Bill, who was rummaging through the papers on his desk. There was something weird going on.

"OK Mike," Bill barked, startling me out of my thoughts. "How far have you gotten on documenting the capture rate of the imager? James tells me," as he looked over at him sliding a book back into place on the bookshelf, "that he has completed the last set of tests before Daniel updates the software platform."

"Uhm, that whole section was put to bed three weeks ago?" I said as a question. You know that, because we went over the final performance stats during the playoff game, remember?"

"Oh yeah, I do remember," Bill said. "I also remember you owe me $50 bucks on the spread."

"I thought you were gunna give me a shot at winning that money back," I said with an evil grin. Again, a pervading sense of some secondary intent lingered in the air.

"Based on how much time you have been 'A WALL'," Bill said as he leaned forward slightly. "I think I may have to reconsider."

Even though our conversation was taking on its normal sparring quality, there was notable tension in the room and I was feeling defensive.

"Ok... so what is really going on here, cuz something is up," I said with experience to back me up. Bill sighed and shook his head a little.

"Mike, you have missed a lot of work lately. You and your team have done amazing things, but they can only cover your butt for so long, then 'Upper Management' begins to take notice."

'Upper Management' was our code word for those who were looking over our shoulder and were definitely not to be trusted.

"You and I both know they are not spending pennies here," Bill grunted. "Also," and he shot a glance at James, "there have been complaints about you leaping past important tests and applying processes not yet cleared by interdepartmental review." I turned and looked at James; he just looked down. "What is more disconcerting," Bill picked up a pencil and began tapping it on the edge of his desk, "is that all the unqualified steps and processes you have taken, have proven to be exact, saving the project a butt load of money."

There was true unease in his mannerisms, as he continued. "When you make advances like that, then disappear, it raises a few eyebrows from other professionals. Not just the ones in research... if you get my drift? Our friends in security are getting very nervous. I have had more than a few of our Human "Intelligence" Resource boys asking some weird questions around here lately. Some, specifically concerning you and... well, friends. God knows, I do not need extra fingers toying with my sensitive anatomy," Bill continued, "so let's be a little more considerate with our lifestyle choices... please."

A sharp pang of anxiety caused the space inside my recently rearranged awareness to churn. Alton had to be their person of interest. It is not like he just blends into a crowd, I thought.

In order to defray the inferences over Alton, I countered with, "We are ahead of schedule by 9 months, efficiency is doubled." Picking up momentum, I slipped into a second gear of arguing to cut off any rebuttals. "We can only move so fast and so far, then ..." I threw my hands up in the air in an expression of frustration, "we must wait for the others to catch up. There is nothing more James, Matthew, Daniel and the rest of the team can do for now and you know how frustrated I get with protocol, when it stands in the way of real progress. The hell with that shi..."

"Yes, yes, I know," Bill cut me off. "That is precisely why I hate to be the bearer of this news."

"What news?" I asked as Alex came in, walked past me holding three packages out at a 90-degree angle, elbow supported in the notch in her hip. She spun like a model on a runway, looked me up and down, as if surprised to see I was still breathing and dropped the packages from an unnecessary height. They made a loud, slapping thud as they slammed down on Bill's cluttered desk.

"Why thank you for your swift response to my request," Bill said sarcastically, bending over to pick up a flurry of smaller case notes that had been swept free of the desk top by the crashing mailers.

She smiled, looked up at the ceiling as if to say, I am soooo far ahead of you guys. Then she walked out of the room slowly, pulling the door closed behind her, until the last inch and then she cracked the door shut with a hard, final tug.

"That also was unnecessary," said Bill, with a wink to James.

"What news?" I repeated, trying to get to the bottom of the mystery that enveloped our conversation.

Bill distributed the notes, then leaned back in his chair and refocused on me. "Mike, I have to release you from this facility, effective immediately." He spoke swiftly and firmly.

There it was... the air crackled with the echo of the shot fired. "Whaaat...? Why?" I coughed out in slow disbelief. I looked at James, then back at Bill.

"We have met all of our metrics and goals. James and the team have performed incredibly well. Daniel has generated the software and manuals without rewrite. I have submitted the project package with uncompromised precision and way ahead of schedule. What else can we do?" I spun and walked to and fro trying to get a hold of the explosion of emotion and anger that was compromising my thinking. Why would they punish us ... me... for overachieving? I could feel an awkward force intensifying from somewhere deep inside me. An odd yet familiar glow. Me, but not mine? It began to churn more intensely and I felt control start to slip. There was no barrier between me and the raw potential it held. Anything I felt, seemed to be translated directly into it.

"Well, that is the thing," Bill said. "They are not punishing you ... exactly." His evasiveness agitated me even more and years of scientific deduction told me, I had no shot at stopping what was developing within me. I could feel my neck burning and I began to sweat. Circumstances were not made any better by a stupid grin I saw spanning James's face.

"This is just bull shit," I said, beginning to pace, feeling my arms tingling. Bill's smirk turned into a full-blown smile and my hands began to burn. I looked at them both and yelled, "What is wrong with you guys? This is nothing to smile about."

What I really wanted to say was... I need to leave. I cannot stop what is happening, but who would have believed me? Fortunately, yelling acted a little like a pressure relief valve, so I continued. "What are we all supposed to do? Just walk away and twiddle our thumbs until whoever made this decision, balances out their meds?" James broke out in laughter, on that one.

"Why are you laughing at this, James?" I said with contempt. "We are a team, if one goes, so goes the lot. You are a far better researcher than me, that is a given, but this cannot be a good thing for you?" The rising energy and anger were reaching a fever pitch. From within, I could feel some sort of shift. A power of a vastly different sort, something outside of my physical body, transitioned into a real, tangible force. It was rising like a volcano, forcing its way to the surface. My concern was no longer just for me, or just the topic of conversation! As I turned toward Bill and the desk, I reached up and ran my fingers through my hair. Snapping noises validated an accumulation of static electricity. I pulled my right hand down from my forehead, afraid of what might follow. I turned toward the door, rising anxiety initiating a panicked need to get away. As I turned back towards Bill, my right hand swept across the edge of his desk. Papers rose in a rough funnel shape and followed my arm out over the floor.

"True," said Bill, as he watched in curiosity as the papers traveled an impressive distance from his desk and gently floated to the floor in a well composed spiral. His simple response interrupted my thoughts and drew my perceptions back to the room and the conversation.

"That is why," he paused making me pay for each word, "we will all... be leaving this facility." I was stunned, everything froze. Bill waited another second and then said, "We also all... will be working in .... Geneva!"

I did not assimilate Bill's last remark for another second and then it slapped me across the face. "Geneva... you mean the particle accelerator?" I said slowly, as my speeding thoughts and feelings hit a perceptual brick wall. On the outside, I must have looked normal, but on the inside my whole being was shuddering like an 18-wheeler slamming on its brakes at 60 miles an hour. I looked for a seat to catch my trembling frame, as I felt the void swinging around in my mind like a massive trailer on that jackknifing vehicle, brakes screeching, wheels smoking.

I looked at Jim, "How... when... ugh... did you know this?" I attempted to sit, but he was already in stride toward me. Cat out of the bag, finally freed to express his excitement, he grabbed and shook my shoulders. "Yeah buddeee," he said as he kneeled next to the chair I had just collapsed in. "Atom smashing, is that cool, or what?" He pumped his fist in the air and then jumped up to punch a ceiling tile. I was speechless. James was laughing and leaping, while Bill was doing some kind of jig around his chair, singing, "I got him... I got him." He looked straight at me, "Ohhh maaannn! I really got you this time... ah ha ha," and he kept on dancing. They were both acting like school kids. I looked down at my sweaty hands. As the overwhelming force which had almost exploded, disappeared as strangely as it had appeared. I was relieved I had not broken into a million pieces on the floor.

The particle accelerator in Geneva was on the cutting edge of our scientific evolution. It was the closest mankind had come so far, to understanding the essentials of the universe, with a cherry on it. There had been mention of a new particle. The essence of all matter called the God Particle. Since the particle was only theory, I liked to think of it in terms that mirrored actual physical discoveries. So for me, the God Particle was in essence, a 'Stem Cell' for the universe. Where ever it was, there was the Universe. It was a blueprint of the makeup of all things. With one particle, you could build anything, maybe even...create new space, in time, wormholes. Stable bridges from one time, in space to another. So, where and even more importantly... when the particle was, at any given time, that was the universal matter it could shift to emulate. The God Particle was still a theory. Only because present technology could not reproduce, or separate it from other matter. If it was a key, a codex to all universal matter, it would truly be an unparalleled discovery once confirmed. Like all new ideas, speculation spun wildly around the potential for worst case scenarios. Ultimate destruction, generated from toying with the fabric of all things, violating universal law, etc. Concerns over the facility having the potential to separate the building blocks of everything and ending life as we know it, were increasing. Just as other scientists formed positive theories and propositions around what was still an unproven discovery. It was all very radical. For some scientists caught up in the fervor, normal parameters defining science and the empirical process, no longer applied. A new conceptual process was to some extent, redefining science itself. More theory, less substance. Still... evidence, the smoking gun, existed to support the quantum concepts that birthed the idea.

I got up and walked around Bill's desk as he headed around the chair for at least the 5th time. I stood in front of him, so that he would have to stop his celebration and look up from the floor.

"Wait... wait a minute," I said and grabbed both his arms. "Why would they want us? They already have imaging equipment in place."

"I know, isn't it craaazeee?" Bill said as he locked arms with me and proceeded to dance around me, bobbing his head from side to side. "Ha ... we showed them," he yelled, letting go to circle his own chair again.

"What ... who? What did we show?" I said, sitting Bill's dancing figure down in his chair. Bill looked over at James ... they both let out a huge laugh.

"What is so funny?" I said again trying to make sense out of the whole thing. "We are like peons to those guys, those scientists over there," I pointed frustratingly out into space. "Their disciplines are so specific, so ... I don't know ... I mean we are like college students, compared to Einsteins."

"I know ... I know," said Bill. "Isn't it insane?"

"How did they even find out about us?" I asked. James had trimmed his reveling back a little as Bill answered.

"Well, that is the $100,000-dollar question, isn't it?" Bill said taking a deep breath, relaxing slightly and shaking his head as if in disbelief. "Remember when you came in to my office and we argued about diverging from protocol and modifying the elapse time on the imaging sequencer?"

"Yes," I said, "I remember."

"Remember how we came to an agreement over discussing, documenting and implementing, all modifications prior to any trials? Especially tuning the sequence just ahead of the curve," Bill said. Yes?" I said

"Remember we agreed we needed to compare our theory, with the actual progressions?"

"Yes, yes," I said, starting to get frustrated

"Remember how you promised to follow our agreement?"

"Yessss... I remember," I said impatiently.

Bill suddenly serious, looked directly at me and said, "Did you?"

The room was deadly silent. I had an immediate need for that body armor Alex had offered earlier. I only had a second to flesh out an acceptable answer. The honest and obvious one was NO... Not exactly...? But I knew if I said that, I would have stepped into Bill's trap.

"So... you know, Bill," I started and James began laughing. I glared at him, feeling like a fish that had already taken the bait and was running up stream for its life, just as the angler snap set the hook.

"That's right... you pain in my ever-loving ass, you followed your instinct," Bill swung an accusing finger at me, followed by a heinous laugh. "James and I knew you would. So, we cataloged and recorded everything, even the entire pretrial and post-trial results. We wanted to catch you in a mistake. Almost everyone on the team was in on it, but we are the ones that got caught. You changed the polarity and the frequency to match phasing with the speed of the particles we were cataloging."

"The timing was incredible," James added excitedly.

"The pictures were perfect", Bill said.

"Ok," I said with a little uncertainty, not sure whether to expect an "ATTA BOY", or a bullet to the back of the head. "Does that mean you're not mad?"

"No," Bill responded emphatically. "I was pissed as hell at you, at first. Then I was watching the films and I saw you add something to the sequencer."

"The strobe circuit?" I asked. Not sure whether I needed to be thinking of alibis or be proud of my actions. Then, I realized the idea for the strobe came from Matthew. I spoke up quickly, hoping to salvage a sinking ship. "You know… the credit for that needs to go to Matt." Happy with the strategy of building a defense just in case the conversation headed in the wrong direction, I continued. "It was his idea. He was watching the monitors while working on circuit dynamics and saw how the cycles on the screen were affecting what he could see. He mentioned it to me. It seemed a simple answer for some of our phasing issues. So, we discussed it and came up with a plan. Matthew built it. I installed it. James and I adjusted for variances in distance. Daniel simply augmented the cycle in the software to accommodate the changes. Just one big happy family!" I said enjoying the continuity of my defense.

"True, I made the call and I am responsible for the decision, so what kind of punishment are we talking about here? You can't demote me and I am too old to be a lab rat? So, are you actually happy, or are you messing with me just because you caught me? Just to get even," I added. "Gotta say, for a smart man it sure took you long enough."

"Both," said Bill . "You see James, along with practically everyone else, was working with meeeee! We may be brothers in a cause but you are also, a pain in my ass. I knew you would try to do it your way. Instead of your way being wrong and all of us getting a chance to punish you and your stupid spontaneity," Bill rose and with two fingers on each hand held high in the air creating the quotes sign. "Mother of god, would you believe it, it worked!" He went back to his chair and spun to face me again. He picked up a pen on his desk and started tapping it on his coffee cup.

"Little did I know... really... believe it," Bill said, as if he had something distasteful in his mouth. "I did not know that agencies with 'special needs' were watching our progress so closely. As we discussed months ago, your team was moving incredibly fast and crossing bridges of understanding in leaps and bounds. Apparently, as you and I had surmised, we are not the only group employed to achieve the same goals. So, when our section brought into application, that which was not even speculated by other teams, they took notice and followed our teams work.'

"Very... closely," added James. "From what I have found out so far, our imaging equipment and processing software, is far beyond what is due to be implemented in the atom smasher later this year."

"We amazed some... as is our job," Bill said, "and pissed others off... really badly. Which is without a doubt your contribution, Mike." James and he both laughed, so did I.

After a second of introspection, I said, "So, you mean this whole time they have been spying on us?" The disapproval in my question was crystal.

"Well, spying is not the right word," Bill said, backpedaling to avoid an argument before it started. "You are not spying on what you have paid others to do for you." Bill shrugged doubtfully, not so sure his statement held up to scrutiny.

"Oh no... here goes the propaganda machine," James laughed. Bill turned to him with a look of... traitor. Bill got red in the face, which was always a sign that he was arguing with his own better judgment, at the same time he was arguing with us.

Bill threw the pencil in his hand, down on his desk as if disgusted, then said, "Hey... what do we always say? They pay us to turn ideas into realities ... right? What we use in raw materials in a month would bankrupt a small third world country. They own it. We just create it."

"No... No... That dog won't hunt, Ole buddy," I rebutted. "This is not Mother Russia, or North Freakin Korea, this is the good ole USA. We are paving the way for a better world with what we do, not funding secret societies, or runaway governmental agencies." Bill turned his laser beam eyes on me. Right then and there, I knew I was done. Bill and I shared a brotherhood and just about everything about our work and lives. The only things we did not talk about were in order to protect each other, coworkers and to distance us from realities that would put us at odds with our work. Realities like technology power structures, clandestine organizations and unofficial military interests, etc. The state-of-the-art technology we created, were ultimately funded and used by these consumers. The aspects and responsibilities involved in Bill's position, weighed heavily upon him at times and he had very little trust for the altruistic motivations or moral compass of the power brokers funding our many efforts. The information I knew made me as guilty as anyone else, so... I changed the direction of our conversation to save both Bill and I embarrassment and unwarranted blame.

I started to retrace our good fortune. "OK, so we came in way below budget and in half the time. Is that the major reason we are on deck?"

"Yes, but for some reason, the HOW is as important to them as the end result," said Bill. "How is it that we all work so efficiently? How did James and Matthew know to take what you were aiming to do and make the equipment do it? How did Daniel know to arrange the software to tell the equipment what to do and when?"

James and I both looked at each other with a shrug. "Well, Bill," I said, "after all these years, you know that is just what we do. Like you and me," I said, "you know exactly what I mean when I say it. You see the plan in your mind, just the way my mind is thinking it and then you provide us everything we need to make it happen." I finished the sentence, fairly pleased with where the conversation was going, but unhappy that I had paid him a complement instead of slipping a verbal counter punch past his defenses. Bill looked perplexed at the complement, when he was prepared for an attack.

Weary of a setup, he said, "Well others want that talent along with the ideas and applications, for their project. They own where we are now and need us where we are not." Then he reached for a button on the phone. "Alex, we need to schedule a team debriefing for 1530 hours on the dot. Make it happen." Bill snapped with intensity as he let go of the button. Then he pushed it again and added, "Please," in a patronizing tone. As he leaned back in his chair, Bill seemed to be measuring something. Then he said, "I would move back a few paces from the door if I were you. Alex should be coming through... right ... about ... now!" The door flung open at the same time Alex flew through it. "If you think I am going to stay here, while you guys JET off to Switzerland without me, you had better think again!"

I had never seen Alex move that fast. I do not think her feet touched the floor of Bill's office between the door and his desk.

"I knew you were listening the whole time," Bill said, head tilted forward like a bull ready to charge. He looked at me and pointed to his phone, shaking a finger at it accusingly. "She took the light out of my extension button so I could not tell when she was listening."

"What," Alex said, "you don't think that I knew that you knew that?" The red in her cheeks quickly coordinated with the red paint on the nail of the finger pointed at Bill. "I asked you if you knew your light was out... oh I don't know... maybe 10 times ... duh! They," she swung her head in an upward motion, "were threatening to replace me if I was not more forthcoming on the progress being achieved. They... were suggesting that I was compromised. I tried to let you know, damn... what did you want... a line of bread crumbs? I keep this room really clean for you. No one knows," she said as she shook her head in disgust. "No one has a clue!"

Cleaned definitely did not mean tidy. That was Alex's code word for removing all undesired technology, listening devices, spy equipment etc. She was really good at it, too. I would not want to go head to head in an Easter egg hunt with her, that is for sure.

"This room was higher tech than the space station! Before I went home some nights, I could hear the orderlies asking each other how you kept finding their best tech. There are more listening devices in the ladies' room, the general's office, the trash compactor and the commissary, than I would want anyone to know. Frankly, I am getting tired of covering your guy's butts. I have run out of places to ditch those things. Also, how else am I to make sense out of all the crazy crap that is going on around here? The guys in black suits ask questions over and over again, acting like I am two seconds away from the brig. It takes everything in me not to shove my fist and their attitudes down their throats, while I use my Muay Thai to send those stupid sunglasses into orbit."

I just stood there with my mouth open, absolutely sure she could take one of them... yeah and probably two.

Alex ranted on. "The guys in gray suits, sit in chairs in the hallway, like no one can see them. The stupid asses... the chairs that no one ever sits in, Ha, brilliant? They watch and listen to everything that is going on. Do you know they even had a custodian with head phones clean around my desk, so he could take pictures with that camera, ID badge thingy you were given in your management pouch?"

I looked at Bill with a raised eyebrow. He just shrugged and smiled, obviously totally enjoying Alex's reckless emotional departure from her normally, very disciplined demeanor. We both returned our attention to her as she continued, smiles hidden just under the surface for our safety.

"So, a girl has to do, what a girl has to do. I mean... again... I ask you, who else is going to watch out for you guys? And now you think you are going to just leave me behind?" Alex leaned over the table and leveled a stare at Bill that would have frozen an army general in his tracks. Bill leaned forward from behind his desk. He went nose to nose with Alex.

I thought, good God this guy has balls. It reminded me of two boxers staring each other down just before a fight. Thank goodness James didn't yell, 'And in This Corner'. I did want to ring a bell, though. To our surprise, Bill spoke calmly with an edge of condescension, as if to a child. "Then get your stuff together and quit... wasting... my time."

Alex, startled by the ease of winning her argument, assimilated Bill's last statement. She realized she had been played. She was never going to be left behind. She looked over at me like a lioness looks at her dinner.

"Don't look at me like that," I said. "I got caught just like you!" Alex moved back from Bill's desk, as if giving herself room to swing. Refocusing on Bill, as the red in her cheeks spread to the rest of her upper torso.

"You mean you knew you were assigning me all along and you didn't tell me?"

Bill sat back down and began to move papers without purpose. He was trying not to smile, but it was all too obvious. He said in a disinterested manner. "Even If I could do without you, which you continue to remind me I cannot, I would be a mouse in between cat's paws, if I moved an inch to leave and not have you along for the ride."

There was silence for a second, only broken by agreement from

James, as he said half under his breath, "Jah... yea that's right."

Then gripping a small pile of papers, Bill shook them at Alex and said, "Next time you get debriefed... like by General Hammel, way before all of us and don't skinny up, we are going to have a serious talk." Like a father admonishing his daughter, Bill had conveyed a serious message. He knew he could not protect her or us, unless he was well informed.

Caught off guard, Alex asked, "How did you know that? You don't have that clearance. And... and that is different. I am military," Alex rebutted. "You know I cannot share classified intel at that level. I am surprised they even debriefed me. For a few days, I was sure it was a set up and I was protecting you by not telling you." I could see that Bill understood that level of deception and felt for Alex on this one. "You know, it would be more than my job, if they found out," she added looking down at the floor.

"Well we," Bill shook papers at James, then at me." We, Weee... are not military... and we do not have to share our Intel either." He followed quickly in a childish manner and somewhat timidly, "Or at least not until we are good and ready."

"Sooo... then, how did you know?" asked Alex, arms now folded across her chest, left foot unconsciously tapping the floor.

"Well... my super sleuth, that is classified," said Bill. "What I can tell you is that these highly trained technicians can fabricate far more than just imaging equipment. What we know would surprise you and let me tell you, these guys could tell those special ops boys, not only what they had for breakfast, but also what color it was when it came out the other side... that is if ... they had a mind to. I don't tell you about our information gathering, to protect you!"

Alex looked down again, then at James, then to me. I put my hand up in the air, just to make sure she knew I was a non-combatant. Bill sat back in his chair and shuffled some more papers. His desk was even more of a mess by now. The air was thick with intensity, but the battle was over. No doubt the smoke would take time to clear. James looked over at me, with a 'Holy Shit' look. Then, he came up from behind Alex and put his hand on her shoulder.

"We could never achieve what we have, without you, Alex. You are more important to all of us than you know. We are a team; we depend upon you sometimes more than any other individual and we would never leave you behind."

"Yes," I said, "you and Bill are like the camp counselors. Without the both of you, we would probably burn the camp down." We all laughed, even Alex. We all knew James was smitten with Alex and, of course, Alex knew it.

She put her hand on James's and I could see tears in her eyes, but they were tears of relief. Caught in the act of being human Alex turned her battle-hardened stare to me. "And you... what are you... thinking? You are suddenly interested in basketball?"

"Basketball?" I said with a cynical laugh, obviously confused.

"Yes." She said it like she thought I was playing stupid. "There was some commotion about you being gone. They track you ya know," she said, somehow slipping 'You Idiot' into her sentence without actually saying the words. "Apparently, you are hanging around with some international basketball star and you just disappeared. Then you show up again near your home, walking with this, too tall guy and supposedly acting like you are drugged up. Some of our boys were undercover as local enforcement and tried to get you away from the guy to take you to a hospital. The guy would not let you go and they weren't authorized to expose their covers and start a scene, so they drifted into the background and kept an eye out. What is that all about?" she finished. Again stressing, I am not your mother, without uttering a single word of it.

My mouth was bone dry and my jaw was hurting from hanging wide open for too long.
I asked, "How close am I being observed?"

"Well let's just say that the boys in the grey suits know what you," and she looked at Bill and smiled, "had for breakfast. The guys in the black suits... those guys, well, they give me the creeps. I have never seen their type before and they are no joke. They are serious and even the General and his staff leave them a wide berth. They are very focused on you, Mike. I do not know why, but the basketball player has something to do with it."

"Why do you call him a basketball player?" I asked still shocked at her revelation.

"I saw a few photos from your file," Alex said. "He is... huge," she exclaimed. "Just a guess, if he is not a superstar, he should be. He would be a rich man. He could just lean over and drop the ball in, nothing but net from that angle," she finished off. "Anyway, a guy that size could not live in this country or any country for that matter and not have an identity. Heck, he could probably have his own zip code." I looked at Bill and silently mouthed, "My File?" Bill looked back at me and shrugged.

"There is no history on this guy, Mike, not any," Alex continued. "The boys in black cannot find out anything about him."

I thought to myself, oh… he has a history all right, not one that you would believe, but he has a long, long history.

Alex snapped her fingers in my direction. "Hey… look at me, this is important. Our guys told me they stopped him one day. The same field operatives that went to help you. In their report, they said he was polite and accommodating and when they asked him where he was from, he pointed down the street. The guys looked in that direction and when they turned back to him, he just was not there. You two really have a lot of people talking, or should I say questioning."

I came closer to Alex and said, "So what should I do now?"

"Nothing," she said flipping her hair to the side and cocking her neck … confirming she was back in control. "They do not want to upset the progress being achieved here, so they are just watching and waiting."

"For what?" Bill asked.

"I do not know," said Alex. "It is way past me, but they are getting impatient". Alex moved away from James and quickly headed toward the door. She turned and looked at Bill, as if over some invisible set of glasses that were hanging on her face. "I better get back to work, a lot to do and I certainly do not want to waste anyone's time." She moved through the doorway and turned to look at me. "Mike," she said, "there does seem to be some kind of threat." She thought again for a second, "From your friend… and now maybe you. I have seen teams like these on alert status before. The men in suits are prepared to take action immediately, to neutralize a threat. My sources tell me they have brought in some very strange equipment, in a van or truck. Keep an eye on your sixes and nines." She smiled kindly and moved down the hall, but I knew she was worried and serious.

I looked at Bill, now sitting back in his chair, staring up at the ceiling. I laughed shaking off the intensity. I said, "You bastard."

Gloating, Bill said, "Yeah, yeah, yeah." He patted his belly saying, "We all pay a price, Rip, ole buddy… and those who snooze… lose… ha ha."

CHAPTER 32

When Bill said, "Effective immediately," he was not kidding. Over the next week our team completed the refining process, documentation and application formats, so that basically the whole department could be packed up and transported to the particle accelerator facility, ready for action.

Bill would walk through the different departments yelling." Pack and Play ... People... Pack and Play ... the hard work now... quick, efficient and professional, once there. Label everything. Oh... and by the way... if you see, Mike, don't let him touch anything and I mean... anything!" His walk through got to be so regular they started calling him 'The Town Crier'. Bill couldn't help but laugh at the label, as he watched his team work like a well-oiled machine. With Alex keeping the management off his back and Bill keeping everyone on cue, the crew looked like a contingent of Santa's helpers just before Christmas. I was responsible for managing the move of our department, which was basically an order to not touch anything.

Let the team handle it, Mike," Bill would say after each update. Standing around giving orders, felt uncomfortable and everyone knew how hands-on a person I was. Yet, their discipline, or more likely their fear, of being accused of letting the enemy (that was me), through the lines, kept them ever vigil. Every time I went to reach for something to pack, or disassemble, any person or persons, within 20 feet would hustle to take over. At times, I felt like a running back being gang tackled and always with a loss of yards.

On Thursday, the first week of packing, I thought I would make sure all of the special lenses were properly stored. The moment I reached for the container, I was surrounded by Daniel, Matthew, and 2 aides.

Daniel was our software specialist. Bill, having an eagle eye for talent, picked him up teaching grad students at Tulane University. As Daniel so aptly put it, he taught others the macro-cosmic secrets to communication software development. He could speak to computers like a therapist speaks to a patient. Both could unravel tangled psyches, but Daniel was effective whether the patient was carbon, or silica based. He acquired the nickname 'The Stone', because we all said that if computers were ever to have a Rosetta stone, it would be Daniel. He could teach computers how to learn, to identify and to correct themselves and mistakes made by others, like me. Daniel could turn the difficult into the understandable and therefore, everyone understood Daniel. He was a born teacher and a damn good strategist. I would often prod him, telling him that he was just being difficult over this matter, or that. He would respond saying, "I may be difficult, but you bring me the impossible… no… wait, maybe it is really you that is impossible," then he would laugh hysterically at his own joke.

I would counter, "Then I am lucky to have come to the right person, so stop talking and make the impossible, possible." I cannot remember a time when he let us down.

Matthew was a resonance expert and an old age tinkerer. He had a way of unraveling ideas, or concepts and laying them out simply. He spent many years trying to develop a perpetual energy wave, using feedback loops and resonating frequency generators. He based his processes heavily on the principles of magnetism, in order to generate, filter and increase wave potential and output. His end use was aimed at propulsion technology. He hoped to produce a never-ending energy source. Once started, it could be maintained, no matter what the demand. He had been achieving success in his efforts until one day, his machine reacted to a spike from an antiquated power grid and lost synchronicity. The wave patterns collapsed and like an earthquake starting a tsunami, the resulting percussion wave flattened a city block. As fortune would have it, it was an old industrial block deserted by all and sincerely in need of renovation. It was there, amongst the rubble of the aging structures, that Bill found Matthew wandering around, contemplating trajectory for parts launched into oblivion from the resonance generator. Bill spent most of that day just following Matt around, talking to him and helping him in his needle in a haystack search. Then, Bill pulled his whole team in to help. After a week of searching, they recovered 60% of the experiment's mechanisms. The rest, well... some farmer in the next state would probably plow up an object glowing slightly blue and still hot to the touch and think he had found other worldly space debris.

Bill saw the genius in Matthew and they quickly became friends. Matt could tell that Bill understood his drive and determination, his passion for science and his vision to help mankind. Through their friendship, Bill mentored him back from disaster, to creative purpose. Bill must have realized that Matt needed a break from his project. A diversion, a place to put his genius, until he was ready to return to it. Bill also knew that Matt's work was directly in line with a master plan overseen by the powers that drove our projects. A self-sustaining engine, running only at startup protocol that could create the power to level a city block? Once that technology was properly contained and focused, could power anything from a city, to say... a star ship, or space station? He knew Matt could return to his work over time and have a better environment and unlimited resources, to rebuild his vision. Bill would make sure of that. So, he gave Matt a temporary purpose and set him to solving imbalances and flaws in design, in new technology. Flaws that caused everything from blurred images, to melted components. Matthew's intelligence and fortitude endeared him to us all. He never gave up. He loved to please and to perform. He was a gentle, kind person, a person that everyone trusted. His sense of humor and unique personality, made us all comfortable with our own selves and therefore, with each other. You might say Matt was a crucial component to stabilizing our team, the glue that binds.

One day while Bill and I watched James, Matt and Daniel work on a processing problem, I said, "Quite a gift, those guys."

Bill said, "Yes, I think we have created magic."

"I agree," I said. "But of all the people you could have chosen to work with, why them?" His response was in keeping with his talent as a leader.

"Like you and I, Mike", Bill said. "They have heart. They have hope. They have faith in the greater good and they will sacrifice to see a vision achieved. With qualities like that, we may not be successful with every project we undertake, but we will sure as hell build something. Right?"

"True," I agreed. "You have built a great team to make it happen."

He simply said, "My friend… this is only the beginning."

Daniel rested his hand on the lid of the container I had just unlatched and started strumming his fingers.

Just as Matthew stepped up and uncomfortably said, "Whoa there, boss, off limits for you!"

A little perturbed, I began to respond, with "You're right … I am the boss. What gives?" Upon looking in his eyes, I could see a hint of a private joke stirring around in the non-verbal communication, a tight nit team shares.

So, I removed my hand and said, "OK…OK." I turned to Daniel, "What is the big deal?"

"Well," he said, "we all got together and figured you got us here, so we can do the grunt work, to get us all," he flipped his head, "over there." He finished with an uncertain, but well-meaning pat on my shoulder.

"Ha… I am not buying that one," I said

"Yea, Yea, Yea, I… I knew that," Daniel choked out. "I thought I would give it a shot anyway. I would never make a penny as a con man."

Matt started laughing, which made us all chuckle.

"All right", said Daniel, shifting his weight and leaning forward a little as if to whisper what he knew could potentially cause me to go ballistic.

James said, "Under no," and he stressed the word No… twice, "circumstances are you to touch the equipment." Then he said, "No… check that, I mean anything!" Daniel looked around to make sure no one was near, and continued, delighted to have something to share that took the burden off of him. "He said you would probably start fiddling with settings, you know… so you would not forget an idea or inspiration when we got where we were going."

Matt shoved his face in between Daniel's and mine. "Yea, then forget to tell us like with the argon sampler."

Daniel leaned back a bit and looked hard at Matt with a "you are not helping me" look and Matt's last words trailed off, "So all the specs would not be off upon our arrival."

Working hard to back pedal, Matt continued with renewed effort." I mean you are definitely not the fly in the ointment."

Daniel punched Matt in the gut with his elbow and then pushed his bent over body out from between us.

"That is not exactly what he said," Daniel relayed with a nervous smile. With another hard glance at Matt, Daniel added, "Hey... let's get this stuff put over with the rest of the optical equipment," jerking his head toward a large group of stainless storage units.

"Right," said Matt. "I knew that..." with a gasp and a grunt. He was very clearly thankful to have a job to evade further trouble.

"What else exactly did James say," I asked crossing my arms.

"Oh... really nothing," said Daniel, looking to follow Matt in the escape.

Not having any of it, I said with authority, "What, Daniel... did he say?" Daniel looked at Matt again, who was moving away from us at an alarming rate with a box.

Finally letting go with a huff, he said, "Something about impressing our new benefactors once we get the project back on track in Geneva."

Noticing the open-ended aspect of his comment, I said impatiently, "Well?"

Daniel scratched the back of his neck, took a deep breath and added, "And ... uhmmm ... not wanting to depress them with unnecessary delays," he finished by scrunching up his shoulders, like someone was scraping fingernails against a chalkboard.

"He said that, did he?" I probed.

Seeing the set of my jaw, Daniel spoke quickly. "I got my marching orders, boss. Don't whip the errand boy and don't go to James and get me in trouble before we even get over there. He is just following orders as well."

I just shook my head and let go of the container.

"Hey, you're the Boss," said Matt, walking back over to move another small container. "Go give some orders to some of the people who don't know any better. We got this; you know we do." He smiled and then moved off quickly after a final look from Daniel.

I took a deep breath, shook my head and accepted Matt's advice. I just walked away. As I left them, my intuition confirmed their sense of relief.

Winding my way through the packing material to my office above the production floor, I was acutely aware of how empty the old place seemed. As I scaled the steps, I contemplated the dynamics of a successful team. There can only be one boss, one leader I thought and that leader has to handle and manage his team with precision. Somehow, I had endowed my team with a guard dog mentality. I just had not considered that I would be the one they were guarding against. On the bright side, it felt good to be protected by others, buffered from the realities that eventually we will all face. Bill, James, all of them, were right to keep an eye on me, considering the transitions I was going to undergo. It bothered me that I might have exposed my team, my friends to a perilous environment. No good leader consciously allows that to happen.

I grabbed the rail on the landing in between the sections of stairs heading up to my office and it occurred to me that in a tinkerer's world, working with an inventor's mind, there was never a time like the present to challenge the concepts our world teetered on. That is what made our efforts and successes so dramatic, so impactful. Inspiration was the godfather of invention. Spontaneity was a key to productive change.

No telling what last minute ideas I may have proposed, I giggled to myself. Boy… do they know me or what? As I came up the last step to my office, out of the corner of my eye I saw a figure disappear around the hall door way, more a shadow than a person.

"Dang nab it," I said allowing the frustration of the past week, to merge with the feeling of the loss of privacy. I stepped quickly and lunged outside my door, just as James was coming in. We banged noses and foreheads. Startled, James backed into the door jamb hitting the back of his head with a resounding thud.

"What the…? Ouch," James yelled. Stunned and clearly not willing to take any more abuse, he dodged back in the hall, poised like a cat, prepared for anything else unexpected. I leaned forward rubbing my nose with one hand and the right corner of my temple with the other. James went limp off to my left, and then mirrored my attempts at soothing his own pain. I looked both ways down the hallway. No one was there.

"That probably made them laugh," I said just above my breath.

"Not me," said James. Then he turned his head a little to the side and added, "Made who laugh?" He tested for blood on his nose and then went back to rubbing his head. "That stings!"

"Yep," I said. "Well no permanent marks, so stop you're whining." I finished with "Paybacks are a bitch," and rubbed my own nose.

"What... paybacks for what?"

I ignored his question and asked, "Did you see anyone out here?" I looked further for evidence of the watcher in the hall.

"No," said James, as he touched his nose again," but I do feel like someone is always just behind me, breathing down my neck. What is going on with that?"

"I can relate," I said with a sigh and then I turned to go back in my office. James walked through the doorway behind me inspecting the frame, worried about additional punishment for entering.

Frustrated at the lack of direct answers to his questions, he asked me, "Are you sure you're OK?"

"Yes," I said. "It takes more than a bump on the head to misdirect me."

"Misdirect?" James said with confusion. "Ok, I do not get any of this and thanks for the bloody nose. Anyway," he continued, "not wanting to waste time, I was on the phone with a Dr. John Schlitt. He is the lead designer, and Bill's new liaison, at the LHC."

"The what?" I said.

"The LHC," said James. "The Large Hadron Collider — the most powerful accelerator ever built," he said laughing, as if just saying the words was magic. "Dr. Schlitt asked if any of us are afraid of heights."

"Heights? I asked. "What does a fear of heights have to do with our imaging equipment?"

"Well," said James, "Dr. Schlitt says they have started the decommissioning of the existing imaging equipment and removal of the present team. He said that they will be ready for us the moment we arrive. He has concerns about our team having restrictions working with heights."

"I don't get it," I said as I plopped into my chair and rubbed my temple again, more out of frustration than comfort.

"Apparently, everything about this place is a leap in technology," James continued with unbridled enthusiasm. "They had to freeze an underground river with probes containing nitrogen. Unbelievable huh, they froze a whole river just to lay the concrete structure. It was a massive civil engineering accomplishment and it reminds me of the book "ICE NINE", did you ever read that? It freaked me out; I was afraid of contaminating everything for weeks after reading it."

"Ok... Ok," I said impatiently. "What does that have to do with heights?"

James went on, frustrated with my negative attitude while he was trying to impress me with facts. "After the concrete cured and the nitrogen tubes were removed, the structure spanned about 5 stories. We have to work all along the different capture points on the collider. Hence," he added with disdain, "fear of heights." He rubbed his forehead again and sat down in the chair in front of my desk.

"So, are we going to be hanging from the sensor stations with rock climbing gear, or descending quickly by bungee?" I said sarcastically. "They have to have proper stations for service and supply ... right?"

"Yes, but I do not know the design or layout of them yet," said James. "The support structure cannot be too roomy if Dr. Schlitt is worried about acrophobia."

"Oh, big words for a big thinker," I said and laughed.

"I am sure we will not have his/her bathrooms and ice-cold beer on tap up there," James said relaxing enough to add in his normal humor. "But I can see how height might be a concern," he responded a little defensively. "Dr. Schlitt says he cannot wait to get us there. He said they are very close to preliminary testing and ... get this... he says all the computer models suggest that at some point, they will be able to cross the bridge from theory to fact, over matter displacement. He says they may even discover evidence of tiny dimensions within existing space."

"I heard that," I said, "an offshoot of the String theory, mini black holes, etc. That is becoming a very popular subject, both pro and con."

"Yep," said James. "So, what do we do, he joked, send out a memo asking everyone to bring close fitting clothing and confirming they are bungee certified?"

"Yea... that works," I said facetiously. "Seriously though, can you get some specs on the service sites and accessibility? We may have unexpected problems with adequate space for our equipment. Oh, and by the way, has Bill heard of this?"

"Not yet," said James, trying to answer each question as it was fired at him. "I just now got off the phone with Dr. Schlitt!"

"Great," I said, "then leave it to us. Oh yea... and do not tell Alex. She is so pumped up about getting everything done in time that if we tell her about this, she will be ordering repelling equipment with our names on it."

James burst out laughing. "Ha, ha... you are so right! Ok, I will get on it."

CHAPTER 33

The rest of that day flew by as everyone was engaged in the move. It was not until exhaustion wrestled my mind into submission, that I finally cried "uncle" and decided to head home. Everyone else was gone. The facility was silent and even though this was my best thinking time, I was put off. The place where exciting discoveries had occurred, now felt empty and a little creepy. I kept expecting a person to step out from the shadows, or from behind a corner. I admonished myself for being childish. Yet, heightened senses told me that there was much more happening around me than I was accepting. Truth be told, I was too tired to explore the possibilities.

Fatigue had interrupted my thought patterns. My inner world, now symbiotically bonded with the void, was anything but calm. The energy within it shifted relentlessly, mutating the foundation upon which my inner balance depended on. I could feel the void drawing energy from me for its own purposes. It slowly gained ground, taking over aspects of my consciousness or subconscious, every time I turned my attention back to the outside world. I felt like I was in the middle of a game of 'I Spy' and losing badly. Only this did not feel like a game and I was pretty sure the moment the inner world gained equality with the outer, both worlds would be dramatically altered.

An impression of danger continued to develop, forcing me to exert mental and emotional influence to keep fear in check. The energy would explode upward at times, like a flare explodes upward from the surface of the sun. As energy rose up from the void, I had the impression that it was attempting to communicate, rather than usurp.

I finished reviewing specifications for changes to our equipment at the collider and relaxed back in my chair. A blistering display of energy and light exploded past my relaxed defenses. I could see faces and recognize personalities. A visage of one of the technicians on our team became clear, in the iridescent light created by the flare. Then the visage fell backward toward the void, but not until I perceived that he was not, what he seemed to be. What he did seem to be, was a spy. He was carrying information on our progress to people I did not recognize. The impression I received concerning their purpose was definite and it was not good.

Although dealing with corporate spies was not an uncommon occurrence in our business, the fact that this person could have invaded our project and done so without the awareness of some of the best security experts, both military and contractor based, had significant implications. I could also discern bits of information on the group he was working with, they knew of some impending danger to life as we know it and they were willing to take any risk to own what they thought we possessed.

What could that be, I pondered? I knew I would need to talk to Bill about this, pronto.

Another flare rose from the void. The iridescent colors were magically clear and crisp. As that brilliance filled my inner vision and obscured any other outer considerations, I saw the village where I had bonded with the young wolves and Lauren. Lauren was crying. I felt a sense of loss and desperation, but I could not see the cause. Lea was clearly in a defensive posture, standing guard over Lauren, but I could not see an aggressor. Lea looked larger now. She looked more like her mom, than a youngster. I had to reflect back on how long I had been away, as her growth seemed unprecedented. The flare began to collapse in on itself. The last impression was of some malevolent, invading force, but why there?

"I thought they were untouchable." I spoke out loud, shaking my head a little. I must be confused, maybe imagining. After the last eruption, it was as if the void had migrated from some adjacent dimension, visible only in my consciousness, to the tangible, real-time, everyday world. Unlike the tapestry images I had seen for the man in the park, the boundaries of the void were no longer fixed. As if fueled by raw physical matter, the void was alive and much more potent, imbued with a separate, yet symbiotic awareness.

Afraid that if I remained sitting at my desk, the experiences would spiral out of my control, I got up, grabbed my coat and headed for home. As I walked toward the exit, nodding to the orderlies that restocked the labs for the following day, I felt like I was walking in another dimension. A parallel to the one I lived in. I could feel time slow down, then like a rubber band, slingshot forward. I had no way to estimate the time segments, but it was unnerving. I walked by a coworker's office, football memorabilia stacked on the shelf beneath a Cleveland Browns clock that hung on his wall. The clock's hands displaying 2:38.

More images and information related to the spy and then to Lauren and Lea clouded my mind. What information had the spy acquired? How could what we are doing, as partitioned as the research was, be worth the espionage? I could see he was very clever. If each research segment of the project had one of those spies … I guess you could put the puzzle pieces together, but for what purpose? When next I looked up, I was passing the same office, this time the clock read 3:25.

That is weird, I said to myself shaking my head, but my thoughts were not flowing in logical patterns. I felt like I was on the other side of the mirror watching life progress on the real-life side. I continued to walk toward the exit. The next thing I knew, I was approaching my car. I pushed the open button on the car remote, the inside lights and the head lights came on. I happened to be directly in the line of site of the headlights and after struggling to see in nighttime light, the irises of my eyes desperately tried to constrict before I was blinded by the brightness. I squeezed my eyes shut in pain, turning away from the light. The afterglow imprinted on my cornea and lit up the vision center at the back of my head, spinning sparkles and the forms geometry must have been inspired from. As the light dissipated, the soft glow remaining resembled the keys my grandfather had left to guide me to Alton's world.

Another vision of Lea anxious over Luka, Lauren next to her, eyes wet with tears, presented itself. The village looked in disarray and I could not sense my grandfather anywhere in the village. Where was Luka? Why were the girls worried about him? Lea's head turned to stare directly at me, fear for me flashed in her eyes, then something outside of my vision caught her attention and she leapt away. The scene swirled like the tempest Alton had evoked at the beach and then ended.

I found myself standing alone in the parking lot, facing the facility, only it was not night, it was early morning. The sun was just over the horizon and cars were starting to arrive at the facility. Good thing I liked to park in the back of the parking lot I thought. What would somebody think, seeing me frozen in the position I was in? I groaned as the rusty hinges holding my torso to my waist, snapped and crackled upon movement. I looked at my watch, it was 7:52. I climbed into my car and the impact of time shifting as it did, really frightened me. What would happen if it occurred when I was driving? Then I remembered the conversation about dark matter, time in relation to space and the makeup of the void.

OK... where was the void now, I asked myself? I could sense it, but it was not present, not part of this moment in time. I looked about me. Everything seemed in its place. I moved my arms and stamped my feet on the floor of the car. Nothing out of synch, everything seemed normal. I even felt rested. I thought back to the night before. I remembered the growing presence of the void and the impression that it was somehow trying to communicate. I stepped back out of my car, locked it and headed back into the facility.

CHAPTER 34

From experience and more than just a few reminders, I knew Bill was usually the first to arrive and the last to leave work. I also knew exactly where he would be. As I entered the observation room above the laboratory floor, I saw Bill sitting comfortably in one of the conference chairs facing the variety of storage and moving units, stacked high in the laboratory in preparation for pick up. He heard a person enter and turned to see who was coming his way. His eyes went wide and he stood up turning to face me head on. He put his coffee down, leaned over and pushed the intercom button while he looked back up at me in astonishment. He stuttered as he said, "Alex… Alex… you there?"

"Yes, I am here and was here before you, as usual. I have far too much going on to play 'Let's annoy MOM', so state your business and be quick about it."

"Alex, come to the conference room, now… now." Alex must have heard the tone of his voice, as all I heard was the sound of her chair being pushed back and quick steps following.

Bill punched in another set of numbers, "Jim… Jim…?"

"Yea, what ya got boss?"

I need you in the observation room, stat. Bill let go of the button and continued to stare at me.

I said, "What the hell is that dumb look on your face for?"

Alex hit the doorway, slowing as she entered. Approaching Bill on the other side of the table from me, she stopped and gaped to match Bill's awe. Jim followed and stood next to them both, they all stood and stared.

Alex was the first to speak. "Mike, do you know where you are… are you OK?" Then she looked at Bill and said, "What has happened?"

Jim went over to the observation window and knocked loudly. Then having caught someone's attention, he pointed to me. I looked down on the floor and there was Daniel and Matthew, they both adopted the same amazed looks.

Alex looked over at Jim and said, "Stop gawking like an asshole and go get Michael some coffee… come on!" As Jim headed to the door she said, "Also get either my, or your phone, we need to take a picture of this for documentation." Jim practically ran out of the door.

Alex rounded the table and approached me with caution. "Mike, when I checked with security last night, you were still here. Is everything OK? Why… I mean… how come you are here?"

After last night's dimensional shifting, I was not exactly confident of my place in things, both in time and in this case… workspace.

"I am fine," I said. "I think anyway… why… what is wrong with all of you? Is there something wrong with me?" I looked down at my arms and legs and then tried to catch my diffused reflection in the observation room glass.

"It is all right, Buddy. Just sit down for a moment until we figure this out," Bill said. Alex took hold of my arm and led me to the nearest chair. Jim came back in with hot coffee, placed it next to me and stepped back. With an amazed expression on his face, he looked at Bill and shrugged.

"I… uh… I made it just like you like it, Mike,… uh… boss," James said. "Careful, it is really hot." Then he slid the cell phone in his hand over to Alex, like he was hiding his actions.

"Ok… Ok. That is enough," I said. "You guys are freaking me out and I have something important to talk about."

"Sure… sure you do, man", said Bill "and we are all here for you, so just relax and tell us whatever it is that is on your mind." A farcical tone peeped out from behind the serious one. They had no idea what had happened to me last night and there was no way I could consider sharing that with them… period.

"Hey, Mike," Alex said. "Do you know what time it is?"

Jim chimed in, "How many fingers am I holding up, boss?"

Alex looked at Jim like he was insane. He is not blind you idiot; he is just here at a normal time!

"You have got to be kidding me. You mean all of this is because I happen to be here on time this morning?."

"This morning," Bill looked at Alex as she slid him a sly grin. "This morning. This is the only morning in your professional life that

I know of, and we have worked together for a pretty long time, that I have ever seen you where you were supposed to be, when you were supposed to be there."

"Well that is stretching it a little, Bill," Alex said. "Remember back in June, when we…."

"All right that is enough," I said. "I get it… I get it!"

Bill shifted his stance and started rubbing his chin. "Uhm… I don't know, Alex. He is still wearing yesterday's clothes. Maybe he is trying to pull a fast one, fool us into thinking he pulled an all-nighter." Bill shifted his gaze to James and then back to Alex, they all spoke at once…

"Nawwwwww!"

"No way… uh, uh," James added. "Look at the clock. It is actually early. He is here before work."

Daniel and Matt had climbed the stairs and opened the glass door, one head practically stacked above the other. "What is going on? Did we have a meeting?" Daniel asked.

"Yea… it must be an important one for Mikey to be here and early," exclaimed Matt.

"All right, let's get it all out. Anyone else want to make a comment? If not, I need to talk to Bill." I stood up and looked at Bill straight on. "I need to talk to you in private. Alex, you probably should be present, too, now that I think about it." Everyone looked at everyone else and with a sharp nod from Bill, dispersed.

"Sure thing… Michael. By the way Alex, please check on the pre-departure psych exams for everyone. Didn't you say Michael was the first in line? Oh… and heck… isn't that for this afternoon?"

I looked at Alex and said, "Really, can we stop now?"

"I do not think he will be a willing participant, Bill," Alex responded. "We might have to restrain and sedate him."

"Oh, I would have thought that would be protocol," Bill smiled. They both laughed.

"All right buddy, let's get to it," Bill sighed. "What is so important that you would upset the natural flow of life here?"

I sipped the coffee James had bought me. "Hey… he did it. He made it just right."

Alex looked at Bill again. "We definitely need the restraints, Bill!"

"Ok, I am getting to it," I said.

Now here was my problem. I had identified the spy as someone I had seen in the lunch facility a few times, but I did not know how to tell them how I knew he was a spy. The guy had seemed well liked and as far as I knew, was a model employee. Based on the reception I received in the conference room, they were never going to believe me.

"Alex," I said, "could you have security close off the exits in the building and call the alert code? Not for nothing, Bill, but when she is in chief mode, everyone jumps."

"Agreed," said Bill, "but I must have a reason to allow Alex to do so. I am going to need more."

"Can I ask you to just trust me? I am telling you it would be a good idea," as I gave him an affirming look.

"You got it, buddy. Alex… you have the com," Bill said, as he cautiously relaxed back in his seat.

Alex put her head in her hand and responded with a hint of the absurd. "Is that supposed to be something new? When have I not had the com?"

Bill and I laughed, because it was basically true.

"Ok… anything else?" Bill asked. "If not, let's get down to it."

"Yes," I said. "Bill, I know you are not taking this seriously yet, but please, as your friend for many years and a partner in many of your professional achievements, you must listen to me. I am not sure how much rides on this, but I feel it is really important."

Bill's face and demeanor had changed. He had known me long enough and well enough to see the serious and maybe desperate side of me.

Alex aware of the shift from silly to serious, pulled a note pad to rest in front of her and began to write the time and date.

"All right, I am just gunna come right out and say this… we have a spy on our project."

Alex laughed, almost spitting out the gum she was enthusiastically chewing.

Bill took on that amazed look again. "Mike, ole buddy, there are more spies in this facility, sometimes more than actual employees. Every section, command, group, division, bureau etc., has eyes on the ground. Come on man, we are burning daylight here."

"I know but they are not real spies, they are, you know, one of the family so to speak. The guy I am talking about, he is a real spy, not connected." I leaned forward and whispered the last two words... "AT ALL".

"Michael, it is my job to vet everyone who walks through those doors," Alex said, "and if that is not enough comfort for you, the people watching over me and us, can chart back to the day and time we reached puberty. OK... Do you have something we can go on here, maybe something to validate your convictions?"

Bill knew my talent for logical deduction and he had rarely seen me so serious. Coupling the fact that I was at work earlier than ever before and that was all it took.

"Al... let's start with identifying this guy. Can you pull up the employee register, along with the ID cards?" Bill asked.

"You sure you want to take the time for this?" Alex asked Bill.

"Yeah... if Michael thinks we have a leak, or a spy, he is just sharp enough to catch it when the rest of us would not. Let's get that roster up on the screen here," Bill pointed to one of the large monitors hanging on the wall.

Alex logged in to the nearest terminal and the large screen hanging on the wall came alive.

"Remember the alert status, Alex," Bill added.

Alex looked at Bill. He shook his head in confirmation. After performing a few functions on the terminal, she got up and left the room.

"Mike, all kidding aside, this is real right? You do have some proof, or some way to nail this person?"

"I am working on it, Boss," I said. "Thanks for having faith in me."

Bill pushed back his hair and said, "Well, you shocked us good this morning. Might as well let you have at the entire facility. Talk to me."

There were three tones on the intercom and a request for a fire check.

Alex walked back in and sat down saying, "All done, sir. The facility is on soft lock and standby as of 0830."

Bill bobbed his head in acknowledgement and then looked back at Alex with a 'I hope we do not regret this' look and focused back on the monitor.

"Can you bring up the assist staff on the monitor?" I asked "I will know the guy once I see his ID card and picture."

Alex began to review the Staff ID information, while I contemplated how James could make my coffee perfect today, but whenever he made it in the past, it was always wrong. "That son of a gun," I said under my breath.

"What, did you see him?" asked Bill.

"No, I just realized that Jim has been playing me for a long time." I lifted my coffee to emphasis my point. Bill looked back at the monitor shaking his head, but Alex smiled from ear to ear. After about 10 minutes, the man I saw in my vision popped on to the screen. "There, that is the guy."

Bill reviewed the information. "Alex, what do you know about him?"

"Well," she said, "he was clean when we vetted him, but I remember thinking he was … oh I don't know, maybe too clean. He was referred to us by another lab, so if he is not what he seems to be, he is very good at being what we want to see."

"Mike," Bill said, "we have to have something solid. If we question him and let him go, he will disappear, along with whatever information he has acquired."

"Do you have any idea what his agenda is?" Alex asked. "Any idea what he was up to?"

I looked down and closed my eyes letting last night's incursion by the void, flow past my memory. As it did, I saw the spy standing by a blue BMW. He was waiving at someone and then he opened the back door, sat in the rear seat and pulled on the seat belt. He stood back up, closed the door and looked casually around while walking into the facility. I watched the flashing scenes in my mind, almost like an old-time movie, as he walked through security and ran his card. "The time and date were only about 30 minutes ago." I looked up at Alex, who was looking at Bill with concern. She shifted back at me and now I could see that she was worried, if I truly was … OK?

"Alex, is there any way you can ask security for the video of the parking lot, say… 20 to 40 minutes ago? Could you also check the system to see if he left and came back in during the same time?" I looked at Bill, and said, "If he has left the facility and gone to his car, I think we can nail him, right now."

While Alex was doing what she did best, I sipped the remaining coffee in silence. Within 5 minutes, Alex had confirmed that the technician had left and returned to the facility all within 25 minutes this morning. She also was able to view him leaving, but the camera with the best view of the visit to his car, was also capturing the early morning sunlight and it degraded the video to the point that nothing clear could be seen.

"OK... That is enough for me," Bill said as he stood up. "Mike, I do not know how you know, what you know. You are gunna need to answer some questions about that." Bill turned to Alex and said," Shut err down... official like. Get a detail to that lab and escort that guy into one of the holding rooms on the bottom level. Have the CO on detail inform his guys to look for other employees, or visitors trying to leave, or at least exhibiting odd behavior. "And, Alex," Bill added, "have them do it quiet, but get it done now. If this guy is that good, we better do this right the first time. He may not be alone, so make sure you have cover in the parking lot and another as back up." "Mike, you stay here where I can get to you once this guy is detained and let's hope you can provide the necessary proof."

Alex was moving to the door with military precision. Bill called to her before she turned the corner at the door." Hey, Alex, be careful and once he is in custody, let General Hammel know we have an intruder." Alex wore the face of a warrior as she left the room and it hit me how quickly they had gone from playful to professional.

"Bill, do you mind if I go out and stand by his car? I need to collect my thoughts."

"Bad idea, buddy. We do not know if he is working alone or in a cell." He started to walk out of the room, then he turned. "On second thought, if you think that is where the evidence is, then let's secure it. I am going to have a few agents accompany you."

Bill saw me start to object and flashed me the "don't press me on this" look. I sighed and said, "Okay thanks."
I passed him as I walked toward the door and added, "As long as they are not going to shoot me if I am wrong."

Bill responded immediately. "Awww come on, buddy, that would never happen!"

I smiled and turned back toward the door as Bill added, "That is my job". I looked back to see him giggle.

As I walked down the hallway towards the entrance, I noticed how normal everything around me seemed. No one would have been the wiser that a breach in security had occurred and that Special Forces were converging on one of the labs. As I reached the main entrance, two casually clothed men met me. They fell in behind me talking to themselves, as if they were just headed out for break.

CHAPTER 35

This was not the first time Bill's team had met with nefarious intent. Once after leaving the Daystar institute, Bill, I and some of the existing team members were brought in to clean up a project and get it back on track. We were directed to work with near earth communication technology. The facility and its projects had been the victim of way too many cyber and security attacks.

We met with IT incursions often, but this was a multi-pronged attack from a mercenary group based out of the Orient. With our team now in charge, the perpetrators had no clue what was in store for them.

The IT incursion was a "seek and destroy" data initiative, which was of little consequence to Daniel. He had the IT bandits ferreted out within an hour of the breach. Then Bill went on the offensive. International news that afternoon reported: "A Large complex caught fire today in Namp'o Korea. It was believed started by stored magnesium ordinance. The fire demolished 2 blocks of an industrial district. The destruction of the 2 blocks of the IT and industrial complex was complete."

Of course, the whisper drone had waited until the complex had closed and was primarily vacant. Then it fired a prototype fission shell that General Hammel was dying to test on an active target. The video was frightening. There was intense light and heat, but very little percussion and noise. The surrounding population was virtually unaffected. I was not at peace until the news stated there were no fatalities, but since the target was a covert op, there was no way to tell for sure. In the meantime, while the attack was being arranged and carried out, Daniel had accessed their database through a porn site visited by one of the hackers. That site run, by of all organizations, the Department of Defense.

Daniel just laughed at the irony. Bad people can do bad things. Why not use their weaknesses against them? At the same time that Daniel was mopping up, Alex, with a little help from one of her clandestine operative buddies, was able to identify and isolate the facility owners.

As I had said before, the attack on the program was multi-faceted. The second initiative of their attack was carried out by mercenaries on US soil. Private arms contractors were offered enticing sums of money for any prototype or solid advancement in science that they could recover. Since they already had individuals in place, they gained entry past security and made their move. I never learned the names of those in the security detail that lost their lives that day, but more than one family lost someone important. Bill was beside himself with anger. Alex was cool and calm and wore the look of a professional. She asked to be dismissed and from what we could find out, went right to General Hammel. A note came across Bill's desk that afternoon, informing him that Alex would be reassigned for a few days for special training and would return after the weekend. In fact, Alex had accompanied a CAG Delta Force Swift response combat unit, called the 'Devils Brigade' named so during World War II by their motto, "Sent here by the Devil, Sent home by the brigade". I never learned what happened, but when Alex returned, she was happy and as sassy as ever. I do not think the private contractors that made the mistake of crossing Alex, made that mistake again… ever!

As the sun beat down upon the pavement outside the faciltiy, waves of heat created small mirages, which tricked the eye. I located the blue BMW at the very back of the lot, parked in the shade of a pine tree that blocked direct line of site from the building. Very convenient, I thought. As I approached the car, I wondered if it could be booby trapped. I judged against it though, if they had gone so far as to infiltrate our group, then the information taken must be worth more than the spies' life. That, in turn, meant there was good possibility helpers were around to collect the automobile. Bomb blasts usually attract a lot of attention.

The two soldiers in casual dress stopped a little distance from me and I could tell they were receiving instructions via their headsets. One of the soldiers ambled over to me, turned to look around and pulled out a cigarette. He asked for a light. Then he said, "The perp has been apprehended and is secure. They are going through his belongings now and Mr. Farrell will be out as soon as they assess the potential for outside interference. He asked us to stay close to you for now."

"OK," I said, feeling a little bit stupid, acting like we were not connected. The soldier walked a few paces away, but did not go any further from me. I walked over to the car again and just looked at the rear seat belt laying across the back seat. Within 5 minutes Bill and Alex showed up. A few more men began to spread out along the perimeter, all very nonchalantly. Alex walked over, then Bill.

Alex spoke first." Ok, soldier, make this good" and she handed me the keys. Bill walked past me closer to the car.

"Mike, this guy seems clean as a whistle. All eyes are on us, so… like Alex said, 'Make this count'."

"Ok, Boss," I said. Then looking at Alex, I said, "Do I need to worry that the car will blow up or something?"

She just smiled and said, "No. No, not unless you are wrong." She winked and crinkled her nose at me. I had to laugh. She was so cool under stress. I walked over to the car and hit the remote. No boom, no bang… just chirp and click. I opened the back door on the driver's side and sat sideways to the seat belt just as I had seen the technician do in my vision. I pulled it out and felt down the length. When I reached the cowling holding the seat belt, I felt material slightly different than the seat belt itself. I pulled harder on the strap. The mechanism clicked and let out one more turn. To my surprise at the base of the belt a small pocket of firm material, abutted the stitching. I reached in the pocket and pulled out a flash drive. It was stainless and by all impressions, just you're run of the mill flash drive. I got out of the car and with uncertainty, handed the drive to Bill.

"Well, this is a surprise, isn't it?" he said looking relieved. Then he walked over to Alex and said, "If it isn't pictures of the kids, or maybe the girlfriend, the wife does not know exists, then it is going to be encrypted. Put Daniel on it and have him duplicate it enough times to allow for destruct protocols. Wait… first have that… prototype laser scan device confirm that there are no contaminants or explosives. It is small, but remember the Argon experiment a few years back?" They both turned to look at me as if I had been the spy himself.

"First Matthew and now you guys. You are never… gunna let me live that mistake down, are you?" They both shook their heads and said "NOPE" at the same time.

As I was heading back into the facility, a tow truck arrived to carry the car to where it probably would be dismantled. I began to think about the series of events that led up to finding the drive and securing the spy. I felt unsettled. I was no detective, even if the void did help to amplify my awareness. In my career, I spent many hours designing experiment processes so that they flowed flawlessly forward and this just felt uncannily like one of those situations. It was all too smooth, almost choreographed. No, I thought, maybe not to that extent, but it just felt too easy.

CHAPTER 36

The holding rooms in the basement of the facility were glorified prison cells. Security was tight and there were not many places for an escapee to escape to. The viewing room was dimly lit as we entered in order to cut down on background light. I walked over to the window and watched the interrogators get up and file out of the room.

"He is a mess in there. I do not think you will get much out of him," said one.

"If I had a dollar to bet, I would say this was a case of friendly fire," said another. "He does not have the nerve to be the guy you think he is."

We all looked at the suspect through the window for a moment. He was sitting slumped over, head hung, sobbing.

"Well, what next?" I asked.

As if hearing my question, his sobbing stopped. We all looked at him again. For another moment his body was lifeless, the silence created a strange air in the room. He raised his head slowly and when he looked around the room, he wore a cynical smile. It reminded me of Jack Nicholson in the movie "The Shinning". His eyes came to rest on the viewing window. He laughed a guttural laugh and then grunted a few times. Not like someone clearing their throat, more like a laugh and grunt at the same time. There was satisfaction in it, like a drug addict feeling his fix after removing the needle. His eyes went from just barely open, to rolling back into his head.

"Ahh haaa... I feel him. I feel the one I seek. Haaa haa," a throaty growl formed his words. "Good job... you followed the crumbs. A babe could have done it, but you did...you did, ha haaa. Yes... I can feel the void now, the open space, the emptiness, just where I need to be, to get where I need to gooooo... ha haaa."

The hair on my neck climbed up onto my scalp and buried itself in folds of skin. I turned and looked at Alex and Bill, then looked at the others. They all reacted with the same sense of dread, as if pure evil had been poured all over them. One of the interrogators caught off guard like the rest of us, started for the door before gaining control of himself. He stood stiff, fighting the unbridled fear, the voice from the technician... our spy, generated.

"Speak again, so I can feel the vibration. I want to know more," said the technician.

"Ok..." I whispered to the others. "Is it just me, or is this like a scene out of a Saturday night Creature feature?"

The technician sat up and then stood up. The shackles on his wrists which connected a chain to the table in the room, clanged as his arm pulled the chain to length. The technician looked down at the chain in a zombie like stupor. He slowly put his other hand on the metal collar and pushed it over his chained hand, his bones crackling, the skin tearing under the compression. There was no sign of pain on his face. He continued to smile with that insane smile. Freed from his shackle, he walked over to the window, with blood streaming out of the torn skin on his wrist and knuckles. He raised the bloody hand to tap the window. The glass bulged in and then out again, as if it were a piece of fabric blown by the wind.

"What the hell," yelled Bill, as startled as the rest of us.

"Uhmmm... shouldn't we do something about that?" said Daniel backing up towards the door.

"Yep, I am," said Alex. "I'm gunna shoot the fucker. Let's see how big a smile he can give me then," as she reached to take the M9 away from the stunned guard nearest her.

"Wait," said Bill. "He is not moving out of the room and this is clearly not the lab technician. This is something we have not encountered, or at least I have not." Bill looked to the General for confirmation. The General looked at Alex and then the ordinance she held ready. I was pretty sure he agreed with Alex, but he nodded back at Bill.

Bill then added, "If he wanted to harm us, I firmly believe he has had the opportunity. He does not seem to find us of importance. He is looking for whoever has this 'Void'. Does anybody here, have a clue to what he is he talking about?"

"I ... Uhm... I may know a little about that, Bill, but I cannot be sure yet."

"Mike, if this is some crazy leap into the dark side experiment of yours, I am gunna be really pissed. This guy scares the hell out of me and that does not happen often. So, if you know what is going on, you better step up here and take charge before Alex smokes this... this... thing, entity, whatever and the lab tech at the same time!"

"Fear... I sense fear. Do not be afraid," the entity spoke kindly, softly, but there was something unnatural in his voice. "I could have taken your lives at any time, if that was my purpose. See...The entity swept his hand across the window. It melted away. It did not melt like molten glass would, it was more like it had been affected by molecular destabilization. What was left of the window fell out of the frame, turning into sand on the floor. I was not sure who yelled and who squealed when that happened, but I know I was one of them. With the window gone, I could see the technician's eyes more clearly. They were totally white, with no pupil. Those had escaped upward into the socket.

"Hellooo... be not afraid. I need the one that can take me where I have to go, that is all. He is the one that can travel through the void. He can draw from it and provide a bridge to where I want to go... where I... must go," the entity added in a very low intimidating voice. "So do not fear me. It would not suit my purpose to damage such insignificant creatures... yet..."

"This is a bunch of bullshit if I have ever heard any," said Alex. "Time to send this anomaly back to the place he calls home." She wrapped the strap of the M9 around her arm and drew the gun to her shoulder as the entity spoke again.

"Home. Yes... the female has it right. I want to go home. Take me there and I will leave you to your world. You can have this one back. He is so frail; it takes more energy to keep him alive than it is worth.

You are the one... the entity pointed to me. Not much training I can see, but I felt you go in and come out unharmed. I cannot do that. I am almost tempted to remain and see what you can do with the emptiness over time, but I want to go home... home... take me there ... take me there now." His last statement hung in the air, dripping of intimidation.

I hated to say this, because it was not science and this entity made my hair crawl, but I turned to Alex and said, "Al... I know you could take out the lab tech, but there is no way a bullet from that gun is gunna stop", I waved my hand at the spectacle before us, "whatever that is. Especially If it can break down the structure of things. I would rather not end up in a pile, like the window. Is it OK if I try to figure this out? He is staring and pointing at me, so I would be the first to go anyway. If that happens… waste him for me, if you can."

"I will not harm you or this flesh if you help me," the entity confirmed.

"We do not know what it is you are asking for… can you tell me what you mean by a bridge and to carry you home?" I asked trying to get a dialog going.

"I have been watching for you since I felt the breach. This world is boring and the lives here hold no consequence for me, only you. The entities focus isolated me and I felt like an amoeba being viewed under a microscope.

"Never before has anyone desired to enter the void. No one can do that without getting lost. No one ever returns from that which is not. Why did you go there? What did you find that brought you back in the flesh? I can see there is another, another of my race around you, but he cannot teach you what he does not know. I cannot teach you what I do not know." There was silence as the entity leaned against the wall, seemingly drained. Then he put his bloody arm through the window opening. Every one jumped and the guard at the back screamed like a child in a horror movie.

"How do you know, human? How did you make something out of nothing? A bridge, your bridge, when there is nothing to build it upon, in the void." A bloody finger now pointed at me and I had to admit, I was scared as hell.

I stumbled with my words a bit, trying to think how to answer him and not give too much information to Bill, Alex and the General. I decided to answer him truthfully.

"I do not know how to answer that," I said.

"It lies unfinished, the bridge. You left it undone. Once it is complete you are the foundation it must rest upon. You are the anchor that holds what is not, within the reach, of all that is. I need it to be done and you," the entity pointed again, "to bring me across it."

I was not happy about the thought of spending time with this guy, or any of his brethren, but I answered as best as I could. "Sir… ah… Sir, I would be happy to help you, but you need to tell me what…"

Alex interrupted with fury, "What in the hell are you talking about?"

The entity was obviously growing weaker, possibly less connected to his puppet, so as he swung his head in an awkward manner towards Alex, his attempted smile resembled a grimace." I like the female. Far too frail for our race, but it would be fun to test her limits."

That got Bill really mad. "That's enough. You have caused enough damage for one day. Daniel, go get Matt. Tell him to bring the Flux generator off his last project to me. I am not sure what is going on, but I can tell a weak position when I see it". Bill turned back to the entity.

"That will take care of this and you. You do not belong here and I do not think you can stay very long. You are losing control already."

It was nice to not feel alone. Bill had recognized the decay. The lab tech's arm was starting to swing out of control. As if it was caught in some kind of whirlpool or eddy, which dragged it around in a circle.

"He is a smart one," the entity said "and his judgment is accurate. I did not expect this ploy to get so far on first contact. If this is how prepared your world is for beings like me, I could conquer it in one morning. Now that you know what I am here for, I will trade. I will allow one important to this one," and he pointed toward me as his arm made a perfect circular pattern, "to come home. In exchange, you take me home."

The vision of the village, Lauren and Lea, flashed through my head.

Fear and anger rose up in me and also drove deep into the void within. Like a bolt of lightning, the void responded. It lifted the entity into the air, driving it into the back wall. The rest of the room was flattened as well. The residual energy highlighted a portal that had been hidden from view the entire time. It was large enough to encase the body of the technician, but not so powerful as to convey substantial physical matter. The entity was using the portal as a connection, a sort of power line. Strings to manipulate the puppet, but that was all. If the portal was any more powerful, both sides of it would be open and exposed. My chest burned, my body tingled and I was shocked by the reaction of the void, through me into the physical world.

"Wonderful, wonderful," said the entity, as he climbed to his feet." Use it, develop it. It will only make our journey easier. I have what you want, you have what I want, a simple trade." Then the entity looked at Bill. "Just so you know… If I do not get home soon, this world will be my very next conquest and I will make it my new home. Chaos will reign."

A tether or connection within the portal snapped and the entities control failed. The technician fell to the floor in a seated position. Where the body was standing, a negative image remained, almost like a reflection in a pond. The surface rippled and within that image I could see a face. It was not horrible or ugly. It was a beautiful face. High cheek bones created a regal appearance and helped to define other features. There were scars, as if created by old wounds, but the face glowed like that of an ancient deity. The entity looked into my eyes, our minds, maybe our souls connected. There, in the depths of those eyes, lay horrors I refused to acknowledge. Sorrow filled the entire impression. The entity opened those bottomless orbs up to me, so I could see how powerful his need was and how desperate he had become. Power driven by desperation, not a good combination when capable of the unimaginable, I thought. As if reading my mind, he smiled and without saying another word, he initiated a vision of Luka being tortured by malformed creatures. His fur was torn in places and blood covered others. It was only a brief image, but the vision produced an anger and vitriol in me that tore through any control I believed I had. My chest burned as it gave way. I could not see what came out, nor do I believe anyone else could, but as it hit the portal, the face grimaced and yelled. Then the portal folded.

A neon fixture swung rhythmically from the ceiling of the holding room, one bulb blinked at half-light, the other lay shattered on the table below. The back wall against where the lab tech, Erin Bowers sat bloody, dazed and confused, was deeply etched with a funneling swirl pattern. The same pattern one might see while watching water drain from a toilet. The cement the wall was formed from was actually indented or swallowed inward around the etching. The emergency lights had come on, but the room and all the occupants, including me, remained frozen in the moment.

Bill was the first one to speak, trying to move closer to Alex and lower the gun from her frozen attack posture. "I knew this was gunna be a hell of a day when I came in this morning. Then you showed up, Mike... on time and I knew... I just knew, I was in for it."

"What did I do?" I said, starting to help those laying on the floor up while rubbing my chest. I had no real answers for anyone just yet and the fact that some other worldly energy had designs on me, actually did not help in that area either.

Bill wrestled the M9 out of Alex's grip. "Shoot the Fucker? Remind me to pay for the human relations course next time it is available, you could use some coaching."

"Human relations," Alex said incredulously. "You call that Human?"

"Maybe superhuman," Daniel said, standing up against the wall the doorway to the hall was on. "Did you still need that piece of hardware from Matthew Boss, because I am ready to go get it now? Then I think I am going to go home and open that bottle of Jack that I have been saving for the night before we head off to Switzerland."

"No, Daniel," Bill said with just a hint of a smile. "The threat has been neutralized. I am not sure how, but it has been neutralized and sent back to where it came from. I presume Mike knows," he added and that was all he said.

I stammered out, "Bill, I know you think I had something to do with this, but..."

"Think is not the right word. The right word would be certain, convinced, positive, definite and I want to know... just like that manifestation, why you? I do not mean next week some time, either."

"I know, Boss," I began, but...."

"That is exactly right, you do know... thank you at least for that!"

"No... I mean I know it looks bad, but I do not know anything about that ... whatever. I mean... maybe it was all like... a magic trick, or sleight of hand? We cannot just presume there was something extra dimensional about this."

Bill looked at me as if I was trying to steal his wallet. "The only thing about all of this that does not confound me, Mike, is that of all the people that some extra dimensional creature came looking for trouble with, it was you. A magic trick can make a rabbit appear out of a hat, not disintegrate a bullet proof barrier and take control of another person. Look at that wall, not much magic there! Tangible energy dynamics at work? You Bet! Wait... maybe you would like to tell our babbling technician in there that this was one big magic trick. Surprise, oh by the way, you were the rabbit?"

The technician was on his feet now stumbling around sobbing and talking to himself.

"Get the medical personnel up here on the double", Bill said to one guard. "And you," he pointed to the other guard wobbling where he stood, "you go help that poor soul. Then find a comfortable room for him to recover in while the doctors put him through their exams." Bill then turned to General Hammil. "General Hammel... ?"

General Hammel was sitting in a chair out in the middle of the room. He was staring blankly into space and non responsive. "General Hammel," Bill called out and walked over and put his hand on the General's shoulder. The general looked up with tears in his eyes. As he spoke, his throat was raspy, as if fighting back those tears." Bill, I have seen many things during my career, some have been horrible, some amazing, some unbelievable, but this is the first time I have been scared beyond self-control. I know we could... be dealing with some new technology that can manipulate solid matter and trick the mind, but everything in me tells me what we just saw was the real deal, not earthly technology. That... thing was not from this world, or any world nearby. My worst fear has always been confronting a life form that is much farther up the evolutionary ladder than the human race. This thing threatened to destroy our world as we know it. I do not have a clue how it could be stopped, if this broke bad."

"I do not think that was his true plan, General," I said." He was more interested in getting away from our corner of the universe. I do agree though, that being seemed to have the knowledge and ability to affect our future, at will."

The medical team swarmed in and confusion ensued. Bill looked at Alex and said, "you all right?"

Alex smiled like her old self again and flipped her long black hair over her head. "I have had better days than this, but hey... at least no one screamed, 'Run to the Light'. I just wish I could have gotten one shot off, just one."

Bill smiled at Alex and shook his head. "All right, let's regroup upstairs." He put his hand under General Hammel's arm and we all filed out into the hallway. "I want a physical carried out for each person in that room," he said. Then he leaned close to Alex and said, "Al... can you make sure the guard is doubled and the door to the tech's new room is to be kept locked, at all times. No one in and no one out, accept the medical people. Maybe, let's get the psychologists up here from the deep space conditioning department. I do not think they will have a clue, but just in case... it couldn't hurt... right?"

Alex nodded and headed off.

"Hey, Bill, it is gunna be a few hours before all of this settles down. I am gunna go out for a while to clear my head, OK?"

"Mike... think about it. We do not have any idea if we will see our needy visitor again. If we do, it is a good bet he is gunna be looking for you. Do you really want to be all alone if he finds you? On top of that, I still need an idea of how you ended up in the middle of all of this. Unless you have it written down somewhere, so that I can grab a very cold beer and a comfy chair, to enjoy what I believe is going to be a doosie of a read. If not, then not just No... but hell No!"

"Yea, I figured that was what you were gunna say, so what if I told you I might find some answers to a lot of our questions where only I can find them, but I need some time to put this puzzle together. As far as our homeless friend is concerned, his doorway, portal or whatever, collapsed. He had a hard time keeping it together to begin with. We have some time before we will see him again, if at all."

"For some reason, I do believe you would know," Bill said, "but today, today was big and I believe... life on earth altering. We need to team up and get as solid a handle on this as possible. We also have the military and those other guys, that are going to be all over this. We do not want to interfere with our move. So do not go far. Clear your head...clear... that means no bars, or disappearing acts, right? And Mike, come back ready to talk."

Daniel said, "I don't care where I go but I definitely do not want to be alone. I think I am sticking with Bill!"

Bill just smiled and said, "I don't blame you at all, Daniel." General Hammel smiled and nodded his head in agreement. "I could use a little of that bourbon if you have it handy?"

CHAPTER 37

As I pulled up to the security check point in my car, I knew exactly where I was going. I needed to find a place that balanced me, put me back together, body, mind and soul. I needed counsel. I needed to know who or what the entity was and why he thought I could help him. Finally, I needed to resolve the anxiety over those I cared deeply for, I had to check on my friends. My inner voice whispered, "If you know where you can go… all right," I said out loud. "I have had it with that saying, I get it. At least I know where I want to go. Getting there, well that might be another problem all together."

I was beginning to wind down from the incredible events that had transpired, as the breeze from the open car window cooled my face and soothed the frayed ends of my mind. That was, until I rounded the corner to my grandfather's street. Large trucks lined the thickets across from his house. They were empty, but there were at least three flatbed haulers, two large vans and one service van, with markings I was familiar with from a few years back. I drove slowly toward the house. What confronted me was unexpected and upsetting. The entire front yard was a tangle of roots, sprinkler system pipes and electrical lines. The yard was marked with day glow orange paint, even the trees were marked with it. As I turned along the side street, I could partially see the back of the house, the basement canopy and steps were torn from the ground. Anger enveloped me. This was not the same anger that sprung eternal this morning. This was not fear, or the need to lash out, not yet. This was hurt, deep rooted and invasive. I parked my car and got out. I stumbled over the wreckage of my grandfather's patio. The foundation had been breached and a broken septic line filled a crater with a toxic looking sludge. I heard laughter and I looked over to a small group of equipment operators. Their laughter echoed against jagged cement and tortured soil. The laughter crawled under my skin and into my throat gripping and abrading it. The moment they saw me, they moved to cut off my approach.

"This is a contaminated site, sir. Please leave."

"Leave… Leave…?" I said still confronted by all the damage and the feelings of violation. "Who has done this? Who… who authorized this to be done to this house and property?" One of the men made the mistake of spitting on the ground where the basement stairs began. That caused me to look over at the landing, where all of us as children had made our mark and where one of the keys sites for accessing the portal to my grandfather had been. The cement had been broken, but lay mostly intact. I could see and smell, where someone had used it as a latrine. A younger operator came forward and seeing me stare at the damage and disrespect, began to look me over more closely. The thought flashed through my head at that moment that I might have preferred the entities company, over these cannibals.

"Sir, you have to leave. There are guards that are supposed to be posted at the corners of the property, but they went to get lunch. We are not allowed to let anybody on the owner's property."

I literally spit the next sentence out on to the ground, along with blood from the lip I was biting, to stay my building fury. "Who… is the owner?" I said in a voice much deeper than I usually speak with. I began to gulp air in response to the feeling of drowning in emotion. "The owner of this property did not hire anyone to recklessly destroy his home. You do not have a right to do this!"

A part of my mind caught a glimpse of the glow. The void was forming around new emotions, infiltrating other aspects of my personality, preparing a clear path to punish those who would take, what was not theirs to take. It felt like a disease that once contracted, grew with each exposure and would never relinquish what it had claimed. It felt smarter than me, more aggressive and much more powerful.

I knew I was assuming a menacing aspect, but I wanted it as much, as I was afraid of what might happen. Acknowledging the intensity of the moment, the workmen spaced themselves out. That was when I realized they were military trained. One of the men began stepping back toward his rig. The void was already ahead of me. It recognized one of the new military issue modular hand gun systems, hanging off of a door hinge on one of the machines. His ordinance was sporting an image enhancing scope, that I myself had created. Now I knew these men were not ordinary forces, as that scope was not available for issue and supposedly in trials.

The void called to me, not in words but in whispers and threats, "the weapon, military, experienced user…" then a laugh… "he won't make it." The void began to move with malice to match the intent of the machine operator. Before I could react, big arms wrapped around me from behind and picked me up. At the same time, a familiar voice patronizingly chided me.

"Come on, Mr. Dumass, you are out of your safe area again." The grip lessened a little as I was placed back down on the torn-up sod. The voice spoke to the operators. "Sorry guys, this is Mr. Dumass. The kids call him Mr. Dum Ass because he runs around his yard in the dark naked. Sometimes… only sometimes, he chases cars. He scared the hell out of his neighbor the other night. He ran after her, when she left her house. At some point she realized someone was yelling at her and she slammed on the brakes. Mr. Dum Ass… uh Dumass… naked as a jay bird, smashed into the back of her car and broke the back window. That was Mrs. Simpson…Really nice old lady. She is eighty. I swear I could not tell if she was enjoying the action, or afraid the only naked man around chasing her, was crazy."

Struggling against a strong clasp, I could see the operators begin to laugh. All accept one, the one who had been heading back to his rig for his weapon.

"Hey, let me get this guy back to his caretakers, they are probably worried. Come on Mr. Dumass, time to go home."

"As we moved away from the three, I could hear the serious one saying, "That guy freaked me out. Isn't that what we are supposed to be looking out for, the strange and the odd?"

"He was that," said one of the other operators, "but he was harmless. Running around naked at night… in the streets no less… Haaa Haa."

"Yea, man… If that was my grandmother, she probably would have gotten out, chased him down and beat his crazy ole ass."

"No doubt," responded the young one, then we moved too far for me to hear them any longer.

Relieved that someone had stepped in to stop what I truly felt was going to be a slaughter, I said, "Put me down… I am OK."

"All righty, Mikee old buddy. Who is always saving your butt?"

I spun around to look squarely in the eyes of Officer Chad Bailey.

Chad had been friends with me since childhood and my grandfather had watched out for him, as if he was his own. Chad had been a football star in high school and college and had the talent to go pro. He wanted to major in sports medicine and then become a trainer as a backup, if he did not get drafted. He loved helping people and worked part time as an EMT for the small fire department in the town. His professional aspirations were cut short, when an ambulance he was riding in flipped on a corner racing to a crash scene. His hip was damaged in such a way that the doctors said it would never hold up against the rigors of professional football. So, Chad enlisted in the marines. He served his country with pride, as a medic and with the Military Police. When he was discharged, he went to work for the local police, his uncle being the chief at the time. He was as strong as anyone I knew and as fast as lightning. We used to run into neighbor's yards, ones that had particularly aggressive dogs and see if we could get back out without a scratch. He always did. Me… not so much.

"Chad… How are ya man," I said trying to shake off the intensity. I hugged him, then punched him in the side. He laughed just like a kid and then faked a punch to my gut.

"Naaaa… might collapse a lung on you, Mr. Dumass, or is it really Dum Ass? Haa Haa". I laughed again wiping the residual tears out of my eyes and sucking on my bloody lip.

"Mikey… you are not stupid and those guys are not construction workers. I have been watching them. It is like 10 years ago all over again, accept they seem confident this time. What the hell is going on? I mean, I am sick about it. Paps would have handled them good, but he is not here and I want to hurt those pricks. By the way, if I did not know you better, that was what you had planned. Although, I don't see a gun, or a knife, not even a bunch of bad words all strung together? What were you planning?"

"I do not know, Chad, but I was really angry!"

"I do not blame you, buddy, but these guys are serious business. If your gunna take them out, let me get changed and wait till night. They won't be in such a good mood tomorrow. I need some payback on this one anyway… ya know?"

"No... No ... Paps would kick our butts just as hard, for interfering. He let me know that this might happen. Some big wigs wanted an invention he created, but you know Paps, they are gunna spend the next 100 years searching for it.

"Anyway, Officer, that would not be official or sanctioned business. No need for you to lose your income over it."

"Well, paychecks in my line of work are never satisfying, but paybacks... they always offer a bonus. Ha Ha," he laughed and slapped me on the shoulder.

"Hey, seriously buddy, they are downright dirty about finding the hiding place of that invention. Didn't you say anyone who gets in their way is toast. I had to drag your Dad away a few days ago. He was hot, hot, hot and he put a beating on at least two of the operators. Boy did they underestimate your dad... oowweee. Someone watching, called the department before he got a real head of steam up, otherwise those trolls would be looking for their mommies or... or.. based on those new-fangled shootin irons they got, your dad would be in a body bag. I got there just as he busted that smart ass one up side his head, knocked him straight... and I mean straight, on his ass." Chad was laughing so hard he was gurgling and coughing, his head and shoulders bobbing like a prize fighter. "Once I saw he was kicking some ass, I took my sweet time getting over there, not to mention the guards on duty were coming around the side of the house. Your dad was smiling like he was having a great time, even though he was getting hit by two of them at the same time. Man... was he getting in some good licks though. One at a time, they fell like statues, then got up shook it off and dove back in. I tell ya, I think these guys liked it, too. It took everything in me not to jump in, but after they realized that getting their butts kicked by a tough ole bird was not all that fun, they tazed him. Don't you know, he got up and kept swinging, then they hit him with it again and he stayed down. God! What I would not have given to have had a video camera and a cold beer on hand... ughhh! I could have made a fortune on the web with that video. Although it would have been so good, I might have just kept it in my private collection. Anyway, after those idiots had had their fill, I hauled your Dad off. They probably thought I was bear hugging him to control him, but I was hugging him and jumping up and down, cuz I was so damn proud of him. He is still one tough buck. Of course, I didn't take him in. I told dispatch I was taking him to the ER to be stitched up. We were in stitches all right… down at Mimi's. I took him home after a couple of cold ones, cooled him down. It was great… just sooo great! He was way too angry to stick in a cell anyway, he might have had a heart attack, stressing out in there. I was proud of him though, he did Paps a solid."

I was both angry and laughing, as Chad told me the story. It took a lot to get my dad mad, but once he was there, he was liquid dynamite.

"Anyway, I knew if he showed up you would be close behind", said Chad, "so I have been staking out the place. The captain hates these guys too, so he cut me some slack, hoping I could catch them violating some ordinance off the property. We filed some grievances, but these people are untouchable."

"Thanks, Chad, thanks for everything," I said as I gave him another hug. "I would stay clear of the place for a while. No sense in losing your job over it and these people can make a single call to make that happen."

"Ahh… boyeee … you know me," Chad posed like a football player running with a ball. "Mr. Slick… can't touch this… Ha."

I started laughing and said, "Yep, you're right, Mr. Slick, and let's keep it that way."

"Hey, don't forget my sis's birthday Saturday. She still has that twinkle in the eye, for you, buddy. All in the family… right?" Chad smiled and winked, then got back in his squad car and as he was passing by me he yelled out, "And stop chasing cars… you Dum Ass."

CHAPTER 38

Since using my grandfather's house as a conduit to get back to Alton's village was off the table, I got in my car and straightened myself up. Like a true OCD candidate, I began running through my responsibilities. I had no clue how to get back to Paps, Lea and Lauren. It was important that I did, because I had seen and sensed danger for them. I also had to go back to the facility to try to explain what happened in the morning, no clue on how I was going to handle that one. Then it dawned on me. Where was Alton? Didn't he say...? "Do not worry, whatever happens, we will handle it together"? I reached out to connect to him, but there was nothing there. "Ok... so I guess I am really on my own with this stuff," I grumbled. I started driving in order to distance myself from the wreckage surrounding my grandfather's house. The loud ring from my cell phone startled me out of my thoughts and caused me to jump in my seat. I picked up the call. It was Bill.

"Hey, Mike?"

"Yeah, boss?"

"I cannot stay on the phone long, so listen up. Do not come back here right now."

Wow... there is one problem solved, I sighed. "Why... what is going on?"

"Remember those guys in black and the other creepy ones in gray that Alex was talking about?"

"Yea, the secret, secret service type guys, right?"

"Yep, those are the ones. Well, they are here along with pretty much all their kin. They are asking questions I really do not think you, or I could answer and I don't want anything to get in the way of our departure to the collider, so stay away until this thing cools down."

"Well, aren't they asking for me? I mean I was there and General Hammel knows what happened?"

"Don't worry about the General. He does not like these guys; I get the feeling they are flies in the ointment to him and there is definitely some bad blood between him and this one guy in charge. Alex is not saying a word accept that you were just a scientist present, like Daniel. He got a handle on the situation without being told and he was clear headed enough to misdirect them."

"He is doing what?" I asked.

"He is making a big deal about the drive, so they are focusing on that. For now, it is as if you were only a bystander."

"Great... but what about the video of the interrogation and what happened after? That has to have been recorded."

"Well... it was, but somehow it was not. The videos show the tech guy being brought in for questioning and everything after that looks like one of those spiral hypnotic forms you see on cartoons, along with static, as if there was some major interference in the room. They are questioning the tech guy now, but according to the med techs that examined him when he was transferred, he has no clue what has happened to him over the past few days and no memory of anything that would suggest ... whatever that whole deal was. Anyway, you sure do have some luck, buddy, so use it and stay away."

"Ok... Are you, Alex and the guys going to be OK?"

"Yeah, we are fine. General Hammel is calling someone up the ladder to get these guys out of our hair. But since they are not supposed to exist, I do not think he is going to work it out. Weird thing is, they want to know more about the entity than about the breach in security. Isn't that strange? It is like they already knew about him or others like him. I am just waiting for one of the guys in black to say that they are from Roswell, or area 51... really!" Bill ended in a nervous laugh.

"Bill, did you ever feel like you were the brunt of some twisted joke and almost everyone knew what was happening, but you?" I said.

"Mike... I work with you, that's what every day feels like."

"Ha... Ok... Ok. Text me when you think it is fairly safe for me to return. I want to talk to you about a few things."

"What do you mean you want... there is no want, you have...I say have… to talk to me. You owe me… big, buddy boy."

"Yes, I do. Thanks for the trust and for being my friend, Bill. It means a lot to me".

"Hey… what are old pals for? Now forget about what I said earlier, and disappear."

"OK," is all I said.

CHAPTER 39

As I hung up the phone, I realized that I had to get to a safe place where I could organize and deal with all the needs and demands facing me. My friends needed answers, ones that if given would probably deem me crazy. The authorities needed what I knew, but at any cost it seemed. Their greed and my response to it, fertilized the growth of the void within me. The void needed ownership, expression and development, to fulfill the purpose energy and matter required. I just happened by coincidence, to be the path of least resistance. Well, in my case, probably the path of no resistance. The only exchange for the right of way the void used at its discretion was that it served my ego, my inner will, as if that was currency I had agreed to. The people I loved needed my help, or at least I felt that was the case, but I could not get to them to find out. The entity needed a ride home, but I did not have the vehicle to get him there. Well, maybe I did, but I just did not know how to use it.

My needs on the other hand, did not seem to fit in anywhere. I needed Paps and Alton for guidance and help. I needed to get control over the encroaching void, because after the encounter at my grandfather's house, it was waiting like universal vomit, just short of my throat and primed to explode the next time fear or anger created upheaval. I needed a place to recover from everything that had happened.

I decided that since I was deemed unimportant by the very people I wanted to avoid, I could just go home. I needed to rest badly. I had been up well over 24 hours. I could not shake the feeling that my experience with the void was not supposed to evolve this way. If I was right in understanding the nature of it, the void was a battery. A massive storage of latent, undefined, universal energy, configured in a form that balanced out the universal matter that was being put to use at the moment. Since what was being used was defined, formed and in the process of being something, it possessed an energetic will, or universal purpose that gave it greater density and magnitude. The undefined matter was without form, without energetic potential and unencumbered by definition, time in space and physical universal laws. Since it was the counterbalance and the constant raw source when new matter was needed, it was fast, immediate, unlimited and could take on any form that universal will demanded. The key to it all was that there needed to be a passageway, or converter for the transition to happen. Of course, it made sense. Both matter and its opposite could not exist in the same form, at the same time. It would be like crossing opposing electrical wires. Uncontrolled, unrestricted volumes of energy, transiting through a limited media... BOOM!

A BRIDGE"? Is that what the entity meant? Did he think I was some kind of conduit, a bridge to carry one form of matter through the opposite of matter? As proposed in Star trek movies and thousands of treatises written on matter/antimatter fusion, controlled reaction between states of matter could fuel almost infinite power sources, like Pulsars, the center of galaxies, or... individual portals? Ok... If I was a bridge, where was the entity hoping I could take him? Home? That could not be a bad thing, could it? I wanted to go home right now. Why should helping him get home be a bad thing? Maybe he would be happy, then not be so thoroughly ominous and creepy at the same time.

No... No... I have no way to know what I am doing here! That... thing, would chew me up and spit me out. He could care less what helping him would do to me or maybe my world. That might be the cost of providing a bridge, the energy to get him to wherever.

The void had adopted me and now it had plans to change who and what I was. I could feel the initiative of it, the scheme. It was not evil, just power needing a conduit, but it reacted with sentience. It had a genetic code formed eons ago. Like a dog driven to seek out a scent, or a match driven to burn once lit. The unlimited nature of the void, was going to have no problem usurping the very limited nature of my humanity unless I had some help. On the other hand, once the amalgamation was complete, maybe I would be something better than I am now. Maybe it was only the inertia of the takeover that had me scared out of ... well. out of myself. One thing I knew for sure, I

217

was becoming more familiar with the void, or it with me. Any prodding with the wrong stick and someone was gunna get a lot more than they bargained for.

Occupied with inner dialog, in a state of exhaustion, the void slipped in to establish a stronger connection. A picture show began to play before my vision, almost blocking out the road. An empty parking lot at a lawyer's office, offered a safe place to stop the car. I parked and rubbed my eyes, trying to get at the irritation that was behind them. In my mind's eye, I could see my apartment building. There was a figure outside and another two moving around inside my apartment. They were dressed in black. Their personalities were dark and slippery. Their intent was specific. The vision began to clear up, as if filtered through stronger light. That light, was the convergence of the void and my physical mind. My vision was now a balance of both the internal and external. I could see clearly and sharply in both realms.

The wind was picking up outside the car and the bushes were shaking under the load. The void was picking up inside me and I was shaking under that load. I observed one of the men pick up the shirt I had worn while in the village, the drool still hard on the collar. A small meter, or resonator, in his hand began to glow and squeal. Anxiety, intensified by what I was seeing and sensing, enriched the void which created a sensation of drowning. The men in black took the shirt and put it in a bag.

"Now they are taking my stuff", I yelled out loud. "Those motha…!" Like a large stone thrown into water, the void responded with an intense eruption. It rose upward past my senses and out of my immediate awareness. At the same time in my apartment, the lights flickered and a half open window slammed shut, just as one of the men leaned out to inspect the fire escape. The window caught the back of his head, shoulder and arm breaking the window pane and knocking him to the ground. He yelled out. The meter in the man's hand flew on to the grate outside the window, squealing loudly, needle spiking. The instrument sparked and fizzled while smoke rose out of it. The other man turned swiftly to the window in response, but there was nothing there. As he turned back, I saw that he was holstering a weapon under his coat. They spoke quickly to each other, then moved toward the door. I could see around my apartment and whatever they had touched, had a residue, a dull red glow.

My vision was drawn down to the street, to a van occupied by men in gray suits. I knew that van. I had seen it before at my grandfather's house. Inside the van, there was complicated sensing equipment. What the heck are they looking for, I thought?

I started the car and headed toward my apartment. The ability to see the outside world, at the same time I saw the inside world, had become easier to coordinate. In one world, I was driving my car. It was familiar and very tangible. In the other world, my attention was occupied by the void, just as tangible and physical to me as the car I was driving. In one world, I had a strong grip on the steering wheel. I was in control of where, how and when I reached my destination. In the other, I could not find the steering wheel and I had no idea where I was going to end up.

I stopped at a light and watched a mother with a stroller chasing her other children across the street. They were hurrying to get home. In my line of site was a building and a stoop outside. It was so similar to the one outside my own apartment that for a second, the two images converged.

Outside my apartment, a man stood fiddling with the mailboxes on the wall, again violating my privacy, exploring where he did not belong. I could hear the steering wheel vinyl crackle under my grip. The sound of someone pushing on their horn brought me back just in time to see the light I was sitting at go from green to yellow. Anger had drawn me much deeper into the vision, upsetting the delicate balance a mind must maintain to function in the moment. Drivers behind me, desperate to avoid delays, were understandably frustrated at missing the light. I ran it and accelerated away quickly. I felt a little guilty over those left stranded.

Upon arriving in my neighborhood, I decided to park a block down from my apartment building and use the darkness of night to see if the invaders had left. I knew it was probably not safe to go too close, but frustration and anger pushed me on. Within a short time, I recognized one of the men that had been inside my apartment, walk casually down my steps, turn and move away. The careless manner with which these men had invaded my home and violated my personal space spawned in me a malicious anger. The combined intentions, generated waves of purpose. I could sense it testing the limits of whatever was left of my self-control. I instinctively knew that if I resisted this convergence of power, I would lose. I would drown in the deluge of energy now substantiated by my inner need. Oddly, I could sense that the power rising in me was aware of the repercussions of a reckless approach. It did not want to destroy the bridge it needed to achieve its goal. Insight filled my mind. The void was not separate. It was now part of me. What happened to me, mind, body, and soul mattered. It impacted what might happen next, for the both of us.

"Holeeee sh.." I breathed out heavily. In the end, this is about me. I am the nucleus. Without me there is no void, there is no bridge from there to here. Without sound mind and body, the void would have nothing. It was only if both worlds burned with purpose that anything could happen. I gave it purpose. My anger at the moment, my emotions had created the opportunity. I had forgotten the lesson I learned in my first experience with Alton. Where there is nothing, where there is nothing...? I was the seed, the something. Like the figure in my dream, I had gazed into the waters of the universal and found my freedom. Only fear could limit me now. I took a deep breath and released my will, into the abyss.

To my surprise, instead of drowning in the conversion, the untamed power lifted me back to the surface of a molten river of potential. Every part of me, every cell was being consumed and replenished in the exchange.

I could feel the power and the intelligence of it, move enthusiastically outward. The power was not of my creation, but it was fed by my desire and my desire was not benevolent. My mind felt sharp and clean, yet it was separate from the will or drive of the void. I thought, could I really hurt others? No... I told myself. This energy containing such intensity and potential was a subjective experience, carrying little physical potential. I could not be a real threat. It might push people around or knock things over, but I am not a killer. I tried to change my thought pattern, to calm down, to let go of the desire to punish those who lacked respect and violated my home and life. Yet, with each wave of the void, the thickness and density of it multiplied. It was clear that I was becoming more of a spectator with every passing minute. Had I flamed sparks into a fire I could not contain? I felt the need to pray, to ask for divine intervention, as the void, the dark matter, geometrically expanded and transformed.

The air in my car began crackling. The energy was fully transitioning into physical time and space. I accepted that I was not going to be able to stop it, but hopeful I could limit it. I was sick to my stomach, yet oddly elated. Could this have been what Alton meant? Once the door was opened? I thought he was speaking metaphorically, perceptually, internally. I did not think he was talking about manifestation, about creating and directing energy. I could feel my will being modified, becoming giddy with potential and the expectation of dealing out some well-deserved justice. I began to yearn to release the amalgam, the stream of antimatter converted into a real-world effect, on those who used and abused power. Those who would violate the innocent nature of others. With that last self-righteous indulgence, control crumbled and a flare exploded upward from my chest and soared past my vision. My head flung back onto the head rest as the energy demanded room. The flare hung in the air above the car. Too late to safely return, it was like a dog, panting anxiously, poised for a stick to be thrown.

Except, this was no game of 'go fetch'. This animal had awareness and a thought process, a reasoning ability that elevated it far beyond performing simple tasks. It could decide its own fate, one tethered and connected to my purpose and my satisfaction. It focused on the men in black, and the men in the van, as it waited for a command. I was no longer fighting against the void; I was fighting against myself.

The two teams of men had unified their efforts. Their instrumentation had sprung alive, the needles were spiking, speaker squealing and lights blazing. The men in black were being directed to walk back toward my apartment. No, they had passed my apartment and were headed toward me.

In the van, the occupants were working feverishly turning knobs and adjusting instrumentation. On the street, two men were crouching over their instrument as they moved. The third was on the opposite side of the street, eyes wide, knees bent, muscles taught. I am not sure whether he was prepared to attack or run for his life.

Another vision solidified before me. The shirt from my apartment, covered in red residue, hung out of a bag being carried by one of the men. That was the last straw. Anger and violence erupted in me and the wave of energy jetted away, like a bullet released from a gun. It rolled towards the men in black as a silent, but deadly tidal wave. A man in a grey suit opened the back door of the van, stood up and waved a probe of some sort in the air, following the path of the wave. A second wave formed and launched into this world like a ballistic missile, headed on its own path, the van. It was different from the first, not as malevolent, but with a power to punish.

From my vantage point, all things followed in slow motion. Although in the outside world, everything happened swiftly and deliberately. The first wave caught up to the men in black as they were working their way methodically down the street. I watched with uncertainty, questioning again whether there would be any serious repercussions, but I was sure they would be impacted somehow. Although a vision of molten energy was clear to my sight, the outline of the wave was only apparent through the meters the men held, dust raised from the street and pieces of paper that were caught in its vortex. One of the men, standing across the street watched as dust and paper moved rapidly toward his partners. He yelled, just as the wave hit its first mark. It caught the man in black around his knees and buckled him like a weak beam. His head hit the concrete with a pop. The meter in his hand splintered upon hitting the hard surface with such force and exploded as the energy raced through its circuitry. As the wave passed the fallen man, I saw blood flowing out from under his head. It matched the red residue emanating from the destroyed meter. My mind took pause at the brutality of the assault. How the energy had sought him out, tracked him like prey. The color of the blood seemed to please some part of me. I felt sorrow at my pleasure.

The second wave was just approaching the van. It caught the open door and slammed it on the man's torso, forcing him back inside the van. His glasses flew through the air, but did not hit the ground, instead they were carried forward by the pulse. The van was rammed sideways against the curb and over on to its side. With a scraping and crashing sound, it continued across the side walk until it fell partially into the opening of a basement stairwell, which crushed the railing and shattered glass. Inside the van, one of the men held on to the console while his feet flew out horizontally. The console broke free and he slammed into the far wall with bone breaking force. His head bounced off the frame of the van and he rolled on to his side tangled in wires, unconscious. The third man in the van had been moving into the driver's seat, apparently hoping to move the van before the wave collided with them. He was crouched with knees bent, stretching one leg into the cockpit, as the van was impacted.

The force sent him through the side window which had been half way open and glass sprayed out on to the street. As the van rolled over, he was thrown back in and across the passenger seat, where the basement railing had forced its way through the sheet metal. The interior of the van was silent, no sign of life emanated from it. The two waves, like packs of wild dog's intent on more blood, combined to focus on the remaining prey. As it hit the man who had tried to warn the others, the energy softened, interacting, choosing, as it flowed forward. With this man, it sensed no aggression, or mal-intent. He was of a kind disposition and not driven by the same agenda as the others. He was a loving father, a teacher of physics and a researcher on this clandestine team. The wave forced him down on the concrete, but without injury. It hung above him and the man rolled over on his back and put his hands up in defense. I could see the meter he held, turn red and he flung it away as it exploded. I could feel the intensity of the wave bearing down on him with authority. The animal in it breathing heavily upon him, asserting dominance and confirming its reality and its warning. The same could not be said about the outcome for the third man on the street. He had begun to run, based on what he had seen as his partners were hit. The wave moved off the grounded man, and moved directly toward its final target. I again noticed how the energy was not blind. It did not damage anything in its path. It did, however, have a purpose. That purpose was about to be employed. Just before the wave caught up to the man, I noticed another figure, tall and slightly hidden in a stairwell, his attention focused on the progression of the wave. I could see no measuring device or meter, but where he stood was dark. I could see a portion of his head moving as if following the energy wave. Could he see it?

The wave connected with the last man and he let out a short scream, which pulled my attention back to the unfolding event. For some reason the energy saw him as the leader, the controller, with a passion for aggression and cruelty. He suffered no concern for others, as he set about performing his responsibilities. It seemed that the energy took satisfaction here. The man was lifted off his feet. He was flipped upside down and hung that way as he was carried forward with the wave. Again, I was sure that he, like the others, were not totally surprised with the energy. Although I knew that was not going to help him with the outcome.

The second story of the building on the corner, which stood directly in the path of the wave, was a seamstress shop. In the windows were mannequins in various stages of dress. I watched in amazement as the man was flipped sideways and head first, then slammed through the window of the shop. I could see him impact the dummies standing in his path. Oddly, they all had their arms out in poses that suggested they were ready to catch him. Unfortunately, the mannequins provided no solace, as the man landed in a tangle of arms, legs and torsos, some unfortunately positioned. The man was out cold. I could feel the wave complete its forward momentum and collapse in on itself, dissipating like mist or fog after a rain storm.

The void went neutral and I snapped back into my surrounding environment. I hung my head on my chest. I wanted to feel bad. I wanted to convince myself that I had little choice in what just happened, or that this was all just a crazy delusion. I sat there caught in an intellectual and emotional nexus, giddy with power, while tremendously saddened by the violence obviously latent within me. I was forced to accept the reality and the responsibility of what had happened. How does one control such power and potential? How was I any better than those attacked?

I slammed my hand against the steering wheel repeatedly, yelling "WHY?" Alton's warning rang true in my mind, "For Good or Bad, once the doorway is open, there is no closing it." I had taken power for my own agenda and employed it to punish those who had misused theirs. I could sense my thoughts sailing over the void, causing ripples across its surface. Had I opened Pandora's Box? It seemed strange to be afraid of the unknown, when it was clear the unknown was me.

Alton was the only one that could answer questions that were forming now in my mind, or maybe Kayla, or Paps, but they were not here and I was alone. A well-known philosopher's warning echoed in my head. "What we create, what we set to plan, must be given the opportunity to overcome that which stands in its way. Only the truly committed can remain in pursuit, for the first barrier to overcome is ourselves." Was I the true challenger, the true enemy here? If I had not allowed my feelings to fuel the void, could I have found a better path for dealing with the men in black? How have I exposed myself and those I care about, by exacting my own justice?

I could feel emotions inside me screaming out... bullshit! A just punishment for those who know better, but do not care. A final quote from the philosopher lingered, "To live embedded in illusion is our natural human condition and each day we confirm that state of being, by allowing desire to recreate illusion in pursuit of our need." I needed to find value in what was happening so that "I" was in control. I held the power, the dominance. So maybe the question should be "Do I have the right?"

My thoughts drifted to the one man the power did not hurt. I had sensed his kindness. The wave had passed him by virtually unharmed. I was responsible all right. The collaboration with the wave had justified forgiveness for some and exacted penalty upon others. Whether it was my will, or uncontrolled desire transferred into will, the responsibility landed with me. For without me, none of this would have happened. "No way to escape the logic," I said to myself, just above a whisper.

The one man the energy left unharmed, lay shaking on the pavement in shock. I got out of my car and started toward the man to help him, just as the void resonated oddly. There was another energy, or person, although not human, but similar and very near. I reached out, curious, just as the strange energy touched me. The void repulsed it immediately, with snake like precision, striking out against a predator. The opposing energy recoiled and withdrew. A lone figure at the far end of the block, stepped out into the night exposed by street lights. The figure very purposely stood his ground and stared in my direction. Like two gun fighters in the Wild West, we faced off at a distance too great to initiate any fight, but I could feel his energy. It was not energy from the void, but powerful all the same. It possessed influence over the dimensions on this side of matter. It was metaphysical, similar to Alton's energy, but more visceral, primitive and therefore, unpredictable. His energy yearned for the void and what it could offer. I expected him to move forward, to attack in some manner, but he seemed confused, uncertain about his chances, or timing. Figuring that I had nothing to lose at this point and no one to turn to for answers, I began to walk forward slowly. What was the worst that could happen? I had created this mess and a little more mess was not going to change what had already happened.

Sirens off in the distance indicated that someone had called for backup. The figure crouched in response and turned as if to leave. I began to run toward him to try and stop him from escaping. I had no idea what I was going to say or do, but I increased my speed so as not to think too much about it. I reached out more significantly with my mind, hoping to grasp some information that would help me when we confronted each other. Something familiar, some recognition of the energy emanating from the figure impacted me. I stopped in my tracks. How could I be familiar with this person?

A fortified military vehicle came around the corner, accompanied by two local police cars. At the other intersection two dark SUVs screeched to stop. A dust cloud spinning wildly came out of nowhere and the figure leapt into it. Too late, I realized, it was no dust cloud at all.

The men in the SUV jumped out of the car and pulled close quarter machine guns from underneath their jackets. Two of them ran to the van teetering on the basement stairwell. I was just far enough into the shadows that I could not be seen by them. I could hear the blades of an approaching helicopter chopping away at the air. They would have night vision capabilities and I would stand out like a sore thumb. Time to leave I thought. I crouched down and ran back to my car. Once in my car, I could see the flood lights from the chopper lighting up the block. I started my car and pulled out of my parking space. There were only two cars on the street. I pulled out behind one loaded with a group of teenagers, laughing and singing to songs on the radio. They stopped in the middle of the road and let one of the passengers out. A few beer cans rolled out of the car. I was in a hurry so I went around, a few unkind words from them ushering me on my way. I turned the corner just in time. In my rear-view mirror, I saw two police cars screech to a halt angling across the intersection, blocking traffic from progressing any further. One black SUV and an army jeep came from the other direction. As I pulled away, the look on the teenager's faces as they were pulled from the car was priceless.

CHAPTER 40

I drove for a while, with the moon barely visible on the horizon, casting its last light across the road in front of me. I needed time to think and the darkness seemed to help. I pulled off the road into a turnaround and parked. I lay the seat back and took some deep breaths hoping to clear images of earlier in the night from my troubled mind. After a few minutes, I slipped off into a light sleep. It was filled with impressions of the entity at the laboratory and then the shadowy figure, possessing a dark and formidable energy. An impression of Lauren sitting on the ground, tears desperately washing fury and hopelessness from reddened eyes, caused me to bolt upright. I wiped sweat from my forehead, feeling claustrophobic and climbed out of the car. I checked my watch; it was almost dawn. I locked my car and began walking. I knew it would not separate me from my thoughts, but I hoped it would grant me some distance from them.

The air was crisp, but not cold. It was moist and smelled luxuriously potent, charged and staged to orchestrate new life. It was time for spring to start its healing process. I took deep breaths and full strides as I walked forcefully, demanding to share in its agenda. After a while, the sky began to lighten, hinting of the new day to come. Unfortunately, the effort I made to unify my hopes and intentions with it, only increased my feelings of being out of sync and far behind the schedule of a changing world. How could I step into a new day, a new me, a new life, if I did not know what baggage I might carry into it?

I shook those thoughts out of my head, combed my fingers through my hair and inhaled deeply again. Feeling stronger for facing a dark road, I took stock of where I had ended up. Clumps of sand ahead, indicated that I had to be close to the beach.

Still drowning in inner dialogue, I stepped off the pavement, climbed a small rise and out of fatigue and frustration, sat down. I put my head in my hands and began to consider the immense amount of change that had occurred in my life in the past few months. It was clear that my life would never function simply in just one world… ever again. I rubbed my face hard with my hands, melancholy sweeping over me. I stayed in that position for a long time in contemplation. I came to terms with how steep and multi-dimensional my learning curve might be. Well… at least I was entitled to one, I thought. Mastering this world, in this lifetime, was far from a certainty for most people, but mastering multiple worlds in one lifetime…" I dunno about that," I spoke out loud to myself.

I began to pray for a new chance to prove myself, prove I was worthy of the gifts recently given to me. I could learn to be a better being? I had to laugh at leaving the word "human" out of that sentence. Where do I belong now?

I raised my head and hands to the sky and as I opened my eyes, I saw the sun climbing out of the ocean, surrounded by soft pink and orange clouds. The brightly colored clouds hung like fluffy towels on the dawn, prepared to dry the sun as it rose from its overnight sojourn in a vast sea. Glistening waves added dazzle to a pristine turquoise sky and I felt the rays of light and heat flow up my chest and warm my cheeks. At least symbolically, I felt my wish had been granted.

The familiar shoreline I had traversed throughout the year stretched out before me. I pondered how I had not heard the roar of the waves, or felt the buffeting wind. Funny I thought as I glanced around me, that I should have wandered back to the very same beach where I first met Alton. The very same group of bluffs I had climbed and the very same salty breeze rushing across the sand.

Another omen, I questioned? Had my 'Second Chance' arrived on the rays of the new day's dawn?

"Maybe" … came an answer from a very weary inner awareness. Omens are the harbingers of opportunity, preparing the way for action.

I felt like I needed to be washed, or possibly cleansed in order to respectfully accept this gift, this reprieve. I watched as the wind gathered the mist, climbing to freedom above the crashing waves, then flying free over the sand and beyond. That will do, I thought as I stood up. I plotted a course back to the beachhead without sidetracking to the parking lot, which had been just over an adjacent dune. Then on to the water's edge. As I angled across the beach, I noticed a figure off in the distance. I continued to walk, aiming toward the surf and spotted movement around what I could now see, was a person sitting in the sand. Another figure was just barely visible behind the dune the person was sitting on. Tripping over a piece of driftwood, as I continued to angle closer to the water, I couldn't shake the feeling that there was something familiar about them. As the distance between us decreased, it looked as if the person sitting was female. Her head buried deeply in crossed arms, which were wrapped tightly around her knees. Her long hair sailed high on the breeze. An animal, still half eclipsed behind a rise in the sand next to where the woman was sitting, moved gracefully back and forth as if smelling the air. Again, something about the scene seemed familiar, but wrong or out of scale. The scientist in me won the moment and after a few steps, I stopped and really focused on them. As I concentrated, I began to hear voices, but the crash of the waves scattered both thought and sound, nothing was clear. After another moment of strained focus, I was able to separate some of the sounds and realized they were not vocal. The sounds originated from a telepathic level and ended up to clearly be my name. My inner voice responded to the call, before my outer person could grasp why. The animal in the distance froze. The sitting woman raised her head and began looking around. The animal began a slow trot toward me, its pace increased until it was at a full out run. Having moved beyond the rise in the sand, the animal was fully visible and seemed massive. The female stood up and began to run toward me as well. If the woman was running after the animal and presumed to catch and gain some control over it, she was simply not going to make it in time to protect me. I needed to make a run for it, so I headed back the way I had come, to escape. Time stood still.

Conceding my plight, I spun around to throw up my arms in a pathetic defense, while the force of the impact threw me back at least 3 feet. I hit the sand, sliding on my back, my belt acting as bulldozer, my underwear the bucket securing a load of cool damp sand to hold me in place. As I coughed and spit sand, I wondered why I was not feeling pain from the teeth and claws that were bound to be stripping my flesh. Everything in me was screaming… crawl, run, escape, but a significant weight pressing down on my chest seemed content in keeping me just where I was. Suddenly, Lea's presence flooded my mind. I looked up to get my bearings and above me, with a front paw on my chest, stood Lea. She looked at me as if to say, it is me ... "you bonehead". Then came the famous taste test. Her tongue reached my cheek and began covering pretty much all the rest of my face. Her massive paw made sure I did not move. All I could think of was, "of course it is!" How could I not have recognized her? All the signs were there.

Once I accepted that it was really her, I was so happy. I felt immediately relieved that she was ok. I tried to wrap my arms around her lowered head and express my happiness, but Lea blasted free of my grip. She ran around and around me with lightning speed, her body in the angle of a dragster hitting the green light. Her race of exuberance displaced enough sand to bury me. Amongst gulps of laughter, I had just enough time to regroup. She stopped and licked the back of my head and neck again. This she did just to torture me, she knew I hated that. She rubbed her nose and shoulders on me, as if she were trying to rub her affection off on me. She pushed her head underneath my chest. With a simple flick of her head, I was a somersault in motion, landing in a heap and with a thud on the sand a few feet from my last position. Then she ran over to me and sat beside me, leveraging her weight against my body.

"Ok... Ok," I said, still spitting sand. "I got it. I won't go anywhere, just give me a moment." She looked at me as if she was about to pounce again, then she looked in the direction of her companion. I looked back at the mess we made in the sand, all except for where I had been laying. Embedded a foot or so into the sand was the perfect outline of my body. I thought how funny, no snow here but that is just about the best snow angel I have ever made. Even down to the smooth sculpted curve from the apex of my lower back and buttocks. Lea stood up to locate her partner, which I hoped was Lauren. I followed her gaze. With a crimson glow back lighting her flowing hair, I watched Lauren take her last few steps then collapse on top of me. The impact forced whatever oxygen I had saved back out of my lungs.

At first, I thought she was happy to see me, but as I struggled to get out from underneath her weight, I realized what I felt was fear, hurt and anger engulfing her. I shook the sand off my hands and pulled her face toward me. She was sobbing heavily. I immediately reached out to her mind. The connection was automatic and like with

Alton, it seemed almost effortless.

Unfortunately, what I saw did not make sense. I saw that Luka was gone ... no... no, he had been taken, but I could not see by whom? Who could take an animal like Luka against his will? I noticed that Lea had been hurt. Knowing her... that injury would not limit her, the true harm was to her pride. I saw the village with damage here and there, but normalcy was returning. I could not see Kayla, Alton, or Paps anywhere. I wrapped my arms around Lauren and consoled her, allowing her to calm down and recover. Her size made such an embrace cumbersome.

Lauren, like Lea, had grown considerably. Even in our telepathic connection she seemed less like a child and more like an adult. I again allowed my mind to partner with hers, while concentrating on soothing her and comforting her. I saw the village trying to pick up the pieces from some kind of calamity ... no... the damage was more purposeful than that, it was more of an attack. As I sat there rocking Lauren back and forth, I caught a more finite glimpse of her pain and what had caused it.

First, Luka had definitely been taken. I could see the beings, or creatures that had taken him. They were about the same size as Lauren's race, but lacked the precision of form and refined features that Lauren's people did. They were maybe, a slightly different version of early Neanderthal man. Their heads were very large, even for the incredible size of their bodies. The forehead jutted out far past the jaw, which was filled with more teeth than seemed possible. Black course hair covered most of their exposed flesh. I tried to see more clearly into their thoughts, or purpose, yet their minds seemed infantile. The village looked like it was caught in some form of stampede, rather than a planned attack. Yet, there was a purpose driving these creatures. They had been set on a path by another force. They were frightened of failure, of disappointing whoever controlled them. Why had they come here? What was their purpose?

The villagers were clearly taken by surprise, as if these invaders were unfamiliar to them and not from the same world. They seemed to take care not to hurt the invaders unless necessary and were more interested in controlling the chaos and any resulting damage. A few of the villagers had gained composure, joined together and unified their power into one force. They focused that joint initiative on the invaders. The scene was surreal. It was as if they were herding a bunch of wild animals or crazed school children. Heading them off here, challenging them over there, driving them back to where they came from. That is when I saw the portal. It was wide by comparison to what I had already experienced. The outline was finely formed and held together precisely. That meant a powerful energy kept the portal rigid and stable. Through it, I could see another world, one of stone and fire, volcanic. It was a wild world, stark in comparison to the world they now invaded. There was some vegetation visible, but it was in a tangle, like a jungle, not at all cultivated. It also seemed obvious that these creatures were not capable of achieving travel through a time/space portal on their own.

The invading horde finally cornered began to huddle down. It was certain they were already familiar with this process.

My attention was drawn to a larger building away from the melee. Behind the larger structure, I could see another group coming. These beings were even larger than the others. Their muscle structure was far more complex; they were frightening. They moved like soldiers, a squad in unison. They embodied aggression and destruction followed in their path. They struck an older woman with what looked like a large bone at the end of a beam of wood. The sound that resonated from that contact was sickening. The invading soldier placed his foot on the prone woman and pried the weapon from her skull. The villagers were not prepared for this threat. They immediately split into two groups. One group, remained in control of the horde, the other group seemed to prepare for a different type of defense. The second group formed a wedge and began generating energy from the focal point of that wedge. The energy was dense and massive. The villagers projected the force outward. Like bowling pins being struck with precise measure, the invading soldiers were tossed quite far into the air and scattered. Where the pinnacle of the force met the invading soldiers, whole bodies became parts. It was clear the villagers had no other choice. The attack was swift and intended to be decisive.

Two of the invading behemoths from the main group diverted from the confrontation and entered a large central building from a side entrance. As they entered the structure, my vision changed to the inside of what looked like a sanctuary. There in the corner I saw Lauren. By her side and in front of her, standing guard, were Lea and Luka. As the two invaders entered, they began smashing whatever was within reach. The taller of the two saw Lauren and headed directly for her. That was all that was necessary for Luka to go on the attack. In one movement he leapt the entire room and landed on the approaching invader. His teeth crunched bone and the attacker's weapon fell to the ground, along with an arm. The second man hearing his comrade scream, leapt into the air and came down with his sledge aimed at Luka's head. Luka, sensing the movement, ducked away from the brunt of the impact but it caught him just behind the ear and glanced off. Luka fell to the ground unconscious. The rage this triggered in Lea was terrifying to watch. She left her feet by Lauren's side and landed with the severed head of the standing invader in between her teeth. She then turned her jaws upon the downed invader. His life ended within seconds.

The remaining invading soldiers had regrouped outside and as Lea stood above Luka smelling his wound, one of them entered through an entrance behind her. Lea, sensing his approach, spun toward him, but hesitated for a split second, uncertain whether to go to Lauren's side or protect Luka. His reaction was fierce and brutal. His club careened across her thigh, the force of the blow lifted her off her feet slamming her against the wall. She struggled to get up but could not.

The invader turned and headed toward Lauren. Upon reaching her, he grabbed her hair savagely, yanking her upward and off her feet. He held her face to face, starring into her eyes and grunting with a sadistic laugh, a laugh that conveyed unwelcome future experiences. He turned, planning to leave the building with Lauren. It was not until the arm holding her in the air landed on the ground beside him that he realized he was not going to be leaving… ever! Luka leapt a second time. His arc carried him above and to the sheered arm side, of the invader.

Watching the wolf sail above his head, he had to have felt the razor-sharp teeth plunge through his skull creating a horrible crunching sound. Luka's momentum carried him past the invader, with the top section of his head clinched tightly in his jaw. With the top of the soldier's skull removed, he fell to his knees, mouth moving and eyes open wide, what was left of his brain still considering what had just happened. Luka walked past the knelt invader dropping the removed parts in clear view, so as to offer the soldier something familiar to look at as he left an unfamiliar world. He walked around Lauren a few times and they both watched as balance departed what was left of the soldier at the same time his life did. Luka's eyes gleamed with a definite satisfaction, the engine of his origins at full throttle inside him. He nudged Lauren to her feet. Once Lauren was standing, he stroked her hand with his nose, then he went over to Lea and smelled her body. He nudged her as well, but she did not move. From outside the building he could hear the grunts and growls of other soldiers. Luka turned to face the sounds. He was in the mood for some payback, but Lauren had to be his priority. He immediately herded Lauren to an exit, farthest from the noise. As they both edged past the doorway, there was a whishing sound. Luka forced Lauren back into the building with his body, just as a net covered him over. Three invaders grabbed the net, one swung his club and Luka fell to the ground unconscious again.

The villagers had herded the main group of childlike invaders back through the portal. Some of them did not want to go. They looked through the portal and saw a threat much greater on that side than where they were now. Although it was tough to differentiate, closer looks at the hoard revealed females amongst the males, even some children. They did not display aggression like the brutal soldiers. Instead they exhibited a crazed enthusiasm as if they had been set free.

The more powerful men of the village rounded up the soldiers and drove them back toward the portal as well. They were not using weapons of any kind, but I could feel their minds focusing energy to a very finite point, like the beam of an invisible laser. The intensity of the energy was causing blood to pour from the closest of the soldier's ears and noses the more they resisted. One invader dropped and his head simply collapsed in on itself, as if it had been filled with air and sprung a leak. Another was staggering but still on his feet. The villagers were not trying to kill the soldiers, but as the soldiers resisted, they created their own fate. The villagers were focusing on three invaders that held the net and Luka. The soldier that was already staggering fell, with more than blood emptying on to the ground from a flattened skull. There were not many invading soldiers left. Those that were left, were blocked from the portal while they held Luka prisoner. They kept trying to edge closer with each move, hoping for a chance to escape with their catch. Another invader fell, nothing left on his shoulders but the hair that was on his scalp.

I could tell the villagers were still holding back, making every effort in show rather than taking final action. The focused energy that was eviscerating the invaders had diminished, but only to give them time to rethink their plan and release Luka. A tall villager that resembled Alton, stepped out from the rest. He reached out his arms and with impressive telekinetic force, yanked what seemed to be the leader of the remaining invaders to the ground. With a pain driven cry from their leader, the others released the net and Luka's unconscious body flopped against the ornate stone just before the portal. The soldiers had given in to a power much greater than their own brute size and force.

Just as it seemed the villagers had succeeded, an explosive wave of energy blasted outward from the portal knocking down everyone in its wake including, the remaining standing soldiers. Out of the portal came a being that looked very much like the villagers, or like Alton. He was clean and refined. His skin was bronzed. His hair golden. He looked like a Greek god but he was dressed and walked like a battle-hardened soldier. He was herculean in musculature and there was an unmistakable magnetism surrounding him. He hunched over defensively, like a prowling lion. He was beautiful and at the same time, terrible to look at. His eyes glowed with evil intention, which was in complete opposition to the kindness and harmonic balance visible in the villagers. He kicked the frightened soldiers and grabbed the net. It was as if he was collecting his dogs as they cowered before him. He threw the net to them, Luka's limp body still flopping around inside. The golden giant ordered his soldiers into the portal and then started backing through, his eyes vigilante and hopeful for a response to his attack. There was no response. The villagers were on the ground dazed and the one villager who had stood alone from the rest, was in a tangled mess with a gash in his side and thigh. As the leader of the invaders spun and walked triumphantly back through the portal, he stopped. He looked over his shoulder as if sensing something more. He stood motionless for a moment and then as if deciding to add insult to injury, he turned completely and took a step back toward the village staring specifically at Lauren. An uncanny feeling swept over me, as if a light from a flashlight had exposed me in a hidden alcove of her mind. It was not Lauren he perceived or focused on. He was looking past her, somehow to me. He sneered and laughed with contempt. I could feel my skin crawl. He spoke with a menacing tone, "Come to me, I will teach you what others dare not."

My mind raced. How is that possible, he has never seen me? I was not here when this happened? Could he see the future, see me connected to Lauren's mind now, or back then? I was confused and more than a little intimidated. The portal closed like the slamming of a door. Then there was a shudder as if something in the mechanics of the portal had been shattered, or broken. I did not know how I knew that; I just did.

CHAPTER 41

In response to the invader's threat, the void went volcanic. I struggled to quell the eruption. Lauren pulled at my arm and even though I looked her in the eyes, my focus was still internal, my mind battling for self-control. She looked at me as if searching for a lost soul. She spoke, but also communicated with her mind to hold me in focus.

We need to help Luka. Will you help us?

I tried to formulate an answer for her, but I could not. Why would they be asking me… for help? From where I stood, I could not even help myself.

It dawned on me that the person that could offer the best help was Alton. I needed Alton now more than ever. My first experience with the void was sink or swim. My last experience put others in real danger and nurtured an aggressive side of me I did not even know existed. If I tried to help and ended up somehow hurting the ones I loved, I would never forgive myself. If I failed them, I might end up leaving Lea, Luka and Lauren at the mercilessness of a being that epitomized evil intent.

Forgetting the connection between minds for a minute, I asked out loud, "Where is Alton, or Kayla and is Paps ok?"

Lauren responded almost before the words left my mouth, "They are far away." Lea let out a small anxious yowl then lay all the way down and began licking a large lump on her thigh. I knew she was in greater emotional pain, than physical and I desperately wanted to make a difference. I scooted closer to Lea, pulling Lauren with me. I put my hand on Lea's leg and reached into her mind.

I asked very gently, "Do we at least know where to find Luka?"

She responded in thought with, "He is my brother; I could find him anywhere in the universe." Her sadness overflowed onto my emotions and my heart wrenched, tears began to form. She dropped her head, laying it across her paws and nuzzling my forearm.

I could feel the void seeking outward, plotting to exercise its right to protect and preserve. As a mother giving birth might bear down through the last throws of childbirth, I could feel the void bearing down on me. Only it was giving birth to emotion and ego, creating the belief that I could overcome this threat, neutralize it and bring Luka home. I resisted, resolved to stop a birth of power ignited by emotion, which I in truth could not direct and could not control. Dried blood on the hair behind Lea's whiskers and the memory of the blood-stained sidewalk outside my apartment bore witness to what a combination of rage and power could accomplish.

Lea looked up at me and the sadness in her eyes found companionship in the limitations we both shared. She was not proud of herself. She felt she had let everyone down, especially her brother. As a potential leader of her clan, she was being groomed and trained to be infallible, to be a leader, but she was still young and lacked the knowledge and experience that age provides.

"No one is perfect," I said as I stroked her nose and her blood-soaked whiskers.

Lauren touched my wrist. With anxious and impatient thoughts revolving around in her head, she said, "We cannot go to Alton, Paps, or Kayla. They are beyond us. We need to go to Luka, now! You are a builder, Alton said so." I just stared at Lauren. I had no clue what she meant, or how that would help us.

"There is no way through… the portal is blocked," she spoke with desperation. "We need to build."

"Blocked… build," I said. "What does that mean?"

"Bad Naphalee," Lauren almost spit. "He broke the path."

"Nephalee?" I said as a question.

Lauren poked a finger at herself and repeated, "Nephalee."

"Ohhh," I said, and a picture of the bronzed giant flinging the net laden with Luka back to his soldiers, flashed through my mind. Luka wrapped in the net, laying at the feet of the soldiers, delivered a sudden pain to my head and spine, which formed into defined pictures. I could see Luka surrounded by a group of Neolithic creatures and brutal soldiers, like the ones from the village. They surrounded him, they taunted and battered him. He would leap out, rearing up on his hind legs, which put him even in height to the largest of them, but he would not attack, he only pushed them down to the ground or shoved them away with his paws. I could tell the warriors had begun to think it funny, a joke.

I was confused. He could have torn any one of them in half? A blow from a shaft of wood the size of a small tree, knocked him to the ground. Luka got up immediately, spun around and caught the shaft in his teeth as it grazed past his head on its return swing. He lifted the shaft up with the soldier attached. Then flung the soldier and his weapon over the heads of the watching crowd, where he landed on top of a cooking fire. Many in the crowd burst out in a twisted form of laughter. Others were enraged as they watched flames engulf the soldier, who then leapt off the fire and ran for the jungle. His plentiful hair fueling the flames of an uncertain fate. Luka then turned and lunged at a group closing in on his flank. That is when it became clear why he controlled his potential. He was protecting a small group obscured by the closing crowd. Any mayhem, would enrage the already excited hoard and cause them to turn on those more vulnerable. At first glance, those in the small group looked human but with the smoke and confusion, it was hard to tell who and what they were.

The crowd backed away from Luka's lunge, leaving what looked like a young male exposed and alone. The lunge carried Luka directly over top of the child. Seeing this, he began to roll in midair, pulling his legs underneath him, determined to avoid harming the child. He crashed down on his damaged side. He let out a yelp and then just lay there. A few of the soldiers inched up and kicked him. Pain and effort had taken the fight out of him for now.

I pounded the sand with my fist and contact with the soft sand jerked my awareness back to the beach and the picture before me disappeared. I looked at Lauren. After seeing the plight Luka was in, I was desperate for a fix.

"What about your mother and father, could they retrieve him before it is too late?"

My hands were already tingling, the hair on my arms was standing on end. I could feel the void creeping its way beyond my feeble barriers. I switched my focus to wrestling the tremendous urge back. The void responded to my restraint in a goading and vindictive manner. A surge of power and flash of insight carried the face of the bad Nephalee and connected the dots. Luka being tortured! The entity at the lab! "I have what you want. You can have it, if you give me what I need."

"The Tech... I mean the entity," I said out loud. "Luka, he has Luka?"

"Holy Shit," I yelled. "They are one and the same, the same evil, the same hatred and bitterness... the same narcissistic prick. All of this is because of me. People hurt, Luka taken and tortured, all because of what I might be able to do for this ... bastard."

Lea understood the revelation almost immediately. She leapt to her feet, muscles taut, hoping that this meant I could transport them to the vile Nephalee, or maybe that she might be able to transport us through my unexplored ability.

Lauren had been watching Lea for a sign, but I was not allowed into the private exchange going on between them. As if given the go ahead, Lauren spoke. "I overheard Alton talking to Kayla the day before you first came to our village." "I heard him tell Kayla that you were a builder, one that could take what was and change it into something new, better. Alton said you could change the way of things to come. He said you were different and we would need that difference. Kayla talked about helping you to learn to travel. Kayla wanted Stella and Thor to be your guides and train, as well as protect you, until you became familiar with the pathways.

Pathways... I knew of portals, I thought, but what exactly... were pathways? Lea motioned with a quick nod of her head to Lauren. Lauren answered my question as if I had asked it out loud. Pathways are older portals, or channels from one place to another. The channel lingers and can be rekindled by one who can sense or track it. Alton, Lea and her parents can do that. They can track them and if the energy is strong enough, they can bring them back to life with their own, uhmmm, will." She looked at Lea for continued support. "They can also join one path to another, to create new destinations."

A vision of my first visit to the void, to the convergence of many channels on many different levels, brought the concept to reality. I remembered passing through older channels. I recalled the impressions I encountered, the endlessness of them, but I did not know their original purpose and I had no basis upon which to understand them.

Lauren continued, "Alton told Kayla that you did not need to travel on paths like some of us do and if you became comfortable with using the energy that way, rather than," she struggled for a moment with her meanings, "being the energy, you would fail to achieve a part of your purpose. Following our way of travel would only delay discovery and limit your learning. Alton said that there had not been a builder that he knew of for many lifetimes. To accept the calling was a choice, one that only you could make once you understood what it completely meant." Lauren looked back at Lea and then down at the sand.

I was stunned and the world seemed to slow to a stop. "I would travel, I would build where I want to go." I said under my breath, connecting greater meaning to the original phrases.

"How?" I asked deliberately. Engrossed in my own momentary astonishment, I must have turned my head towards Lea, because I suddenly realized I was staring directly into her eyes. Her wet slippery nose pressed against mine. I drew my head back a little and still all I noticed were her eyes. An endless revolving treasure of gold and bronze.

We shared so very much in that single glance. It was clear in that instant that she did not want to force me to do anything that I was not ready for. She had been monitoring her brother's strength and he was running out of time. She needed to move. If I was not going to be able to help, she would have to find another way. Lea also knew there would be death and destruction once she got to where Luka was. She did not want Lauren to see any of it or put her in any danger. Finally, she did not know if she would make it back alive, from where her brother was and she did not want to leave us both separate and alone. In truth that is why she agreed to come. She knew I would protect Lauren to the best of my ability and if I was ready and able to accept my purpose, then all the better. With those considerations shared between us, she looked at Lauren. Her eyes returned to focus on mine. Her thoughts said, stay and protect... yes?

"Ahhh... Hell No!" I yelled out without hesitation. "There is no way you're going without me! I want to go... I want to help. I just don't know how! I don't know! But, even if we find a way, I have shown myself to be dangerous to others. I do not think I can be trusted!"

Lea and I remained locked in thought, but I could still feel the confidential connection she shared with Lauren. It was like a special language. One not defined by words, but by feeling, need, attachment and familiarity.

I turned to Lauren just as she implored out loud, "We need you to take us to Luka... "NOW," and she placed her palm upon my chest to emphasis it. "Our way is blocked! You are our last hope!"

Well I thought, there is no way I am going to just sit by and let this happen. I have to try. Maybe Lea can use some of what I can do, to get us there.

I turned to Lea. "OK… I need you to show me how! Can you show me how to get us there?"

Lea focused intently on me. There was something different in her eyes. I felt her somehow reaching out farther beyond the connection we now shared. I could feel her probing, trying to understand why I was so different and how I was limited in experience and ability. The blending of our consciousnesses was comforting. I felt a weight, a burden of responsibility and fear being shared through love and trust in another. I started to give into the union, allowing Lea freedom to explore. I was as curious at what she might find as she was curious to find it.

She began exploring feelings, thoughts and recent experiences. Each time she confronted the energy created through the void, she evaded it as if conditioned to avert it. I took one of those moments to probe her aversion. I could see that the dark matter was a no man's land to her. A quicksand for consciousness. If caught within its matrix, it could pull energy, matter, or awareness into it, disintegrating the entire substance of the being and the energy that composed it, like universal acid.

When traveling through a portal and its funnel, the vortex, or walls of the tunnel were the matter being drawn through anti-matter. The anti-matter acted as a repelling force to matter, providing a dense wall keeping the tunnel and the matter in it moving within the structure. If the vortex were to collapse because of an imbalance, or for some other unexpected reason, all would be lost. Older pathways remained intact because matter was of time in space, creating volume, density and defined potential. That potential remained as long as it was in balance with the potentials opposing it. If it had exhausted its matter stream, it could be re-energized by applying enough latent matter to create an energy exchange. Energy consuming energy, time displacing space, space rooted in matter, was compelled through the exchange creating a conduit to some far-off point or dimension where the energy would balance. The more energy displaced, the further the travel through time in space or the larger and more defined the portal could be. Lea, Alton, the bad Naphalee and others so endowed, could manipulate that energy, but only on the matter side of the equation, not on the anti-matter side. They were able to feed the matter forward and balance the process if the pathway was already in existence, or still viable, by simply adding more. Oh, it was more complicated than that, but like Paps had said, "A universe far too complex to ever understand, but simple in its form, application and laws."

Now I understood the aversion to the dark matter for Lea. It had no place in the efforts they made. But where the energy was not in balance that was where danger lurked and Lea could sense it intuitively. Anti-matter, black matter, was a mechanism at the base of what drove the universe. A power grid, a massive universal system, positive and negative. Without both, there was no flow of energy and no life. Lea's charge in travel was one of balance and control, sensing, tracking and adjusting how the energy was used. The void, even if accessed within me, was off limits.

Wherever Lea applied what she could do through me with the void, created an immediate exchange of energy. I could tell it was more reactive, raw and dangerous than she had ever experienced or believed she could handle. The matter side was finite, limited to physics and the mathematics of all things that exist in physical form. The power from the anti-matter side was staggering in comparison to the matter side. The void, anti-matter had no exact solid form, no limits, no boundaries and no dynamics that defined its potential. It was rather unlimited raw material, the stem cell of cosmic creation. It existed in the background; a shadow of the potential hidden in direct sight. Anti-matter was only defined once it was engaged with matter, a true, never depleted, universal battery.

I began to understand what Lea was searching for. She knew that the void was defined within me somehow. She recognized that the unlimited nature of the void offered immensely more power than what she managed within her own capacity as she traveled on familiar pathways.

I felt Lea step back away from me, both physically and perceptually. I could hear her thoughts. How does this human withstand the destruction? How is this human a... she thought for a second... a part of such an undefined reaction?

"That's it!" I said out loud, startling Lea and Lauren. "I ask myself the same thing? Do you see how it is primed to overwhelm me? What happens if that takes place? Have you seen what I have done to those who I feel threatened by? What happens if I spin out of control and the energy consumes everyone and everything? Yet... I am a medium, a bridge, which allows the void to displace matter without destroying both."

Lea remained quiet for a moment, she was thinking, reasoning and then she offered her impression. "At some point, we must all confront our fears. How we confront them, is another thing altogether. You are a builder. I am not sure how it is done, but I understand the idea. You can become the crucible for the darkness, so that it can be used to make the light. There is a place within you that is vast and unexplored, a universe itself."

Her words brought back my first experience with the void, initiated by Alton.

"Yes," I said, "I think I see what you mean. I created my own place, almost my own dimension or mini universe in the void. I am part of it, yet I have a place of origin outside of it. I am a spark of life in both worlds. Unfortunately, I am a master of none. I think what I created while in the void, was driven by some will or drive to be, to exist no matter where I was, as opposed to choose simply not to exist. God...! That even sounds ridiculous to me, but that is how I remember becoming one with the void. I became reborn in it. I began as a nucleus of willed life that demanded a place where nothing else existed and began using the dark matter to create it. It began building me cell upon cell, using the matter side of me to fuel the growth. From spark of life, where nothing existed, to embryo, to a babe unborn in a womb of undefined potential. I am still not delivered Lea, I am still suckling on the individual life supplied through matter only."

Lea's thoughts, gentle as a whisper echoed in my psyche with emphasis. "I understand the concern over your limitations, but you cannot know what they actually are unless you commit to your purpose. It is from that place of purpose that you are able to exist within the darkness. That place is a home, a middle ground, an oasis, allowing the darkness to flow, rather than destroy. You must be reborn completely to have any hope of success!"

I could grasp her meaning, but I did not think she could see how frail my control over the transition of that energy was. Empowered as it was, who knew what it could become. It already proved itself to be unaffected by violence or fulfillment of base need. A specter of the Bad Naphalee immersed in his power and hate, flooded my vision. I shuddered.

"No… no," came an immediate response from Lauren, who had slipped her way into our private conversation. "You are not like the vile one," she continued. "He is driven by the need to escape his pain at any cost. You are driven to understand your pain, your place in all of this. There is no evil intent that underlies your need."

"Ohhh… There will be! If I find this Naphalee and his legions. Knowing how I responded to the men in black, I can't wait to crush him when I see him. If Luka is hurt in any unrepairable way… if I do have the power, I will wipe them all out of existence. I know it. I can feel the potential! What if I hurt you or Lea in the process? What will I have gained? No, I dare not even think of letting that aspect of me loose."

I heard a voice from the past, my grandfather teaching my brother, his namesake, about believing in himself, reaching beyond his present potential. He said, "Hugh, a closed mind and heart are a limited mind and heart, therefore too small to accept concepts that stretch the imagination. We cannot know what we are capable of, if we are not prepared to let go and explore the potential life has to offer. Believe in that potential, employ faith. It will set you free. Let go and let God, my boy.

Lauren placed her hand upon my chest. "I believe you are greater than what you see. I believe that whatever you treasure as the person before me, you will also treasure above any darkness. For in darkness, that which we treasure becomes the light that guides us home. I remain by your side."

Tears began to fall from my eyes. I kissed Lauren on the cheek.

"I am willing to do the same," offered Lea.

I could feel the bond that connected us. I was not willing to let that be destroyed. Then, it hit me. I was not willing to die, to give up, to fail. I was not willing to accept the chance that anyone else would get hurt. Unwilling to let go… and let God.

"I get it. The bridge is built out of sheer will and nothing drives will more powerfully, more intensely, than… love!"

I looked at Lea, who saw it all unfold in my mind. She understood and joined in that concept. I could feel her start working with the energy around me. As she did, I let the barrier I had built to block the void start to erode. I let my love for her, pace the erosion. Lea faced the void and the destructive force of the dark matter.

A large section of the barrier crumbled and I came face to face with myself.. At first I was the scientist with insights into the workings of energy and matter. Then, I was Paps and his never-ending spirit for finding truth. The person staring back at me then changed to the bad Naphalee, in all his anger and need to punish. Who was I really? Lea had the faith and the truth of it. It was not until I was tested at my core, until I was reborn that this tug of war would be resolved. Then I would know who I truly was and what I was capable of.

I could see a reflection of Alton in my mind. I visualized what he would say. It was, "Where do you want go? Know it and go, Michael. It is time for the sleeper to truly awaken!"

As I watched my reflections in the void, I felt Lea by my side. Then I felt her reach out into the void, through me and through my physical energy, as her buffer. Just before she reached out, she looked at me. I could see the essence of her, her strength, her will and her unwavering love. I realized I would do anything, sacrifice everything I was, to protect her.

As she pulled my being further and further into the void, the air began to crackle, a massive charge began to build. I was immediately fearful. Before I could respond, convey the possibility she might be destroyed, the void broke through. As the energy flooded and surrounded Lea, she felt immense pain. I raced to surround her with myself, cover her with every last cell. That only fanned the flames of the process, expanding it exponentially.

The pain she was experiencing, the burning, seemed like every cell in her flesh was being stripped from her bones. I called out to her, "Stop, run away. This is what I was afraid of. She turned again to me and I could see the sacrifice in her eyes. I could see the love she had for me and Luka. I could see the idea that set her upon this path. The wall of energy building before us was massive, a title wave cresting as it met the shores of physical matter.

Instead of pulling away, Lea opened herself up. She reached out into the void. I raced furiously to place all I was, between her and the full force of the dark matter. Like a mad weaver, a desperate spider whose web was being destroyed faster than it could weave a new one, I fabricated substance from the convergence of the matter and anti-matter stream. I surrounded her with it. I did not flinch. I did not have that luxury. I could not let Lea surrender herself in this way; the loss would be too great to imagine. As I wove the bridge to support her existence in both worlds, I lost sense of time. When the demand reached what I thought was beyond my limit, I continued on. At some point, I was no longer the mad weaver, the agile spider struggling with the thread. I was the thread. There was no effort now. Momentum, will, maybe some principal of a continuum, endowed me. I was not the fabricator. I was the steel substance that bridged the chasm between energies.

There was intelligence or maybe just universal laws in motion. Life in this existence was simply energy given function, purpose. The beginning already connected to the end. We were just the elements that the potential flowed through, a universal circuit, one end connected to the power, the other connected to unrelenting need.

Lea was energy in motion, powered by will and desire. As she applied that will, the energy did more than light her way, it became the way. The voids unlimited potential overwhelmed the limits of that confronting it and the title wave began to crash. Lea took the leading edge and brought it into form, allowing it to draw in on itself, fuel itself, employing the dynamics that allowed dimensions to blend, space to fold, time to transition at a converted pace.

She hid nothing, shared everything. The honesty of her need was overwhelming. The energy received her as a liberator, a crusader and it awaited her command. It moved to her, responded to her as a child to its mother.

It suddenly seemed so natural, as she took her place in the center of my awareness, joining my source to her desire. I could feel what she felt, sense what she sensed and see what she saw. I watched and learned as she created for me what I was unable to conceive.

Lea stood beside Luka in her mind, her love for him paramount, her desire to help him grew with each violent act he endured. As I stood with her, I could again see how powerful his body had become, how he was nearly the size of his father.

As he regained some awareness, two of the invaders began wrapping straps around his nose and jaw. I could feel the straps being wound painfully with malicious intent. The pressure was cutting off his ability to breathe.

I started breathing heavily, my body jerking in unison with

Luka's movements, caught in the same fight, one with him. I felt Lea reach out to her brother and in the madness of his pain, hanging in a limbo between life and death, he embraced her love and our strength. Through his pain, hope blossomed and energy flowed into him from our bond.

Lea began leveraging the emancipated dark matter to finish the new portal, building a new doorway to where Luka was. She could not have done it herself. The old one was broken, destroyed. A builder though, did not need what was, he only needed what was to be.

Alton had said, the essence of the universe was the will of love, in all its forms. I had released the void and its long-contained energy into the hands of one I trusted and loved. I might as well have handed over my very spirit to her and at that moment, without fully understanding all that was happening, I might already have. The pain turned to ecstasy, a release, an expression of energy united with purpose. As it flowed through Lea, she gathered it, but did not possess it. She nurtured it and directed it. My fear for her safety relieved, I refused to be a spectator any longer. I was inspired to go on the offensive. I reached into the void and using the concept taught to me by Mr. Brown, my elementary teacher, I made it big, vivid and greater than imagination could bear. I began consuming the dark matter at its source, driving the transformation as an enthusiastic participant in a dance of unlimited creation. I was fury in a storm, the crack in thunder, the force in lightening, power incarnate. Will, driven by desire, honed the energy, focused it and refined it into a stream stronger than any laser I could have ever dreamed of building in my laboratory.

CHAPTER 42

Wave upon wave of energy forced its way beyond the walls that physical matter and life experience had built. The dark matter now driving its energy inward formed the walls of the vortex. With Lauren and Lea's consciousness tied to mine, we flowed forward toward a widening rift, a canyon deep, filling beyond its capacity. I could hear a roar off in the distance but coming swiftly closer. I was having a hard time catching my breath. Light blazed past closed eyelids, sounds were immense as if we were in the middle of a huge engine, pistons pounding, energy flowing, the roar of immeasurable potential. The sound of something solid being torn apart cascaded through my awareness, as if the flow of the energy were stretching the fabric of space itself, driving a wedge into what was, to make what would be. A massive vortex opened up around us, drawing us forward. Everything seemed to elongate; the noise began to fade and disappeared into a background hum. Light of all colors followed the noise, stretching around the edge of the vortex, then elongating as it moved down into its core. As the light funneled away, the colors brought to life the fabric of my vision, with flashes as fierce as bolts of lightning in a hot summer's night sky. Then, all went silent. The suffocating sensation faded and was replaced by the absence of need for breath at all. I perceived, as if from within and from without, from on top and bottom. I stood up, or maybe down. I was not sure. There were no bearings to anything that was happening. I was acutely aware of my earthly surroundings, but integrally tied to the vortex that stretched to where my friend and brother lay beaten and bloody.

I stomped my feet in the sand I stood in, but there was nothing solid beneath them. I put my hand on Lauren's shoulder and realized she was captivated by what stood before her. Within a few feet of us, a massive spinning vortex churned. It stood about 15 feet around and at different places it rotated at different speeds. Random patterns of light flashed and blended, then disappeared as they were consumed by the vortex. The outside trailed off into dimensional confusion, but the inside was like a picture frame, a doorway filled with the place the invaders had come from. Smoke rose up from the ground and was swept into our world. Sounds of a prehistoric jungle flowed uninterrupted through the connection of worlds.

I was standing in that other world, just as I stood next to Lea and Lauren who were dwarfed by the scope and dimension of the portal we had built. I looked out upon that primitive world now intimately linked to Luka. I also looked out upon the beach and those I cherished there.

My perceptions began to coordinate with the rest of my senses. My psyche began a cleanup job, collecting all the pieces of a jumbled puzzle, fitting them into one place. One physical point of origin. The portal now complete, belonged to itself, subject to the laws of matter and space in time. Like a painting or sculpture, the vortex was truly a work of love and a work of creation.

I was also now separate, but I still held the energy which manifested it. I could close or open it at will. Lea was proud. She had faced her mortality and had not flinched. She had created what no other of her race had, an original pathway, a new portal. In her own way, she had become a builder. She looked at me through the eyes of one empowered.

There was a synchronization still evolving within and around me. The difference was that now I was confident that I would gain and maintain control. The scientist at my core knew we had reached a point of no return and was pleading for a moment of contemplation and consideration before we physically breached the barrier between worlds. The experimenter in me, the challenger, and the person eternally faithful to Luka, was intent upon ending any and all threat from this place, period.

A familiar voice reverberated in my mind, commenting with sarcasm. "Destroy, the destroyer? Well, that may very well be you." My inner voice fell on unconcerned ears. I stepped toward the event horizon, then turned to Lea and Lauren to instruct them to stay put. Lauren was already by my side and Lea was leaping through the opening, her goal solidly in line with mine. We were now partners in the hunt. Thoughts of retaliation, of unrestricted action, of revenge, seemed natural and completing.

CHAPTER 43

As I moved through the portal threshold on to a new and hostile world, the smell of sulfur and smoldering rock burned my throat. Lea was already in front of me. Her nose to the ground, canvassing the area for information. She stopped and froze in place. Her body quivered under the stress of the primordial energy she now channeled. Keying into Luka's position, the fur on her back began to rise up her spine like an uncoiling snake. I could tell it was taking every ounce of her will not to bolt off in pursuit of her brother. After a moment her powerful frame relaxed and she moved to Lauren's side, nudging her hand. It was clear, that Lauren had to come first.

Grimy patches of gas and smoke floated past us like an airborne disease belched up from some deep caustic stew, bubbling beneath the ground. Drawn toward the ever-spinning portal, the patches of dense smoke seemed eager to pass through and contaminate another world.

Lauren, blindsided by a puff of that acrid smoke, bent over and coughed. I turned to put my arm around her, to comfort her, but she had straightened up and stood like a warrior, fists clenched ready for battle.

I looked over at Lea, she knew to come to me immediately. She lowered her head even with mine to make strategic eye contact.

"I am concerned about Lauren," I said to Lea in a what I thought was a private moment. "I am not sure what I am capable of... or what may happen. I am afraid both of you might get hurt."

Lea leaned forward and pushed her forehead firmly against mine as if to enforce, 'No turning back now!' In contrast, her fur was soft and comforting against my face as we stood locked in thought.

"Did we come here to share doubt?" she offered. "We must let our fate be decided by our faith." I looked down, feeling a little ashamed, and noticed her claws had dug deep holes into the soil where appropriately, steam bled out.

Well... I thought, as I raised my eyes and my expectations to meet hers. "If you can stand the heat in the kitchen, then I sure can do a little cookin!"

At that moment Lauren intruded, "Hey... hey... what's going on here? I will not stay behind. We go together," and she started to move past me in a huff.

"Lauren," I said, "what will we have accomplished, if we save Luka and lose you? I could not bear that!" Lauren stopped and leaned close, her eyes burning a hole in mine until I could feel the intensity of her resolve in the back of my head.

"Stop wasting time," Lauren said. "Lea is ready. I am ready. Let's go get Luka."

Lea cast a glance back at the portal. "There is no longer a barrier between worlds," she said. "A pathway for escape exists if we need it."

I sighed in resignation. Knowing they could leave without my help, made me feel better.

The intensity of the moment reinforced the attitudes of those with me, the energy being held back surged. The portal shuddered in response and grew by a foot or more, emphasizing the raw need to consume anything that was in its path if not held in balance.

"OK, no turning back. We need to move," I growled. Before I could take my first step, Lea had launched herself in the air, as graceful as a gazelle and as powerful as a saber tooth tiger. She sailed over a small rise of smoldering boulders and was gone from site.

Lauren and I looked at each other with a smile of that embodied release. There was no fear in her eyes, only purpose. She bent down and picked up a rock considerably larger than my head. It was still smoking, as a dull red glow faintly emphasized the anger that burnt deep within each of us now. She bounced the rock in her hand, judging weight against probable use. She lobbed it in the air a few times and smiled at me again... a dainty smile. She shrugged her shoulders, then said, "This will have to do," and followed Lea up and over the stones. I leaned back, laughing loudly and yelled, "Yesssss…!!!"

The hunt for our friend was on.

EPILOGUE

The facility was unnaturally quite as Dr. John Schlitt, managing director for the LHC (The Large Hadron Collider), proceeded down the hallway past the final phases of construction on the adjunct laboratories. Conceived and constructed as the world's largest and most powerful particle accelerator, John had not expected this incredible career opportunity to become the world's largest pain in the ass. It was a constant struggle to deal with so many individuals, organizations and governments, demanding everything from access to secured documentation and rights of participation, to claims of violation of patent or intellectual property. Every demand was a potential nightmare.

If those were the only interferences usurping his time and energy, he could handle them. But it had become obvious that he was in a moral and ethical conflict with the power structures that envisioned the project.

Soon, hundreds of scientists would occupy these halls. They would diligently assimilate untold millions of bits of data collected from ground breaking experimentation, with the hopes of gaining insight into the very fabric of the universe and that, was certainly worth the effort. He thought about his many years pioneering exploration in the sciences. Throughout it all, he had sadly discovered that money, power or both were always the foundation principles funding the research.

"Would the discoveries made confirm and support the theories that inspired the project?" John asked himself. "They had better," he answered. In order to substantiate the incredible costs incurred in building this one of a kind facility, someone, some group, or some connected organization was expecting a big payoff.

John turned the corner that led to the administration wing. As excited as he had initially been with this opportunity, he was now angry and frustrated. The level of secrecy surrounding the facility and the suppression of a truthful agenda was not acceptable. He stopped for a moment and calmed his emotions. They would not be helpful in the meeting he was on his way to. He leaned against the wall thinking, "The discoveries realized through this project should be shared with the world, distributed amongst the most brilliant minds, no… all the minds and creative souls of mankind. If for no other reason, than to allow collaboration and exploration into a universe that every human being interacts with, every second, of every day of their lives."

There was hubris and corruption in the power structures directing this enterprise. He had seen it before and knew the progressions of behavior and paranoia. Secrecy was more important than discovery. Domination of everything from information to individuals was more of an imperative, than say… finding a key to unlocking the Cosmos. John shook his head in disbelief.

The facility was allowing more government representatives, military contingents and influential private sector operatives in each day. Most frustrating though, was the intrusion of a group of men, highly secretive, highly trained, that wore only black. It did not take a scientist to deduce the importance of a project, if they were involved. Everyone was intimidated by them. They were at best, untouchable. At worst, a shadow government that was good at eliminating the word 'Free' from Freedom.

John remembered the very point when the project crossed over into uncharted territory. He had been briefed on a development that was to be the major initiative once the facility was in good order. It seemed only a slight deviation from the facilities planned purpose, so he did not see the harm. Then, during a debriefing for the staff managers and scientists fitting out the facility, one of the speakers made a mistake. He mentioned a change in production time lines, to allow for study of a new element. The staff in attendance demanded to know more. Of course, they were scientists! John happened to be behind the curtains of the stage when the speaker had asked for clarification on describing the sample for study. He had walked off the stage, out of site and addressed Mr. Randolph, the director of the men in black.

He said. "Sir, can I tell them the sample is believed to be anti-matter?" Mr. Randolph almost spit out the water he was sipping.

"No, you idiot! You were not even supposed to mention the element. These are scientists. They know the significance of such a change in agenda. It would open up questions that would take us a year to answer, even if we could, which we can't. We are going to have to deal with each individual, in each department, to assure project integrity."

"I understand, sir, but they are asking for more information so they can provide for their departments. Can you make a suggestion on how I could best handle that?"

"Just tell them they will be informed individually and in plenty of time as to how this will affect their departments. Then, they can begin their preparations."

"Yes, Sir, is that all?"

"That is all, get it done and if there are any... and I mean any dissenters, I want their names and departments... right?"

"Yes, Sir, I will take care of it."

"Good," was all Mr. Randolph finished with.

John knew that to win the hearts and minds of the staff, the powers that be needed to control their minds first, or at least control the reality those minds functioned in. He had seen this type of operational 'Ends justify the means' approach before. He would not be a part of that. He respected the collection of scientists that had begun this project and they trusted him.

Then and there, John took every opportunity to defy propaganda and deception. Someone or some group had supplied this new element. If they did, they knew what it truly was. Where had this unknown element or matter been collected from? Who besides Mr. Randolph knew of its true characteristics? How did they maintain the elements stability and prevent it from interacting with a physical world? Every budding scientist and every science fiction buff knew that matter and anti-matter were incompatible. Contact between just two opposing particles could start a chain reaction that would consume all that mankind possessed.

With information so well kept, so well-guarded, solving this mystery would be hard. Any deviation from security protocols meant that someone might disappear. At present, a small number of his staff had simply gone missing. He was assured by Mr. Randolph that there was no reason to be alarmed, but that was all he would say. These people were John's responsibility. After arguments with Mr. Randolph, men in Black had shown up at his office, or shadowed his car, or positioned themselves in suggestive ways, so as to confirm their commitment to a secret. Mr. Randolph was flexing his authority and making sure that John knew who was in control.

John had nowhere to turn. The military was only there to enforce a DEF COM status set in place by no other than Mr. Randolph. They did not know what the dangers were and so had become an unwitting pawn to those who did.

As John rounded the last corner to the suite of offices he and his staff occupied, he noticed two tall men dressed in cleanly pressed black suits, their stature, undoubtedly military, their serious and almost dead to the world nature, a declared threat.

John passed the men without any sign of recognition, but cautious not to seem disrespectful or provoking. He entered his office and saw Diane, his assistant, diligently working at her desk. She looked up and smiled with a crooked smile, one that he had become very familiar with over the years. It was a smile that said, "The big wigs are here and as usual brandishing their little brains and devious minds."

John returned the smile as he approached her desk, picked up the mail and asked, "Anything important that I need to know about?"

"No," she said nonchalantly as she finished stamping a group of papers on her desk. Then she leaned forward and whispered, "John, I was asked to leave the suite in order for someone to enter unseen, so I have no idea who is in there. Although I do not think there is anything to worry about, they seem somehow anxious to talk to you."

"Great," John said as he took a deep breath and set the mail down. "I will go in then." He looked back at Diane and said, "If you feel threatened… leave and do not return."

In response, Diane said, "If they drink the coffee I made, we won't have to worry about them… after today." Then she flashed him an innocent smile.

As John entered his office, he saw that the drapes had been drawn. The room had just enough light in it to make out a few faces around his desk, but the rest of the room seemed eerily dark.

"Well, Dr Schlitt, it was good of you to put your work aside and meet with us so quickly."

"Not at all," John responded. "I got a call from Director Samuels. He said it was of immediate importance. How can I help you and the WSA, Mr. Randolph?" John headed for the chair situated behind his desk with a strategic view of the entire room.

"We seek an update on the arrival of your new team and the

time frame for installation of the equipment they are bringing. Also, where are we on the departure of the team from China?"

"Mr. Randolph," John said with a patronizing flow "I am far removed from the detail in communications and level of information gathering that you and your staff share. I can only guess at what you already have full knowledge of, but since our last communication with a researcher named James, overseeing some of the transitional issues for the American team, they are packed up and ready to go. Dr. William Farrell, their project director, is one of the best in the world at successful cycle production. So, we are in good hands from the start.

Mr. Randolph interrupted impatiently. "Dr. Schlitt, do you not find it interesting, that this group has made so many historic discoveries in the past few months?" Mr. Randolph stood up and moved in the direction of the shadows in the back side of the room. As he turned back to look directly at him, John noticed slight movement in the very corner where a conference table had been. That table was now on the opposite side of the room, along with the chairs, as if they had to make room for something big to fit there.

Very strange, thought John as he answered Mr. Randolph. "Yes, as you have suggested some of their discoveries are very impressive, leaps and bounds. It all seems to funnel from one man. Their main team lead... his name is Michael. In reading his dossier, he is very unpretentious, a solitary individual known to be a good scientist and a good team leader. He has been with Director Farrell on many projects and they are a 'Go To' team for their country's military. The team is made up of a ragtag group of extremely talented but undisciplined prodigies. Yet, the whole package seems to produce incredible results. I am both excited and worried about their arrival."

"Why would you be worried, Dr. Schlitt?" asked Mr. Randolph.

John cautiously sat down at his desk and rubbed his temples. He looked up and stared into the shadows at the corner of his room, feeling like he was on stage, now sure there was another person concealed in the darkness that Mr. Randolph was playing to. Having had just about enough of the cloak and dagger stuff, as well as having lost some talented scientists and friends, John reacted with anger.

"Why do you ask me questions, Mr. Randolph? You are far more capable of answering than I." John shifted in his seat and refocused his questions to the corner of the room obscured in shadow. "Why does it matter who arrives and when, if they are just going to disappear like others dedicated to this project? How are we even to complete this project if there is no one left? Why am I worried, you ask? You already know the answer to that one as well, Mr. Randolph!"

Caught off guard by John's outburst and realizing he was losing control of the conversation, Mr. Randolph moved back to the desk to sit down.

There was the sound of a throat clearing in the corner at the back of the room and a deep low almost menacing voice said, "There can be no mistakes from this point forward, Doctor. We are running short of time to reach the goal this facility was designed to achieve."

John was now the one caught off guard. "What goal would that be exactly, sir? Because I have yet to receive one that is different from the misdirection fed to the world at large."

There was no response, only silence. John continued, "I am expected to run a facility that could render much that we now know to be as ignorant as believing the earth to be flat. How am I to achieve any objectives, if those who will perform these groundbreaking discoveries keep disappearing? How am I to achieve any specified goal, when I do not even know what that true goal is?"" Silence continued to rule the moment. Where are my people? Why have they been removed?"

The deep voice vibrated at a level that rattled something inside John, saying, "Doctor, if you feel unequal to the task you have been appointed to, please let Mr. Randolph know now, so that we can make other arrangements."

John laughed, relieved by the comment. It proved that they were guilty of manipulation on even the simplest of levels. He picked up a pencil on his desk and rotated it in front of him so everyone in the room could see it.

"This pencil is a tool, employed for writing. It allows a person to erase what has been written, to erase mistakes, so to speak and start again. You, Sir... do not own this tool. The project we are on cannot afford this tool. It is too simple a tool to operate in the complex environment required. You cannot simply erase your mistakes and start again. You are committed to that which you have conceived. I am also a tool, Sir. I am a tool that has been employed to build and run the facility envisioned. I am the right tool for the job. Both you and Mr. Randolph know that! I have the experience, the knowledge, the security clearance and the understanding of what is absolutely required to provide, not just for the present, but for the future. Knowing my dissatisfaction with the short-sighted, idiotic approach to security that Mr. Randolph has employed, if you had other choices you would already have replaced me. So, let's agree to put the simple tools at our disposal away in order to work and communicate on the same level. If we are all, and I mean as a team, not up to that task then this project is already lost." This time there was dead silence, not even a breath.

"I would also prefer that you do not threaten me ever again," John continued. "You cannot afford the time and expense replacing this proper tool will cost you."

Mr. Randolph's eye bulged out of his sockets in anger, as he half stood above his chair.

Laughter from the corner shook the room. Outside the door, John heard footsteps, followed by knocking.

Diane called out, "Is everything all right, Dr. Schlitt? John?"

"Everything is fine, Diane. Lunch time is not too far off. Why don't you spend time with the budget office on this month's P & L and then eat. I will review any concerns you have over it this afternoon. Ohh... and Diane, check on the delivery of the last super cooler to be installed in the stabilization chamber. Make sure they triple check the seals for pressurization and document the additional tests once it is installed."

"I will attend to it immediately, Dr. Schlitt."

"You truly are the best tool for this job, Dr. Schlitt." The deep voice said, still laughing. This time it held a comforting quality, almost benevolent. "I am sorry to have created an environment of mistrust. Be at peace about your colleagues. They have been removed to another facility to prepare for, as you have aptly stated, 'the unknown agenda'. You can understand the need for secrecy in transporting these professionals to another location, can't you?"

"I presume you mean the need for secrecy concerning the outside world, because it would make no sense to hide that information from me." John looked directly at Mr. Randolph and finished, "Now would it?"

Mr. Randolph did not reply and John knew he had created a greater enemy than had existed before the meeting.

"Have you eliminated the good Doctor from the 'Need to Know list', Mr. Randolph?" the booming voice asked.

Mr. Randolph rose from his seat and turned to face the corner. If John did not know any better, he would have thought that Mr. Randolph was cowering.

In a somewhat shaky voice, he answered. "I felt the information would distract Dr. Schlitt from his duties."

"And how was Dr. Schlitt going to collaborate with, and support our agenda, if he was kept isolated from those he was to integrate with? It does seem unbelievably counterproductive, Mr. Randolph."

Mr. Randolph stuttered a little bit, then said, "In light of the circumstances we have been monitoring, the occurrence at the other facility and the injuries to some of our operatives, uh... field representatives, it seemed prudent."

There was a hesitation and a huff that indicated impatience from the dark corner. Then in a lower tone than before, the voice said, "I do not presume to tell you your job, Mr. Randolph, but Dr. Schlitt is obviously a far better asset when trust and cooperation are fostered, as opposed to the dynamics you seem to value at present. Can we fix this?"

John felt a little light headed from the vibration the voice emitted. He was beginning to understand why Mr. Randolph seemed nervous.

"Yes ... Yes, Sir," said Mr. Randolph.

"Dr. Schlitt," the voice continued. "You are a perceptive and intelligent man. I hope to spend some time with you in the future. I believe I could open your eyes to some of the more pressing matters facing us. Until then, please accept our deepest apologies for the way you have been treated. You may speak with any of your relocated staff members at any time. Mr. Randolph knows how to get in touch with me as need arises and rest assured, I will prioritize your request for time to talk. Until then, this new team coming in from the US is of vital importance to us. Let us just say that the personnel on this team may become the crucible, within which this project flourishes."

John put his head down. He was uncomfortable with the anger he had displayed, compared to the sincerity and genuineness the voice in the corner expressed.

"Dr. Schlitt," the voice added, "thank you for your time and excellent service. I believe you and all of your staff will realize substantial reward for your efforts in the days to come."

Mr. Randolph turned to face John. His eyes were intense and his mouth was drawn tight, as if holding back a tantrum. "Dr. Schlitt, please exit your office. We will need a few minutes to confer with our guest before he leaves to attend to other matters."

John looked to the corner then down to his desk again. He was trying to figure out how he could get more information on the voice in the corner before the opportunity passed.

"Do not worry, Dr Schlitt," the voice spoke plainly. "I understand your concern for a more familiar relationship with me. Today is not the day for introductions, but soon, very soon."

John was shocked that the man in the corner had read his thoughts, or maybe he had just been obvious. In response, John said, "I would like to thank you for taking the time to address my concerns and I am relieved that those whom I have known for many years are in a safe place and well cared for. Thank you again for your consideration."

"Not at all, Dr. Schlitt. Your professionalism merits that level of respect. Until we meet again."

"Yes," said John as he moved toward the door, "until such time."

John moved out of the room, past the outside office and started down the hallway. He felt as if he had been freed from prison. He shook his head and thought, what have I gotten myself into? Sure, they will let me talk to my staff. What a great opportunity for them to observe our interaction and listen into our conversations. Mr. Randolph will have already arranged that!

This is the end of Book One. Book 2 will follow Michael, Lea and Lauren as they struggle to free Luka. It will follow the research team and what they find at the LHC and finally the book will explore a Universe unrestricted by dimensional limitations.

Thank you for joining us in the adventure.

ABOUT THE AUTHOR

A native of Virginia, living in the beautiful Blue Ridge mountains with Lori his wife. Robert is a father to five beautiful children and a friend to the many animals that share his farm. He has lectured and taught on varying subjects surrounding meditation and human potential. He believes that every individual is endowed with a pure connection to God and is never alone.

Gods Last Giant was at first an imaginative idea. Over a number of years, it took on a life of its own.

As a series GLG hopes to share with the reader that what we determine to be imagination or speculation today, in a universe that is truly unexplored, may be reality tomorrow. Enjoy the read.

SDC Publishing, LLC was established to promote and encourage aspiring writers and artists. It is a family oriented vehicle through which they can publish their work.

Contact SDC Publishing, LLC at allenfmahon@gmail.com

Or on the web at SDCPublishingLLC.com

73781716R00164

Made in the USA
Columbia, SC
07 September 2019